*Attack me! I'll f...
out!* Short-Son's th...
he could say noth...
teasing him, playing with him before they
killed him. His fangs were sticking to dry
lips, frozen by his grin.

"Our coward stinks of fear," said Puller-of-
Noses, ready for the kill, charging himself for a
single leap that would rip the life from his prey.
"You smell like a fattened grass-eater." When
his opponent didn't respond, he couldn't resist
the final, ultimate insult. "I'll make a deal with
you. Be a herbivore. Put your head in the grass
and eat it, and I'll spare your life. Or fight like
a Hero and I'll give you honor."

While he taunted, his only caution was to
reestablish his crouch. The pause gave
Short-Son a fatal moment of thought.

Puller-of-Noses had tendered a verbal bargain: eat grass and live or be a Hero and die.

His word of honor would force him to
keep that bargain.

Puller-of-Noses was also too stupid to
understand that he had actually offered
Short-Son a *real* choice between life and
death. In the challenger's mind there was no
choice at all between honor and eating grass.

Trembling, full of disgust for himself, Short-
Son sank to his knees and began to eat the tall
strands of green—crawling, ripping it from its
roots with his fangs, chewing, though his teeth
were not meant for such chewing. There was no
way for his throat to swallow the fibrous cud,
but he kept chewing and chewing.

THE SURVIVOR

MAN-KZIN WARS IV

Created by

Larry Niven

with

Donald Kingsbury

Greg Bear

and

S.M. Stirling

MAN-KZIN WARS IV

Copyright © 1991 by Larry Niven

A Baen Books Original

Baen Publishing Enterprises
P.O. Box 1403
Riverdale, N.Y. 10471

ISBN: 0-671-72079-1

Cover art by Stephen Hickman

First printing, September 1991

Distributed by
SIMON & SCHUSTER
1230 Avenue of the Americas
New York, N.Y. 10020

Printed in the United States of America

CONTENTS

INTRODUCTION

Last month a stranger in New Jersey asked permission to use the kzinti in his fanzine. (Fanzines, fan magazines, exist strictly for recreation.) Gary Wells wanted nothing of Known Space, just the kzinti, embedded in a Star Trek background.

I wrote: *I hereby refuse you permission to use the kzinti in any literary property.*

The last guy who did that involved the kzinti in a sadomasochistic homosexual gangbang, badly, and published it on a computer network. A friend alerted me, and we spoke the magic word and frightened him away. (Lawsuit.) I'm still a little twitchy on the subject, so don't take any of this too personally. . . .

Wells persisted. He sent me the Fleet bio for his kzin: a crewman aboard a federation battlewagon. He's got his format well worked out. It would have been fun to see what he might do with it; but I'm going to refuse him anyway. I don't want the playground getting too crowded.

I hope the network bandit doesn't turn up again.

I wouldn't be so picky with a story set in someone else's territory . . . but when you play in my playground, you don't vandalize the equipment. Jim Baen and I have solicited stories which we bought and then rejected because they didn't fit my standards.

The bandit's kzin was ridiculous. Large warm-blooded animals that have to fight don't have big impressive dongs. There's no flexibility in their mating habits. (We have some partial understanding of why humans are an exception.) Humans will smell wrong; this is established as important to kzinti.

Yet such matters can be handled with taste, or at least versimilitude.

If you once read Donald Kingsbury's *Courtship Rite* . . . but the nightmares have since gone away . . . "The Survivor" is your chance to get them back. Kingsbury writes horror stories for bright people. You will come to understand his cowardly kzin, and even to sympathize with him, but not, I hope, to love him. Grass-Eater is not *normal*.

"The Man Who Would Be Kzin," as portrayed by Greg Bear and S.M. Stirling, isn't normal either.

There are writers out there who know considerably more about the kzinti than I do. The *Man-Kzin Wars* authors have already delved deep into normal kzinti family life. The kzinti are mean and dangerous and intelligent. I fear I've been taking them too lightly.

—**Larry Niven**

THE SURVIVOR

Donald Kingsbury

CHAPTER 1
(2391 A.D.)

His tail was cold. Where could he run to?

The Short-Son of Chiirr-Nig fluffed the fur inside his suit to help him keep warm. At the airlock exit he hadn't had time to appropriate better surface garb from the public racks. The suit was non-standard, too large and good only for a limited surface excursion. Eventually he would freeze. The oxygen mask and support pack should last indefinitely.

Ruddy light from an enormous red sun gilded the snow-swept rocks. A dim rose cast itself across the hunching sprawl of atmosphere-tight buildings that spread down into the valley gloom. The scene demanded infra-red goggles to penetrate the shadows, but Short-Son had no goggles. Could he run to the mountains? The jags against the sky had been named the Mountains of Promised Victory by the founding warriors of Hssin, but they were mountains of death.

Dim as R'hshssira was, the sanguine glare from the snow peaks drowned the stars along the horizon. But above, undismayed by the pale glow of R'hshssira, the

3

heavens peered from a darkly mauve sky, seeming to give more light than Hssin's litter-runt-of-a-star, even as they peered through wisps of cirrus.

If there was little light, there was warmth. But one had to be standing out on the open plain of Hssin in full daylight—forge-red R'hshssira looming full round in the sky—to feel the warmth. Nevertheless it was real warmth that soaked into space armor—if one was willing to freeze his backside and tail.

Short-Son of Chiirr-Nig turned his back to the sun, his tail held up to the radiation.

His warrior elders sometimes joked about whether Hssin was a planet or a moon because no kzin was really sure whether the pitiful primary, R'hshssira, was a father star or a mere lost whelp with slave. R'hshssira was too cool, too small to be a star, already having collapsed, without igniting its hydrogen, to the density of a heavy metal. Still it bathed them in a bloody warmth.

A star-beast in hibernation, its metabolism inactive.

A beast with no rotation, no magnetic field, fighting nothing. It slept and the slave satellite Hssin patrolled protectively close to the master's lair.

Short-Son couldn't go to the mountains. He had to escape back into the city he had just run from. He stared up at the constellations, at five brilliant, distant giants that lay across the River of Heaven. If there was no place to run to then let the Fanged God Who Drank at the River of Heaven take him to the stars.

Hssin served as a forward military base of the Kzin Patriarchy, barren as a moon, yet with atmosphere like a planet. The gas was thin, wicked, noxious, sometimes as stormy as the surface of R'hshssira was docile. The temperatures ranged over extremes impossible for life to endure. Nothing worth hunting could live in those hills and plains of shattered rock and ice. The kzinti who stayed here were pitied by the kzinti who passed through on their way to greater glory.

. . . *And,* thought Short-Son bitterly, *who mock and torture the loyal kzin whose heroism keeps this wretched base open for the use of the Patriarchy.* He envied the outward-bound warriors their journey, their wily females, the wood and leather and tapestry in their starships. He scorned their petty complaints about the hardships of space. He openly hated their sons who used him as sport, but kept private his thoughts about violating their soft-furred daughters.

The Short-Son of Chiirr-Nig knew where *they* were running to. The brightest star on the horizon of Hssin was the beacon that made them endure both their travels and the tedious duty at bleak military bases along the way. Looking at it, he refused to call that white binary by its Kzin name, Ka'ashi—he always called it by its unpronounceably exotic alien name, *Alpha Centauri.* What did those weird sounds mean?

An old warrior had once told him that the monkey aliens had named it after a beast that was half monkey, half herbivore; four cloven hooves and two hands. Just the name could make him smell the hunting and stalking of strange beasts! He had salivated over smell-pictures of the six-legged underland gagrumphers.

But it was *he* who was being hunted!

The Son of Chiirr-Nig thought of himself as a freak, as the only kzin in the Patriarchy who had ever felt fear. Perhaps others had felt fear—but *they* did not run.

What was a half-grown kzin youth doing on the surface, hurrying in a pressure suit so hastily donned that he had forgotten his thermal underwear? He had also forgotten his oxygen. His mask-pack was rumbling to make up the lack by the dissociation of atmospheric carbon dioxide and his fur was not keeping him warm. His tail was already numb. Heroes as stupid as he was, died, he castigated himself. He was alone. He didn't even have his mother to protect him.

I'm a coward, he thought, using a particularly vicious word from the Hero's Tongue which referred to scurrying animals too small to bring hunt-honor. He would never have let another kzin know that he used such a word to describe himself. Nevertheless, he wished he could understand why no one else was afraid to die.

Puller-of-Noses and Hidden-Smiler—he had his own private names for his youthful comrades—were hunting him and they would catch him and kill him. A game. His father was always pushing him into such games before he was ready. His father wouldn't care if he died stupidly. It would please Short-Son's sire not to be embarrassed anymore. That noble one had a name and many sons to do him honor, enough sons themselves to earn names and make themselves rich on the labor of monkey slaves.

An old warrior friend of Short-Son had told him that there were octal-to-the-octals of the man-monkeys to be had out there, swarms! herds! forestfuls! You could kill them by the army and eat them by the feast and still have enough monkey slaves left over to make you rich! For a while Son-of-Chiirr-Nig held his furless tail between his legs to warm it and, shivering, found Man-sun, a radian to the right of Wunderland's two stars, at the edge of the constellation Raised Dagger. It was almost touching Victim's Blood, a distant red giant star that the man-beasts worshiped as lucky Mirach or simply as Beta Andromeda. They had a rich vocabulary of hauntingly soft sounds.

Sometimes it awed him to be on the frontier. From within the Patriarchy, it was said, one could gaze at the night sky and be unable to espy any nearby unconquered stars—but out here the sky was filled with unspoiled herds and grass! So much monkey meat; too

bad those kit warriors were going to kill him before
he got his fangs into it. What a waste! His claws
extended and retracted.

Short-Son had a problem. As long as he was outside,
he was probably safe. But Puller-of-Noses was one
organized kzin, a born commander. Already Puller's
father was arranging to send him with the recruits to
Wunderland for the fourth assault on Man-home. By
now there were probably two octals of his fur-licking
sycophants waiting at the entrances to the city with
their wtsai daggers ready to clip ears:

Looking for me.

But the base was enormous. The original assault on
Wunderland had been staged from here. And the base
had grown fivefold since then as the news of the coming conquest of the Man-system spread back deep into
the Patriarchy. New ships arrived constantly and new
facilities, tunnels, buildings, floater landing sites were
springing up with disordered proliferation. Surely
there was a place to hide.

The kzin youth began stumbling his way in the
direction of some newer diggings, taking deceptive
shortcuts that only led into mazes of walls. He had
certainly not been prepared for this frantic expedition.
He was already too cold to continue. When the pads
of his feet began to go numb a more local solution
seemed in order. He almost turned back when he
found his advance blocked by the great Jotok Run, an
extensive collection of domes and subterranean war-
rens used for the breeding and hunting of the Jotok
slaves. He was going to freeze to death before he
worked around it.

Why didn't he get it over with? If he went back
through a main residential entrance, they'd catch
him—there would be a fight and he would be killed
or hopelessly maimed. Maybe he could surprise them
with a terrible rage and kill one of them before they

got him? He could smile, but the rage paralyzed his leap. He had never been able to leap. It was hopeless. Why not let them kill him today? Even if he escaped today, they'd find him tomorrow and kill him—to purify the race.

That was when he remembered that kits were not allowed to hunt in the Jotok Run without a guardian. Puller-of-Noses could not be there with his gang. Of course, Short-Son was not allowed in the Jotok Run either, and if he was found there he'd be mauled, but at least the adults would not kill him.

There were no windows, and the walls were thick, self-repairing mechanisms which would give warning of malfunction. He found ways to climb up over the walls, with four fingered hands that had evolved for rock climbing.

In his mind, as he climbed, he dreamed that he was clandestinely attacking a monkey-fort. At every corner and ramp he brought out an invisible beam-rifle and poured light into the swarming man-monkeys. By the time he was overlooking the central loading courtyard, vast enough to take twenty floaters, he had killed octals and octals of the furless beasts. He gazed down upon the shadowed landing area and planned his final assault on Man-home.

Doom for all mankind! Then he could hunt giraffes!

He saw surface elevators big enough to take a floater down into the city. He could dimly make out some small kzin-sized airlocks. But a freight entrance would be the easiest to jimmy. There were good locks on the inside to contain the Jotok, who were clever and sometimes treacherous, but no real barriers from the outside. There was no need for barriers from the outside—a kzin did not break and enter without a reason he would be willing to explain to another kzin.

Short-Son did not have the normal entering tools, but he did have a toolkit on his suit and he had always been curious about mechanisms, probing them until he understood their function. He could no longer feel his feet when he dropped into the courtyard, and his fingers were so frozen he took an eternity to release the outer freight door. Stupid mechanism! A female could design a better latch hold!

The black wall slid open. He entered the freight chamber to swirls of condensation while the outer door rolled shut and the purifiers hummed to life—cleaning the nitrogen of carbon dioxide and methane, and adding oxygen. It took him seconds to disable the alarm. By virtue of kzin habit he was battle ready when the inner door released, ready for the five-limbed Jotok leap, or an adult custodian, or even a follower of Puller-of-Noses.

What he found was three of the baby five-armed Jotok, about the size of his hand, crawling around the loading area, totally confused by the stone floor. He squashed them with his foot. He passed through the barrier maze of opaque glass walls into a verdant bio-cology—tall trees, the babble of a brook, and when he removed his oxygen mask, the rotting steamy smells of a pampered rainforest and the hint of a distant pond with rushes. Some of the smells he couldn't classify.

CHAPTER 2
(2391 A.D.)

Short-Son of Chiirr-Nig shivered in relief at the
warmth. He packed his face-mask and holstered his
tools with stiff fingers, dropping one of them. Just
having to pick it up brought his fear and rage out in
a grumbling snarl—not too loud. He didn't want to
attract attention. He assessed his location and picked
out a cluster of bushes and trees where he could hide
without leaving a trampled trail. Assume an imminent
attack.

He removed his boots and began to massage blood
back into his feet. Another of the baby Jotok was trying to climb a thin tree, unsuccessfully, three spindly
arms waving impotently, while the other two double-
elbowed arms pushed against the ground. Short-Son
did not kill it—his rage was subsiding. *Stupid leaf-
eater. You'll make a stupid slave when you grow up.*
The bark was too smooth. The soft-boned fingers of
the tiny infant needed to catch on rough bark. He
noticed more of the creatures. They were probably
coming from the pond.

Leaves rustled, and he looked up quickly, scanning the branches. The ceiling lamps that imitated a tropical sky did not make it easy, there were too many of them and not enough shadows. Had to watch out for those Jotoki. They were *smart* when they grew up—and big, too. They had five cunning brains, one in each arm, and they never slept without at least one brain on the alert and in control.

Short-Son did not feel too threatened. The Jotoki ran from danger and the wild ones were used to being hunted. Give them an escape route and they ran. But they were said to have no fear at all when they were hidden. Caution was still called for. The father of Striped-Son of Hromfi had been killed in seconds when a wild Jotok dropped on him from above during a hunt. Yes, they knew how to hide. A nose couldn't even find them because their skin glands imitated the smells of the forest.

What to do now? Rest. Catch some game and gorge—even if it was poaching. Short-Son was famished. The odors were turning his mind toward its natural ferocity, but he had no intention of hunting Jotoki without training. Any small dumb animal would do. This vast array of domes and caves was made for hunting. It was the best he'd ever do on Hssin, much better than buying frightened *vatach* in cages at the market, and lugging them home on his back for his father.

What he found on the second layer down was a slithering snake as long as his leg. He made a fool of himself catching it. Kzinti enjoyed hunting anywhere, but they were not built for hunting in the forest, and tree climbing snakes were not their natural prey. Nonetheless it made a good morsel and the blood had an interesting tang. The bones were unpleasantly crunchy.

He had to think about getting out of the reserve

even though he didn't want to leave. If he stayed,
some adult would find and thrash him; if he left, his
peers would kill him. Finding refuge in his father's
compound was, perhaps, not the best idea. His brothers were allies, even though they taunted and humili-
ated him, but his father would just throw him back
into the jaws of his peers—to make a good warrior
out of him. He could hear his father lecturing him in
the sonorous formal tense of the Hero's Tongue,
"Make every use of the games to hone your skills."

He found a large fungus the size of his head, growing between two rotting trees, with microscopic flowers flourishing on the black patches. He sniffed in
wonder. He found the trail of some small animal and
he saw a wild Jotok sitting high above on a lamp, its
elbows in the air, watching him with an armored eye
that poked up out of a shoulder blade. The eyes of
the other arms were retracted, probably asleep.

And he wandered down to the pond and waded
among the reeds, looking for fish. All he found were
pre-Jotok arms swimming about, the size of his finger,
the gill-slit red. Each arm was an individual creature,
only joining in a colony of five when they were ready
to crawl upon the land. The polliwogs had an armored
eye already, but only graceful fins where the fingers
would develop.

What a distraction, wading in a pond. He should be
thinking about the mock battle of the game. He
shouldn't be alone here. He should have a whole
squad working with him, or at least be on the team
of some other squad. But he didn't mind the distrac-
tions. It was probably his last day alive. His father had
forgotten that the games weren't fair. The kits tested
each other—and there were rules of honor and honesty to keep the exchanges from being lethal. And
then something happened that had no rules.

A consensus developed about who was the weakling.

And from that day he was hunted and marked for death. The unweaned were "after ear." There was no escape. No act of bravery was good enough. The consensus was a death sentence. Short-Son knew. He had himself helped hound a "designated" weakling into a trap to be torn apart by eight of his peers. So much for being swift to do the bidding of Puller-of-Noses.

Death. Standing to his ankles in the water he found three of the Jotok arms locked together in a union that would last a lifetime, their thin-filament head-feelers waving, sending out a chemical call for two more mates. At this stage they were particularly helpless, unable to dart away, unable to escape onto the land. He pulled them apart, curiously, to see how the head was formed. It bled because the circulation system was already joined. The intestines of the head spilled out. When his wonder was satiated, he popped the arms, one at a time, into his mouth.

CHAPTER 3
(2391 A.D.)

"You devour my charges!" came a rough voice from the shore.

Before he turned, Short-Son of Chiirr-Nig heard in his head an inane lullaby tune that his father sometimes sang to his sons when they had scampered and tussled too much and were very tired.

> "Brave little orange kzin
> Brave little striped kzin,
> Turn to the din
> And if it makes you smile,
> Leap
> But if it is nothing at all
> Really nothing at all
> You may turn-in;
> And droop your eyes while
> You sleep."

The fear was there again. Short-Son faced his challenger obediently. "Honored Jotok-Tender!" And he clouted his own nose to indicate that he knew that he had offended, and stood willing to take the consequences. Inwardly he cringed, waiting for a clawed fist to smack him. Standing among the reeds, he couldn't roll onto his back and expose his throat. His stance was too defiant, but that couldn't be helped in water. The huge scarred kzin wasn't smiling, so at least there was a temporary truce.

"I was enjoying the smells of this delightful Run," he said absurdly.

"And killing Jotok, which is forbidden!" The *voice* was smiling, and *that* was bad.

"*Tiny* Jotok," the kit blurted out, knowing this was the wrong thing to say before he was finished speaking.

"Little ones, hr-r? The size of your opponent is a measure of your warrior skills?"

I'm dead, thought Short-Son. "My inferior warrior skills badly need the attention of a great scarred warrior such as yourself!" Maybe flattery would help.

The right ear and what was left of the left ear of this giant fanged kzin flapped in amusement. "I am no veteran of any war. My scars were earned as a kit in the games, at which I did very badly or I would bear no scars. Out of my reeds—now!"

So he knows what is happening to me! thought Short-Son wonderingly, quick to obey the command to come out of the water.

"I will have to report this transgression to your father."

"Yes!" agreed Short-Son quickly, glad that the thrashing was to be postponed—though perhaps it might be better to be "disciplined" by this orange giant than to be "disciplined" by his father. He followed the Jotok-Tender closely, trying to match his long stride.

After working their way through the swamp and

then making a gradual climb through many turns
within the arboretum, and finally passing beneath a
chattering of Jotoki from the trees, they came to a
rock face. The blast and cutting tool marks were still
in the stone. Some stunted trees were trying to make
it in a bed of flowering vines high on a ledge. A door
in the rock face led into a more conventional kzin
interior, stone-walled like a fortress keep with skins
on the walls.

They were met by a silent Jotok slave, in yellow-
laced livery, who walked leisurely upon the pads of
his primary elbows, thus freeing his hands. When a
Jotok ran, and they could run very fast, they ran on
their wrist pads, with their five-thumbed hands locked
out of the way around the wrist. The centerpiece of
the room beyond the hallway was a replica of ancient
kzin battle armor of the kind that had been supplied
to the kzinti by their then Jotok employees. The bat-
tlewear had, tied to it, ceramic tokens of kzin
manufacture.

*Something to humble the Jotok slaves who dusted
it*, thought Short-Son—except slaves were never
taught their history. This yellow frocked dandy who
preceded them would not even know that his kind had
once had a home sun or that they had been stupid
enough to hire mercenaries to fight their battles for
them.

Jotok-Tender relaxed himself on his big lounge. He
did not invite Short-Son to sit, and the youth, taking
the hint, stood at attention, alert, his ears respectfully
raised to catch any wisdom or approbation that might
be sent his way.

"Your father will not be pleased with you, youngling!" he growled.

"No, Tender."

"I will have to offer him an explanation."

"Yes, Tender."

"Younglings have been known to tell the truth by remaining silent. I wish the true story *without* the silent parts. It will save me beating it out of you."

"My tongue is at your command!"

The giant's ragged ears rippled in amusement. "In the meantime you may sit and relax."

He turned his great head to the waiting slave. "Server-One, refreshments. Grashi-burrowers in the iridium bowls!" Above the arms, full of intestines, the slave's warty head could show no expression. His invisible undermouth clicked acknowledgment. One eye was fixed on the Tender, a second eye fixed on Short-Son, while three other eyes wandered.

Short-Son did not dare to sit down and put himself at ease, but he had been ordered to do just that! He sat and tried to stay at attention. This Jotok-Tender seemed to like him despite gruff ways. Why? It was suspicious. He scanned all the hypotheses he could think of.

The slave reappeared on three elbows, two arms carrying a black lacquered tray with legs, upon which sat two small but tall ceramic sacrificial bowls, inlaid with iridium, and set in carved wood. Short-Son could smell the spices in the sauce—imported, expensive, inappropriate for a thrashing.

A second slave in blue livery brought the squirming Grashi-burrowers, who were mewing softly, handing one of the animals to Server-One, keeping the other. Expertly the animals were beheaded and their blood drained into the cups to enrich the sauce, the Jotoki squeezing/releasing to help the failed hearts move the blood. Then each slave sliced open his delicacy, swiftly removing the intestines, feet, and other inedible parts. The small beasts went back into the bowls, neck down; the slaves curtsied, and left the room.

For all this while Jotok-Tender had not spoken. He pushed one of the cocktails slightly forward toward

Short-Son, taking one himself, to pick up the burrower and munch on it delicately, without using his ripping fangs. Then he dunked the beast back in his bowl for more sauce. Short-Son watched carefully. To him the morsel in the cup was but one mouthful, but he had no intention of displeasing his host—he ate his gift one tiny bite at a time, returning it again and again for more sauce. He was too anxious to actually enjoy what he was tasting.

"You are brave to have Jotoki for personal servants," he said to make polite conversation. He knew that his father detested the five armed creatures and thought of them as treacherous liars fit only for the mines and factories.

"No. There are rules to training a Jotok. Do it right and one can find no more loyal slave among the stars. A competent kzin wins his battles; a kzin in a hurry loses his life—so goes the saying and few pay attention to it. A kzin troubled by his Jotok is a poor trainer. However, you need not listen to me. You are an impetuous youth and impetuous youths do not have the time to listen to an old kzin."

"I am indeed impetuous in my ways and lacking in the wisdom that so great a one as you could impart to me—but not so impetuous that I would leap ahead of your stalking. There is pleasure in following the pads of a graceful gait."

The ears fluttered again. "But I doubt that I would have anything to teach you about flattery. Your tale, youngling!"

Short-Son was already aware of his good luck. He had by now deduced that this old kzin, who had never made a name for himself and had never been allowed a household of females, dwelled upon the pleasures of fatherhood. Living alone, he lacked all knowledge of how much trouble kits and grown sons and pampered females could be. So he longed for a son. It was plain.

Just as plain as it was that Short-Son of Chiirr-Nig longed for a protector.

This was a delicate situation. Jotok-Tender would want a brave warrior for a son, and that was something that Short-Son could dream about but never be. Yet he couldn't lie about himself to this potential protector—only slaves and monkeys lied—but if he told the truth . . .

"We young trouble-makers play games," he began carefully.

"I remember," said the old kzin gruffly.

"Today I was at a disadvantage. Seven well-trained warriors were arrayed against me."

"Seven adolescent kits—short-tempered, with the brains of pre-adolescent Jotoki—were arrayed against you, yes," snorted the kzin. He was insulting Short-Son's companions; a pre-adolescent Jotok had no more wit than a female—animal cunning at best—and did not acquire male reason until after full growth.

"Brawn without brain can be quite effective in some situations," the youth sidestepped. "There have been times when an immature Jotok killed his kzin hunter," he added.

The old kzin was grinning. It frightened Short-Son into a state of heart palpitations, even though he could see the faraway look in Jotok-Tender's eyes. "I faced such a group as yours once. I also stayed and fought. I didn't die. They only got half an ear for their belts." Then the Tender did a strange thing. He stopped grinning, and he rippled only one ear, the ear that was half gone.

What could Short-Son say to that? He quoted military history. "It is recorded that the great Hanash-Grrsh at the battle of the Furry Nebula, when faced by a superior Jotok fleet, disengaged."

"Ah, you are telling me, with oblique honesty, that you *ran* from your attackers."

"Hanash-Grrsh defeated the Jotok fleet some octal-to-three days later!" said Short-Son defensively.

"With a command that included octal-to-six of tested warriors, don't forget. I suspect that you, on the other paw, are acting alone. If you were indeed surrounded by these seven ferocious youths, how then were you able to escape?"

This discussion wasn't going at all well. "Through an airlock," he said meekly. "They weren't thinking of the outside as a battlefield and neglected to cover that option."

"Not likely. You surprised them. They didn't suspect that you'd run. Kzin warriors don't run from honor. You surprise even me. No need to explain to me why you chose to re-enter through the Jotok Run—they wouldn't be here or even have spies here."

"I will train myself and fight them to victory another day!" Short-Son half-growled defiantly.

"Not likely. I know the games. You are marked for death. They have smelled your cowardice just as I smell it now."

Short-Son was stung. "I could stay here and work for you. I'm good with machines."

"No. You are cruel with my helpless Jotoki. Cowardice makes a kzin cruel, always, always, always. I cannot shield your cowardice. You are your father's responsibility." He drooped his eyes sadly.

I'll never have a protector, thought Short-Son. There was no place to hide. "My father will thrash me for trespassing."

"I suppose he will."

"I would rather have you thrash me, old one."

Jotok-Tender cuffed the youngling gently, as if he were a brother. He growled for Server-One, who came scuttling in on five wrists, one armored eye on Jotok-Tender and another eye on the tray and bowls. After a whispered conversation, the eyes focused on Short-Son. The slave returned with a thin, polished switch.

"This will make welts that will impress your father," the kzin growled, "but it won't do any damage, and the pain will be gone within days. Three welts should be enough. Are you ready?"

Short-Son could endure anything when he knew he wasn't going to be killed. "Yes, honored warrior."

Thwack! Thwack! Thwack!

Strange—when this giant beat him he was not even afraid. "You would make a good father." He was trying to tempt the old kzin.

"We will never know. I will take you home to your father's compound so that you will not be waylaid before you get there. I will explain your situation to him, and convince him to give you one last course in bravery. Listen to him. Do not listen to your false emotions. Your life depends upon that."

"You speak the truth, old kzin."

"I myself can teach you little about combat, not being as skilled a warrior as your honorable father, but I can teach you one maneuver that saved my life. Do you sometimes find it difficult to leap?"

All the time. "I have found it difficult to leap at seven smiles."

"Hesitation is the essence of this maneuver. Studied hesitation is best, but hesitation induced by fear can serve just as well. This trick was never taught to me. I learned the whole thing at once, by chance, and killed my attacker. I practiced months to learn what I had done and how to repeat it. It is the only real warrior skill I have. Come."

The giant took Short-Son through rock tunnels to a domed arena which was used to train many Jotoki at once, seducing them to the discipline of taking orders. An eight-and-four of the Jotok were there, practicing the physical arts in a game of move-ball. Their master shooed them to the sidelines where they clustered in a chaos of arms.

He placed Short-Son in front of him, then backed away, crouching. "Now leap at me!"

The youngling tried—but fear paralyzed him and he couldn't leap.

Jotok-Tender roared. "This is only a demonstration! Leap!"

He leapt at the giant, feebly hoping to please him.

The huge kzin sidestepped, turned, and reached out an arm. Short-Son felt his leap go awry, felt his arms fling out from the attack posture in an instinctive attempt to regain his balance, felt himself twisted to flop onto his back like a carcass of flung meat. How did that happen? A fanged face was grinning down at him. When he moved his dizzy head in an attempt to get up he saw along the wall an array of armored eyes watching him from the shoulders of a tangled mass of limbs, undermouths tittering.

Jotok-Tender was unconcerned. "If my claws had been extended, you'd be lying there with your throat ripped out, temporarily a very surprised kzin. Standing over my first victim, I was very surprised myself. Get up. Now *I* will jump *you* as soon as I have shown you how to swivel the pads of your feet."

CHAPTER 4
(2391–2392 A.D.)

In the social protocol of the Hssin Fortress, Chiirr-Nig, the elder, would never have entertained Hssin's nameless Jotok-Tender—but a matter of father and son always took precedence. There was no better way to enter a named-one's household than to voluntarily take upon oneself the son-duties of an absent father, and, while doing so, protect the father's reputation. Since the Jotok-Tender had handled the son's transgression discreetly, without public humiliation for the father, with disciplined kindness for the son, he was welcome, even to a seat, in the great front room of the Chiirr-Nig compound.

Awkward kdatlyno slaves were in attendance and two wives lounged on the rug beside the rippling dance of the infrared warmer. Chiirr-Nig took the opportunity to unburden his disappointment and frustration at Short-Son's inability to master the basics of self-defense. While he lavishly fed his guest fresh Jotok-arm with fish, passing the fish from his own dish down to his youngest wife, he grumbled, first raging and then growling about the lack of self-discipline in the younger generation.

Quietly, Short-Son's mother had slipped into the high-ceilinged room, sensing from wherever she had been the emotional tone of the conflict. Gracefully Hamarr wandered over to sniff the welts on her kit's back. She paced about the reception room, eyeing the two males and her son, ignoring the kdatlyno. With a low growl she drove off one of Chiirr-Nig's younger wives.

She nuzzled Chiirr-Nig in a way that interrupted his conversation, trying to tell him that she was concerned about her son. Idly he scratched her head, paying her concerns no heed. She had fiercely protected the runt of her litter from his brothers and scrappy sisters, and especially from the sons of the compound's other kzin-rretti—but Chiirr-Nig himself had too many sons for him to even think of playing favorites.

Frustrated by her inability to gain her named-one's attention Hamarr turned to Short-Son, nuzzling him. Playfully she began to shove him from the room, blocking his every attempt to return, to get past her, to stay.

Chiirr-Nig watched the display with amused ears. His son was acting properly in attempting to stay while his fate was being discussed—but a kzin indulged his females. They always provided good excuse to break the rigid rules. "Go play with Hamarr!" he dismissed his son, waving a hand. "She's bored. Take her for a run."

Presently Jotok-Tender and Chiirr-Nig were exchanging stories about the escapades of their youth, when Hssin was a dynamic new base on the frontier. Chiirr-Nig offered honors to the giant for bringing his son home, and the giant tactfully suggested that the son needed an intensive crash workout on the finer points of the martial attack.

A playful mother herded her son down to the recreation dome, loping ahead of him, then backtracking to hit him from behind, then facing him—still and silently—poised to run or attack. When she reached the recreation room, she chased away the other kzinrretti with low growls and threats, and bowled Short-Son onto the floor, where she could sniff and lick his welts. She stared at him with admonishing eyes, asking a question whose answer she would be unable to comprehend.

It bothered Hamarr that he was so passive. Her other sons weren't passive. She belted him to his feet, approached, withdrew, surprised him with a cuff that shook his head but was designed not to hurt. She smiled at him and rippled her ears at the same time. She retreated so fast that he had to come after her, but when he got too close she cuffed him again with enough force to rattle his fangs. He enjoyed playing with her, but he was already bigger than she was and he didn't want to hurt her. Nevertheless she forced him to leap and attack until the juices of the fight were running in him savagely. Once he almost bit her too hard.

That evening Hamarr refused to leave him; she refused to return to her own quarters and insisted on sleeping at her son's feet, sometimes waking up to lick his welts, worriedly. She remembered how greedy her other sons had been when they were suckling, how she'd had to growl and cuff the others away when they'd had their fill so that the runt wouldn't starve to death. He was an odd child, and she didn't understand him.

The father dutifully talked to Short-Son's brothers, and the brothers good-naturedly set up practice sessions for their runt sibling. It gave them a chance to show their warrior skills, and to make the training so rigorous that the runt was hard pressed to meet their demands. They could cuff him around, goad his rage, tease him, work him over, all for the virtuous cause of improving his warriorness.

Short-Son merely endured the practice, resigned to his fate, knowing that the one-on-one combat was not preparing him to face a whole *gang* intent on killing him for his ears. The only thing of possible use that he had learned recently was the trick shown him by Jotok-Tender.

For a while he escaped the games. His father used his son's interest in machinery to get him apprenticed to the shipyards where he went to work on the gravitic motors being assembled for the Prowling Hunters. Many octals of them were being shipped out to the Wunderland System. He found himself working with Jotoki slaves, even being taught by them.

Zrkrri-Supervisor had short words of advice for him. "The slaves will save you work, use them, but never put yourself in a position where a slave knows how to do something you do not. That is fatal. I will not consider you competent until you can replace at any time any slave under your command."

There was nothing new in the motors they were building, a four hundred year old design. The Patriarchy had long ago set up standardization so that no matter where a ship was assembled it could be serviced at any other base. How else could the Patriarch run an empire? When a ship needed repairs it might be a lifetime from its mother shipyard, as light traveled, totally dependent upon locally manufactured spare parts.

Innovation, anywhere except in the Admiralty labs of Kzin-home, was discouraged. Heroes, always chafing under inappropriate rules forged at a distance, tended to ignore the decree. But such insubordination was balanced as unauthorized invention was stripped out of weaponry and replaced by standard issue due to lack of spare parts for the innovation.

The engine work was not easy, the conditions of the shop impossibly dark and noisy, made for the needs of Jotok rather than kzin. He had a desk and console beside the superstructure that surrounded the motor being built or refurbished. The desk had never been cleaned and when Short-Son tried to clean it, the edges and pockets still stained his hands.

The superstructure seemed to have been designed by Jotoki; they could swing from platform to platform with ease—trees were their natural medium—but it seemed to shake under kzin weight and frustrate his attempts at climbing. He didn't like to look down. His ever-present Jotok companion always watched him patiently with one eye, other eyes on handholds and general surveillance.

The language he had to learn drove him crazy. It was a corruption of the Hero's Tongue that didn't hiss or rumble, but flowed and chirped. Worse, the expressiveness of the Hero's Tongue had been disemboweled—there were no more insults, the military idiom was gone, the mollifications and flattery were gone. What remained was a utilitarian ability to describe, to point, to anticipate. With a language like that, a slave wouldn't even be able to *think* about revolt—but it was annoyingly bland for a kzin to speak.

However, learning the patois gave Short-Son the first power he had ever had. If he asked a question of any of the Jotoki who worked for him, the slave would stop working and explain very carefully whatever he wanted to know. Nobody teased him. Nobody insulted him. Nobody told him that a warrior didn't need to know *that*. He didn't have to phrase his questions to flatter, or worry that they might insult. He just got answers. If he grinned, he got answers quickly.

So absorbed was he in learning the craftsmanship

of gravitics and puzzling over the theory and mathematics of it, that he forgot the games that young warriors play, forgot that they were still hunting him down. They almost found him. After one of his shifts at the motoryard, while he was hurrying toward the shops that served the local factories, his mind occupied with the remembered taste of a *vatach* snack he was about to buy, he spotted a member of Puller-of-Noses's pride, waiting, watching, seeming to be busy doing nothing while he lounged beside the empty cages outside of the meat shop.

Short-Son backed up, fear driving him to return to his dim little desk on the vast floor of the motoryard. He couldn't think. He couldn't stay here. He couldn't leave. He chose instead to go up—the yard maintained a grassland park up there for their kzin workers. It was empty at this hour, but the tall grass soothed him and he had an overview of the shops and the giant freight elevators that rose to the surface. He stayed here under the artificial light, repressing the growlings of his hunger, waiting, waiting until he was sure his enemy was gone. Then he sneaked back home to his father's compound, ashamed.

It didn't matter. He was sent with a crew into space to install new drives in a Hunting Prowler that had recently come in from Kzrrosh on its way to Wunderland to join the armada forming against the monkeys. It was his first time in space. And it was the first time he had ever seen a Hunting Prowler whole. Nothing of the experience was familiar, the deep space armor that constrained him, the sled that was bringing him closer, the bulky Jotok armor that extended his slaves' reach by a full metallic hand.

The spheroidal warship was one of the smaller kzin naval killers. Short-Son's chief slave pointed out a larger battleship in the far distance, a red dot moving in the light of R'hshssira, but their Hunting Prowler, close as it was, seemed far more formidable, studded with weapon pods, sensor booms, control domes, drive field ribs, and boat bays with a shuttle drifting alongside. Still, for the moment it was helpless—its motor was gone, the new one still held in the claws of the shuttle, uninstalled.

Hssin rolled beneath them, clotted red, like another giant battleship. It was more than illusion. From Hssin, Wunderland had been conquered. Hssin still attracted warcraft from ever more distant regions of the Patriarchy as the news of the monkeys spread at the unhurried pace of light. The kzin fought their battles that way. Reinforcements arrived for a generation after the battle was won. Sometimes they were needed, sometimes not. In this case the latecoming Conquest Warriors were needed, for the star-swinging monkeys still owned unconquered systems.

Under the stars, maneuvering the giant gravitic motor into this lethal ship of conquest, Short-Son first thought that perhaps he too might be able to join the armada being thrown against Man-sun. His power gave him the illusion that he was a real warrior. It felt very good. With magnetic boots on the hull of the kzin ship, *his ship*, he could look up and imagine what it would be like to destroy the ships of men.

But the very same day he returned from space, the watcher for the pride of Puller-of-Noses was there, waiting patiently by the meat shop, waiting for him. He had thought that the glory of space had reformed him. He had given the power to travel between the stars to a valiant ship of prey, juggled that monstrous motor in his own arms! Didn't that give him the power to crush all fear? to become a warrior?

Yet it took only a second sighting of the watcher to trigger all the cowardice he had ever known. It meant that they had found him. Fear! An image of himself that he had brought from space, crumbled. He was no kzin who could carry a star engine on his shoulder—he had been no more than an insect carrying a stone. How to save himself?

Again he retreated back into the motoryard and climbed. It was all he could think of now, waiting them out a second time, hiding. Tomorrow he would think of some better plan. It was a miserable feeling. He stepped out onto the roof into the still tall grass. Why didn't they leave him alone?

Only when the grass moved did he realize his terrible mistake. First he faced one casual kzin, in the shirt and epaulets favored by the young of Hssin. But there were others; he smelled their exertion. When he edged back toward the door he confronted the brown striped watcher who had followed him. To his right a third kzin rose from the grass. Before he could run, a fourth blocked his way. Two others guarded distant exits. He was trapped by six grinning kzin who wanted his ears.

"Now you'll *have* to fight," said Puller-of-Noses, already crouched and waiting for his leap.

CHAPTER 5
(2392 A.D.)

Short-Son tried to look over the edge of the roof but he was too far away and he already knew there was no escape in that direction. He glanced toward the pair of almost ship-sized elevators that rose into the artificial sky. Much too far away. Could a kzin fly?

Never had he felt such a rage. His mouth was wrapped back over his fangs in a death grin and he couldn't have erased it from his face if he'd tried. His claws were out. His haunches were primed to leap at his tormentor and tear him to bits with fang and claw and hatred. He breathed. Only the fear kept him rooted.

"We hear you do it in trees with Jotok playmates!" taunted Hidden-Smiler whose smile was not hidden.

He remembered clearly through the rage how Jotok-Tender had told him the usage of fear, and practiced with him. Wait for the first leap. Apply that body-twist while extending the claws just so. A strange part of his mind was noticing that he had no control over his claws now—they were unretractable.

31

"Your father was a *vatach*!" rumbled another kzin who was not coming too close.

"His *mother* taught this toothless kit how to fight!"

Puller-of-Noses was relaxing now, sensing that Short-Son really didn't have the courage to fight. That emboldened him. He wasn't going to need his friends. He motioned them away. He'd take these ears himself. "You're tied up like a *zianya* on the table, ready for the feast. I smell your fear, *zianya*."

Short-Son snarled.

"Oh, we disturbed you! You came up here to feed on the grass. Don't let us stop you." Puller-of-Noses was enjoying the repartee.

"The grass is choice for one with a double stomach," jibed Hidden-Smile.

Attack me! I'll flip and slash your throats out! Short-Son's thoughts were ravening, but he could say nothing. He hated them for teasing him, playing with him before they killed him. His fangs were sticking to dry lips, frozen by his grin.

"Our coward stinks of fear," said Puller-of-Noses, ready for the kill, charging himself for a single leap that would rip the life from his prey. "You smell like a fattened grass-eater." When his opponent didn't respond, he couldn't resist the final, ultimate insult. While he composed it, the tip of his pink tail flipped back and forth. "I'll make a deal with you. Be an herbivore. Put your head in the grass and eat it, and I'll spare your life. Or fight like a Hero and I'll give you honor."

If Puller-of-Noses had attacked then, a desperate Short-Son might have unbalanced him and slashed him to a quick death, but the pride leader was prolonging the agony, waiting for a reply, enjoying his wit too much to begin a battle that would end instantly and thus instantly end his fun. While he taunted, his only caution was to reestablish his crouch. The pause gave Short-Son a fatal moment of thought.

Puller-of-Noses had tendered a verbal bargain: eat grass and live or be a Hero and die.

His word of honor would force him to keep that bargain.

Puller-of-Noses was also too stupid to understand that he had actually offered Short-Son a *real* choice between life and death. In the challenger's mind there was no choice at all between honor and eating grass. He *thought* he had Short-Son trapped.

Trembling, full of disgust for himself, Short-Son sank to his knees and began to eat the tall strands of green—crawling, ripping it from its roots with his fangs, chewing, though his teeth were not meant for such chewing. There was no way for his throat to swallow the fibrous cud, but he kept chewing and chewing.

Six kzin came forward with stunned eyes. Their ears twitched in amusement, but it wasn't amusement they felt; what they felt was disbelief. And only then did Puller-of-Noses realize that he could gain no honor by killing this sniveling coward. Worse, he would be condemned to death if he broke his word. The ears of his intended victim were worthless.

From that day on Hssin's "herbivorous" kzin had a new name spontaneously bestowed upon him—Eater-of-Grass. There was no suppressing the story. It spread like grassfire throughout the Hssin base. The Chiirr-Nig household disowned him. The naval shipyards no longer trusted him to work on their gravity polarizers.

He had no place to sleep, no place to eat, no one to talk to, no work. For a while he lived in corners and on roofs and in tunnels, hunting escaped rodents. It was hard to keep clean. Once he was mistaken for a wretched telepath. He even tried chewing on roots to ease his hunger, but in his stomach they turned to gas and indigestion. He begged—and grown kzin pretended he didn't exist. He robbed a cage once of its live *vatach* which had been hung out for fresh air, a death offense if caught. He made it look as if the *vatach* had escaped. They all expected him to walk out onto the surface of Hssin and disappear into the mountains to die but he had no suit.

When he begged for a surface suit, yes, then they paid attention to him and charitably granted his wish. Eater-of-Grass didn't walk into the mountains, however—he used the suit to break back into the Jotok Run, mostly because he wanted a bath. Soaking in water wasn't the best way to take a bath, but it would do. He spent a day cleaning and grooming his fur. When no one came to throw him out, he saw no reason to leave.

This time he was more covert. He knew how to hide. He kept away from the hunting parties and he knew much more about Jotok manners. He stalked the wild Jotoki up in the trees and they hunted him when he wasn't looking. He studied Jotok anatomy for lack of anything else to do—the lungs on the inner arm that fed the heart and doubled as a singsong voice, the strange-tasting brain tissue that grew in a cortex around the heart, the leaf-grinding teeth in the undermouth that made great spearheads when sharpened.

Eater-of-Grass built three hidden lairs. He pretended he was an ancient kzin, before language or iron or gunpowder, spraying and defending his territory. According to the Conservors that was the era when kzin fathers often ate their sons to keep down the competition. Wryly, he wondered how different it was today. Then a kzinrret hid her children and defended them fiercely. Kzinrretti *still* tried to be protective. He remembered his mother fondly—without her he would not be alive today.

When the lights came on one morning, green and yellow through the leaves, he lifted his ears to listen for kzin hunting parties but heard only insects and the fall of a branch. Broad leaves dumped their water. Swooping from one branch to another, a firg cackled every time it took to the air, visible because of the red scales down its back.

He sniffed—detecting no kzin smells—but he wasn't alone. He could never pick up the scent of a Jotok, because of a Jotok's ability to mimic any aroma, but a forest is full of clues. With nostrils flared, he was catching the tang of lush broken cells, sugar, acid, spice. The rind of the pop-spray. A Jotok was out there, eating fruit.

Yes—there he was, many eyes watching from a rocky ridge, one hand already around a branch ready to shoot himself up into the growth above, and far enough away to escape. Prey for today's meal, perhaps. But the creature would be hard to track. Best to ignore him for now. But not totally.

Eater-of-Grass found a tree being garroted by a pop-spray vine and shimmied up the bark to tear off a bunch of ripe balls. The rind was tough but that meant nothing to a Jotok's grinding molars. He placed the balls on a stump in sight of his prey and retreated far enough away to be out of fear's range, trusting the animal's natural curiosity to induce it to examine the offering.

He wasn't quite sure how to spring a trap. This Jotok's limbs had the bulk and shape of an adult, but the skin wore a youthful shine. The beast might still be too young to have intelligence, yet must be about the age at which its kind acquired (very quickly) kzin-like deductive powers, becoming both hard to catch and dangerous.

After eating the fruit-balls his prey didn't move away. It sat on its mouth, watching him, elbows in the air. He approached and it retreated, he casually distanced himself and it followed—peculiar behavior for a wild Jotok. The animal was still there the next morning, much closer, sitting in the tree above him and watching.

He fed it again. "Some pop-spray for you, Long-Reach. Hai! Long-Reach!"

When he had retreated the required distance, it dashed to the ground to devour his offering, shoving the balls one at a time into its undermouth with a weird lateral chewing motion. All the while it stared at him with two eyes, focused one on the fruit, while the others jerkily kept a cautious watch on the neighborhood.

Then . . . "Long-Reach," it imitated from a lung slit on one of the arms. "Long-Reach," replied another arm.

Fan-like ears suddenly erect, the amazed kzin recognized what it was saying from his recent verbal exchanges with Jotok slaves. Its voices were musical, muting the hisses and gutturals of the Hero's Tongue. He listened, fascinated, as the arms began to play with the words, chatting to themselves in harmony. "Long-Reach. *Long-Reach*. Long-Long-Long-Reach. Reach . . . Reach . . . Reach!"

It tittered, pleased with itself, shifted to the mockery of the chirping of various insects, then sat down to await the orange-yellow kzin's response.

"Come here, Long-Reach," he said in his most ingratiating manner. "Stupid animal, I want to eat you."

"Want to eat you. Want to eat you," it replied.

How remarkable, he thought. He had found a Jotok in transition. Jotok-Tender had told him that if he fed one of the beasts at this stage, it would follow him around and imitate him. The Jotoki were very peculiar, indeed; children were not raised in a family, they had no household keep, no patriarch, no mothers, no brothers to terrorize them, no teachers, no discipline, no toys, no warrior games. They just grew up in the forest, and when an adult wanted a family he just took a trip to the forest, picked out a healthy youth who had managed to survive and took him home.

The transitional Jotok was "programmed" to bond to whoever adopted it. Unfortunately for the Jotok race, the transitional mind, having evolved on a planet where the Jotoki were the *only* intelligent life form, couldn't easily differentiate between an adult Jotok and an adult kzin. Any intelligent parent sufficed. Thus they made excellent slaves.

Days later Long-Reach was still following him around, no longer afraid of its kzin parent at all. Astonishingly, it had acquired a vocabulary of more words than it could count on its five-times-five thumbs. He tried to remember himself as a small kit; certainly he had never learned the basics of the Hero's Tongue in so short a time.

After catching a rodent to eat, and being astonished when Long-Reach promptly dashed off into the woods and came back with another rodent, he became challenged to find out how much he could teach the creature. Could it learn to use tools? He sharpened a stake with his knife and handed the blade to one of the five arms.

"Long-Reach, now you try."

"Long-Reach, try." The Jotok didn't succeed. It wailed in consternation, but wouldn't return the knife to Eater-of-Grass, demanding the right to continue to try. Half a day later it was still trying, by then more pleased with itself. The stake was sharp, if very short.

The kzin youth became delighted with the absurdity of their relationship. He found himself struggling up trees, which sometimes tottered under his weight, to gather delicacies for his Long-Reach, while Long-Reach got tangled in the underbrush chasing rodents for him. He no longer thought of Long-Reach as a meal, or even as an "it." What he appreciated most was that Long-Reach never slept—at least one arm was always awake, watching for danger.

There *were* dangers. The wild Jotoki, who had passed through the transitional phase without being adopted, were antisocial beasts, protective of their territory, and, though hunter-shy in the daytime, were vicious at night. They had no language or learning, but were quite capable of inventing tools and devising intricate revenges for remembered transgressions. They *knew* that the kzinti were their enemies. They backtracked to deceive, they laid traps, they played jokes.

Of course, the worst danger was the kzin hunting parties.

Eater-of-Grass was amazed at how well Long-Reach knew the Jotok Run and how quickly he could take them away from danger. He was a very useful companion.

CHAPTER 6
(2392 A.D.)

Thumbs were pulling at his fur. He did not mind because Long-Reach was fascinated by his hairiness. The thumbs grew more insistent. They pulled his eyelids open. "Hunters, hunters, hunters," the arms whispered, sometimes interrupting each other.

Eater-of-Grass was on his feet instantly, soundlessly moving. But it was soon evident that they were being tracked by experts. They hiked from the tall trees under the domes, ducking through tunnels, wading across dark swamps, climbing over blasted rock faces, squirming down through a crevasse to the treetops of the level below. Mostly Long-Reach chose their route. But evasions didn't shake their pursuers for long. All the while the desperate kzin youth gauged the hunting party, sniffing the wind, sometimes sending out a circumspect Long-Reach to reconnoiter through the rainforest's canopy.

The fugitives were being tracked by three Jotoki scouting among the branches and one kzin on the ground, in an unhurried manner but diligently.

The final backtrack was a mistake. They fell into the center of the Jotok shepherds, and the triangle moved with them—no matter where they turned. Pinned. He caught a flash of yellow livery in the trees—and knew who was hunting them.

"Long-Reach, we won't escape. Stop."

His Jotok slave did not fully understand. Arms waving, the beast ran ahead on three wrists, returned in confusion, ran up and down trees, and finally stopped close by, primed to run on five wrists, swaying with fear.

Eater-of-Grass waited, death resignation on him at the same time that his mind was trying out various phrases of flattery. Eventually the giant kzin appeared in the copse below, his age showing in his lame pace. He approached the youngling.

"Ah, you," he said.

"I had no place else to go, honored warrior," explained Eater-of-Grass sullenly.

This excuse for his crime was ignored. "You no longer have the youth-name of the house of Chiirr-Nig. How shall I address you?" asked Jotok-Tender.

"Eater-of-Grass," replied the ostracized kzin, defiantly.

"An inappropriate name," growled Jotok-Tender. "Names must bear on the day's truth. Have you been eating grass? I think not—you've been hunting and eating my Jotoki, and various small warm creatures. Eater-of-Ferocious-Jotoki might be a better name." He glanced down at Long-Reach.

"We run!" said Long-Reach. "Now!" admonished another of the arms, but the beast stood its ground.

The giant reached down gently to pop an eyeball out of its armor as far as it would go, examining the lubrication petals. Then he took one of Long-Reach's arms and examined the thumbs. "Exactly the right age.

You will have an absolutely loyal slave if you train him as I shall instruct you. You didn't frighten him away?"

"Honored oldster, I had some recent experience with Jotoki at the shipyard. I speak the appropriate patois. Long-Reach, here, found me more than I found him."

"Perhaps we could call you Trainer-of-Slaves. A good trade-name that. Does it suit you?"

"Better than Eater-of-Grass."

"Never use *that name* in front of me!" snarled Jot-ok-Tender. "I asked you a civil question. Answer! Does it suit you?"

"Trainer-of-Slaves at your service, honored half-ear!" He paused. "Am I being offered employment?"

"A slaver like me offering *employment*? Perhaps I could give food and shelter in exchange for unquestioned service."

"I am loyal to the warrior who gives honest leadership!"

"Said well for a recidivist." He let his ears flap for effect. "We can't parade you around, of course, but I can keep you busy and out of sight. We have mutual needs. Are your ears erect? Have you been in contact?"

"In hiding one is deaf."

"The startling news, then. By lightbeam, Hssin has had advance warning of a small armada coming through, long on its way, ruled by High Conquest Commander Chuut-Riit of the Kzin Admiralty. He will be stripping Hssin of Heroes and warships, including all the Jotoki slaves we can provide. His Conquest Campaign against the monkey-worlds has been *authorized* by the Patriarchy itself. The Patriarch!

"I have already received my advance demands, and dare not be lax in meeting them. Who knows how this Chuut-Riit deals with failure? I am not of a mind to find out. I will be busy and I need help. No one will begrudge me your services. As for those moralists who would have you wasted, a mere wave of Chuut-Riit's orders before the noses of such kit-eaters will lay flat their pompous fur."

"Chuut-Riit?"

"Obviously a member of the Patriarch's family. Other than that we know nothing."

"Coming *here*?"

"In truth, we don't see much of the Patriarchy in these dismal regions, and do quite well without it, but evidently news of our contact with the monkeys seems to have filtered inward and given our wealthier Heroes Long-Journey fever. The families of Ka'ashi"—he gave the Kzin name for Wunderland—"will not be pleased."

"Not be pleased by the attention of the Patriarchy!"

"Youngling, for lifetimes this outback of the Empire has attracted only adventurers driven from the richer worlds by their fathers, by debts, by a desire to be where the Patriarchy isn't, driven here sometimes by kzin hubris, and sometimes, like me, by cowardice. Heroes with ragged fur. Who else would tolerate the cramped quarters of stinking ships for years on end? Wunderland was a gift of the fanged god. Why should its Heroes desire to roll on their backs and expose their throats to those who already have vast wealth? In rage they will challenge Chuut-Riit, but if Chuut-Riit proves able, they will submit. Chuut-Riit will prove able. Do you know history?"

"I listen to the Conservors."

"Not them! The Collected Voices. Last night I put the memoirs of the Riits in my scanner. They scent victory and track it down at the leisurely pace of starlight. Then they impose their victory upon the victor. The Riits are the conquerors of successful Conquest Commanders. If we obey them, we get to keep a goodly portion of what we have conquered."

"And if we don't?"

"Then they begin by taking our daughters. After that the air parches and the fur gets wet with fear."

"I see many duels."

"Yes, and as you watch the mayhem—if you are wise, from within a thick bunker—remember that only fools who wish to cleanse the race of their own fool's blood challenge the Patriarch's family. This is the *Patriarch's family*, not some wandering warlord. Are you with me?"

"I begin to serve your needs at this very moment, wise and merciful Hero! I will make no mistakes!"

"You *will* make mistakes, arrogant kit, and for that I will cuff your brains hard enough to rattle them in your skull, but not hard enough to damage them. Before you follow me, soothe your slave. Disarming his fear at this stage of his development is very important. He must feel free to leave us, though he has already hormonally locked-on to you and cannot leave you. And it is essential that he take direction from *you*, not me. As we travel back to my lair, make sure that your slave is *always* closer to you than to me. Do you understand that?"

"Yes, honored teacher."

"I will try to trick you into violating my admonition. No matter what I do, keep your Jotok closer to your side than to mine! Your training has begun." Jotok-Tender made a high *Rrwrowr*, and his liveried slaves dropped from the trees and formed a point for their return procession.

As Trainer-of-Slaves followed his new protector, he thought about the mysterious Chuut-Riit. An armada! The mythical Patriarchy was coming to Hssin! Because light was faster than the gravity polarizer, it would be impatient years before the High Conquest Commander arrived—but the good in that was the time it gave Trainer-of-Slaves to make himself ready.

He would produce slaves for the Patriarch's family!

The thought returned his attention to Long-Reach, who was following them with all the enthusiasm of a monkey tied to a nose-ring. He patted the beast's warty head and threw a stick for him to fetch—in a direction which would keep him away from the giant.

But Trainer-of-Slaves was having a difficult time thinking about slaves. His mind was on the bridge of a Prowling Hunter, following Chuut-Riit through the starry reaches, seeking prey. His soul had already vowed eternal allegiance to this Hero whose miraculous message from space had saved his life. The miracle of it was an omen: Chuut-Riit was the light leading him to Heroism.

Back in the slaver compound, Jotok-Tender tattooed a black splotch on Trainer-of-Slaves's facial skin so that charcoal could be discreetly seen through the fine hair, and he ordered fitted for his charge a purple and mauve tunic of the distant W'kkai style, unfashionable on Hssin. None of this was a disguise, but it made it possible for a local kzin to face this pariah and say "Trainer-of-Slaves" and not think *Eater-of-Grass*.

The old slaver warned his youngling apprentice never to discuss his cowardly past. That way the subject would never come up. It was dangerous for a kzin to mention another kzin's former life under a different name before the subject kzin mentioned it himself.

"In time you will have your own army of slaves, who are owned by others but loyal to you. You will need no other name than Trainer-of-Slaves to bring fear into the feet of kzin warriors. Dress well, pretend to no honors beyond your station, honor your timeless word—and keep your slaves close at hand."

Trainer-of-Slaves was shown to his sparse lair, and taken on a tour of the Jotok dormitory, poles and platforms under a windowless dome. On the level below, underground, were the training simulators where Jotoki learned their trade.

"Why will Chuut-Riit want so many Jotok slaves? Many families of Hssin will not permit Jotoki in their houses."

"I imagine that Chuut-Riit values them as mechanics."

"They handle tools well! In the shipyards my supervisor commanded that I learn all that my slaves knew, but I must admit that when *I* needed three arms, I was at a loss! One plus three-octals of thumbs!"

"Recall that the Jotoki evolved the gravity polarizer while we were puzzling over flint. We were hired by the Jotoki for our abilities as warriors, not for our way with machines."

"Is it really true that the Jotoki once ruled over us?"

"They commanded the ships that first took us out to the stars. But order evolves from disorder. Vegetation evolves to dominate the rock, the herbivore evolves to dominate the vegetation, and the carnivore evolves to dominate the plant-eater. Intelligence evolves in males to dominate the female. In the natural order of things the warrior rises above the mechanic."

"And the wisdom of age rises above the untutored youth. Have I got that right?"

"You've had a bad beginning, but you may yet live to an age when your fur sheds without replacing itself—if your flattery doesn't get you into trouble first."

CHAPTER 7
(2392 A.D.)

Long-Reach was collectively puzzled by the strange
chambers to which the yellow-one had taken him. It
was a frightening world, more because there were no
trees in it than because of the slabs that slid open in
the world-boundaries. The first big discussion he had
among himselves was: how would his mouth eat if
there were no leaves? His eyes kept looking for leaves,
and each of him kept asking to stare through another's
eyes to see if there weren't leaves in that direction.
Skinny(arm) was especially apprehensive.

And for another thing, in this world there were too
many of the yellow-orange carnivores. They made all
of him anxious. He didn't know why his own yellow-
one was special except that the nervousness disappeared when they were together. Then very interesting things happened.

Among himselves he referred to his special carnivore companion as Mellow-Yellow, which was not a
vibrating-word but was a pastel image-word of the
kind used to communicate between his selves. Mel-

46

low-Yellow was "world-lights filtering down through mingled leaf-tissue." It was the best forest image there was. His companion did seem to have a voice-name, but the rules were confusing. Sometimes he referred to his body as "Hero," sometimes as "Warrior," sometimes as "Kzin," sometimes, when he was dangerous to be with it was "Eater-of-Grass," or "Fangless." The voice-names changed as night and day. Lately it was "Trainer-of-Slaves." Simpler to think: Mellow-Yellow.

The furry Mellow-Yellow had a game with the low-frequency sounds that was so exciting to play that Long-Reach couldn't seem to stop playing. If Mellow-Yellow quieted his vibrator (which seemed stuck in his mouth where he couldn't chew it) Long-Reach felt compelled to hum and rumble and chatter in order to provoke more of that game. When he deliberately tried to keep one of his lungs silent, another was sure to interrupt the hush. Big(arm) had more restraint than skinny(arm).

The game had rules. Each eye-image had an ear-sound that only Mellow-Yellow knew and Long-Reach had to guess. Since the kinds and varieties of image were endless, it was a never ending quest to find the voice that fitted the image. What was exciting was that if his selves were clever he could use words to provoke the new sounds out of Mellow-Yellow, or even better, use the words *themselves* as an aid to discovering the new words. His selves carried on an internal race. Which lungs would first utter the true sequence of sounds? Sometimes they all spoke at once. Short(arm) was best at such races and tended to dominate the role of talker. When short(arm) was asleep, Long-Reach was less glib.

In this world beyond the trees, there were many new images, many new words.

"Leaves," said short(arm). "Leaves, leaves," repeated skinny(arm) because there weren't any.

"Ah, you're hungry." Mellow-Yellow left the cave through . . . an elevator? Door, door, corrected short(arm). When Long-Reach tried to follow there was no door. Anxiety.

But Mellow-Yellow came back with leaves in a container of grass. Big(arm) thought about the right words for the sight and made suggestions while feeling the weave of the grass blades that were entwined in a very regular way. His eye had never seen anything like it. "Leaves sit on grass-floor," said short(arm) while communicating the thought that flat-"floor" could not be a good word for hollow-container.

"It's a *basket*, not a floor. I got it from the slave quarters. Say 'basket.' "

"Basket, basket. Basket of grass. Grass basket."

"And don't take it apart! Don't you *ever* stop being curious?"

Long-Reach picked up the basket with two arms and dumped the leaves on the floor. He sat on them, elbows in the air, and began to masticate. "Good," exclaimed all the arms in unison.

"My ears ripple when I watch you sitting down to eat."

"My ears ripple when I watch you sitting down to excrete. One-mouth better than two."

"Long-Reach, *your* ears don't ripple. Your ears are in your wrists."

"Ripple? Ripple?" Big(arm) rose so that its eye could look at the resonance cups on its wrist which analyzed sound.

Trainer-of-Slaves rippled his ears to demonstrate. He was genuinely amused. "That's what *I* do when I tell a joke. How do I know when *you* are telling a joke?"

"Joke?"

"Some other day!"

Trainer-of-Slaves needed to sleep—so Long-Reach

hooked himself to a wall rack and slept himself, with only freckled(arm) awake and watching the door. Freckled(arm) had things to mull over but that was difficult with sleep-silence on four channels.

Thinking did not go rapidly without question-answers from other-arms. But questions were themselves interesting. What had happened to the forest? Why did the absence of trees make floors flat? What was glass? How could something invisible resist the push of a hand? How was R'hshssira attached to its ceiling? Did all worlds have different colored lamps?

There were more questions in the morning when Mellow-Yellow led Long-Reach to a cavern full of weird shapes and vines that swallowed eyes and arms. The giant carnivore was there with the smell of leaf-eater flesh on his breath. Frightening.

"You won't be able to put him in the machine—they panic when their arms are constrained—and his vocabulary isn't big enough so that an explanation will register. We'll have to shoot him up with trazine. First, we'll let him watch a Jotok come out of the trainer unharmed."

Long-Reach stayed as near his yellow companion as he could get. They put him too close to a big leaf-eater like himself who was suspended in mid-air, his arms in thick sleeves, with vines coming out of the caps over his eyes. His limbs convulsed as if he were running and flying among the trees—but he wasn't going anywhere. Terrifying.

The big kzin unhooked the eyes. The sleeves came off. While the beast was being liberated, three of Long-Reach's brains came to the simultaneous conclusion that *he* was going to become the replacement. Three arms started to back off—and couldn't move.

"The trazine won't harm you. Be gone within heart-beats." They were putting him into the sleeves and he couldn't resist. His eyes had retracted to their armored state in a reflex at the shock of paralysis, but he could not keep them closed while the giant popped out each eye in turn and stuck them into caps. He was blind and paralyzed. Was this the death he had been avoiding all his life?

All of his minds went into escape mode. But before he could even think of escape . . . suddenly . . . he was transported to a forest. There was a precision smoothness to each detail and no smell. He had not passed through any walls or doors. Did one die and go to an odorless forest? He still couldn't move, but his thumbs were wrapped around branches and he wasn't falling. He saw no kzinti. When the paralysis wore off, he took the chance and ran; he zipped through the trees like flying, barely touching a branch before he was reaching for another.

The landmarks were unfamiliar and there were no odor clues. The trees were too tall. When he climbed as high as he could go there were no ceiling lamps. White moss floated overhead where the roof should have been. Nothing he did seemed to orient him, even his acceleration senses were subtly contradicting his eyes and the feel of his skin. He couldn't backtrack because the world changed behind him as it passed out of sight—what was behind was as unknown as what was in front. It was wrong.

A lake appeared through the trees, larger than any lake he had ever seen, bluer than it had any right to be. He skittered among broad branches that had been able to reach outward along the shoreline, afraid to let the lake out of sight lest it disappear. High above the beach he paused.

His tree developed a lung-slit and spoke. "I am a tree."

Startled, he leaped into another tree, nearly missing it. "Nice leap," said a bird who had been watching him.

He was gaping at the tree (with three eyes) and the bird (with two eyes). How many different kinds of worlds were there? asked freckled(arm) frantically. After a while Long-Reach got used to it. The world patiently gave him lessons in speech with the same image-sound codes as Mellow-Yellow had used. Stones talked. Stumps talked. Animals talked. It was very disconcerting.

The predictables had shifted. And not to be able to predict meant *danger*. Hide and meditate upon the consequences. Idly fast(arm) plucked some berries in their leaf-cones and shoved them up into the undermouth to placate hunger. But there was nothing for Long-Reach to chew on. Shock. In this world food was going to be a problem. Too many problems.

"Eat me," said a leaf.

He tried. It was only a strong taste, still nothing to chew on.

"Bitter," said the leaf which had miraculously regrown. "Eat me again."

He did so. It tasted like the caps of marsh-reed, or even seed-berries, but again there was nothing to chew on.

"Sweet," said the everlasting leaf. "Eat me again."

Right now he wanted Mellow-Yellow. "Trainer-of-Slaves!" he bellowed.

His call produced an immediate twilight, fading into a night darker than the deepest cavern.

Beside him, Mellow-Yellow appeared slowly, like a ceiling lamp at dawn, without casting any light into the darkness. The carnivore's image was too sharp, too orange, and flickered a little. A furry hand reached out and touched the eye of big(arm). Then—weirdly with only one eye—he was back where he had started; Mellow-Yellow was the right color, the giant kzin was beside him and so was all the machinery in the cavern. His selves jumped to look through big(arm)'s eye.

Long-Reach could now feel his arms in their tight trap. Panic. Death . . . he began to struggle.

The giant kzin backed off but Mellow-Yellow efficiently freed the capped eyes and removed the constraints. Long-Reach walked away, miffed, with only freckled(arm) watching the big yellow trickster curiously.

"Joke," said Trainer-of-Slaves.

"You have brains where your intestines should be!" sulked Long-Reach, who had begun to assimilate his anatomy lessons. "Joke," he added, having no intention of insulting a carnivore.

But for the rest of the day he refused to speak. At night while Mellow-Yellow slept, his minds debated what they had seen. The whole event reeked of danger. Hide, said all of his instincts. And yet the curiosity was overpowering! Talking trees! Moving through walls! Seeing different worlds with each eye! The wonder of it!

At the first sign that Mellow-Yellow was awake, he herded him toward the door. "More joke," he said.

During his second session in the confinement rig he learned numbers and image symbols for numbers. Released, he enthusiastically counted everything—still amazed that the region between three and many could be divided up endlessly into distinct parts, that no matter how high he counted, there was one more. He counted kzin, he counted lamps, and he counted the leaves he ate, one by one because freckled(arm) wanted to know how many leaves it took to stop hunger.

The virtual worlds of the confinement rig were of two kinds. The moment he tired of one, he was shifted to the other. There were the work worlds where he learned practical mathematics and the art of maintaining machines and proper ways of addressing his kzin masters. There were the play worlds of forest and dungeon where natural law changed whimsically, sometimes in frightful ways, sometimes amusingly. When capricious play taxed his minds, a shift to the tuning of gravitic force fields was a relief; when tedious machining drove him to singing mental tunes in harmony, a shift to the free world of play was pleasure.

Time blurred. He saw less and less of Mellow-Yellow, yet the hours he spent with his kzin companion were rich in conversation. Trainer-of-Slaves admitted that Jotok-Tender was a hard taskmaster while Long-Reach taught his friend geometry and how to disassemble machines. Once they couldn't reassemble a machine because the slave hadn't got that far in his lessons. For that sin Jotok-Tender had them both scrubbing floors together.

The best days were spent hunting. Long-Reach wore a special uniform of cloth that distinguished the slaves of Mellow-Yellow, green and red stripes, ruffles. They swept through the Jotok Run searching out new slaves, leisurely, with no special command to return. To the senses of Long-Reach, the familiar woods and ponds and rock faces of his youth were better than the virtual forests of the confinement rig. There was fresh forest odor and the trees didn't talk. The ceiling had lamps and the caves led only to the level below.

Long-Reach would flush the prey, knowing where the young gathered. Then Trainer-of-Slaves would seduce the youth while Long-Reach hid in the trees. The hunt was not always successful. The Jotok they stalked might prove large enough, yet still untouched by curiosity-hunger—he'd have to be released until he matured. Or he might be wild, past his prime, good only for the dinner table, his intelligence lost to language, metamorphosed into cunning.

Trainer-of-Slaves kept the best of the Jotok captives for himself. Three became his personal retinue: Long-

Reach, Joker, and Creepy. The three had the usual training in mathematics, mechanics, and gravitic device maintenance. But they were also Mellow-Yellow's hunting companions. They noticed that he had enemies among the kzin, and chattered about the danger to him among themselves, covertly. Inevitably they became his bodyguards, the eyes who watched his back.

CHAPTER 8
(2396 A.D.)

The armada was arriving. Like all things in the Patriarchy, there was no great hurry.

First the swift *Victory at S'Rawl* fell out of space into orbit around Hssin. It disgorged no warriors, and made no diplomacy, but imperiously took over the duties of the local Orbit Command by Authority of the Patriarch. Traat-Admiral was acting as point-liaison for Chuut-Riit, Warrior Ambassador Extraordinary. The Admiral was under strict orders to dominate the local kzinti from the moment of first contact—they were considered to be fierce but not reliably obeisant.

An inner-world kzin, however territorial, was used to the formalisms of hierarchical command, but out here in the wilds a less disciplined breed of kzinti were notorious for the way they fought over and defended the spoils of their adventuring; crass in their willingness to defy a messenger of the Patriarch if he gave any appearance of weakness. The Patriarch was thirty years distant by lightbeam and forty years distant by ship,

The Hssin fleet might have responded arrogantly. The Conquest Heroes of Hssin were brothers of the Conquest Heroes of Wunderland. They could have ignored, or even ordered an attack on the *Victory at S'Rawl*—after all, it was a mere command warcraft heavy with electronics but deficient in armaments. But would the Hssin household of Kasrriss-As have dared such disdain, knowing who was to follow Traat-Admiral?

No action was taken against the *Victory at S'Rawl*. Space traffic control was relinquished with grinless self-restraint.

Ships began to drift into the R'hshssira System in ones and twos, every few hours, over months, the transports with their time-suspended warriors, the warcraft, the auxiliaries—all that Chuut-Riit had been able to exhort, to tempt, to command from five systems. No ship debarked a single warrior to Hssin, taking orbit instead in a great ring around red R'hshssira. To awe Hssin at a distance, that was Traat-Admiral's intention.

In time Chuut-Riit himself arrived, his flagship a spherical dreadnought of the Imperial Ripper class, larger than anything that the barbarians of Hssin had ever seen, the first new battle design from Kzin in centuries, ominous, weapons-laden. These out-world adventurers of the borderlands would fawn all over him for its specifications—and he would sell those details for a price.

During the six days it took for the gravitic drive field of the *Throat Ripper* to collapse from a cruising speed of six-eighths light down to the velocity of R'hshssira, Chuut-Riit had been in post-hibernation training—massage, fight simulation, strenuous amusements with a favorite kzinrret. Hibernation was good for neither muscle tone nor quick reflex. Swift repairs to the physique, he never neglected.

Most confrontations Chuut-Riit handled with a logic that cowed his foes, but if that failed he used wit before falling back on an awesome rage that could subdue opposition with the sheer stench of his anger. Still, he liked to be in prime physical shape for those times when it was necessary to bloody an irrational enemy with fang or claw.

The work den adjacent to his stateroom was small, paneled along one wall by holographic savanna mismatched to the ceiling pipes. Above his data-link hung a modern pulse-laser and an antique crossbow. The floor beside the data-link provided place for but a single kdatlyno-hide rug—this one bare along an edge, old, a trophy of his first hunt as a servitor of the Prime Household. In those days, having more strength than sense, he had aligned himself with a Patriarch who was too young to have remained alive long, but live he did, to grow old and perish while Chuut-Riit served him as military trouble-slasher, first on Kzin, and then among the stars where the endless years of hibernation had slowed his aging.

He was not old but (having outlived his regal pridemate) he felt his age. He remembered things vividly that his subordinates knew of only through the distortion of imaging and writing. These kits thought of the Asanti Wars as one battle and knew nothing of the treason of Grrowme-Kowr. They purred of the Long Peace, as if there had been no battles before they were weaned. Unshared memories made a kzin feel old, old, old.

Ah, though perhaps not as old as the Riit crossbow. Chuut-Riit had on his electronic spectacles and was staring at it—Jotok light-alloy, forged by kzin ironmongers, inlaid with blueshell by a semi-professional kzin artist. The leather strapping had been replaced but all else was original.

It was said by his grandfather that this crossbow was

the weapon of choice carried into space by the first Riit ancestor hired to battle off-planet. The family genealogy traced him back through to the household of one of the almost mythical Riit Patriarchies, but the truth was probably less romantic—perhaps he was a game-keeper at some distant hunting reserve who scandalized his household (even endangered their lives) by vowing fealty to the Jotok infidels.

Those spider-armed monsters arrived with wealth and magic. They had swords of fire and gravitic machinery and dreams of hiring mercenaries to conquer them a stellar empire, preferring someone else to do their dying for them. In the aftermath of the siege of the Patriarch's castle and his ignoble defeat, Jotok wealth could have bought these spacefaring animals any number of wretched kzinti.

This crossbow and a letter (written in what competent historians had charitably called an "illiterate" hand) were all that remained of the ancestor. The letter was a wonderful attempt at trying to describe stars to a kzin father who was convinced that the stars were the souls of Great Heroes embedded in the Fanged God's Dome.

The Riit medallion engraved into the crossbow was supposed to have been the family mark since pre-historical time. Popular notion held that it was a stylized carnivore's grin, but Chuut-Riit's careful historical research had shown that it was really the shoulder patch assigned by the Jotoki to their elite kzin warriors. It represented a dentate leaf. The dots and comma motto that surrounded the medallion was, however, a later addition: "From Mercenary to Master."

The most invidious sentiment that Chuut-Riit had ever heard was voiced while he was recruiting support for his armada at Ch'Aakin. "If these monkeys put up such a fanatical fight, we should hire them to do battle for us, to be killed in our place. It is time we enjoyed the Long Peace we have created. If a master is truly a master, he can buy life for himself and death for his servants." Said by a fop who had never challenged his father to combat, a fop who owned his share of Jotok slaves yet had never seen the forest-buried ruins of the Jotok worlds, looted by trusted orange mercenaries.

Chuut-Riit was both a mathematician and a historian. He was a student of the rise of the Jotok Empire. It had attained less than an eighth the size of the modern Kzin Patriarchy, yet could still teach important contemporary lessons. How had their purely commercial fleets developed, to such a fine art, logistic battle support over interstellar distances?

Once the Jotok had been military geniuses.

The ancient kzin commanders, using deadly ships thoughtfully supplied by the Jotok, had been enthusiastic plunderers—the language of their teachers was destroyed, lost even to the surviving Jotoki. Nothing but the melancholic forests and foggy lakes remained. For his studies, Chuut-Riit was forced to rely on secondhand kzin texts by kzin warriors who had never mastered Jotoki five-stream grammar. Only with the aid of queueing theory, delay-prediction analysis, intent-result resolution, did the anecdotal fragments provide insight into Jotok military strategy.

The Jotok should have won any war that pitted them against their strategically immature hirelings, except that at the time of the confrontation kzinti warriors were already the mainstay of the Jotok military. The Jotok overwhelmingly preferred commerce to military service. Why that was so was a deep puzzle to Chuut-Riit, but the records that would have answered his questions could not be found in kzin archives. If one had lifetimes to rummage in all the distant places . . .

Enough reverie. He had work to do before he went planetside.

The armada was closer now to Wunderland than it had ever been, with the Alpha Centauri binary effulgent in the heavens of R'hshssira. A very bright Mansun was the new central jewel of the constellation the kzinti called The Water Bird. Hssin Tracker files would contain the most recent information about the Man-Hero war, even if the news was years behind the current situation. He called up everything that Hssin Central Command was willing to transmit.

Assessing only the bulk of the material and its general nature, he began to ferret out a list of the Hssin staff responsible for tracking. He marked off five names from Chief Intelligence Officer to Spoor Level Collator, then contacted them personally, checking their answers against each other's statements. He wanted to know that he had *everything*. He was polite, firm, to the point, and appreciative. That was the way to secure cooperation.

He tapped the phone link. "Gis-Captain, give orders that I am to be disturbed by *no one*."

His youthful kzinrret, Hasha, stuck her head through the oval door, huge yellow eyes lambent with appeal, sensing that he was busy, testing her welcome. He gently purred to her a few simple words of encouragement in the Female Tongue. She did not qualify as a taxing distraction. "My Hero," she replied traditionally, then slunk to his side where he stroked the back of her neck while he growled and spat information out of his data-link, organizing it on his spectacles. She was well trained and said nothing, but she let her tail flirt with him. Sometimes his other fingers flicked purposefully over the command plate.

He was not here on the direct orders of the Patriarch. There was no time for that in an emergency. Because of the snail's pace of light, the Patriarch's awareness of what was happening on his border was more than thirty years out of date. Chuut-Riit had general orders and made his decisions without consulting Kzin-home; in essence he was a traveling Patriarch. When the diameter of the Patriarchy was a whole lifetime, field commanders had broad authority. They did what they did and reported when they could. Once an obligation was assumed, they honored it or they trained their sons to honor it.

Chuut-Riit came to the boundary of the Partriarchy on a hunch generated by electromagnetic spoor. Rumors. Strange signals. With hardly more than hints picked up at a hunting match, he had set out from W'kkai as if his nose could read a wind of scent from across the interstellar reaches. A new starfaring species?

Four years closer, at Ch'Aakin, he learned that his nose was good. An obscure little border fortress circling R'hshssira had mustered a fleet of irregulars, attacked and actually conquered one of their worlds. Tree-bred omnivores with ten fingers. It was a major victory. Who would have thought that a planet-grinding binary system would contain such Kzin-like richness?

He knew then that the consequences for the Patriarchy might be immense—and not all of the consequences were necessarily good. Inept military leadership on the borderlands was always a possibility and always an invitation to disaster.

The Tracking Teams at Ch'Aakin had given him their reading of the lightbeams. He spent days with those documents. The Conquistadors of Wunderland were indeed reckless Heroes, but he already knew all about that. What interested him most was the nature of the man-animal's resistance. The details of *that* campaign fascinated him.

In his journal he made a prediction—already fourteen years out of date. He *guessed* that the local warriors from Hssin would settle down, become

Wunderkzin, then grow restless and make a reckless strike toward the hairless-beasts' home system—a tempting five-and-a-half years away by warship. They would fail, too. Their tactics at Wunderland had shown not the slightest understanding of logistics.

Years passed. Chuut-Riit spent time in hibernation and brief periods of frenzy adding to his armada. The closer he came to the Alpha Centauri double system, the fresher became the scent.

Now at Hssin he was close enough for the kill.

(1) He already knew that the First Fleet probe into the man-system had been a disaster. That was as he had predicted, long before he had known that a First Fleet had been launched.

(2) He already knew the numbers and deployment of the Second Fleet. He had obtained that information when he passed through miserable Fang. Given the facts about the man-system obtained by the First Fleet, he had been predicting a second disaster.

Now he was curious to see how well his prediction had held. He began to dig into the Hssin files. These out-world kzinti might be recklessly brave, but they were poor strategists, gland-strong bunglers. An early victory would be welcome, however unlikely, but such a success would also complicate his mission—winners were more reluctant to accept help from the Patriarchy than were losers.

Ah, there it was. With grunts and finger-waving he flicked the relevant documents over the surface of his spectacles.

He was not surprised to read that the attack of the Second Fleet had also failed. Still the details galled him. His claws were out; his rage was such that he would have slashed to death commanders who had already died for their incompetence. Why hadn't they attacked the laser batteries of the inner planet from below? He spent some hours doing careful calculations, but his insight was useless—the Third Fleet was long launched, already near Man-sun, and probably marked for destruction. Save the Patriarchy from these Hero irregulars!

The news, even though it was cold meat, pressed urgency upon Chuut-Riit. His stay at Hssin would have to be short.

With the proper timing, he could arrive at Alpha Centauri during the slump just before the formation of the inevitable Fourth Fleet. It would give him leeway to staff that Fourth Fleet with all the resentful enemies he was going to make on Wunderland and with the hot-heads who had swarmed to the battle-scream of his hastily collected armada. They were expendable.

But the best of his Heroes he intended to hold back and discipline into a real naval threat. The hapless man-beasts, slaves-to-be, would have to wait for the arrival of the Fifth Fleet before they tangled with their first professional kzin army.

CHAPTER 9
(2396 A.D.)

The excitement!

The recruiters weren't just taking volunteers; they were conducting tournaments and selecting the warriors who were to accompany the armada to Wunderland. Competition was in the very air that wafted through the ventilators. The warriors even smelled different. They cuffed each other and tussled. They boasted about their skill and about the number of man-animals they would own when they were their father's age. They invented new and wonderful insults.

"My Near-Sighted Hero!" roared a kzin youth to a myopic friend at the feast between the jousts. "You say you see yourself on an estate in Africa hunting elephants? You have selected an elephant as your prey, I presume, not for his bravery but because he is big enough to see?"

"Will you wrestle the tusked beast to the ground with me, or will you shoot at him from a tree while he waves the tree over his head?" retorted the myopic friend, peering, not quite sure who it was who had challenged him.

The challenger directed his booming voice to the other orange-red tournament contenders who were devouring their Jotok arms noisily. "Let me recite to all, to this gathering of noble Heroes, the illustrious saga of my stumbling friend who is too tall to see his feet!" He stumbled in imitation, rousing a flurry of flapping ears and good-natured growls.

"Well, don't fall over before you've read me my fate!"

"You'll make it through the fiery battles in space. You have courage and quickness to compensate for your weak eyes! You'll smash ships and disgorge the boiling hairless corpses to the vacuum. We know that you have *blind* luck and the cunning of a *mole!* You'll stagger through the traps that explode in space. You'll drop on your grav-platform to the surface of Africa, there to slaughter battalions with your broad-beam fire!" The raconteur was spitting and snarling with relish as he described the fights, purring through the compliments.

"Get on with it!" taunted the myopic friend. "I demand the glorious day of my elephant hunt!"

"Ah that. Hr-r. You see the elephant-beast's gray bulk looming in the distance. You stalk him. You leap mightily! But what is this? You have dived, headfirst, into a gigantic gray boulder! The boulder takes the first round. Birds land in your mane, singing. Uniformed beasts, wearing the colors of the UNSN, crawl out of hiding, intrigued by your sudden stillness. Alas, they skin you, and there you are, Conqueror of Manhome, cured and spread upon some floor in Africa to tickle the feet of monkeys!"

The audience roared approval. Some waved Jotok bones in the air.

Trainer-of-Slaves was uncomfortable in this crowd—there were too many of his old enemies present. He was here only because he desperately *wanted* to volunteer, *wanted* to follow Chuut-Riit to glory. His courage was not permitting it. He didn't dare enter the tournament, even though claws were padded and no one could attack outside of the circle. In all this time of preparation for the coming of his savior, it had never occurred to him once that he might have to fight for the privilege of following!

I'm doomed, he thought. He would have stayed longer at the meet, struggling to find a way around his fear, but he spotted Puller-of-Noses moving through the crowd.

So he caught a jerking auto-car through the tunnels back to the Jotok Run. Back to work. It didn't matter. Hssin would be emptied after the armada left, and most of his enemies would be gone. There was that.

Jotok-Tender spotted his apprentice in the dome near the main entrance of the Run and moved to greet him, animation in his gait. Hssin was indeed in a state when even the giant caught its fever! The giant didn't stop as he usually did but came right up and cuffed Trainer with force enough to half-knock him down.

"Look at this!" He showed a golden honor card. "Chuut-Riit has commended us for our slaves! Our work groups have been overhauling some of his fleet's worn gravitic polarizers. He is pleased. A small thing, but we have honor!"

Trainer took the arm of his master, almost gently, and walked him through the trees and grass of the plaza. There was nothing much to say, but they made purring noises at each other. There was no question of working for the rest of the day. The old kzin fussed about, providing sparkling water and tasty hard bits to chew on. He talked quietly of his best memories. Trainer-of-Slaves listened fondly to the familiar tales.

The next day was not so quiet. Kasrriss-As, the Patriarch of Hssin, who had never said a word in his life to Jotok-Tender, using underlings to deal with him, made a personal voice call. Chuut-Riit was interested in the response range of the man-beast's physiology and had bought two Wunderland monkeys from Kasrriss-As which he wished to hunt. An elaborate hunting party was to be arranged immediately for the Jotok Run, which was the only really large hunting run on Hssin.

"They don't make good prey," Kasrriss-As grumbled. "They're badly designed. Weak. They can run, but not well; they can climb trees, but not well. Good to eat, though." Sulkily he added, "I wanted them for my menagerie."

"Noble Hero, when shall we have the hunt ready?"

"He hasn't given me enough notice!" complained Kasrriss-As. "It takes months to exercise them into fit enough shape to make a good run! Terrible muscle tone! Ah well—could your kit possibly do something with them, teach them something in a day? Anything to make the hunt more interesting! I'm so distracted. I have so many things to do. Take care of everything. The honor of Hssin rests upon your accomplishment."

At the instant of disconnect, Jotok-Tender reached out and pulled down an enchiridion—not a data capsule or an eyewriter—but a slim, lavishly illustrated book, bound in Jotok hide and printed on the finest fiber paper in subtle colors and everlasting scent. "Read it now! Learn everything you can." It was the most popular kzin manual on men.

Huem-Sergeant and two of his assistants immediately brought the rare beasts around to the Jotok quarters. Trainer-of-Slaves, still with the book in his hand, saw three battle-ready kzin, so enormous that they could enter through the door only one at a time, roughly nudging two helpless charges between them. The hairless bipeds, together, couldn't have massed as much as the smallest guard. The monkeys looked much less formidable than their pictures, and they didn't smell like flower-water. They were far more vivid. They wore the smell of fear.

He tried to fit on them the details he had been reading in the enchiridion. The one without facial hair was a young male? Trainer-of-Slaves stared intently; yes, that must be right. The one *with* the facial hair had looser folds in his tail-like skin, and tiny wrinkles—signs of age. It was the youth who was radiating the essence of fear most strongly. That must account for why his genitals were retracted.

"Aowrrgh," said Huem-Sergeant, "strange lot." He was reminding Trainer-of-Slaves to relieve him of his guard duty.

Trainer forced his eyes off the monkeys. He gave the swift transfer-of-contract sign with his hand, and the kzin warriors left him, one at a time through the door.

Alone with his deformed charges, he felt his own fear stirring, the need for a grin. But he had a strange sympathy for the frightened young one—there was no need to frighten the doomed animal further. He suppressed his smile and kept his face as expressionless as possible under the circumstances.

"I have a stall for you," he hissed and spat, but they understood nothing.

"I think he wants us to go with him," said the bearded biped.

"Should we resist?"

"Don't be crazy, Marisha."

They followed him through the corridors to the stall. "This is where you will sleep and defecate until the hunt. I have orders to make you comfortable." The spits were mixed with the atonal inflections and burry rumblings of the Hero's Tongue.

"I think we've been demoted."

"What's happening? Look at this place! I thought we were getting along with the Chief Kumquat?"

"There's a big buzz stirring up this ratcat trap. I think we've been sold."

"You have a theory that we are slaves. Are we really slaves?"

"I don't know *anything*, Marisha. Nothing at all. I'll see if I can get us some food. Big Yellow Lineman here is just standing around staring, wondering where the football is." He made finger motions to his mouth.

"Long-Reach, some food for the slaves."

The Jotok scuttled into the stall. "Honored kzin, what do they eat?"

"Sol's Blazes, what is that *teufel*!" screeched Marisha.

"I've seen them at a distance—and once close up. That was in a kzin engine room. I think he has a better deal than we do."

Trainer-of-Slaves was consulting his book. These rotting manuals never seemed to carry what you needed in the place you were looking at! "Omnivore," he clacked and hissed. Not very helpful. "Try one of everything. Water, too."

Long-Reach returned with a variety of warm, raw meats on a skewer and a bowl of leaves with a side dish of leaf sauce.

The older man sniffed the meat but tried the leaves first. "Tastes like eucalyptus. Same texture, too." He spat it out and tried the meat with a sour expression. "We're going to have to teach them how to cook all over again."

"It's raw? Gottdamn!"

"And tough."

Trainer-of-Slaves was impressed when he watched them chewing on the meat and rejecting the leaves.

"Can you ask him for some clothes?" whimpered Marisha.

"I don't think they have our size. Maybe something in yellow lace with five arm holes?"

Trainer-of-Slaves busied himself with professional questions—asked of himself because it was impossible to ask *them* anything. He examined the bottoms of their feet, clawing the sole gently, and decided that the skin was too soft. Had they been carried about by machines on Wunderland? Maybe on the two-year trip to Hssin in the hibernator their feet had grown soft? Certainly they wouldn't be able to last out the hunt on those!

Item: provide them with makeshift sandals. The giant was frugal to the point of insanity and had all sorts of hides around that had been softened by Jotok mastication.

He wasn't sure what to do about the rest of their skin. It had no fur to protect them from heat and cold, and would be useless against brambles and branches. Nor was it thick like a Jotok's hide. Just running his claws along their skin made them flinch in pain and make noises that didn't sound like polite conversation. Had they been shelled out of their carapace? Or was it just that Man-home was a paradise?

Item: provide them with leggings. With their build and fragility, what they really needed was a military suit of armor.

At first light he took them into the forest—with Long-Reach, Joker, and Creepy following in the trees. He tried to teach them the lay of the caverns, how to run and where to run, how to backtrack and hide, what to rub on their bodies to disguise their rank smell. After frustrating misunderstandings, he decided that they didn't understand that they were going to be hunted. Were they stupid?

For a while Trainer-of-Slaves entertained the notion that they might be females. What did he know of monkey anatomy? They certainly didn't understand him when he quite carefully enunciated from his man-talk phrase book. They behaved exactly like kzinrretti he'd tried to converse with—lifting their faces attentively, listening, all attention and no comprehension. Females for sure.

But they *did* chatter. Was it mindless chatter? Some sounds seemed ... meaningful. "Notsofast!" was a demand that he stop demonstrating kzin reflexes. "Let's-restaminute!" was a cry of weakness. "LunkheadOverThere" and "BarrelRibs" was a way of referring to a dominant slave master while deferentially averting one's eyes.

At twilight he tried an experiment. Painfully he copied for them words from his phrasebook—using manscript.

day tomorrow run fast
= = = = = = = = = = = = = = = = =
4/8 day hunt catch—man die
6/8 day hunt catch—man die
8/8 day hunt end hunt—man live

"Holy Mother Earth, he's telling us that tomorrow we're going to be on the wrong end of a kzin hunt!"

The young one paled.

The older one turned toward Trainer. "Jack, she's only fifteen!"

They understood! He could smell their sudden fear. They could read! Ah, males for sure.

CHAPTER 10
(2396 A.D.)

Trainer-of-Slaves took the game animals out into the darkness of the caverns before lights-on. This time they were far more receptive to his instructions about sneaking away, dodging, and hiding. It was fascinating to observe the sudden increase in their intelligence. Now he owned an essential fact: a motivation-prompt accelerated a man-beast's learning rate.

Interesting.

He compared this with what he knew about the Jotoki. A Jotok's intelligence depended upon a hormone that was triggered by body-size; they were all geniuses during transition. You couldn't stop them from learning! Then, at adulthood when the mass of their arm-brains stabilized, their ability to learn began to taper off rapidly. A mature Jotok could always retain what he had mastered during transition, but he learned *new* facts and *new* ways only slowly. Motivation was a minor variable.

He wondered if a motivator triggered some kind of intelligence hormone in a man-beast? A kzin who controlled such a hormone directly would have a useful tool. Perhaps that could be accomplished through a chemical bypass-block that shunted around the motivator. The slave-master could induce a rapid learning mode, teach a specialized behavior to his monkey, then turn off the monkey's ability to self-modify that behavior. A compulsive slave. No chains. No threats. Very economical.

As he watched them, Trainer-of-Slaves began to catalog in his mind the motivators he was observing. Certainly these beasts were able to modify their behavior rapidly when their lives were threatened. *They're like me*, he thought as he helped the Marisha-beast lay a false trail through the marshes.

But, of course, they were different, too. He doubted that they had a concept of honor.

Sometimes life was *not* valuable. Trainer-of-Slaves was beginning to resent the hunt. These slaves were valuable *alive*. Study your enemy—who had said that? What was valuable in a pile of stripped and bloody bones?

When it was still dark he released the game at a multiple divide of caverns which Long-Reach called The Place of Many Ways. He felt sad. He needed at least ten more days to toughen them up, to learn enough of their language to train them in the more subtle evasions.

"Long-Reach," he said to his companion when the man-beasts had disappeared beyond hearing, "as my special hunter, I have a service for you to perform. Who knows these sprawling forests and caves and liquid ponds better than you?"

"Only the Fanged God," replied Long-Reach in the formal ritual of their conversations.

"Your official function in this hunt is as my scout. I have specific orders."

"I am five ears."

"The monkeys won't survive until twilight without help. You will scout for them, not for me. Appear to me from time to time, for the sake of appearances, but scout for the beasts. Give them aid, but be careful *never* to tell me what you have done! I don't want to know."

"As my master commands."

At first-light the hunting party began to assemble under the primary dome of the Jotok Run. The thin banners of Kasrriss-As hung in brilliant color, carried by four kzin servitors who were experienced hunters in this Run. Trainer-of-Slaves was without colors but he had been hastily outfitted in the light armor of the Kasrriss-As household. Three Jotoki in green and red striped livery remained respectfully on call but at a distance.

Chuut-Riit's party was less formal, but nevertheless elegant. He wore a pale peacock-green armor of a leather style that pre-dated spaceflight. He had decreed no weapons and no devices and carried none. He had brought with him only Traat-Admiral—and a young recruit, Hssin-Liaison, proud of his new cognomen.

Trainer-of-Slaves felt one moment of shock—and then repressed, invisible rage. He stared straight ahead. *How does my enemy do it?* This pest had the persistence of a fur-tick! Could he lead even Chuut-Riit around by the nose?

Hssin-Liaison, whatever he was called, was never subtle. He did not return disregard. In front of Chuut-Riit and without preamble he grinned at Trainer-of-Slaves. "You will not live out the day—Coward-of-Cowards."

"What is this?" inquired Chuut-Riit mildly.

"This Animal is unfit to carry the duties of a Conquest Hero."

The ears of Chuut-Riit flicked in amusement. "I believe the tournament is settling such matters."

"This cowardly Animal won't be found in any tournament ring. I challenge him here."

"I see." Chuut-Riit seemed aloof from the menace and anger. He turned to Trainer-of-Slaves matter-of-factly. "Hssin-Liaison has been using his contacts among the young warriors to enlist troops for my Fourth Fleet." He lapsed into silence, waiting, perhaps curious that Trainer-of-Slaves had chosen to ignore the challenge.

"Voice of the Patriarch, my duty is to the execution of the hunt," Trainer replied stiffly.

"Good." Chuut-Riit only glanced toward his liaison underling, then addressed the others. He was obviously not willing to interfere in local squabbles about which he knew nothing. "I am here for a slow hunt— no quick kill. We flush and pursue. We challenge and fall back. We play. We save the kill for twilight. Yes, I'm anticipating my first taste of human flesh, but I am far more interested in observing the response of the enemy under attack. No weapons. No devices. Those are the rules."

Every other kzin at the meet added another rule silently. The harassing would be enjoyable, but the final kill must be given to Chuut-Riit alone.

The banners were staked into a circle. Noiselessly the hunters moved into the woods under the arching ceilings. Chuut-Riit loosened his leather armor and gave Trainer-of-Slaves one last noncommittal gaze. "So the hunter becomes the hunted." Then he was gone.

Deeper into the trees a five-limbed beast dropped beside Trainer. "Hssin-Liaison threatened you with death."

"He won't be able to find me. Only you know the Run better than I. He's good on rooftops. He's a city-kzin." Contempt. "I'm Mellow-Yellow, remember, who floats among the leaves like lamplight. I'll take him in circles." But the plan wasn't to take him in circles; the plan was to lead Puller-of-Noses away from the man-beasts. It was the least he could do for them, to neutralize one of the hunters.

The man-beasts were trapped, and allowed to escape, twice before midday. Jotok-Tender's slaves brought in a simple lunch for the hunters, served on collapsible canvas tables. Chuut-Riit paced about their vale making intellectual pronouncements upon the evasive tactics of the day's game. "Innovative," he called them. He liked that. Hssin-Liaison managed to mix some leaves into Trainer-of-Slaves's meat. Kasrr-iss-As spent his time ingratiating himself into Chuut-Riit's favor and discussing the textile trade with Traat-Admiral. He was the one who had stayed behind while the other warriors raided Alpha Centauri.

The canvas tables were folded and whisked away by the slaves. Chuut-Riit amiably resumed his tracking. However old his eyes, his nose was a marvel at spotting spoor, his mind superb at guessing the moves of his prey.

"We'll wound them this time, and watch how they handle that."

When Chuut-Riit smiled beside a craggy lava outcrop—and then moved left instead of right—a secret pleasure rippled under the fur of Trainer-of-Slaves. Last night he had not been able to determine for sure whether his man-beasts had understood this intricate back-track and feint move. A perfect execution. The maneuver had been taught to Trainer (too many times) by a wily old Jotok who was probably still at large, up there in the trees watching them, keeping his distance. It worked well on the kzin mind.

Trainer-of-Slaves followed the real trail, "carelessly" obscuring what spoor he found. He knew where they had gone, a broad and growth-sheltered ledgeway along the wall of a cavern that had all the appearance of a dead-end. It led to three good escape routes, but to anyone unfamiliar with the layout of the Run, the wide ledge smelled of trap. Prey avoided it—and hunters avoided it because they thought prey would be avoiding it. Trainer was in no hurry to get there, perhaps to lead another hunter to them. They needed a rest from terror. He urinated. He smelled the flowers which reminded him of his mother.

With a rustling of leaves, Long-Reach dropped from the branches bearing the news that their game was safe but exhausted, laying low. He had other news. Puller-of-Noses was following and had cut around and in front to intercept Trainer-of-Slaves.

"Where are Joker and Creepy?"

"I have given them instructions."

"I'll have to do a decoy. What do you suggest?"

"Climb up along the trinity hill—he will see you from there, being on the other slope. Then drop down through the Burr Crevasse to The Lakes. He will have to follow, so you'll know where he is, but you'll already have passed through, so he won't know where to find you."

"I like it." The slave-trainer kzin became Mellow-Yellow, half Jotok, slipping along swiftly through all the little shortcuts he knew, until he came to the hill with the three giant trees that could grow here because of the ceiling vault, carved by tons of rock that had collapsed during the excavation, and now supported by a cathedral of arches. While he climbed he was looking intently into the woods across the depression for an orange-red blur.

Disaster is always abrupt. He met his enemy. In the wrong place. Five kzin-lengths in front of him, wearing that persistent grin.

They both fell into an instant crouch.

His mind reeled. What had happened—a light breeze? for critical moments blowing in the wrong direction? Had his enemy smelled him coming? and simply waited? He made an instant tactical assessment. Puller-of-Noses was unaware of the Burr Crevasse or he would have blocked off that escape route. It was still available if he could dance his enemy a few paces downhill.

"There's no grass to eat here, Defecator-of-Undigested Grass."

"You swore before witnesses that you would let me live."

"That was then. We have many lives and one death. You've already lived an extra life. Today I have sworn to kill you."

Chuut-Riit had talked about the value of the unexpected tactical option. Trainer leaped, without grinning, without screaming, while an incredulous Puller-of-Noses shifted just too late to save his balance—simultaneously, a reflexive swipe, accurate, deadly, disabled Trainer's right arm. They were both bowled over, taking out a tree before bouncing to their feet. Blood poured from the arm. But the coward was now on the right side of the Burr Crevasse. Facing the wrong way.

He couldn't run toward that escape. He had no way to defend his back.

Five kzinti screams descended from the trees, four arms wrapping around the enemy warrior while the fifth ripped his nose open. Before the attack was over, Long-Reach was jumping out of harm's reach. He skittered away, then turned to face the kzin. Motionless. It was a draw. The kzin could run him down, but he could climb a tree faster than any kzin could follow.

"A slave who attacks a kzin is warm meat!" snarled Puller-of-Noses while the blood ran into his mouth. "I'll kill you later!"

"There are three of us," said Long-Reach.

The kzin's eyes scanned the treetops rapidly, looking for the others. Nothing. When he turned back to his kzin target, he was alone. Chagrin. Both coward and slave were gone. No matter. All he had to do was follow the blood.

Trainer-of-Slaves jimmied himself down through the Crevasse at a record pace, one-armed, rocks ripping gashes out of his hide, leaving a trail of fur and blood as he bounced to the level below. He felt no pain. He ran. At first he gave no thought to obscuring his trail. What was the use? Hssin-Liaison or Puller-of-Noses or Second-Son-of-Ktrodni or whatever in hell was his name would follow him to the ends of the Partriarchy right now, fangs ready for the kill.

In neat livery of green and red stripes, Joker swung out of the sky. "Follow me." He scrabbled along the ground, picking a route by some criterion Trainer-of-Slaves did not understand. What greater mortification could there be than to have a slave lead him in flight! "Make for the water," said Joker before swinging back up into the sky to disappear.

Bolting, driven by the fear, all else lost to his mind, he reached The Lakes, exhausted, bewildered that a relentless Puller-of-Noses had been unable to follow. His arm was torturing him. His disgrace was complete. Of course, there was always humor in every situation. He had been a successful decoy.

Are the man-beasts doing any better than my wretched self?

He trudged a circuitous route back toward the ledgeway where the hunt's prey had been hiding. They were gone. He found a happy Chuut-Riit instead, relaxing, playing a poetry game with Traat-Admiral, which wasn't going well for the Admiral.

"Where is everybody?" asked the Conquest Commander amiably. "Is it the custom on Hssin to take afternoon naps?" He noticed Trainer-of-Slaves's arm. "I see that my righteous Liaison officer hasn't been able to put you out of action." He came over and examined the wound. "I've seen worse." And he began to dress the slashes.

It was only then that Trainer-of-Slaves realized how dazed he was. He was just standing there, letting one of the highest military officers of the Patriarchy fuss over a minor clawing.

"I'm all right, sir. Have we relocated our prey?"

"One is wounded. He attacked me to let the other escape. I let them both go but in such a way that they will remain separated. We may now destroy them one at a time. You're from Hssin. You must know these monkeys better than I. It is said that as a mob they fight bravely. Do you have any information about how they fight alone?"

"These man-animals are the first I have ever met, sir."

"Yes, they're rare. Curious beasts. Trainer-of-Slaves, do you have an idea of what kind of slaves they'll make?"

"I have a theory that they might be controlled through biochemistry. I would need to have a large sample size upon which to experiment in order to confirm or deny my hunch."

"Of course. I'll have to take you to Alpha Centauri with me. There are monkeys on Wunderland, sufficient I should imagine."

"Dominant One, I am not qualified. Hssin-Liaison will tell you why."

"Hssin-Liaison will tell me *nothing*! He's dead. Not far from here. He was found by a scout of Kasrriss-As who was following a trail of kzin blood." Chuut-Riit glanced knowingly at a certain wounded arm.

Trainer-of-Slaves maintained a shocked silence. His enemy—dead?

"His legs were broken and there was a stake through his eye," said Traat-Admiral.

Like the incoming whine of a bomb, Trainer realized what had happened and who was guilty.

"He broke his legs when he ran full-paced into a trip wire, since removed. The trip wire was set across the trail of your blood. The stake was buried in the ground and set to pierce anyone unfortunate enough to fall upon it. He missed, but his head was later *lifted* and *rammed* down onto the stake. Through the eye."

"A terrible way to die, your excellency."

"I'd take you there now, but twilight would overtake us and our prey would escape by virtue of my lenient rules. We'd go hungry. Let's make it simple. Do you admit that he was murdered?"

"Yes, sir." Trainer had anguished images of Long-Reach—all of his slaves—being hacked to bits.

"Since Hssin-Liaison was my servitor, I will pass judgment on you. Let's be clear about the circumstances. Hssin-Liaison widened the circle of the tournament to include you against your will. The rules of the tournament require gloved claws. He neglected that detail—as your wounds testify. He who so broadens the rules cannot complain when his life is forfeit as the consequence of his rules."

"He was not killed in face-to-face combat," said Traat-Admiral. "He was murdered."

"Wait, Traaty. There is a military lesson in this which we should consider. If a force stays to fight, knowing that it will be slaughtered, yes, there is honor in that defeat. But what if the same force retreats and lures the enemy into a trap in which he can be slaughtered? Can we call such a victory, dishonor? I find a contradiction here. If defeat is honor, does it follow that victory is dishonor? Save us all from such logic!"

He thinks I did it! He can't conceive of slaves murdering kzin. Neither can I.

"I say the tournament was fairly fought and fairly won. Hssin-Liaison made new rules without consulting our Hero here. Trainer-of-Slaves replied with his own unorthodox rules, also without consulting our now dead warrior. I see a balance."

Truth was always sacred. Trainer-of-Slaves desperately searched for the kind of courage that would allow him to speak the truth.

Ignoring the youth's sputterings, Chuut-Riit continued with his line of reasoning. "Yes, there is a just balance. However, my young Hero, you have done me harm and owe me recompense. I have lost a warrior for my Fourth Fleet. You have won this unusual tournament fairly and so you must join my service. I will be assigning you to Traat-Admiral who is building for me an elite corps I choose to call the Fifth Fleet." He nodded to his Admiral. "Doesn't he have just the qualities we need?"

Long afterward, a dazed Trainer-of-Slaves was still pondering the consequences of Jotoki who murdered kzin, barely able to keep his attention on the hunt. Fortunately the hunt seemed forgotten. Long-Reach was nowhere to be found, hiding probably. Should he execute Long-Reach? Should he bring up the perils of slavery to Chuut-Riit? Yes, that's what he should do. The coward in him shuddered.

Kasrriss-As appeared from the direction of Burr Crevasse. "The body has been removed. Since there are fewer of us, I suggest an immediate resumption of the chase before twilight overtakes us."

"Your arm looks bad." Chuut-Riit's voice carried a fatherly tone. "No need to follow us. There will be other hunts."

"This hunt is my responsibility."

But he couldn't keep up. They stalked and killed

the wounded man-beast first. Before the lights dimmed they had the young one cornered. The animal's wailing cries of rage turned to screams before Chuut-Riit tore the body apart. Trainer shared in the feast when it was his turn to gnaw and rip at the carcasses. What else could he do? At least the meat was delicious.

He spent half the night wandering in the forest.

Later Trainer-of-Slaves found his three personal Jotoki cowering in their stalls. How could he talk to them about their crime? Shouldn't he just destroy them? Shouldn't he speak to Jotok-Tender? When he remembered the giant musing about the depth of the loyalty found in a Jotok properly adopted, his heart curdled; was that what was meant? Murder? Had Jotok-Tender known all along?

Long-Reach was huddled arms, head hidden by arm stalks, eyes barely peeping out of their armor, silent. As the kzin master of these slaves he had to say something. Yet how could he even mention such a crime? It was too horrible! "I'm angry!" His fangs were bared in a grin. "You disobeyed my instructions! Specifically, I told you to protect the man-beasts, and what were you doing instead?—you were watching over me. The man-slaves were lost! I take care of myself! I'm a warrior! I'm a Hero! Do not violate the wishes of a Hero! Obey!"

The subject was never mentioned again.

CHAPTER 11
(2399–2401 A.D.)

The warships of the Patriarchy were large but cramped. Sub-light supply lines don't exist in an interstellar empire. Every need of a conquest had to be thought of by the Ordnance-Officer and brought along. The storage took space. Hydrogen took space. Purifiers filled the ship with ducts. The hibernation vaults took space. Machine shops took space. The gravitic drives and their shielding alone took up *half* the space in the ship.

No savanna-roaming kzin could ever have created, or imagined, such a claustrophobic horror of passageways and pipes and tiny rooms, where even the ceilings had to be used for storage and the doors stayed locked for years. But long ago, as mercenaries, the kzinti had fallen into this hell-in-heaven as penance for their sin of impatience.

Light took two and a half years to travel between the R'hshssira infrared dwarf and the Alpha Centauri binary. Kzin warships spent more than three years on the same journey. Chuut-Riit's flagship, from the first scent of man-animal rumor, had given seventeen years to this single mission.

The voyages were grueling. Without their hibernation coffins, touchy and argumentative warriors lacked tolerance for the time-gulf between stars. Trainer-of-Slaves would have none of that. He took ship duty for himself. All his life he had been bound to an essentially uninhabitable rock of a rapidly dying star. How could he not stay awake to relish his adventure?

To prepare himself for Wunderland, he devoured the written sagas of Kzin. After all, his race had been born on a planet. Roaming a planet with breathable winds was a kzin's natural maskless state. Wasn't it truth that Wunderland was desirable *because* it was so Kzinlike?

He followed the patricidal tragedy of *Warlord Chmee at the Pillars*, almost squeezing the wetness out of his fur after the Storm at the Pillars. When the Hero blinded himself in remorse, he stopped reading—he wanted to *see* Kzin-home, first, before he searched his soul.

There were many sagas. He imagined himself with Rgir's pride in the Mooncatcher Mountains. He felt the drifting snow and vapor breath at warcamp in the Rungn Valley.

And there were heroic poems. He listened to the boiling-fat sounds from the *Poems of Eight Voyages* as he recited them aloud, marveling at plains of waving grass, at a winter wind whose chill claws could ice a Patriarch's fur to the white of age.

The sagas always spoke of the wind. The hunter's wind. Death's wind. The howling wind. Sweetgrass wind. The seasalt wind. The wind of many messages. Running with the wind. Wunderland had winds, too, he thought.

Trainer-of-Slaves soon found the confined spaces of the warship intolerably full of smells that machine-made winds never took away. Nor was a diet of meat-biscuit conducive to an even humor. He snarled. His temper was short. He had a broad comment to cover every ship deficiency.

One warrior became irritated enough at this ire to grasp him by the vest, repeatedly shoving him against a bulkhead. "Let my ears hear more of your foul insults! I'm here to inspire your mouth! I demand more!" Finally Deck-Officer interfered and ordered them both to the Vault, where they were antifreezed and stacked with five hundred other suspended Heroes.

All trips come to an end. The Vault was unloaded at the grimy Fortress Aarku orbiting Alpha Centauri B and when Trainer awoke he wondered why he had ever left Hssin. Aarku was only nine-hundred kilometers in diameter and it didn't even have amenities like a poisonous atmosphere. The Fortress itself had been started as a major installation a generation ago after the invasion, and then left unfinished. It was a "strategic position" thought up by an admiral who didn't have to live there.

Alpha Centauri B would have been an outer planet if it had massed a thousand times less. Instead, it had grown into a healthy orange-tinged *star*, but with only three quarters of A's mass and a quarter of A's luminosity. The two stars orbited each other with a period of eighty years, coming as close as eighty-eight light-minutes and moving away from each other as far as 280 light-minutes.

They had disrupted the formation of one another's outer planets, leaving nothing circling A but Wunderland and three dense inner worlds, plus the myriad rocks of the Inner Swarm. A ring of rubble surrounded B that included ten major asteroids. In between lay the bulk of the Serpent's Swarm buzzing in an intricate dance of resonance rings, pseudo-trojan orbits, high inclination orbits, and other exotic solutions to the problems posed by forced cohabitation with two major stars. There were vast gaps in the Swarm where no asteroid could survive without being pumped into another orbit.

To view the Wunderland on which he had expected to serve, Trainer-of-Slaves had to tune up the base's electronic telescope and blot out the blinding spear of Alpha Centauri A. His unit was stationed about as far away from its forests and grasslands and mountains as they could be sent, dashing his dreams of loping over the surface of a planet under an open sky.

War was war. Each warrior had his own emplacement and his own fight. Trainer's fatalistic companions had a saying that even the rocks around Centauri B had their duties. His duties were to turn out slaves for the engine rooms of the Fourth Fleet. The conditions in the hastily prefabricated tunnels were appalling. He was stuck with his smelly Jotok cages, with his wire-mesh runs and masses of Jotok babies crawling all over each other without enough space and never enough wind to carry away the smell. Hssin seemed like paradise.

A berth on the Fourth Fleet began to seem more and more desirable. He began to dream about Man-home. If he couldn't have Wunderland, then why not Earth? Earth, too, had winds and an open sky. The winds had fascinating names culled from Wunderland libraries. Nor'easter. The icy candelia of the Andes Mountains. Trade winds. The dry chinook wind that blew down the slopes of the Rocky Mountains after depositing all its moisture on the western slopes. Mediterranean sirocco. Whirlwind. Tempest.

Trainer-of-Slaves began to take a personal interest in the fate of the Fourth Fleet. He was too busy with Jotoki, and too far away from the center, to face politics from a crouch. But he followed Chuut-Riit's duels and celebrated every win. The locals were resisting the economic burden of preparing a new fleet. They made loud claims about the ferocity with which the Third Fleet would slash the Solar System, though that battle must already have been fought and won or lost.

Chuut-Riit was adamant that the burden continue. It was, he told his Heroes, the Patriarch's policy that in any war a backup fleet was always in preparation to follow a battle-fleet, no matter how sure the battle-fleet's victory. That was the only way a slow-motion interstellar crusade could be fought. Better to send expensive reinforcements to a victory won years ago than penniless faith-in-victory to a defeat. The kzin had a saying, "Don't count your fingers when your claws are sheathed."

Alpha Centauri B was a favored space for Fourth Fleet maneuvers. As a result, Trainer-of-Slaves met many gung-ho captains who had driven their gravitic-polarizers past normal specifications and needed urgent maintenance. They liked him because his crews did a good job. They also liked him because he served Jotok meat and that was a treat hard to come by.

Ssis-Captain took a special liking to Trainer-of-Slaves. They shared an avid interest in Earth. It was he who introduced card-tricks to Trainer's slaves. The monkeys used a peculiar set of plastic symbols, five plus an octal of cards in a suit, with four suits. The Captain never ceased to flap his ears while Long-Reach did his five-handed shuffle, rotating half the deck clockwise and the other half counterclockwise while sitting on his mouth. He didn't like to play poker with Long-Reach, though, because the Jotok always took the pot.

On one run in from the A star, Ssis-Captain brought in some Wunderland musical instruments and they put together a combo, a rather cacophonous effort. Creepy managed the twelve string banjo with three hands, Long-Reach played the drums and did harmony with all five lungs, while Joker handled the cymbals and xylophone. Trainer-of-Slaves did his imitations of Heroic Poetry on the kazoo.

"I've got to have you *animals* on the *Blood of Heroes*! Do you want to pledge honor to my ship? I'll pledge all of you! We've *got* to be playing together when we march under the Arc de Triomphe in Berlin!"

"The Arc de Triomphe is in Moscow," corrected Trainer-of-Slaves righteously.

"You must be wrong. The red monkeys got out of that war early. I distinctly remember that the Arc de Triomphe was built by French-beasts to honor the victory of their Kaiser at Berlin. The High French Conquest Commandant Hitler marched under it with his whole army when he defeated the Huns. I've seen the daguerreotype!"

On another trip Ssis-Captain smuggled in a kzinrret inside an old polarizer housing. She was a beauty with a luminous red sheen to her fur and streaks of tan in her nose, but she wasn't at all pleased with the ride and studied them both from sulky, undecided eyes.

"Jriingh, meet your new mounter."

"My hero," she purred.

Trainer-of-Slaves was horrified. "You stole an illustrious one's wife? Or worse, a daughter?"

Ssis-Captain's ears flapped while he rumbled in his throat. "He gave her to me. She's a little terror. She spits and hisses at his wives and fights with them. She kept chasing his favorite off into the woods of his estate where he couldn't find her. She boxes the heads of his daughters and tries to take his sons down under the bridge."

"An ideal mother for great fighting Heroes!"

"It didn't work that way. All her sons got killed as

kits in rage-fights. Crazy, the lot of them. Her mate backhand-cuffed her often enough, without profit, but he's too soft-clawed to kill her. I reasoned that you and I could solve his problem."

"Do you suppose the man-beastesses give their males as much trouble as ours?"

"Worse! A manrret is smart enough to pick the lock on her door!"

Jriingh stepped gracefully from the polarizer housing, haughtily exploring her new abode, sniffing warily. She was half the size of a male kzin and probably twice as agile. She snapped up a baby Jotok that had escaped from its wire run, and swallowed five arms in one bite and then peered into the smelly tank, pondering ways to catch more.

"She's being boarded on the *Blood of Heroes*, of course."

"Against regs. *You'll* have to keep her."

"It's against regs to keep her here, too." Trainer-of-Slaves was beginning to feel angry.

"Hr-r, yet you do have the space, a corner somewhere with a lock and key."

"But I won't be able to keep her pheromones out of the air!"

"You won't have to. That's the whole beauty of this sally."

"I'm supposed to give this little hissing terror the run of the place?!"

"It's not a problem. She likes males. She just doesn't like females. Fix up a room. Give her some nice things. We'll run a beneath-the-grass pride to keep her happy. Let her keep your feet warm. We *need* a beneath-the-grass pride out here: card-tricks, music, war stories, ch'rowl. Do you think a Conservor will come *here* and give you a lecture on the One True Way of Honor and the nature of the Furry God?"

Trainer-of-Slaves settled into himself—giving way

just a little. He was not used to such camaraderie and
he liked it. Yes, he wanted to conquer Earth with this
warrior and own a huge hunting preserve in the Ama-
zon next to France with hundreds of pink, tailless
slaves tending to his animals. Of course, Long-Reach
would always be his top slave.

For two years High Conquest Commander Chuut-
Riit had been caught in the snare of a painful power
struggle. Then the first news from Man-sun burst from
the lightbeams, 4.3 years after the fact: the Kzin had
dealt a great surprise victory in the first skirmish. The
Third Fleet was positioning itself for battle.

Wunderland kzinti forgot all else. Even Chuut-Riit
paused. Infighting died. The Radio-Operators became
the Heroes of the Moment, drifting in space at the
instruments of their huge antennae pointed at Man-
sun.

The good news did not last.

By the end of the month the extent of the disaster
was evident. Trainer-of-Slaves was outraged at the
man-beasts. Kzinti became morose. They grinned
more often, thoughts of monkeys on their minds. And
Chuut-Riit's situation changed dramatically. There was
no longer any question that he was Governor of Alpha
Centauri. There was no longer any opposition to *his*
design for the Fourth Fleet, or to his date of
launching.

Trainer put in for a transfer to the *Blood of Heroes*.

CHAPTER 12
(2402 A.D.)

Ssis-Captain arrived at Fortress Aarku with a new uniform, slightly non-standard. The padded under-armor vest was a too-rich shade of mauve with sapphire blue trimmings. The buttons on his epaulets were Wunderland jade from mines in the Jotun Range. The eight-pointed captain's star radiated from a real diamond. Pagoda style three-quarter sleeves were of the satin one might find on a kzinrret's bed. The arcuate leather cuffs of the undershirt, setting for his chronometer/comp, were tooled from high quality kz'eerkt—the tanned hides of Wunderland criminals, selected to be without blemish or lash mark.

"Impressive," said Trainer-of-Slaves.

"I am determined that you shall have your fleet rating!" Ssis was flicking the tip of his tail back and forth in agitation as he paraded to show off his tailoring.

"Hr-r. Yet I have sworn enemies who would make it difficult."

"Harrgh! I have proper papers here for you that

will make it all easy, letters of introduction and recommendation." He began to purr. "And a pass to Wunderland! I don't dance around, I just leap right in. They have to give you to me. I need you."

"Friend, I shall be satisfied with the trip to Wunderland."

"Not after you've served as my gunner!" The elegant captain lifted his bushy head and with a great grin emitted a spitting-yowling imitation of the sounds of battle. "We're going to carve up some asteroids on the way in. Great sport."

Trainer-of-Slaves decided that he could leave Long-Reach in charge of polarizer repairs, and took his chief slave on a tour of the shop. One giant field-generator was suspended in the light gravity of Aarku while two of the five-armed Jotoki slaves worked to replace its laminated planars.

Long-Reach stood proudly on four wrists while pointing with his fifth arm. "This unit will be ready for testing in two days," said skinny(arm). "I am honored by your trust in me, brave master," interrupted short(arm), checking various screens by taking control of three eyes. "All will go well with the polarizer repairs. We are expecting another unit for overhaul at the end of the day. And my duties among the juveniles?"

Trainer-of-Slaves trusted Long-Reach with all but one thing—the Jotok transients. "Just keep the life-support functional. Change the filters again." It would never do to have one of those curious five-armed, five-brained fledglings fixate upon a mature Jotok as parent. "Third-Teacher-of-Slaves will be in charge. Your first duty is to the shop."

"You will be traveling to Wunderland? The crew has checked over the engines of the *Blood of Heroes* from finger-tip to elbow. They hum. Do tell Ssis-Captain to stay within specs."

The gravitic polarizer was the foundation stone of the Patriarchy and of warrior military superiority. In its stationary version it made artificial gravity possible, but its most useful application was as the reactionless space drive which allowed vehicles to accelerate in "free fall": one gravity for the lumbering freighters, sixty or seventy gravities for the faster military warships.

These kzin craft bewildered the Wunderland defenders at the time of the 2367 A.D. conquest. They darted about with incredible velocity and acceleration changes, yet ejected no reaction mass, and didn't seem to need refueling even after maneuvers that would have exhausted the tanks of a torchship. The kzin warships could be goaded and provoked and then harassed like a bull in Old Spain, they could be burned, but they couldn't be chased. They didn't seem to obey the laws of physics.

For years after that terrible six months, war-impoverished professors from the Munchen Scholarium gathered in the cafés along Karl-Jorge Avenue in Old Munchen, writing equations and speculating with preposterous assumptions while they sipped their schnapps. Research equipment can be confiscated. Equations and speculation are free. When Alpha Centauri B was in the night sky, wan but brighter than any streetlight, each new theory about kzin technology was carried like an epidemic between the sidewalk cafés until second sunset when the nightlife of Munchen died.

Given that a reactionless drive *did* exist they eventually sketched out the beginning of an understanding that had a sound theoretical footing by the time Chuut-Riit arrived as governor. The human mind, unlike the kzin mind, is obsessed with resolving the contradictions between what it observes and what it thinks it should be seeing.

Momentum did not *appear* to be conserved by the reactionless kzin ships, but the gravitic field equations upon which the polarizer was based invoked negative space curvature, a necessary element of any reactionless space drive. Normal *intuitions* about momentum fail in the presence of negative curvature—momentum then has a direction opposite velocity—but the equations of momentum conservation still hold.

Trainer-of-Slaves took up his gunner's berth on the *Blood of Heroes*. He was outfitted with mask-goggles. They imposed diagrams upon his visual field which supplied all that he might need to know while firing. During check-down he had time to make simulation runs—with his goggles feeding him the dangers of a virtual world. It gave the liver a jolt to kill monkey-ships even if they were only program-generated ghosts.

The five spherical ships of the hunter-pack drifted into position. There was ear-bulb chatter as the captains readied themselves for the three light-hour sweep from Alpha Centauri B across to Alpha Centauri A, roughly the equivalent of a run from the distance of Uranus to Man-home. The Serpent's Swarm would give the sweep realism, though it contained hundreds of times the mass and debris of the Solar Belt.

Because of this plethora of asteroids, the Kzin Training Command was able to designate as many target asteroids as it pleased without disrupting the economy of the Swarm. Fourth Fleet attack-training stressed destruction of the kind of asteroid defensive installations which the monkeys used extensively to protect the north and south approaches to Man-home.

At maximum acceleration the *Blood of Heroes* could make the three-light-hour trip from B to A in less than two days at a turn-around velocity a tenth the speed

of light, but this was not common practice because of
the density of matter in the Centauri System which
created field energy losses.

The gravity polarizer of the kzin high-velocity drive
contained a natural mechanism to protect the ship
from impact by gas and micrometeoroids. The
offending particle was violently accelerated as it
entered the field while, at the same time, the ship
reacted to the added mass by recoiling. In the
exchange, field energy was re-converted to mass. The
particle size was not critical—unequal masses accelerate at the same rate within *any* gravitic field.

Unfortunately, atoms impacting into a polarizer's
field generated a weak electromagnetic interaction
which drained field energy into radiation. Inside a
planetary system this could have been a serious problem if high velocities had been desirable. Between the
stars, where high velocities *are* desirable, kzin ships
weren't able to travel much above eighty percent of
light speed through normal densities of interstellar gas
without bleeding to death from "blue shine."

While a gravity polarizer was accelerating it converted mass to energy, when it decelerated it converted that same energy back to mass. Its power
requirements were orders of magnitude less than a
torchship, needing power only to make up for the
losses involved in field interactions with the local
media.

The hunting pack was practicing the standard
maneuver. Come in high over the Swarm, then attack
down through it at a moderate velocity. There was
much bantering back and forth between the offensive
team and the defensive team during an "engagement"
debriefing. All kzin insults weren't delivered in
anger—the real meaning lay in the inflections of the
spit-hisses. Ssis-Captain was fond of calling his oppo-

nents baboons because they had been ordered to "think like monkeys." Amiably they dubbed him "Kshat-Lunch," referring to a herbivore who was known to eat offal.

It took them twelve days, not two, to work their way across the Swarm on patrol/attack status, instruments scanning at full vigilance. The *Blood of Heroes* recorded static from the Tiamat industrial world: instructions to some lonely rockjack in his torchship, calls for part replacements, a medical emergency. Doppler shifts alerted monitors.

Of the man-ships they saw only glimmers flicking across detection screens. Somewhere among the stones armed feral humans grubbed about, plotting revenge—but the *Blood of Heroes* saw none, though its instruments were looking. These sullen beasts were mostly no more of a nuisance than fur-ticks but they made good target practice when found. On this run the Heroes sparred only with tumbling rubble.

Trainer-of-Slaves was an experienced gunner by the time they reached the cloud-streaked globe of Wunderland. He was not yet an experienced politician.

CHAPTER 13
(2402 A.D.)

In its simplest design, the kzin gravity polarizer just floated. If it was shoved *toward* a mass, energy was fed into its polarizer field—which forced it to rise. If it was pushed *away* from a mass, energy was drained from its polarizer field—which forced it to fall.

The shuttle "platforms" that transported freight and passengers into and out of Wunderland's mass-well were straight modifications of this primitive device. Descent was controlled by electromagnetically *bleeding* the field to charge molecular distortion batteries. Ascent was controlled by *feeding* the field from those same batteries. Horizontal velocity was controlled by a torsion field interaction that spun-up or spun-down Wunderland's rotation.

The cycle was highly efficient, leaking some spillover energy at the electromagnetic-gravitic interface and some in tidal friction. When dropping from orbit around Wunderland to the surface, the shuttle's polarizer rose only a few degrees in temperature.

Munchenport was a depressing introduction to the

fabulous wealth that Trainer-of-Slaves had heard about all his life. A proper spacedrome had yet to be constructed. They settled onto an open field that was serviced by extruded buildings of recent fabrication, all square and ugly, all laid out and finished by forced labor. The Wundervolker wryly called it the "himmelfahrt"—both because it was from here that one ascended to the heavens and because so many of them had "gone to heaven" building it.

The number of unleashed man-beasts was appalling, lined up with their baggage, milling around, shuffling through the weapons scanners, arguing with attendants. Most of them were looking for work in the military industries of the Serpent's Swarm, needing the wages badly enough to be willing to build weapons that would be used against their father system. They smelled of unwashed bodies and poverty, a peculiar sweet-sour odor blending with the machinery-and-synthetics smell of the building and the residual ozone from cheap electric vehicles.

Ssis-Captain knew the routine. He hired some man-beasts of burden to carry his and Trainer's luggage to the aircar terminal. The clean cool breeze inside the car was a relief. "We'll go to the old city. It's better there," he said.

To a Hero born in space on a hostile outpost near a dying star, Munchen was odd for a city. This was a city? The low-pitched tile roofs weren't airtight and the windows opened to the atmosphere. From some views the buildings were hidden by the trees that shaded streets. The broad blue waters of the Donau cut through parks of palms and blooming frangipani. Of what use was the steel steeple of the Saint Joachim cathedral?

Ssis-Captain found a room for them in an old four-story brick mansion that had been converted for kzin use by knocking out the tops of all the interior doors.

He gave their luggage to an old man-female who staggered under the load, finally setting it down to breathe before dividing her job into two trips.

"She's ready for the glue-factory," commented Ssis, who was three times her size.

"It's a she? But she took your instructions!"

"Of course."

He stared at the old lady. Dumb male-animals, Trainer-of-Slaves could understand, but females who comprehended sentences? He tried to imagine his mother speaking in whole phrases. He had talked enough to her, and sometimes . . . sometimes he had imagined that she was listening, such big round eyes she had.

It was a powerful deception. A kzinrret always gave the *impression* of being intelligent. Once as a spoiled kit in the Chiirr-Nig household he had been so taken by this illusion that he had given his mother an adventure picture-book to read to him at nap-time. She had chewed the book to pieces.

But enough of amazement. They beeped their automatic car on its way, settled into their room, and set about to pad the rest of the way to the Admiralty by foot.

Trainer-of-Slaves had been close to only two monkeys in his life and found a city-herd of them disconcerting. Ssis-Captain just ignored the animals while they scurried around him or waited against a wall. They all wore clothes—a fact somehow surprising to Trainer—though obviously they belonged to no military unit. Since Chuut-Riit's hunt on Hssin, he had imagined that naked was the natural state of all man-beasts.

The Admiralty could have whatever it wanted. At the time of the occupation they had wanted the Landholder's Ritterhaus. It stood with great Gothic arches and stone buttressing at the head of the cobblestoned

Grunderplatz. The victorious Heroes had not bothered to demolish the crowded bronze memorial of the Nineteen Founders, perhaps because the Ritterhaus dominated the group and the kzinti were in the Ritterhaus. Down there, those laboring bronze figures looked like hard-working slaves.

The Fourth Fleet bureaucracy was at a frenzy with the final logistic preparations and assignments just months away. Trainer-of-Slaves was received by a harassed kzin officer who kept having to duck under man-height doors as he busied himself trying to find his files. He couldn't remember which computer he had fed them to. Finally, in distraction, he reset his bat-like ears and offered the absolute certainty of his help tomorrow, at the same time, if Trainer would be so good as to return.

They retreated to their lodgings in the old manor house. A dignified kzin passed them on the stairs with two leashed kzinrretti. Females could be dangerous in a city; they tended to spat with any unpleasantly odorous animal who dared approach them, and man-beasts with alcohol on their breath were always likely victims. They would even attack a male kzin twice their size if the lives of kits were at stake.

"Reasonableness does not control female emotions," explained their patriarch. "Have a good night. You'll have to fold your ears against the kzin at the end of the hall—he growls and fights ghosts in his sleep."

A return to the Admiralty in the morning produced puzzling results. The kzin clerk dismissed Trainer-of-Slaves, and when Trainer politely persisted, another kzin ducked out of an adjoining office.

"You are not qualified for the Fourth Fleet and your rating application has been refused."

"I have these recommendations . . ."

The huge red officer with yellow splotches in his fur hissed. Trainer-of-Slaves immediately took the hint, saluted with a sharp claw-across-face, and retreated.

That evening Trainer and Ssis-Captain were considering their other options at a trunkshuppen off one of the side streets that led into the Grunderplatz. There were no other kzin present at the Mondschein. The waitress was clearly terrified to serve them but she was brave in her order-taking.

"Guten Abend, ehrenvoll Helden," she trembled. "Haben Sie gewahlt?" When they were slow to reply, she suggested a popular bourbon with milk.

"Ich ... nehme eine ... Coca Cola," said Trainer-of-Slaves, twisting his tongue around his teeth with his best animal imitation.

Ssis-Captain's remarks in the Hero's Tongue were meowls and spits of derision and approval. "The place smells like vatach-in-a-cage." He was referring to the humid scent of furless fear. "Nice little planet, Hr-r?" He nodded his mane at the waitress while playfully punching Trainer. "I'll take one of those to curry my backside in my European castle." Then, he consulted his translator. "Ich nehme einen Whiskey Kentucky mit Milch," he ordered, before he returned to business.

"You have some slandering enemies here in Munchen so we shall go elsewhere—which will lead directly back to higher lairs." Ssis-Captain had an invitation to the base at Gerning in the isolated northern province of Skogarna. "Friend Detector-Analyst is pleased with his post. The vast woods are isolated both from man-beast traffic and the arrogance of kzin patriarchs who are so well fed with land that they guard their holdings against the likes of us as if we were one-eyed kzinrret bandits."

Ssis-Captain rearranged his ears knowingly and flared his nostrils to hint that what he knew about the base was special. "Chuut-Riit established the Gerning station within months of his ascension as governor. The officers there are all kzin who sided with him in the struggle. Good contacts."

As he leaned forward with more conspiratorial details, Ssis-Captain's chair—suddenly—collapsed, and milk-in-bourbon arced to slosh onto his mane and vest. His massive head rose above the table with a fanged grin. When he was fully erect, his mane touching the low ceiling, he snarled in the direction of the pale bartender.

The other patrons, who had been uneasy, were now no longer even twitching.

Their waitress calmly dried her hands, sauntered to the door as if there was nothing more important going on than quitting time—then fled.

Ah how the liver rules the mind, thought Trainer-of-Slaves, noticing both the man-beast behavior and Ssis-Captain's rising rage. How much different was rage than fear? He knew enough not to touch Ssis for he could not hide his amusement, and too much tail whacking would turn the rage against himself. He appealed to the Captain's vanity as he, too, rose, "We'll have to wash your vest right away before the milk dries. Come." To the bartender he raised his glass, careful not to smile. He wanted to put that apprehensive creature at ease. "Zum Wohl!" he said, proud of his growing facility with animal grunts.

Ssis-Captain did not come right away. He took his rage out on the chair, taking the remnants of its poor wooden frame apart with bare hands and teeth as if it were a United Nations Warship.

CHAPTER 14
(2402 A.D.)

In an aircar over the province of Skogarna the social structure of Wunderland stood out in a way that never would have shown from the ground. It was clearly a wilderness dominated by a manorial elite. Coming into the kzin base they passed over the Nordbo estate at Korsness, huge, isolated from Gerning by hill and primeval wood along an expanse of beach. A ribbon of roads leading to Korsness clearly showed who was master of Gerning.

The light armored aircar carried the two kzin Heroes above the forested hills, past the hillside scar of recent kzin construction. It was afternoon but sunset hues of red washed over the clouds along the horizon where Alpha Centauri B was disappearing. The sea showed an astonishingly clear blue that faded into pastel shades of green where the shallow coastal waters had flooded a crater and left a curving string of islands.

Many such craters littered Wunderland. The planet suffered continual impact from meteorites straying out of the Serpent's Swarm so that some nights were aglow with falling stars. A major strike every few million years had left Wunderland's lifeforms permanently poised for adaptation. The navy that had defended Wunderland from the Conquering Heroes had consisted mainly of a Meteoroid Guard unit.

Gerning Base was created by kzin who loved to hunt; the actual station that monitored the high atmosphere for thousands of kilometers around to detect feral spacecraft seemed more of an afterthought. Some cunning kzin had his eye on this area, anticipating the time when honor and heroism would earn him the right to a full name. In the meantime he was serving Chuut-Riit's purposes.

Detector-Analyst was a local kzin from a background that gave him a Hssin heritage, though he had never been to R'hshssira. He gave Trainer-of-Slaves special consideration out of curiosity for the planet of his patriarchs. Ssis-Captain grumbled at all this talk about a place he had passed through while in hibernation and kept interrupting to turn the conversation into a lighter vein.

Jokes: "How do you stop a monkey from running around in circles? Nail his other foot to the floor."

Zoology: was a Wunderland tigripard faster than a Kzin krrach-sherrek? Or only more cunning?

Better than he liked stalking through the forest, Ssis liked to sit in the lodge on the carved logs, supping fermented milk. The political intrigue was all in the lodge. He speculated with Trainer about the identity of the ambitious kzin who was "pissing around the borders of this territory," looking for a noble name so that he might found a household here. They decided it must be Yiao-Captain.

Yiao-Captain was an unlikely candidate. He was as short as Trainer and as slight, not the kind one would expect to dominate a fight, but he had a cautious cun-

ning to him—and an *energy*—that would make any
challenge to his honor dangerous. But it was his ambition that struck them both.

Trainer-of-Slaves first sniffed around its edges when
he was invited to share a kill with four of the local
kzin. The kill was a forest herbivore, headless, and
carved in places that facilitated sundering, the fresh
blood still running into the table-gutters where a spout
delivered it to a bloodbowl. The tang of bloodscent
was overpowering. On a sidetable stood green
homeblown bottles of the local akvavit, ready to mix
with the blood.

Trainer learned in conversation that the akvavit had
been seized in Gerning for unpaid taxes and its distill-
er's daughter sold into factory slavery at Valburg. The
normal procedure was for the indigenous *Herrenmann*
to handle such details but the kzin purposefully
audited estates and villages when taxes seemed low
and found simple ways to encourage ardent taxpaying.
After all, the taxes were set at fair levels.

The conversation changed from such mundane top-
ics when Yiao-Captain arrived to rip off a hunk of
meat for his own fangs. He dominated the conversation with his enthusiasms. He added fire to the tinder-
dry debate over Chuut-Riit's *Logistical Preparation as
the Key to Victory In War*. He provoked insults and
countered them with witty insults of his own that
both needled and defused. When he tired of that,
he turned the collective attention of his coterie to
tales of adventure.

Adventure, to Yiao-Captain, meant astronomy. His
haunch of herbivore held motionless, he stopped
eating while the sputtering of the Hero's Tongue
quickened to an almost battle intensity. To know the
stars! There were rumors of strange beings who lived
in the depths of space, rumors of ancient empires that
had casually abandoned tools upon the ice of comets

long before any of the giant stars of the constellations
had yet flamed to life.

Hr-roghk! The hints! The spoor untracked!
Starseeds that spawned at the galaxy's very edge.
Where did they come from? Where did they go? Mysteries! What were those moon caves deep in the outer
planetary gloom around red dwarfs? Caves so ancient
they must have been carved by disintegrator beams?
Wealth! Honor!

Then silence to let all this sink in while Yiao-Captain noisily stripped his morsel. He left, reminded of
duty by some new passion. The conversation drifted
back to kzinrret jokes, to who had just received a
name, to the honor duel between Electronic-Systems-
Upkeep and Builder-of-Walls, the spike on yesterday's
scope, the taste of space rations. And finally, finally,
the tongue-wagging licked around that most degener-
ate bone of speculation—fleet rivalries; who would
reach Man-sun first?

Days of hunting brought Trainer-of-Slaves and
Detector-Analyst together in a friendship broader than
the commonality of Hssin. They often went out at
dawn without Ssis. Detector had been hunting in the
woods around Gerning since the opening of the base,
and knew the ways and the smells of the forest. He
knew the waterholes and the places where a tigripard
might be found stalking its own prey.

The aroma of Wunderland, the expanse, the open
skies, an evening standing on the beach by the sea—
all of this overwhelmed Trainer with joy. He had been
a hunter himself, moving daily out into the Hssin Jotok
Run to cull the wild Jotok or lure a transient into
slavery, or measure the salinity of the marshes where
the Jotok larvae wriggled among the reeds. He had
thought the Jotok Run a capacious relief from the
cramped city, but this! This Wunderland went on
forever!

Once the hunting through the woods took them as far as the Korsness estate. Trainer saw from the hill Yiao-Captain helping a man-beast and his child move a fallen tree from the main road. He went to help the Captain. It seemed like a political thing to do—ingratiating himself with this officer could only prove useful. But why was he moving a tree when there were so many slaves and machines?

"Rrrr, we have welcome help," purred Yiao-Captain to the tiny child who had been trying to lift the tree at its center.

Trainer recognized the larger of the tame animals as the local king of beasts. He couldn't tell one monkey from the other but this one was tall for a man, with a hideous hooked nose. Unfairly, he had an unearned name, Peter Nordbo, but that was the way of the monkeys who did not know the value of a name.

"You're big," said the *Herrenmann*'s child to the new kzin. "What's your name?"

Trainer-of-Slaves could hardly understand beast talk, and he knew the child would not understand his. He had not yet grasped enough words in the slave language to translate his name. But Long-Reach's name for him was an easy translation. "Mellow-Yellow," he said. Those two words he did know. He added stiffly, "You are Short-Son of Nordbo."

The boy cocked his ear. "I'm Ib Nordbo, ehrenvoll Yellow." He put his three-year-old back to the tree. "Push!"

After the two kzin had carried the log to the roadside with token help from their human vassals, the child found a nest of petal-pickers that had been disturbed by their activities, the tiny scaled creatures dashing grief-stricken around their paper home. Ib Nordbo, not the least bit afraid of the kzin, took Trainer by the paw and made him stoop to his haunches while he explained the social life of petal-pickers with three year old seriousness.

Peter Nordbo watched his son anxiously while Yiao emitted a purr to reassure his vassal. Trainer-of-Slaves listened intently to everything Ib told him, even understanding some of it. He was fascinated. The man-beasts he had seen were very badly organized into slavehood. There had to be a better way. Learning animal psychology by direct communication with their young was a source of important clues to domestication.

Mellow-Yellow let a petal-picker climb onto his stick, waving its long front legs. Ib laughed. "They like roses. I feed them roses but it makes them sick." And he got up and staggered around for Trainer like a petal-picker drunk on the alien essence of rose.

"Do you have petal-pickers on Kzin?" asked the child curiously.

"Never . . . been . . . Kzin-home," Trainer struggled with the language.

"I go to Kzin," Ib pointed at himself. "I will tell the Patriarch to be nice."

Peter Nordbo had been licking his lips. He hastily picked up his son who was as much of a chatterbox as his young wife Hulda. "Maman wishes you for naptime."

"No!" The boy struggled.

"Sir," apologized Nordbo, "he is young yet to learn the proper forms of respect."

Kzinti have a soft spot in their liver for sons who struggle. Yiao-Captain nodded his mane. "If ever I reach Kzin-home, I will deliver the katzchen's message with great respect to the Patriarch."

Only days later Yiao-Captain appeared at the lodge with his Nordbo *Herrenmann*, violating all protocol. Kzin and beast came there to play some sort of man-game. Bored with fleet gossip, Trainer-of-Slaves tried to follow the moves and the logic of the game. It was played out on an octal by octal board, with stationary combat pieces. There seemed to be no action, no attack. The pieces stood there, sometimes without moving for minutes. One piece was moved at a time, to some trivial advantage. Sometimes, very gently, a piece would be set aside.

Yiao-Captain seemed fascinated by the game; his eyes never left the pieces. He asked questions roughly, and would cuff *Herrenmann* Nordbo as if he were a son, and he would purr happily when he captured a piece. But the stationary nature of the game obviously took its toll. When beast-Nordbo spent too much time on his moves, the Captain would pace restlessly, and if his opponent, even then, had not moved, he would stand towering over the small slave and impatiently suggest what the next move should be.

"Ach, that would give me too much trouble with your bishop when you jumped your knight. I think I'll move my pawn. I see advantage there."

"How do monkeys ever win a war? You'd be slashed to pieces before you decide which trench to sit in!" He turned to Trainer-of-Slaves. "You've been watching. Do you understand this ponderous wargame?"

"It is much too slow for me. I'm looking for fast action around Man-sun."

"You have a conventional mind. Five and a half years in hibernation is action?" Yiao-Captain roared in good humor. "Do you have a ship yet? Chuut-Riit is always looking for Heroes who want to get their tails singed."

"I have a ship, but the Admiralty is being slow with my rating."

"Hr-r, that's easy to fix. I'll tell you who to go to."

Yiao-Captain seemed to be at ease anywhere. When Traat-Admiral arrived for an inspection, Yiao took him hunting and entertained him without the slightest hint

of propitiation. He appeared to be very well connected. Ssis-Captain hid in the bushes so that when
Traat-Admiral came for his aircar on the day of depar-
ture, he could step out along the path and pass the
Admiral with a sharp salute.

It was a glorious day. A chill wind blew in from the
sea that ruffled the fur and took away the heat of
exertion. Ssis was in a mood for celebration. He chat-
ted excitedly about what Yiao-Captain could do for
them, counting sons before they were born. Trainer
guided him north to the creek where they wandered
upstream on the boulders. Ssis leaped very carefully
not to get wet—stone by stone—but Trainer didn't
mind wading when he had to.

"Shissss!" the Captain whispered, freezing. "I've
caught a scent."

They skulked downwind over a lightning-felled tree,
silently on pads. Bent underbrush led around-hill. A
splash of white through the leaves. There he was. They
had a man-beast. A youngling with a spear. He saw
them and started to run. In a flowing gait Ssis-Captain
cut him off, drove him back toward Trainer. He fled
in a perpendicular dash, away from them both. Ssis
flanked him, around a gray outcropping, grinning. The
boy-beast turned. Futilely. The natural carnivorous
leap of the kzin was awesome in the low gravity. Ssis
was blocking his way again, not hurting him, not coming close. Toying with his prey.

Trainer-of-Slaves had flashes of the poor monkeys
he had tried to save back on Hssin during that fatal
man-hunt. He stood, frozen with fear, not for himself
but for the wretched animal. Ssis was only playing,
having fun, but the beast didn't know that. Trainer
reached a hand up, trying to think of something to
growl at his companion that would restrain him.

The terrified boy, unable to retreat, charged with
his spear. "Die Zeit ist um! Rattekatze!"

Ssis whacked him aside with unsheathed claws, but instead of picking himself up and running, the animal charged again with berserk energy, spearless. His body rebounded from the massive bulk of the moving kzin. He no longer had a face.

"No sense of humor," said Ssis-Captain, rolling the corpse onto its back with his foot.

Trainer-of-Slaves lowered his hand. They were so frail! He stooped over the youngling-beast to check for signs of life, the heady blood-odor stimulating his hunger. "He's dead!" There was no help for it. They stripped the clothes off the body and took turns ripping it apart with their fangs. What they left was a pile of bloody bones, half the flesh still uneaten, the braincase smashed open for the delicacy within.

One day later a grim *Herrenmann* arrived at the kzin base desperately trying to hold his rage within a propitiative framework. Yiao-Captain greeted him, at first not reading Peter Nordbo's state of mind. The hints of rebellion only raised Yiao-Captain's ire. Nordbo shifted his argument. Gerning was a small town. If the taxpayers were hunted, who would pay the taxes?

"I have supplied your base faithfully. How can I collect your tithe if this goes on?"

"I will conduct an investigation." Yiao opened a switch on his desk. "Data-Sergeant. Get me information. Who was hunting yesterday?"

Later Yiao had Ssis-Captain and Trainer-of-Slaves ordered to his office. He left them standing at attention. His mouth was twitching around its fangs. "You have been guests here at this base," he growled, making it plain that they no longer were. "I have let you roam freely. You have been serving in cramped quarters and I have sympathy for those who do their duty under trying circumstances. You have no authority to kill my taxpayers. Nor any reason. The woods abound with lower game." Contemptuously, the tip of Yiao's naked tale flicked back and forth. "This youngling you attacked, was that the best test of your prowess that you could find? Next you'll be devouring suckling kits!"

Yiao-Captain let the warriors stand while he attended to other matters. Finally he pulled out papers for Ssis-Captain. "You have been recalled to the fleet, immediately. I have seen to it that you will not return to the surface of Wunderland. You'll have to do your hunting on Man-home. I hear that there they have a surplus of taxpayers."

He had even worse words for Trainer-of-Slaves. "And I have investigated you, too. You have been toadying around the base seeking a fighting position in the Fourth Fleet, slithering behind the command of those who have been appointed to consider the staffing of the Fleet. You have a record of cowardice. Your presence aboard a fighting ship would endanger its Heroes. I have seen to it that you are being recalled to your duties at Fortress Aarku, immediately."

CHAPTER 15
(2402–2403 A.D.)

When the Fourth Fleet convoys began to assemble, stripping Centaurian space of its slaves and Heroes and warcraft, the Fortress Aarku became a tomb smelling of the Jotoki pens burrowed into the rock. The trained slaves were gone. The maintenance hangars were empty.

After Wunderland, Aarku was a coffin.

Trainer-of-Slaves suffered for another year at Alpha Centauri B. He tried to keep his contraband kzinrret happy, but she missed the flirtations of the warriors who were on their way to Man-sun and became moody and demanding. She did not comprehend the war. She only knew that she had been abandoned. She wanted attention. She rubbed against Trainer while he was trying to work. When he rebuffed her, she took to stalking his personal Jotoki and actually killed one of his trainees. When Long-Reach discretely approached his master for help, they decided to store her away in a hibernation coffin and only bring her out when Trainer felt the craving.

Months after the Fourth Fleet was gone, remnants of the Third Fleet began to arrive at Alpha Centauri. Hangers at Aarku filled. Polarizers improperly maintained for a decade needed a fully stripped overhaul, but more than that there was much old battle damage too drastic to have been repaired in transit.

Trainer-of-Slaves personally crawled through the last of the stragglers. Eight survivors out of a crew of forty had brought it home, three of them dying of injuries en route. Inspection showed that *The Vindictive Memory* had taken a near fatal internal explosion. The ship's command sector had been pierced in three places by x-ray bolts. Space desiccated kzin were still trapped in one compartment. In the main gunnery turret three carbonized kzin lay melded to their weapons. The ship was not salvageable.

It was enough to chill the liver. Trainer-of-Slaves was reminded that he was afraid of death. How had he let Ssis-Captain mesmerize him with dreams of valor?

Orders relieving him of his duties at Aarku came as an electric surprise.

Some young son of a noble name had annoyed Chuut-Riit and was being given the Aarku assignment as penance. Even though Trainer was to be allowed three personal slaves, the new post didn't look appetizing—the commission involved a permanent position, not on Wunderland or Tiamat, but in deep space. Another dead-end for a coward? Yet the commission script bore the seal of the Fifth Fleet.

The tiny ship that brought him out, all gravitic drive and no armor or armament, was called a *Ztirgor* after a long-legged browser of Kzin that could run and dodge skillfully through brush and hills but had no other defense against attack. They were two light-days out, a six day trip by *Ztirgor* at 70 Kzin gravities of acceleration with a turn-around velocity a third that of light. Alpha Centauri had been reduced from suns to a coruscant pair of stars in Andromeda.

They were drifting in to dock. By starshine the great hull of the communications warship was dwarfed by its extended antenna. The transmission/reception fabric, shimmering in the palest of rainbow colors, dominated the heavens. From a distance there were no clues as to its size—binocular vision is erased by space.

This great antenna faced Man-sun, now brilliantly overlaying the constellation that the man-beasts called *Cassiopeia* and the kzin called *God's Fang Drinking at the River of Heaven*. The Father-sun, appropriately, lay in the constellation of the *Dominant Warrior* that, to monkeys, was not a warrior but represented a ferocious bear.

Strange, thought Trainer-of-Slaves, how little the constellations varied over the whole of Patriarchal Space. The brightest stars were too distant to move. The stars of *God's Fang* were all giants, the brightest a red giant, the others, massive white giants, furious forges of the heavy metals.

They were met in the shuttle bay by an efficiently formal Master-Sergeant who recognized Trainer-of-Slaves by the slaves he brought with him. "Grraf-Hromfi will see you immediately. Lesser-Sergeant will settle your slaves. Welcome aboard." Trainer was already missing his kzinrret. He'd had to sell her on the sleight-of-paw market, too quickly to get a good price.

The warship was maintaining a light artificial gravity, just enough to settle dust and lost objects. They glided through the passageways effortlessly. It wasn't much different from Fortress Aarku. During the journey Trainer-of-Slaves deduced that Grraf-Hromfi ran a disciplined ship—the smell of it was remarkably clean.

At the Command Center, the Sergeant snapped off

an alert ripping-salute. He was dismissed. Trainer-of-Slaves imitated with his snappiest claws-across-face and Grraf-Hromfi replied with a salute that wouldn't have taken the hide off a kit's tail. He wore a soft vest over his robe that he must have repaired himself, but he smelled like a hard task-master.

"I don't think that on the *Sherrek's Ear* we can provide you with the kind of feral life to which you have become accustomed; nevertheless, we do have interesting duties. You haven't smuggled aboard a kzinrret, have you?"

"No, Sire!"

"I thought that I'd let you know that we don't tolerate such irregularities here."

"Of course, Sire!"

"I've been reviewing your record, Eater-of-Grass." He returned his heavy duty data-goggles to his eyes which didn't prevent him from seeing, through the data, the sudden stiffness in Trainer-of-Slaves posture—or the way ears folded against skull—or the lay-back of the fur on cheeks. "Yes, youngling, I know everything. At ease!"

"My cowardice has shamed me, Dominant One! I sought to restore my honor by volunteering for the Fourth Fleet."

"I assume that you believe the Fourth Fleet's mission would be more successful with cowards in key positions?"

"No, Sire!"

"I also have here, printed across your face at the moment, a report on a recent conversation of yours. You were speculating that old enemies from Hssin sabotaged your efforts to join the Fourth Fleet by telling stories about your legendary cowardice."

Trainer thought frantically for a moment, scanning his memories. He damned his loose mouth. "I admit to that conversation, Sire."

"That's hardly necessary since I have an audio recording of it. The stories are true; you do have enemies, as my files will testify. They *have* made depositions unflattering to your bravery, but those reports were filed on Hssin. In the meantime those enemies you cherish so close to your liver, have forgotten you. In their memory you have impugned the efforts of those who sought to grant your self-seeking application to join the *Blood of Heroes*. Your application was accepted at all levels, even by those who disapproved of you. The 'enemy' you are so bitter about is Chuut-Riit himself."

"Then I abase myself!"

"Shall I read to you what you said about this enemy? I particularly liked the one about him speaking with his anus and beshitting with his mouth."

"I have made a grievous error!"

"Beshitted with your mouth, did you? Hr-r, but you will be sufficiently punished. You have come under my command by the orders of Chuut-Riit. That is punishment enough for any sin. I make Heroes out of kits. It is easier on me if you do all the work."

"I volunteer immediately for any duty you may assign me!"

"Excellent." Grraf-Hromfi pulled an antique flint-spark pistol from a belt holster, and raised the goggles to his forehead, out of the way. "I prefer this to a wtsai knife," he said wryly. "It gives me several octenturies over my opponents. That makes me feel modern." Since the pistol could fire only one musket ball at a time, it had skull-cracking knobs on the barrel so that it could be used as a club. "Disassemble and polish my weapon while we talk." He handed Trainer-of-Slaves a polishing kit.

"Yes, Sire!"

"Chuut-Riit has been building two fleets for the last three years, not one. The Fourth Fleet was a full attack unit. The Fifth Fleet, to which you are now an honored member by the personal order of Chuut-Riit, was conceived of as an elite seed. With the launching of the Fourth Fleet, the seed is being planted. The Fifth Fleet is to grow into a fully operational attack force—assimilating warriors and warships only as fast as they can learn its strict code. It will not be a loose confederation like the Fourth Fleet. Any breaks in discipline will not be tolerated."

"Already I feel the juices of obedience in my liver, Dominant One!"

"Do you have questions?"

"Will we see action, Wise One? Or are we just a Fourth Fleet backup?" For a moment, Trainer-of-Slaves stopped his vigorous polishing of the ceremonial pistol.

"Let's take an example. Your brazen friend, Ssis-Captain, takes what he wants and does what he wants. Once he has an idea in his head, he acts. If his ears are tickled, he acts. His liver stops at nothing. If it took his fancy to put a kzinrret in command of his bridge, there she'd be pacing about and purring!"

The ears of Trainer-of-Slaves had to be consciously immobilized as he polished. He was imagining *their* kzinrret in command of the *Blood of Heroes*.

"Am I not right about your friend?"

"Hr-r, absolutely!"

"Yes. And he has never commanded a ship in battle. He sees an enemy position and he takes it, right?"

"The *Blood of Heroes* has a valiant crew. They are totally loyal to Ssis-Captain."

"What will his battle-lifetime be? An octal-day? Two if he's lucky! Then again he may have no more than the time to *see* a monkey before he is dead and his ship, cooked meat. Chuut-Riit has assigned all such commanders to the Fourth Fleet. *If* they survive he may be able to teach them something. They *may* even kill a few monkeys. Perhaps not even that. What have the first three fleets of you outworld barbarians accomplished, you screaming berserkers of Hssin, you borderland ragpickers? Bloody nothing!"

Grraf-Hromfi was now stirred up enough to clutch his planning-surface. "Hr-r, perhaps you wild barbarians have been teaching the monkeys military strategy in your own cunning way, one fleet at a time, never making the problems harder than a monkey can solve? The next thing we know, you Imperial-border scavengers will be hiring man-beasts to do your fighting. Why waste the talents you have taught them? Put them in command of your warships!"

"Sir, you speak of my father, not me."

"Hr-r, and you are different?"

"I admire firearms. This is a fine pistol, Sire. I believe I'm ready to reassemble it."

"Picked it up on W'kkai. That's where Chuut-Riit found me. We were both bored and listening to rumors in the marketplace to see if we couldn't sniff up some action. I had just bought the pistol from an old warrior who needed the gold. Chuut wanted the pistol, too, being a collector of pre-space weapons. He swears that he added me to his retinue so that he can keep track of this pistol. Notice the mark of Kai, a famous forger for the Riits."

"The Fourth Fleet will have glory with such a great weapons collector as Chuut-Riit."

"You are clawing for fish? The flattery does not disguise your question. Let me be blunt since my position allows it. Chuut-Riit is not the leader of the Fourth Fleet. He is here, mere light-days away, sitting in a palace on Wunderland. You can have no idea of the difficulties he has had in trying to shape Fourth Fleet discipline. Every border Hero thinks of himself as Heaven's Admiral ripe to pillage the wealth of the unexplored frontier. The Fourth Fleet is a fleet of admirals!"

Hromfi was raving again. "And let me tell you something else, youngling. It will be Chuut-Riit who will be taking the Fifth Fleet to Man-sun as his personal armada. That's where *his* confidence lies. But we won't be stalking that path of victory until he is certain that both you and I are ready. I am ready; you are not."

"I am instantly ready to take any assignment!" Eagerness flamed.

"Hr-r, now. Finish the pistol first. I keep even the flint ready to spark, so test that." He checked the weapon, then returned it to Trainer-of-Slaves. "It must have been a cramped journey in the *Ztirgor*. Take some rest. Then report to Duty-Sergeant at lights-on. We'll have time to talk again. What else to do but exercise the Hero's Tongue? We have heaven above and stars below and years of time. An interstellar warrior's main duty is to wait."

"Have I been dismissed, Grraf-Hromfi, Sire?"

"Not on this ship. Your duties never cease. You will, of course, take charge of maintenance immediately. But there will be many other tasks you will have to learn—besides the polishing of pistols. Correct communication protocols. How one coordinates an interstellar war. And we have fighter craft out here with the *Sherrek's Ear*. You will learn how to defend a deep space base such as ours. Coextensively you will be learning sound military strategy. To cudgel that into your Hssin head, you will be teaching what I teach you, in turn, to my sons, a thankless and trying task, alas, for which I need help."

"Is that all, Sire?"

"I detect a note of sarcasm in your hisses. No, that is not all. That is the beginning."

"I look forward to your regime. In the end I shall

become convinced that I am one of Heaven's Admirals, a worthy goal for a Hssin barbarian."

"Claw your face and begone—Eater-of-Grass."

Trainer-of-Slaves took no notice of the insult for Grraf-Hromfi had spoken it with a purr. What could one's liver make of it all? He was terrified of this old kzin battle-ax—but he wasn't *afraid* of him.

Grraf-Hromfi called other engagements to the screen. Ordnance had arrived at the battle of Ceres when there were no longer any functioning warships to be supplied. Since the warships were already derelict, no warriors rallied to defend the late-arriving kzin freighters. It was a recipe for massacre.

Further sunward, against orders, the Second Maintenance group had found, and enthusiastically attacked, a target of opportunity. They were not equipped to blitz a major laser battery and were so crippled by the attempt that they lost the capacity to refit damaged *Scream-of-Vengeance* fighters—their appointed assignment. Without fighter cover, the *Victory-at-Swordbeak's-Nebula* was destroyed by a suicidal squadron of *Darts*.

"Think before you leap," Grraf-Hromfi admonished the Heroes who had died in those battles. His was the funeral voice of a father reprimanding the corpse of an arrogant son.

Trainer-of-Slaves had been all too willing to leap aboard the Fourth Fleet. He recalled the carbonized Gunners of the Third. Whatever flesh hadn't been burned had been mummified by space during the desperate journey home. The images were vivid. Fangs grinning through fried face. The black ash of fur along a pair of legs. Yet each of those Gunners must have had his ambitions of liveried slaves, of estates on the pampas of Central France or on the great steppes of England. For the first time Trainer-of-Slaves felt a real contentment with his own simple, unexotic servants.

And sometimes, when he was in a bad mood, Grraf-Hromfi used the practical arts to illustrate his motto.

With gloved claws, he took his seminar group into the tournament ring. None of the young kzin could touch him while the cameras were active. He always drew them into a fatal move and then stopped the fight for review. Full-sized slow-motion holos of the contest flickered in the ring. The master's pointer jabbed at the swimming image of his last opponent with caustic comment.

"By launching his assault from here, he gave me too much time to react. Look at my feet anticipating. He can't change his trajectory. Here—keep your eyes on my feet—I'm braced for the attack and"—the pointer whipped upward—"see my arm coming to grab his wrist? There, I've got it, and all I do is flick him around his axis just enough so that his own feet trip him when they touch the ground. Three seconds later he is dead." Grraf-Hromfi cuffed the young loser while the youth's holo image leisurely impacted the mat. "See? *Think* before you leap! Develop your brains beyond the level of a sthondat ganglion!"

And sometimes Grraf-Hromfi used the dry rhetoric of formula to hammer home his motto.

The *Sherrek's Ear* was the nucleus of the Third Black Pride that was to go out with the Fifth Fleet. What was a Black Pride? Black was space's invisible color. Grraf-Hromfi scratched his nose with a claw. That was a sure sign that he was going to hold their ears for hours explaining, in detail, how every action-of-the-moment had a future consequence. Yes, he would repeat it again and again. Warriors who won battles could actually smell consequences, could read the spoor of distant consequence in current events.

What startled Trainer-of-Slaves was the depth of Chuut-Riit's long-term planning. Two stripped-down and experimental Black Prides of the Fifth Fleet had *preceded* the Fourth Fleet to Man-sun. They would stand in place to assess the coming battles from two positions at distances far greater than the aphelion of Neptune. If the latest armada met with valorous defeat they alone would remain, undetectable, monitoring the electromagnetic fetor of man's activities, photographing the solar planets, mapping the asteroids, waiting . . . brooding the ultimate avenging strike.

Kzin equipment was competent to find large defensive systems. Grraf-Hromfi showed his students what the *Sherrek's Ear* could do from such a distance. He had photographs of ships docking at Tiamat in the Serpent's Swarm. He showed them street maps of Munchen, fuzzy but readable by a trained hunter. He played for them an overlay composite of the fusion power station at Wunderland's Wachsamkeit, done in twenty frequencies from gamma to ELF.

Think *before* you leap.

Before the Fifth Fleet attacked, five full-strength Black Prides would be girding Man-sun at distances too great to be observed without already knowing their location, unreachable by torchship even if detected— each a fallback and resupply base for a sustained operation, each a spoor gathering center.

Grraf-Hromfi outlined two main flaws in the previous conquest attempts: (1) local logistics dependent upon pillaging the fruits of the battlefield, and (2) long-distance logistical support which was nonexistent.

The Black Prides were designed to serve local logistic needs. A Black Pride was to comprise: (1) a communication ship such as the *Sherrek's Ear*, (2) for defense, a Carrier and its litter of *Scream-of-Vengeance* fighters and *Ztirgors*, (3) a combination manufacturing ship and floating drydock which could tool up for—and build—any spare part within hours, (4) four fast ships to mine the comets, (5) a warehouse, and (6) a hospital ship. The antenna was to be assembled by replicating robots after arrival. Prefabricated and expendable rest-and-exercise modules were to be built in the case of a protracted battle.

Long-distance logistic support was to come from Alpha Centauri. For a full six years Wunderland and the factories of the Serpent's Swarm would be launch-

ing a monthly convoy of supplies and hibernating warriors, divertible either for battle or occupation use.

But talk and diagrams never really reached the liver
of a kzin warrior who had survived the quarrels of
youth. Sometimes, to teach what he had to teach,
Grraf-Hromfi called in a student to assign special duty.
Then he would repeat his motto, *sotto voce*, flicking
his tale leisurely. There was always a trap in such duty,
some hidden factor to waylay the over-hasty. Doing
was learning. A brush with death stimulated thinking.

Grraf-Hromfi turned over the education of his sons
to Trainer-of-Slaves. The sons learned little. Trainer
learned how to anticipate lethal pranks. He even had
to kill one of the fiends. The Conquest Commander
did not reprimand him for that. It was the first trophy
he had ever earned for his belt.

Over the next few years the primary duty of Trainer-of-Slaves remained—to train Jotoki for Pride maintenance as the group built up to strength. Pre-
transient Jotoki were shipped out to him from Fortress
Aarku. He took each one of them through their parent
fixation, and when they were trustworthy, he introduced them to the simulators.

It was difficult to remain aloof from his creatures.
He couldn't talk to them about their history or about
military strategy, but they were so curious that they
often tricked him into conversations he didn't know
he was having. One of his charges he found skittering
jerkily across a forbidden corridor on his second
elbows; a shoulder eye was following an insect with
great puzzlement.

Another eye caught the appearance of Trainer.
"Master. What is?"

"An insect. Probably from Wunderland, and wondering how it got here."

"Alive or machine?"

"It's organic, like you or me."

That took Trainer-of-Slaves into a discussion of the differences between the reproductive cycle of life and automated factory production.

His Jotok charge wanted to know if machines were "made up" in the imagination.

"Of course."

"By us?" He meant intelligent life, including kzinti.

"Of course!"

The Jotok scratched his undermouth and wondered about the mind that had made up the "assembly book" for kzin.

They had to retire to the arboretum to handle that one, Trainer-of-Slaves gently bringing the virescent insect with him. Mellow-Yellow gave his lecture on evolution to a rapt audience.

"How did *I* evolve?"

And there they were, right up against Jotok history.

One time when he was playing cards with Long-Reach they were discussing the marvelous estate they would have together after the conquest of Man-home. Long-Reach asked him about the forests of Earth.

"How different could they be from the forests in Hssin?" countered Trainer, looking through his hand for the ace of clubs.

"Will the Conquest burn them to charcoal?"

And there they were, right up against the subject of military strategy. Conversation was spherical—no matter whether one headed north, south, east, or west to avoid a subject, one always navigated right into it.

filed reports and played cards. He sniffed for trouble. During one of those lulls he learned to fly a *Scream-of-Vengeance* fighter. That was safer than dreaming about Grraf-Hromfi's harem. Dreams about kzinrretti tended to fill idle moments. Sometimes he was back in the Chiirr-Nig household on Hssin, in the study, with his mother's loyal head in his lap, scratching her forehead. He regretted having to sell his sex-demon, Jriingh.

It was natural for a kzin to want a household. But Trainer couldn't understand why *he* wanted sons, not after he'd had to teach the Terrible-Sons of Hromfi. Nor was it moral for a coward to pass on his traits to sons who would disgrace the Patriarchy. Nevertheless he wanted sons. He supposed that his real sons were the Jotoki he took on during their fixation phase.

Sons challenged their fathers to physical combat. His many Jotoki "sons" wore him out by a different kind of challenge. The curiosity of a pestering Jotok in transition demanded that Trainer keep learning. It wasn't that he needed to learn. It wasn't that he was curious. He never asked a question whose answer didn't have a solidly rank smell. But he hated not to have a ready retort when a slave asked a stupid question like, "What is the minimum size of the universe?" The answer to a question like that not only didn't have a smell—it couldn't even be seen or heard.

Long-Reach started it all by telling four of his young apprentice polarizer mechanics about the black dwarf R'hshssira. It would collapse forever without fusing its hydrogen because it only had seven-eighths of the mass needed for ignition. But R'hshssira would *still* have a finite radius when there was no longer any radiation pressure pushing out from within.

The four youthful Jotoki had been learning gravity polarizer mechanics together under the supervision of Long-Reach and Creepy. That was twenty freshly curious brains in concert in teams of five-to-a-body. To rebuild and tune a polarizer one did not need to master unified field theory, but such practical constraints never appealed to an eager transient.

The "terrible four" roughed out the calculation that gave them the minimum diameter of a white dwarf star as a function of its mass. They didn't do nova mechanics—that was beyond their youthful abilities, but they did work out the mass range and size at which neutron stars existed. For each mass they could calculate a number for the diameter of the neutron star.

Masses large enough to collapse behind a light barrier were more difficult. Before those calculations were done, one of their brains infected all the others with the burningly important question, "If the *whole* universe collapsed, what would be its minimum diameter?"

Mellow-Yellow tried to give them a practical kzin answer. "The universe is expanding."

But all *four* Jotoki (twenty voices) wouldn't let him get away with that. Tuning polarizers was practical. *This* was recreation. *What if* the universe was contracting?

Data-link texts on gravity shouldn't be allowed. Worse, gravity polarizers were constructed all too elegantly. They should have flashing lights and be built along the lines of a W'kkai wooden puzzle. Then his Jotoki would be kept too busy to go off onto one of their wild chases.

Alas! Let it slip that the polarizer worked with negative space curvature and immediately they were delving into the tensor equations. From there insanity was only questions away. What is the difference between negative and positive curvature? Since positive curvature is common—and that means everything attracts everything else—why isn't the universe imploding?

When will it start to implode? *If* the universe imploded, how small would it get? Tell us, Mellow-Yellow!

Thank the Fanged God that Long-Reach and Creepy and Joker had outgrown such questions. Nevertheless, Trainer-of-Slaves gave up an interesting card game to examine the matter. His data-link surprised him. It asked him to rephrase his inquiry several times, then produced the answer which had been known for some octal-squared generations. It was a theorem named after Stkaa-Mathematician-to-S'Rawl.

Stkaa, of course, was one of those kzin who wrote the commas and dots of the Hero's Tongue in the blood of martyrs. For the return price of an equal amount of blood, he made himself clear. On the data-link screen Trainer had to run the theorem's equations with different boundary values. He had to call up the definitions of words he'd never seen—sometimes because unified field theory was an arcane subject with its own hisses and snarls, and sometimes just because the language had mutated since the time of Stkaa. As often as not the definitions required that he run even more equations before he could make sense of the definition.

Three days later . . .

It was an easy enough theorem to declare. "A universe cannot contract beyond its lowest state of information." But it required a hackles-raising use of the uncertainty principle to find the temperature at which *every particle in the contracting universe had an equal probability of being anywhere in the fireball*—the required lowest state. But once you did that: out-popped the minimum radius. Very neat.

Trainer-of-Slaves dutifully lectured his four "sons." He set up the unified field equations. He contracted to the essentials. He pulled a trick out of his ears that allowed him to apply the uncertainty principle to eliminate all the singularities.

If you knew the velocity of a particle you didn't know its position. Was it still approaching the central point or had it already passed through? If you fixed the position of a particle you no longer knew its velocity. Was it inward or outward bound? All information about whether the universe was contracting or expanding had been lost.

Presto! A minimum radius for the universe. (Thanks to Stkaa-Mathematician-to-S'Rawl, but don't tell them that.)

You knew you had the attention of a Jotok when three eyes were focused on you—when you commanded all five eyes you were a sensation. Big-Undermouth skittered off to bring him some squealing Grashi-burrowers in a bowl, which he munched while other arms curried his fur. Why couldn't kzin sons be like this?

He was beginning to understand his success as a Jotok trainer. At the onset of intelligence a Jotok bonded to anything that gave the basic verbal cues. He'd seen a machine-bonded-Jotok cripple its mind trying to be the son of a machine. The bonding moment was critical—but it wasn't enough. The Jotok was looking for a father, and you had to *be* a father if you wanted a reliable Jotok slave.

This was a confusing concept for Trainer-of-Slaves. He couldn't be a real father to his Jotoki because he couldn't give them combat training. They were herbivores, not Heroes. Only a father who was a coward would sire sons who were unable to fight. (Did Trainer still remember the murder of Puller-of-Noses? Perhaps. As an inexplicable aberration.)

Trainer-of-Slaves liked his isolation, mostly because it kept him out of fights. He had to maintain a delicate balance between dueling and not dueling. He preferred to be obsequious—older warriors appreciated subservience because it allowed them to delegate duties—but younger Heroes tended to mark a deferential kzin as potential prey.

To keep that nuisance at bay he had to maintain a reputation in the tournament ring. That he was Grraf-Hromfi's favorite opponent was enormously useful to him. The proud warriors of the Third Black Pride, awed by their Commandant, didn't see that Hromfi would never have hurt or humiliate Trainer, that the old warrior was only interested in providing an able disciplinarian for his sons. He was training Trainer-of-Slaves as proxy to cull his sons, a fatherly duty for which he had no liver.

A warrior who smelled Trainer's fear was restrained by the ear of the Commandant's son he wore on his belt, and by the many scars Trainer carried on his arm and body from contests with those same sons. The scars were a badge of sorts which Trainer appreciated, however painful had been their healing, because they warned others to keep their irritation in check.

Nevertheless, despite his growing skill as a combatant, he preferred his isolation. In the old days he would have hunted the savannas of Kzin-home alone.

CHAPTER 18
(2410–2413 A.D.)

Isolation can never be complete within a military machine, no matter how remote the posting. Trainer-of-Slaves might hide behind his work, but his superiors always found him because they needed him. In time, Chuut-Riit came out for an inspection. The Black Prides were the bones of his Fifth Fleet, and he liked to keep his tail around developments. While his officers were with him in the maintenance hold of the Pride's floating drydock, the *Nesting-Slashtooth-Bitch*, and looking out over a dismantled *Scream-of-Vengeance* from a catwalk, Chuut-Riit turned to Trainer-of-Slaves.

"I recall our conversation at that hunt on Hssin."

"Sire, I was young then, of shrunken liver and rattle-brain."

"But you showed the talents of a fine captain, a gift for feint and kill," Chuut-Riit replied diplomatically. "Let me refresh your memory about the topic which intrigued me. You had a theory that male humans might be domesticated through their biochemistry. I

135

recollect that you talked about a trigger to control the pace of their learning, then a block to freeze that plasticity once they had attained the desired slave behaviors."

"Sire, I have speculated thus—but never with any experimental animals upon which I could test my ideas. Mental physiology can take strange twists. The turns cannot be followed without sniffing the trail. Nor can the males be domesticated without providing the proper kind of breeding female."

"I have a partial-name for you if you succeed in this venture."

"Sire!"

"Too many of our humans go feral. I suspect that on Earth, with its very large population, the problem will be worse. Hunting those humans who can't adapt to slavery is a limited solution. The feral human is covert and has the ability to pose as a slave. When he strikes he can be deadly. There was a recent massacre of kzinrretti and their kits. It reminded me of your proposal. If you have the time to pursue the subject I can send you all the experimental animals you can use. I should like to take such knowledge with the Fifth Fleet."

"I am eager to accept!"

"You have the space out here?"

"I can set up feeding cages."

"Good."

Trainer-of-Slaves had a wall of clean cages erected in a munitions area that was unused—they were not on a war mission yet. The cages were small by kzin standards but quite adequate for a man-beast who wished to stand erect or lie down, and more than adequate for children. When the first group of experimental animals arrived, he established a fixed regime. They received five-eighths of the water and food they needed simply for keeping their cages clean. The

remaining rations were given for appropriate cooperation. No other pressure was placed on the animals for
refusal to cooperate.

They were very noisy.

Included with the first shipment was the best
human-tech autodoc that Chuut-Riit's officers had
been able to locate, complete with instructions in Ger-
man, English, and Japanese. Its computer was essentially a full compendium of human biochemistry,
though not in an easily decipherable form. The autodoc had been supplied so that he could recycle animals damaged in experiments.

First he tackled the autodoc's exotic computer and
set up a program to translate its records of human
biochemistry into kzin-symbolics so that they could
be transferred to his data-link and integrated with
the generalized model of all known organic alien
brains. He was amazed to recognize one of the
human neuro-transmitters as similar to a kzin neuro-
transmitter. Its peculiar chemical form gave him a
clue as to why kzin reflexes were so much faster
than human reflexes.

Within weeks Trainer-of-Slaves had his first experiments running. Long-Reach was proving to be a tal-
ented surgical student. His initial try at removing the
top of a male's skull had provoked massive hemorrhag-
ing—a mistake that was being repaired in the autodoc.
Long-Reach's second attempt was a success. His animal was restrained in a comfortable chair, the dome
of her cranial bone sliced off at the top to expose the
brain, her human head cramped rigidly to prevent her
from hurting herself.

Trainer had upped the room temperature in defer-
ence to the female's furless skin. He had tattooed a
dots and comma identification on her arm so that he
wouldn't mix her up with the other animals. Delicate
probes were already embedded in her brain, measur-

ing transmitter chemical activity, mapping the neural circuits involved in sensory input, monitoring blood flow, measuring neural activity changes as basic emotions were chemically switched on and off. He needed to get a paws-on feel for the brain structures he had extracted from the autodoc.

But he hovered around his experiment nervously. He didn't want her to die of shock while he was still so unsure of the human performance envelope. He had special catfish ice cream to give her when the data gathering was over in appreciation for her discomfort.

In time he would learn how to erase her inquiring mind while retaining her ability to bear children and perform her sexual functions. He wasn't yet quite sure what would be the best use for the males. If he was to domesticate them as work animals, he would need a different approach than if they were to be domesticated for food.

Thus the years went by uneventfully. Experiments on slaves. Biochemistry studies. Neural map deciphering. Polarizer maintenance. A bit of fighter acrobatics in exchange for a fast repair job. Another lethal fight with one of Hromfi's sons; another ear for his belt. More lectures on strategy. An embarrassing incident with one of Hromfi's coy daughters, fortunately in the dark. Gunnery practice. More Jotoki to train. More questions to answer. Another round of brain experiments.

His most productive line of research came after he deciphered the autodoc records which gave him the switching codes that turned neural growth on and off. He found it useful to know under what conditions human neurons could be made to reproduce or to bud-off new neurons. It fascinated him when he found that he could cause dendritic sprouting.

That was only one of the enthusiasms for which his

kzin impatience got him into trouble. He was wildly hoping to astonish his peers by fabricating a genius slave—but when he increased the number of neural connections in a man-male's brain by an order of magnitude he succeeded merely in killing off his animal. Depressing.

Occasionally excitement broke through the drudgery of incremental scientific advance. Yiao-Captain visited, his fervor so persuasive that the Pride actually moved their great antenna forty degrees away from Man-sun to observe some sort of freak gamma source.

The wonder never lasted. Always they returned to the monotony. Yes, he *was* having solid if exasperatingly slow success with his experiments—but the work was so tedious! Yes, he *was* getting so expert that he could recycle most of his man-animals through many brain operations before they died—but the finicky detail work constantly left him on the edge of rage. He wasn't sure that he could have gone through it all if it wasn't for Chuut-Riit's promise of a name. Thank the Fanged God for the high spots that broke the ennui.

There was that second vacation on Wunderland when he was able to set up steady arrangements to restock his cages from an orphanage—he couldn't just pirate experimental animals out of the war factories without the risk of a duel with some touchy kzin manager. Criminals and political prisoners were too much in demand for the hunts.

His Jotoki kept his mind busy. Sometimes it was a racy card game. One of his Jotok discovered a mathematical theorem that was not in any data-link. Another of his slaves did an excellent project on the biochemistry of pain-accelerated learning in humans. That cleared up a whole lot of puzzling questions about human brain function. He didn't know how he would have survived if his incurably curious Jotoki weren't taking so much of the load off his mind. Sometimes all he had to do was ask a question, and one of his Jotoki would experiment with an orphan and come up with the answer. They had more patience than a kzin.

Trainer-of-Slaves knew he had been with the Third Black Pride for too long when their antenna began to receive news of the gigantic battles in the Man-system. He had been at this post almost ten years. The battles that were juicing up Wunderkzin livers were themselves more than four years dead. Of course, with light-speed messages it never seemed that way. If a space battle lasted a month, it still took a month to play out—four years after the fact.

The Fourth and Fifth Black Prides were stationed up ahead, listening, too. The Third Black Pride was behind Alpha Centauri as the last backup. The Prides frantically compared messages, filling in the transmission gaps, but they were all light-days apart, and it took days for the final compilation to be authenticated by the communications officers.

None of the news surprised Grraf-Hromfi. Stoically he repressed his rage. But Trainer-of-Slaves was surprised.

The *Blood of Heroes* was destroyed on the eleventh day. Vaporized. Trainer, tired from following every new bulletin, was stunned by the heroic death of his best friend. Four years ago. His ancestors were whispering. It was as if he had been living four unearned years. *I'm a ghost*, he thought, but that was silly. He felt pathos. Then the kzin anger took him. He wanted to fight, and there was no one to fight. He wanted monkey ears on his belt. But they had Ssis-Captain's ears on *their* belt.

Something about these humans that he did not understand. He went to his cages in a foul mood.

"Hey, Dr. Moreau," jeered a female with long black hair, "when do you sew on my wolf's head?"

"Svelda! Clean up your cage!" he snarled with his

best animal pronunciation. It was just a matter of feeding the suction nozzle.

"You come any closer and you get shit in your fur!"

His mouth was twitching over his fangs. "Be careful. I'm in a vile mood."

"That's news to me? What do I care? What have I got to lose? Kill me!"

He purred to disguise his ire. "I'll give you ice cream if you clean up your cage."

She was weeping. "You've mucked around in my brain so often I can't think straight. Ice cream! Do you understand anything? Open the cage door and I'll kill you. Do you know what happens to a woman when you cut up her brain? All the emotions come out! She loses control. She becomes an animal." She held onto the bars and snarled at him, gnashing her teeth.

The orphan children in the adjoining cages began to wail. They were so much easier to manage than these political ferals.

So—another failure; she was still capable of connected reason and the only obvious result of the experiment had been to produce a state of constant, poorly controlled rage. These man-females clung to their reason even after drastic surgery. And when he *was* able to delete their intelligence they showed grave, and sometimes startlingly weird behavior deficits.

Once he had tried to eliminate curiosity and had produced instead an idiot who compulsively asked questions with no interest at all in the answers. Another experiment in intelligence reduction had produced a perfectly rational woman with a deadly lack of common sense. He had tried for docility, using the autodoc's knowledge of human brain chemistry, and achieved only passivity leading him to the discovery that there wasn't much difference between passivity and sloth. Passivity neutralized intelligence, but it neutralized everything else of importance, too. Docility, on the other hand, seemed to *require* intelligence if a kzin was to get any use out of it.

He was still missing some essential key.

"You *like* ice cream," he stated firmly, hoping to motivate the Svelda-female toward cleanliness.

"Suck it up your nose!"

Was that a *reasonable* statement? Borderline. He wanted to make her happy so that she would clean her cage and stop disturbing the other animals. Ice cream wasn't going to work. Perhaps she could no longer understand the concept of ice cream? If reason was failing, he should try something emotional—a kzinrret always responded to emotion. What would she respond to since she did not like him? since she was fixed at rage? Victory? He thought about that.

Victory was very emotional; it stirred the purring vibrations. Kzin and animal alike all relished victory. "At this moment your race is happy and I am bereaved," he said.

"Happy?" she shrieked. "A finger in your eye! That would make me happy!" She rattled her cage some more and snarled some more. "*Gottdamm Urin-Pelz!* You stink! *Urin-Pelz!* Take a bath!" When he tried to reach in his hand, unclawed, to give her a soothing pet, she snapped at his black fingertips.

A remarkable display. Svelda had come to him shy and quiet and properly propitiative. He had been delighted into thinking that very little modification of her mind would be necessary. But his surgery had evidently de-inhibited a whole layer of vicious instinct. Puzzling. Reluctantly he dismissed his latest theory about human brain function.

How far could she still reason at the abstract level? She was having trouble connecting victory with joy. He enunciated his animal call imitations more carefully as if he were talking to his mother. "You monkeys have done grave damage to our fleet attacking Sol.

Noble warriors have died valiantly. That is why you are happy and I am bereaved."

"Sol?" The beast began to weep hysterically. Another singular transformation. "The Solarians took you out . . ."—the sobs were racking her body—"you *Rattekatze* father-suckers?" she asked between sobs. "At Sol?"

"Another fleet will be sent."

He was observing that the she-animal's brain damage was extensive. All the emotions seemed to be operating at once, uncoordinated. Tears of grief were streaming down the furless face. She was grinning the way humans did when they were radiantly happy, but the way she bared her teeth seemed to have a kzinlike ferocity. Some ancient hardwired instinct had been severed from its inhibitory subprograms.

"Kill! Kill! Kill!" she screamed happily through her grief and through the bars to drown out the wailing of the children.

Later, with the she-Svelda under sedation, Trainer-of-Slaves tried to repair the damage to her brain by regrowing neurons in the places where they had been excised, but it didn't work. She went into a coma. The autodoc could keep her alive but she responded to no outside stimulation, could not groom or feed herself, or even eat. He had to give the meat to Grraf-Hromfi's sons for good behavior, but he kept the head and sliced up the brain, feeding its neural circuitry into his data-link in the hopes that someday he could make sense of what had gone wrong.

He couldn't resist clipping one of her ears to his belt. After the Fourth Fleet disaster, he *needed* a monkey ear at his waist.

He was thinking more about his mother than ever before. He had always thought of his mother as non-intelligent. All the idioms for *stupidity* in the Hero's Tongue were references to females. If one kzintosh said of another kzintosh, "You kzinrret," what he meant was, "You brainless *stupid* fool!" And yet . . . when Trainer-of-Slaves had tried to replicate, in human females, that endearing kzinrret *stupidity*, what he had achieved was bizarre non-functionality.

Still in a rage induced by the defeat of the Fourth Fleet, he took his rage out in an aggressive attack on this problem which had been plaguing him. He thought about his mother. He was thinking about all the times she had saved his life.

His experimental mistakes had confronted him with strange facts. He'd had to question his ideas about intelligence, to break that concept down into its many parts. Now he analyzed what his mother must have been aware of while she was actively protecting him, and he came to the remarkable conclusion that his mother *had* to be intelligent.

But that was impossible. He flashed on his cherished image of catching her chewing on one of his first books, chewing it to a pulp.

The Fanged God had given souls to the first kzinrretti but at the crucial Battle of Hungry Years they had betrayed both Him and their mates while the males stayed loyal to their God and so He had taken away the female souls and given their bodies over to kzintosh masters so that the race might continue to propagate itself. That was mythology, tales of events that had happened before science, before writing. What *had* happened? What had the kzinrretti lost at the Battle of Hungry Years if it wasn't intelligence?

Trainer-of-Slaves was sure that he loved his mother—whatever she was. *What* she was remained locked behind silence; she seldom spoke and when she did speak she used only the elementary vocabulary of the Female Tongue, no more than a few octal-squared words. Was it a contradiction in terms to call an animal intelligent if she couldn't use language?

Grraf-Hromfi conceded in one of his seminars that the Wunderland Admiralty was reassessing top strategy. Chuut-Riit had cynically expected the Fourth Fleet to fail because of its arrogant commanders, but he had also expected it to demoralize the monkey hive—and drastically weaken human military capability. Now Chuut-Riit was opting for a few more years of preparation. He wanted Centaurian industry built up to the point where it could keep an interstellar supply line filled. And he needed that extra crop of warriors that more time would provide.

In the meantime the Third Black Pride kept track of Sol through the distant transmissions of the First and Second Black Pride communication warships. Those scoutships of the Fifth Fleet had remained in place, well away from the battle zone—undetected as of 4.3 years ago—keeping their vigil out where Man-sun was only the brightest star in the heavens.

A steady flicker and hiss of messages came through to be filtered and cleaned and analyzed by the kzinti spoor specialists back in the Centaurian system. Fuzzy pictures of UNSN Gibraltar Base. Specks that looked like a fleet moving in the asteroid belt. Some new markings on Mercury. The trace of search beams scanning the skies. Non-military beamcasts giving the tone and morale of the monkey civilization. Better and better maps of the cities of Earth.

Trainer-of-Slaves often flipped through the images. He gave only a glance to one of the earliest post-battle transmissions. It was a single crude picture of a vehicle being assembled in the asteroid belt. The scale markings indicated enormous size but its size was deceptive. Most of the structure seemed to be a flimsy magnetic funnel: one of the monkey ramscoops of no military utility. To be noted and ignored. Perhaps it was to be an emissary to one of their local allies.

Months later there was a second flurry of activity

when more pictures of the ramscoop came through. Now it was equipped with massive disposable hydrogen tanks and was actually being launched toward Alpha Centauri! To what possible purpose? This time Trainer noticed the furor only because Grraf-Hromfi used the item as the inspiration for a seminar lecture on human technology.

Trainer-of-Slaves was not to recall that seminar for another five years. Immediately when he left the briefing room other worries occupied his mind. He had a sick Jotok to tend and he was in the middle of a card game that he was losing to Long-Reach.

In that five years the Fifth Fleet doubled in size. The effort caused great hardship among the vassals of Wunderland, more than Chuut-Riit thought prudent to impose. Such stress created an alarming increase in feral activity. But there was no help for it. Extraordinary war efforts always cause hardship, both among slave and Hero. Sacrifices had to be made for the Long Peace, always. Peace did not exist without war to impose it.

Trainer-of-Slaves developed a lucrative sideline. It did not pay off in coin, but it paid off in favors. His Jotoki became experts at modifying warships and fighter craft to better than standard performance. This was not particularly difficult to do.

"Kr-Captain, your *Screamer* now gives us a perfect check-down. But I do know ways its performance could be improved." While unbinding the terrified zianya who was to be their dinner, Trainer paused to let his message sink in. It was against regulations to make non-standard changes. Waiting without comment, he watched Kr-Captain tear out his hunk of flesh to an anguished animal cry. Trainer was not going to mention the subject of irregular modifications again.

"I'll take any edge," said Kr-Captain, blood on his jaws.

"Of course, any alteration can be restandardized."

"A laudable way to deal with fussy bureaucrats."

"Useful too, in case non-standard parts are unavailable during an emergency."

"When might such work be done?"

To avoid equipment chaos, standardization had been rigidly imposed since the time of the first interstellar Patriarchs. All improvements, by decree, had to come out of Kzin-home. In a subluminal empire, sixty light-years in diameter, new standards diffused slowly.

Brilliant innovations built to serve a need during the heat of some local war tended to die in the files. First the innovation had to reach Kzin-home. Then it had to be tested by a bureaucracy which considered itself to be the sole font of all change—and was understaffed. The ideas that lived often took ten or fifteen generations to become the new standard authorized by the High Admiralty, not because the Admiralty was particularly senile, but because the pace of light from star to star was pitiably slow.

Still, many such battle-tried ideas could be found hibernating within the labyrinthine network of lairs inside the data-links. Finding them took maze-tracking skills, and battle-cunning to know what was wanted, and an engineering background to know what was possible. Having fanatically loyal Jotoki technicians also helped.

The *Flayer-of-Monkeys* was a three-kzin fighter-scout. They were well away from the *Sherrek's Ear*, testing the illegal modifications, when they got an emergency message. "*Flayer. Flayer. Flayer.* Record. Record. Record." Kr-Captain was at the leading point of the delta-shaped control chamber. He switched on his combat communications memory. Trainer-of-Slaves happened to be riding in the Sensor's harness, and Long-Reach was uncomfortably seated on his mouth in the Weapons-Operator chair, peering at his instruments. He was used to maintaining them, not reading them.

Sherrek's Ear continued urgently. "Acknowledge and Execute. Time Lag too Long for Confirmation. Will Repeat Message. Ramscoop Coming Through. Intercept and Destroy. *Flayer* is only Warcraft in Combat Range. Repeat: Intercept and Destroy. Ramscoop Coming in Much Faster than Predicted." The excited kzin controller spat out a number. "We See Target: Three Octal-squared Light-days Out, Coming In. Real Position: Passing A-star; Perhaps Already Outbound. Possible Collision A-star. If So: Cancel Intercept. Now Read Coordinates for *Flayer* Intercept."

They were given a position which placed Man-sun almost in occultation with Alpha Centauri A, on a circle surrounding A at a point thirty degrees north-east of a reference longitude through Kzin-sun. If they couldn't intercept within forty-seven hours, the ramscoop would escape.

". . . We Assume You Are Unarmed. Destroy-mode Your Choice. Message Will Now Repeat. *Flayer*. *Flayer* . . ."

A startled Kr-Captain swung his outer antenna toward the *Sherrek's Ear*. "*Flayer* Ack. Will Intercept. *Flayer* Ack. *Flayer* Ack. Moving out." He switched off the comm—they were too far away to carry on a conversation—pulled down his goggles, and took a brief look at the heavens while he rolled *Flayer-of-Monkeys* in the direction of the line joining Man-sun and Alpha Centauri A, now separated by about seven degrees.

"We've got to close up Man-sun and the A-star. That's shaving the hairs. Hope your juiced-up polarizer really will do octal-squared g's. What the sthondat is a ramscoop?"

"Hey, two missiles!" said Long-Reach's short(arm) after checking the weapons readout.

"*Camera* missiles," snarled Kr-Captain, lolling his tongue. "For maneuvers."

Trainer-of-Slaves was suddenly remembering Grraf-Hromfi's long forgotten seminar on ramscoops. "I know what a ramscoop is."

"Good. Whatever it is, can we kill it? We're disarmed." They were already accelerating at sixty-three g's, yet it would be hours before they began to see Alpha Centauri creeping across the starfield. Kr-Captain turned to calculating orbits on his screen. They were going to have to cross the line-of-flight of the man-thing at ninety degrees. "We have just enough time to decelerate and stop on their line-of-flight. Should we stop or do a flying pass?"

All of Grraf-Hromfi's lectures on tactics crowded into Trainer's thoughts. *Think before you leap.* "Stop if we can. We get one try. We don't want our fire crossing the line-of-flight at an angle—not at those velocities."

The old seminar room on the *Sherrek's Ear* was filling Trainer's imagination. The smell of frame-beryllium and old fur. The wet sniff of algae. But especially that room five years ago. Grraf-Hromfi was the same benevolent tyrant that he had always been, mane a bit scraggly. His holo mockup of the ramscoop floated to one side and he held his shamboo pointer tipped with slashtooth tusk that he liked to jab into his holos—and sometimes into the bellies of his less attentive listeners.

"We do not know its intention," the ghost-memory was saying to Trainer. "It is probably coming to sniff spoor around our boundaries. It cannot have an attack capability."

Trainer tried to reevaluate: was that still true?—and drew a blank.

"It cannot defend itself."

Yes, thought Trainer, *its speed is its only defense, running like a fangless herbivore.*

"The most interesting fact that this mockup reveals about the United Nations Space Navy is that they have not—as of four years ago, I repeat—learned how to build an interstellar-grade gravity polarizer. Otherwise they would not be launching such a massive low-performance device. The magnetic funnel"—he pointed—"is used to collect interstellar hydrogen for the reaction drive. Can any of you tell me its major constraint?"

There had been silence in the classroom. Today it was the silence of interception through soundless space.

Trainer remembered himself prompting, mischievously, "Ask Long-Tooth. He knows."

Long-Tooth-Son of Grraf-Hromfi jumped out of his reverie. "Honored patriarch, a ramscoop is too slow."

"Its *acceleration* is too feeble," corrected the father. "And why is that?"

Long-Tooth cast Trainer a venomous look for getting him into this dialog. "There's not much hydrogen for it to use."

"How much?"

"Sire! I don't know."

"Trainer-of-Slaves?"

"Please accept my surrender if I am wrong. Between here and Man-sun the density is about an octal-squared to four-octal-squared hydrogens per fistful of space."

Grraf-Hromfi again passed the slashtooth tusk of his pointer through the fuzzy holographic ramscoop in front of him. The spout of its funnel was burdened by racks of spherical tanks. "They need these huge hydrogen tanks to prime their reaction engines since they can't collect much hydrogen at low speeds. The tanks will be dropped off once they are moving fast enough to devour more than starvation rations of the interstellar hydrogen."

He was grinning at monkey folly. "They can't collect much at high speeds either in spite of the fact that the main funnel collector surface seems to be about as large as the Patriarch's private hunting estate. Their maximum speed is a quarter that of light if they use a ramjet design. With a more sophisticated flow-through design they are only limited by relativistic effects which are considerable. I doubt a top velocity beyond a half-lightspeed."

. . . and you were wrong . . . The *Flayer* was at the center of a sphere of stars, intercepting some manthing that was coming at them close to the velocity of light.

"At really high speeds they would have to know how to burn proton cosmic rays—an unpleasant diet." Grraf-Hromfi got an amused ripple of ears when he added that this might be to the taste of a herbivore.

. . . yes, and the monkeys have managed to thrive on that unpleasantly lethal diet . . .

"Those are engineering details and I presume they can be mastered. Ramscoops are a primitive solution and we've never used them, so we know little of the details. The major problem is not an engineering one—it is a flaw in the concept. A fusion funnel cannot attain high accelerations, first because it is fuel-starved, and second because reaction drives produce *inertial* acceleration. How do you build a gossamer funnel that can take even one gravity of inertial acceleration?"

. . . but at a fifth of a gravity, year after year . . .

Grraf-Hromfi did not mention in his lecture that a fighting kzin warship could accelerate at sixty gravities with the pilot floating in his cockpit and thus reach its maximum cruising speed in about five days, because all of his officers knew that. "How long would it take this funny-funnel to attain six-eighths the velocity of light?"

"Six months?" ventured a bored officer who leaped to conclusions before thinking.

"More like eight-ten years—with most of that time spent at low velocity. When will it reach Alpha Centauri?"

"About the time the Fifth Fleet has occupied Manhome," said Long-Tooth-Son with a grin for the poor beasts.

. . . but it is here and the Fifth Fleet hasn't even started yet . . .

"That's a reasonable estimate. I'd like to remind you that these pictures are more than four years old."

. . . it took them only nine plus years to get here . . .

"The monkey-funnel is already out of range of both the First and Second Black Pride. But even after all this time"—the 4.3 years the Pride's message took to reach Alpha Centauri—"the ramscoop will still be close to Man-sun and just beginning its journey. It is not something we'll ever have to worry about. We'll keep an automatic tracker looking for it—that's our duty—but I doubt if we'll ever sniff it again. The monkeys will decelerate and sulk around outside Alpha Centauri well out of our range."

So even Grraf-Hromfi could be dead wrong.

Trainer-of-Slaves did a calculation on the Sensor's data-link. The automatic tracker had detected the first trace of the ramscoop two-hundred light-days out—yet years earlier than expected. Which meant that its maximum speed was far higher than kzin engineers had anticipated.

Kr-Captain finished his trajectory plot and put the *Flayer-of-Monkeys* on automatic. Turnaround was in twenty-three hours. "*Sherrek's Ear* gave us orders to be creative." He meant that they were unarmed.

"Best little mechanic in the galaxy sitting right beside me," said Trainer-of-Slaves.

"So how are we going to kill this what-ever-it-is?"

"We may not have to. Grraf-Hromfi proved that a monkey can't stay alive in a ship moving at that speed—cosmic sleeting."

"Give old red-mane an ear," he purred sarcastically. "We don't have to fight because the enemy has already suicided! A nice philosophy until a monkey leaps out of the funeral pyre." He returned to a commander's inflected spits and growls. "*We* shall assume they have a gravity polarizer shield and are still alive."

"A gravity shield is the same as a gravity drive. Then they wouldn't need a ramscoop."

"What's a ramscoop?"

"A magnetic funnel that collects interstellar hydrogen and ejects helium as reaction mass."

"Is a monkey going to stand at a porthole and shoot arrows at us?" Kr-Captain flapped his batwing ears.

"Maybe the magnetic field protects them," suggested Long-Reach, two arm-slits speaking in unison.

"Slave! Shut up," growled Kr-Captain.

"Does he play cards?" whispered the arm nearest the relaxed ears of Trainer-of-Slaves.

"Don't eat your seat, Long-Reach. I'll need your brains in due time."

Long-Reach hunkered down on his undermouth, petulantly. He was muttering along internal channels to himselves that he *was* Weapons-Operator. That started an argument among the arms about who was to take charge of the camera missiles.

"The line-of-flight cuts right past the A-star," said Trainer. "They'll already be dead. The starwind is fierce at that distance. It will have hit them like your father's claw." Kr-Captain seemed unconvinced and so

Trainer used an analogy from a virtual horror-adventure they had both lived together under shared eye-caps. "It's like a hurricane wind in your sails."

Kr-Captain bared his fangs. He didn't like being reminded of that horror-story world covered with water, trying to survive in the company of five war-stranded Heroes on board a fleeing sloop in typhoon weather. His liver was still recovering. "I will not repeat myself again! *We* shall assume that the monkeys are alive, you miserable fur-tick fleeing-the-skin-of-a-dying-sthondat!"

"As you command, brave Hero!"

"Now how shall we kill them? It was *you* who took out my particle-beamer for this test!" The thought of being disarmed put him back on the edge of anger. Not even a nuke. "Shall I slash at them with my *wtsai* as they zip past?"

"This combat couch is very uncomfortable, revered Hero," muttered short(arm). Listening to himself gave Long-Reach perversely practical ideas. "We could toss my combat couch at the enemy."

"Silence!" roared Kr-Captain.

Trainer-of-Slaves was looking around the cockpit for things that might be ripped out. "Gold dust is what we need, but your honor-bearing *wtsai* blade is powerful enough to destroy even the most invincible monkey battleship."

Long-Reach gave a good imitation of a kzin "hisssss" of profound inspiration. "We leave our noble Hero on the line-of-flight, waving his *wtsai*. He leaps," said short(arm). "He strikes!" exclaimed freckled(arm). Then a chorus of arms imitated the spits and snarls of a kzin fight. Skinny(arm) intoned the denouement, "In one blow the enemy ship disintegrates in a blaze of shame! and ever afterwards Kr-Hero radiates bluely from the honor roll of the Patriarch!"

Discretely, fast(arm) gripped a rod on the back of

Trainer-of-Slaves's combat couch in case he had to
yank Long-Reach to a safer place.

His lips twitching, Kr-Captain eyed his more yellow-
orange than red-orange kzin companion. "Where did
you find this five course lunch?"

"We've been together since Hssin. He really is a
good mechanic."

"We seem to have reached a consensus," grumbled
the Captain. "Some massive object left along the line-
of-flight."

"Perhaps not massive. If we sprinkled gold dust in
its path, each grain of dust carries the impact energy
of a medium nuclear strike," said Trainer.

Kr-Captain did not believe him. Kzin are not used
to combat passes at relativistic speeds. But he did the
calculation on his screen. The numbers convinced
him. "A little dust in the monkey's path and—nuclear
fireball! Easy."

"Not so easy," moaned big(arm). Long-Reach had
been consulting among himselves. "It is not just a bigger high-velocity kinetic impact," stated the practical
fast(arm). "We now pass into a new realm of the
unimaginable where our intuition fails," expostulated
the expansive short(arm).

At relativistic speeds, kinetic impact becomes a cosmic ray shower.

Visibly, Alpha Centauri began to creep across the
glittering heavens toward Man-sun. The stars shim-
mered unnaturally through the strengthening polarizer
field. Long-Reach, as "honorary" Weapons-Operator,
busied himself with a simple project. He removed
cameras from missiles. Then he built two makeshift
warheads out of bottled oxygen and half their water
rations and a few grams of tungsten-carbide grinding
powder from his toolkit.

The *Flayer-of-Monkeys* was well equipped with sensors. Seventeen hours from their rendezvous it began

to pick up the ramscoop which had an "apparent velocity" of 120 lightspeeds. Electronic amplification constructed a foreshortened image. The scoop was gone. That was a shock. Trainer-of-Slaves thought, at first, that it had been "burnt-off" during the close flyby of A-star, but when he had the *Flayer*'s data-link rotate the image to a side view, he saw that the funnel was simply folded-in to a vastly reduced scoop area so that its magnetic field was being used only to protect the crew. In the high mass regions around Alpha Centauri they had simply "furled their sails"!

From a standstill, *Flayer* aimed and directed its missiles down the line-of-flight toward the oncoming UNSN ramscoop which was now occulting Man-sun. The makeshift warheads bled a lethal mist of oxygen and ice-coated tungsten. Then *Flayer* moseyed down the line, away from the ramscoop, bleeding its helium coolant, its cabin nitrogen reserve, plus a bottle of argon—and for good measure the talcum powder that Kr-Captain used to bathe his fur. They returned at full acceleration, stopped, rolled and dropped to the side, rotating to face the coming action. Trainer-of-Slaves mounted the salvaged cameras.

"All they have to do is dodge!" complained Kr-Captain, who was an expert at sixty-g maneuvers.

"They are blind in front. Their course is laser-true. Do you know how much lateral-thrust energy it would take to deflect them a whisker's breadth? They don't command that kind of energy. They are committed!"

The Heroes strapped in to do the warrior's greatest duty—wait.

Half an hour later the nameless ramscoop, its mission still a mystery to its attackers, zipped by, moving faster than any explanation can describe what the eye saw.

The first missile missed.

The second missile ticked through an edge of the

folded scoop, ionizing into a fireball genie that lashed a flaming arm out after the ramscoop—too late, too slow.

The ramscoop plowed ahead into the mist.

Valiantly the magnetic field tried to cope with the overload but wasn't equipped to handle the dust or the oxygen. Superconductors overheated. Electrical resistance began to vaporize the surface of the scoop. . . .

Meanwhile hydrogen and oxygen and tungsten, helium and nitrogen and argon, even talcum powder, were ionizing on impact to become tiny superdense nuclear projectiles sleeting through what to a nucleus is mostly empty space: the bulkhead, the air, the life support, the instruments, the protein, the fusion engine, hardened lead-tungsten radiation barriers, everything—and on out to the other side, leaving behind ionized trails as spoor.

A few of these "cosmic rays" collided with the relativistically massive nuclei of the ramscoop, scattering, smashing nuclei into a spray of particle fragments. Mesons flashed into gamma rays and gave birth to muons. Muons lived out their leisurely lives and died. Positrons blinked into existence. Anti-matter screamed out of collisions. Wildly exotic nuclei spat out particles in a desperate search for a new equilibrium. Neutrons bounced and bled into space.

But it was the energy of the stripped electrons that destroyed the monkeys' ramscoop. The ship was essentially transparent to the impacting nuclei—but opaque to the electrons. The kinetic energy of the electrons was instantly transformed to heat.

The flare blazed, then was gone at near lightspeed, doppler-shifting into the red. It had left them. Inertia is implacable. What is moving continues to move.

The UNSN vessel was destined to travel on through the universe as a dense cosmic ray packet, slowly disintegrating and falling apart from its contact with the interstellar medium, from collisions with gases and particles. Billions of years later, in some distant galaxy, scientists might note its passing as an increase in the cosmic ray count from some strange quadrant of the sky. There would be theories about the high metallic content of the rays.

On the return of the *Flayer-of-Monkeys* to the *Sherrek's Ear*, they learned of the ramscoop's mission—a bombing run. From a great distance it had launched precision pellets at specific targets. The relativistic pellets carried the wallop of a nuclear blast.

UNSN spoor was dated and their gunner's accuracy terrible. Whole areas of the arctic zone had been blasted without a single kzin or human casualty because there was nothing there. One lucky hit on a kzin base had killed four thousand Heroes. The human-beasts had taken gruesome casualties, only five percent of which were military related. A miss had impacted the ocean and created a tidal wave that had rolled over four seaside communities.

Kr-Captain was furious. "Why didn't we get it *before* it attacked!"

Alas, warriors were always reminded of the fortunes of war. Only the Black Prides carried the really long distance detection equipment. Both the *Tigripard's Ear* of the Fourth Black Pride and the *Patriarch's Nose* of the Fifth Black Pride had detected the ramscoop two days before the *Sherrek's Ear* had sniffed the electromagnetic scent, but each was almost two light-days from the line-of-flight. By lightbeam they didn't have time to warn Alpha Centauri, and by their fastest fighters, they didn't have time to intercept. The ramscoop was following too closely behind its own electromagnetic arrival notice.

Sherrek's Ear, though it was behind Alpha Centauri, was stationed only eight light-hours from the line-of-

flight. Even then, interception would have been difficult had the *Flayer* not been out on a maintenance
run in the right direction.

Grraf-Hromfi gave a diagnostic lecture. *Think
before you leap.* Never underestimate an enemy. He
was furious at himself for assuming that no ramscoop
could fly faster than half lightspeed. He was so furious
that he set up a whole day of tournament to clean his
liver of rage, taking on all comers.

Only months later they learned the covert mission
of the ramscoop when Chuut-Riit was assassinated.

CHAPTER 20
(2420 A.D.)

Detection-Orderly-Two summoned Grraf-Hromfi immediately, rousing him from a curled sleep. Hromfi was not the kind who made life miserable for warriors who interrupted his rest. A Hero on duty had the obligation to wake the dead if he felt it in the interest of the Patriarchy. The Commander of the Third Black Pride appeared at the Command Room, naked in his copper red fur except for slippers, grumpy, but not angry.

Analysis began promptly, without preliminaries. The small object had appeared in the heavens out of nowhere, near Rh'ya in the House of the Fanged God's Kzinrretti—the Pleiades. Only light-hours away. Very anomalous gravity pulse. That had set off the alarms. It was also a neutrino source.

Another strange event.

The Third Black Pride was up to full strength. Its Commander ordered a discrete reconnaissance probe. If the mystery pulse came from a small ship, he wanted it captured for interrogation. Quickly. And *not* destroyed.

Instantly, he chose for the mission three pilots he could trust: the first an old warrior with gray in his pelt who had flown *Scream-of-Vengeance* fighters for Chuut-Riit since he was a kit, the second a wild-eyed Hssin barbarian who liked to pick the meat out of his fangs and comb his mane *before* he leaped, and the third, Grraf-Hromfi's most promising son.

They, in turn, were shaken out of their sleep. Each hastily donned goggles so that he could receive his orders. "The intruder is to be disabled, not vaporized!" growled their Commander. "And while I have your attention: a warning." He shifted into the menacing-tense of the Hero's Tongue to jolt their livers. "Our instruments tell us that this object *appeared* out of nowhere. Instruments can be deceived. The best kzin minds can be deceived. *However*, regardless of how irrational the concept, *expect* the object to defend itself by *vanishing* into nowhere. Attack without warning! Disable it immediately! Prisoners are to be taken! If it is an automatic ship, the brain is to be salvaged!"

While the three crews scrambled, he called ahead to make sure that Fighter Command was ready to equip them with *Screamers* modified by Trainer-of-Slaves. He wanted them to have whatever edge he could supply.

Grraf-Hromfi's nose was beginning to sniff the odd-ness of an alien technology lurking about. On the bor-derlands of the Patriarchy that could be *extremely* dangerous. But how to put these enigmatic pieces together? He thought of the wooden puzzles of the kzin Conundrum Priests of W'kkai. Eight ways there were to put any puzzle together, and seven of those ways always left an awkward shape protruding.

In the meantime, decisions never waited for a fin-ished puzzle.

How had that unnaturally fast ramscoop dropped

off agents? No obvious mode of deceleration suggested itself. At an incoming velocity near lightspeed any agent would have carried the energy of a continent-smashing bomb; the energy release from *any* kind of capsule-braking would have been observed. And how had they penetrated Chuut-Riit's security to juggle creche feeding procedures so that Chuut-Riit had to face his own ravenously hungry sons behind locked doors? It seemed like magic. Of course it wasn't.

But now—an unauthorized ship that wrote its own unique gravity pulse. Could it be that the ramscoop hadn't delivered the agents? Was there a new player? He remembered Yiao-Captain's visit and his infectious insistence that they point their long distance antenna toward a possible "alien" artifact. Another orphaned piece of the puzzle that "protruded."

This was indeed a time of troubles. After the launch of the three *Screamers*, Grraf-Hromfi brooded briefly on the other troubles while he did his warrior's duty, waiting. . .

. . . troubles enough to incline Grraf-Hromfi to leap off for Man-sun immediately and let these slashing Wunderkzin rip their own faces apart. Octals of the kzin nobility, who had been chafing under the rule of the outsider Chuut-Riit, had seized the assassination as license for them to seize power. Traat-Admiral's claws had been busy with duels. Political chaos.

Regrettably, border barbarians were uneducated in honor! They thought of duels and Ascendancy as honor. They thought of death as Opportunity. They knew nothing of the honor of Loyalty After Death.

Leaving them to their own murders was a warm, meaty idea, but impractical. The Fifth Fleet needed Wunderland as its supply base. They couldn't use Hssin. It was extra light-years away and Hssinkzin were all related by blood and warrior oaths to the original Centauri Conquest Heroes anyway.

The ramscoop attack, itself, had done little damage—but it had brought hundreds of honest slaves to a state of feral defiance. Now *open* defiance was spreading like a plague as the squabbles among the kzin became public knowledge. Ferals had even attacked the Gerning base from space and put its detectors out of commission for three days, long enough to land supplies for some of the renegade animals.

Grraf-Hromfi was in a bad mood because he was just back from a political tour of Wunderland estates. He had picked the most obsequious of the power hungry back-stabbers first, cleverly led them to state the claims they believed to be true, challenged them to a duel for false claims, and killed them. After three such contests of honor, the rest of the Wunderkzin learned more quickly the value of careful reason. The power hungry always made the same mistake—they built their True Case, the case they were willing to defend in public, upon false logic.

Detection-Orderly-Two appeared at the oval bulkhead door of the Command Center of the *Sherrek's Ear.* "Sire! May I have your attention again?"

Grraf-Hromfi glanced up. The orderly mock-slashed his face sharply. "You look like you've just bested your father at arm-tug. Found something new? I hope not another of those objects."

"No, Sire, not in this system. But I have something for you to consider, if you will, sir. May I use your data-link?" Without even waiting for assent, he switched on the wall screen and spat-hissed commands to the retrieval slavecrystal. Ribbons of telemetering appeared. "These are mystery signals which the Second Black Pride has been relaying to us from Mansun for analysis. They started arriving about three months ago, off and on. We have never been sure that they weren't noise, or the artifact of some instrument malfunction."

"You've found something there besides noise?"

"Yes, sir! They all have the same signature as our mysterious visitor. I did a comparison. It came out at the seven-eights confidence level—excellent, considering that the signals we have are only whiskers above the noise jiggles. The *Patriarch's Nose* has been seeing what we have been seeing—but just inside their maximum range."

"*And* 4.3 years ago," muttered Grraf-Hromfi. "We must *never* forget the lightlag. A lot can happen in five years. The Fifth Fleet has doubled in that time. Who knows what cunning they have been up to at Man-sun."

"What do you think the mystery object is, sir?"

"A scout."

"Do you think they've found a way to travel at lightspeed, sir?"

"We'll find out. All detection squads are on full battle alert?"

"Yes, Sire!"

Grraf-Hromfi was now very worried. Was the pulse-object a visitor from Man-sun? He turned up the gravity in the Command Room so that he could pace. On impulse he called Trainer-of-Slaves for a goggle-to-goggle conference. "You paw around with those agonized shrieks-and-spits of demented mathematicians? Their water-hole tracks describing unified field theory?" The virtual image of Trainer-of-Slaves hung in the air like a ghost, fixed in position.

"Dominant Sire, I've inflicted some of that torture upon myself, yes. Do you want an opinion on that pulse?"

"What would this sudden appearance of mass mean?"

"You are suggesting that the pulse tells of the creation of mass out of nothing?" asked Trainer.

"Yes."

"That's impossible, sir. My opinion of the pulse . . ."

"Mate yourself to a sthondat! I didn't ask your opinion, Eater-of-Grass, I asked what it meant!"

"To avoid your insults, I will tell you what you wish to hear. Any mass passing *through* the light barrier would appear as if it had been created out of nothing."

"But this one wasn't moving at relativistic speeds."

"Light barriers can be stationary. I refer you to the work of Ssrkikn-the-Juggler: 'The Event Horizons of . . .'"

"Yes, yes, yes. Can mass pass through an event-horizon?"

"Mass pops out of black holes all the time—but it can't bring any information with it. Your faster-than-light ship would fry its occupants down to their unreadable parts. You couldn't find out where they came from—not even the direction."

"You think we'll have a simpler explanation for this pulse?"

"I do, but my opinion is worthless beside your own, Lord Commander!"

"In a few days I may have the object for you to examine—if it doesn't play *hide-the-copper-penny* with us, or worse, put us in cages for some alien zoo! In the meantime I suspect that our visitor may be from Man-home. I want prisoners. There may be injuries in the attack. You are our veterinarian. Take a *Ztirgor* with that autodoc Chuut-Riit gave you, and follow the attack force. Do not attack. Your only function will be to handle human casualties."

Grraf-Hromfi broke the contact and lifted his goggles above his eyes. His ears were folded and buried, his lips trembling over fangs. He didn't like to wait!

CHAPTER 21
(2420 A.D.)

The United Nations Space Navy *Shark* materialized at a radius of 335 AU, some 50 billion kloms behind Alpha Centauri—the location picked to keep them hidden from kzin eyes which might be watching Sol. There was minimal danger at this distance but UNSN Lieutenant Nora Argamentine was still filled with the dangerous excitement of her first combat patrol. She had a special reason for wanting revenge against the kzin.

"It's looking okay, Charlie. Clear field," she said. The detectors were in the green.

Charlie was captain. Prakit was hyperdrive engineer. The other two in the cramped cargo capsule didn't belong. They were special forces, checking out the fate of the *Yamamoto*, silent, untalkative, to be dropped off in their tiny torchship if a closer approach was possible, their mission to kill Chuut-Riit if that ratcat had survived the attempt on his life by Captain Matthieson and Lieutenant Raines. Efficient killers.

Once she got her telescope operational they'd be

167

looking at Wunderland. The *Yamamoto*'s relativistic pellets should have left marks—perhaps not visible from this distance. They intended to move much closer, in stages.

Nora wasn't so sure that the *Yamamoto* had even passed through Alpha Centauri yet. It might still be hell bent on its mission, delayed by a patch of low density interstellar gas or a magnetic field breakdown or tanj knew what kind of trouble. The arrival time of a ramscoop was not highly predictable. Raines and Matthieson would be shocked by the level of technological progress since 2409. Wunderland might be liberated before they even arrived!

Prakit fussed over his hyperdrive unit, tuning it up for the next jump. Nora could turn around to encourage him, but there wasn't room for her to help him. She reached out a fist and banged him affectionately on his helmet with her wrist, grinning at him because he was so sober.

"Betsy giving you trouble?"

"Naw, Betsy's just a baby. If I feed her every four hours and bounce her on my knee, she calms down."

Betsy was a new crashlander model and they were lucky to have her. We Made It had been in the hyperspace-shunt engine business two years earlier than Earth, having bought the technology from incomprehensibly alien spacewanderers. The quality of the product from Procyon was better than Earth's—for all of Earth's vaunted technological superiority—and the UNSN crews fought over every shipment from Crashlanding City.

This model could make the transition between relativistic and quantum modes in half an hour when it was fined-tuned. When it wasn't fined-tuned, when Prakit couldn't get the hyperwave functions of the atoms into the proper phase relationship, Betsy just wavered and whined and if you were looking at her you'd feel as if pieces of retina were peeling off the back of your eyeball. Prakit didn't mind.

"She's fastened down," he'd say.

"If you guys need to stretch your legs just stick them up here!" Nora joked, shouted into the hold at the "special forces." Argamentine was a good-natured woman who liked to take care of her men even if that wasn't the style of military women. Her father had been fried in the Battle of Ceres during the Fourth Kzin Invasion when she was a teenager, and somehow she could never give enough love—or hate enough.

"We've got lots of room. There's room for *you* down here," said the first killer because there wasn't.

"Are we there yet! Are we there yet!" cried the other killer.

Nora fixed her two commandoes ration crackers with a little smuggled Camembert, and passed her gift down the "hole." "Don't get crackers in your bed!"

Charlie and Nora spent more than a day between naps taking photos and scanning the volume of space they wanted to move to, about 50 AU farther in. Nora spent a few moments off duty just gazing at the Serpent's Swarm through the electronic image amplifier. "God, Charlie, you've got to take a look at their Belt!" There was no hurry about tasks and no frantic priorities. They were making a very cautious approach. It took only about five minutes to move across 50 AU in hyperspace, but they didn't want to jump into a nest of kzin, not when they needed a minimum of 30 minutes to set up another jump.

Sometimes she had nightmares sleeping in the cockpit. As a teenager on the Iowa farm-city she had imagined such a cockpit around herself at dusk while the stars rose above the trees, imagining herself killing kzin before they got to Daddy, wondering where he was, what he was doing out there—and if he was safe. It had been a nightly ritual, murdering imaginary kzin.

Charlie woke her up with a gentle nudge. "Bandits, at eight o'clock, twenty degrees high. Hey, Prakit, get us the tanj out of here!"

Lieutenant Argamentine was instantly awake and reading the flowing graphics on her screen. She asked her machine questions and the graphs changed in response. "Bandits coming in fast. The doppler reading shows a deceleration of sixty-four g's. Three fighters. They carry the *Scream-of-Vengeance* signature. That's the fighter that got my Dad."

"How much time have we got?" Charlie's voice was rapid-fire, impatient with chatter.

"Easy, Charlie. This is a different war. We aren't fighting the last war. They are *hours* away and we'll never have to engage them." Daddy had had no choice—in a fighter with only a fraction of their maneuverability. "We have time for coffee and crullers." But she was nervously straightening a strand of curly hair. "I used to play this game with my little sister when she was three. I'd let her almost catch me—then I'd disappear." She turned around to smile at Prakit. "How are you doing?"

"I'm doing! I'm doing," snapped Prakit.

The phase-change built up while Prakit counted off the minutes. They fell into a silence of suspense. War was waiting for those few seconds of action. "We love you, Betsy," said Nora when she couldn't stand the suspense any more.

"Shut up. Let Prakit work."

The hyperdrive suddenly went into a vibration that built up over three seconds and then died. Prakit cursed. "She just reset."

"Plenty of time," said Lieutenant Argamentine.

"I'm going to take five to make an adjustment. We don't want Betsy to burp again."

Charlie was thinking of defensive action now. He

rolled the *Shark* so that the jet of its piggy-back torchship was pointed toward the *Screamers*.

"It won't do any good," said Nora. "Those devils are maneuverable enough to get out of the way of anything."

Charlie called down to his special forces. "We're under attack. Get ready to fire the torch. When I call for fire, *fire!*"

"We're going to be out of here!" said Prakit.

This time, as the phase-change built up, nobody broke the silence. Nora stared at the engine even while the sight of it started to "peel" the rods off the back of her eyeballs. *Go!* she prayed. But the *Shark* stayed suspended, agonizingly. Too long.

Betsy shuddered and reset.

"I should rebuild her," said Prakit frantically.

"You had all day!" snarled Charlie. "Time?" He was asking Nora how much time they had to live.

"They're still decelerating. Looks like a boarding. If they decide to take us alive, Betsy will have time. If they decide to make a fast pass, we are dead meat."

"Suits sealed," said Charlie. He meant helmets and gloves. They were already wearing airtights under their uniforms.

"Can't!" Prakit's voice was frantic. "I can't afford to be encumbered. I'm taking her up manually. I can shave off minutes that way. I can keep her in the canyon. I've done it before. The autoguide has been hitting the walls. Shouldn't happen."

They began a third countdown. "Can we do a short tunneling?" Charlie was looking for straws.

"Doesn't work that way. Don't talk to me."

They waited. Again. Finally Charlie could wait no more. "Attention. All crew. I'm arming the self-destruct." If they got into hyperspace, each officer knew how to deactivate it before it blew. If they didn't . . .

They waited. The kzin continued to close.

"Down below. Get your torch primed." Charlie turned to Nora. "You and I are going to practice keeping our ass aimed at the kzin."

"There are *two* bandits coming in. One is doing a boarding maneuver, the other seems to be setting up a fast flyby." Nora twisted that ringlet of hair with her free hand, then found she needed both hands for her combat duties.

"And the third?"

"Hanging back. He'll be able to board *or* kill."

"We'll practice wiggling our ass between the two lead *Screamers*." The *Shark* began to oscillate between two points—the aiming precision-controlled by the ship's computer.

They waited.

"We're going to make it," Prakit said, calm certainty in his voice.

"Fire!" screamed Charlie to his torchmen.

Fire blazed out at the dancing kzin, seeking while the *Screamers* avoided. The countdown continued.

A lurch as the torchship was blown away. Nora saw it cartwheeling across the heavens before it detonated. A moment later the cabin took a hit. She didn't see Prakit sucked into space, helmetless. Her faceplate was triggering to opaque on cue from the explosive glare while actinic light burned the unshadowed half of her uniform. In the instant of death's visitation she saw, not the father's battle doom which had, until now, never left her mind, but a baby sister running toward her with ruffles around the bottoms of her tiny pants . . .

The Hssin barbarian had already flashed past. The second *Screamer* dropped from 60 g's down to a fraction of a g and was only nudging the alien object as the old warrior jumped out with a backpack into the hole that had been opened for him. He knew what he was looking for, but it took him precious seconds to find it. He slapped the backpack down. Its electro-gravitic vibrators cut a clean hole through the floor and the backpack disappeared at 230 g's carrying an amputated hunk of the *Shark* with it. The battle-armored Gunner leapt into the cockpit with two air-bags, and in a choreographed economy of gesture the old Hero and his Gunner each stuffed a body into a bag, and then hunkered down, waiting for the explosion.

Chuut-Riit's warrior was grinning through his face-plate. "Maybe the acceleration killed it."

But no—the destruct bomb lit up the underside of the *Screamer* and the wreckage of the *Shark*.

The engine was intact. Give that wild Hssin barbarian credit—he could shoot straight! While the old warrior was examining the salvage, Hromfi's son drifted to within hailing distance. The veteran Hero made hand signals to Hromfi's Son: *Where was that laggard, Trainer-of-Slaves?*

Double arm motions signaled back: *On his way*.

The *Ztirgor* rolled and locked onto the bottom of the old warrior's *Screamer*. Its insides had been stripped out to accommodate the autodoc. The body airbags were delivered efficiently and opened. *Messy*. Trainer-of-Slaves had a choice. There was room for only one prisoner in the autodoc. He chose the man-male because he was a male, then changed his mind because the male was dead, space-boiled blood clotting a neck wound, half his back carbonized to the bone. The female would have to do—after all, the man-females *were* intelligent and information could be tortured out of them.

He didn't know if the autodoc could save her. He slashed away the remains of the green UNSN uniform with his claws. He slit, and then peeled off, the airtights. Some of the melted flesh came with it. He didn't know what to do with the bra, trying various techniques of puzzle-solving to unleash it, then in exasperation cut it off. The rest was easy.

The first time Lieutenant Argamentine rose out of her dark delirium she was proud that she knew exactly where she was—she was in the womb-like care of an autodoc. She could feel it all around her and, if she moved her right side, she could feel the needles and the jell. But where was the autodoc?

Memories were elusive. When she struggled with their vapors she saw corncobs cooking in their husks in a bonfire. That didn't seem right. It was too distant. She saw a starving man in a red shirt selling cow dung. Damn! She wanted to remember yesterday! What had happened to her?

She struggled to remember where she was, almost getting it and then forgetting. General Fry! A flash! That was the right clue! The sudden jubilation of knowing. But then it all went away. All she could remember about General Fry was being caught naked in a space-hammock with him by a laughing Colonel who wrapped them around and around in their netted prison.

But that was it! Revelation! Sobs of relief! She was at the hospital in Gibraltar Base and the *Shark* had blown up trying to jump to Alpha Centauri. She faded back into delirium with a desperate need to tell her baby sister that she was all right, and when she woke up again she was talking to General Fry, not sure that the conversation wasn't a dream, trying to convince him that he should still let her go out to fight the kzinti.

The delirium went away. The autodoc became more real. She could feel herself healing. She slept normally. She knew her life signs were good. They would open the box and talk to her. General Fry loved her and he would be there when they opened the box, tenderness in his flinty old eyes. Maybe not. Maybe just a nurse.

When the box opened it was a kzin face staring down at her, tall, massive, hairy, fangs as large as the wolf's in Little Red Riding Hood. It was the first kzin face she had ever seen. She still remembered nothing.

"Sprechen Sie Deutsch?" the ratcat asked. "Ich spreche nicht sehr gut."

Had the kzinti conquered Germany? Had the Fifth Invasion begun just as the *Shark* launched for Wunderland? She was still certain that she was in the Solar System.

The yellow-orange monster brought out a portable translator which began to recite the same phrase in many languages. Finally the cultured electronic voice asked, "What languages do you speak?"

"English," she said.

"My English also is very nasty," spat-hissed the kzin. "Might be machine help us. I learn English. You teach?"

"Thomas Alva Edison!" she swore in utter amazement.

"Brain injury," he growled. "I am decorous and able veterinarian. Skilled with female brains." His ears unfolded proudly. "Much experimentation. Fix all animals."

He set the autodoc to raise her to a sitting position and then held out a dish for her, a stemmed sherbert glass with a spoon. Nora noticed that she was ravenously hungry. Her kzin continued to babble without making much sense. "Please be decorous slave and clean cage," he said. He held a spoonful of his gift to her mouth.

It was vanilla ice cream flavored with chunks of fish.

CHAPTER 22
(2420 A.D.)

While Lieutenant Nora Argamentine recovered in the autodoc of the slave quarters, Hrith-Master-Officer maneuvered his *Nesting-Slashtooth-Bitch* to pick up the wreck of the mystery scout. The floating drydock's maximum acceleration capability was ten g's, thus they took much longer to reach the scout than had the original fighting triad. After grappling the wreck into the repair hangar, Trainer-of-Slaves and his Jotoki mechanics began a meticulous study of the vehicle.

The structure of the engine made no immediate sense. Trainer didn't expect it to. His first priority was to determine its function and limitations, his second, its manufacturability. Then, at leisure, he could reverse-deduce its operating principles with the aid of a team of physicists.

Long-Reach came up with a preliminary assessment of pieces that were clearly gravitic manipulators. That tended to confirm Trainer-of-Slaves's suspicion that the monkeys were now building a sophisticated gravity polarizer that could travel very close to the speed of light, somehow bypassing the "blue-light" bleeding effect that limited all kzin drives.

Such a conclusion fitted the data. The peculiar pulse patterns observed at Man-sun and transmitted by the *Patriarch's Nose* were five years old. They looked like a series of tests of a new vehicle. And here, 4.3 years after the completion of the tests, was one of the test vehicles on a test combat mission. Simple. Grraf-Hromfi's fear-hope of faster-than-light magic was just that.

Non-scientists like Grraf-Hromfi, in spite of their admonitions to others, were always leaping to conclusions before they gave their science speculations deep thought. The rumors about an ancient lost civilization that had spanned the galaxy before the birth of the sky's brightest stars provided just the kind of fantasy universe in which to dream of superluminal travel.

Spread the rumor that fossil relics survived on some wrinkled moon of a red star forty light-years thither and kzin, by the herds, would set upon an aimless life of wandering to track down the chimera. The *older* the empire, the *grander* its mysteries. The *deader* the empire, the greater the heights to which it *must* have risen. The Hero's Tongue had a short word for such fantasies: the-forest-bush-with-leaves-that-smell-like-meat. Somewhere there were always kzinti hunting that bush.

Trainer made the rounds, feeding the naked children in the cages. His experimentation schedule had been destroyed by recent events, but animals had to be fed no matter what. Tired, he retreated to his cramped quarters, putting off Long-Reach, who wanted a game of cards.

He rubbed in the talcum to get at the dirt and smell. He worked the powder into his fur, and then massaged himself down with a good vacuum vibrator.

That felt good! He found a hard pillow for his head, and stretched out on the bunk. Now for a liver-jolting virtual adventure to get away from life's problems! He popped the goggles over his eyeballs with a little squirt of lubricant.

Would it be possible to find out what Grraf-Hromfi had been watching lately to get him so nervous about superluminal superstitions? The Lord's access file was restricted, but that didn't stop some shrewd guessing. Vocally, he keyed in "faster-than-light," then, after some thought, "ancient empires." He already knew that would give him more than a thousand titles, so he narrowed it down even farther by adding to the list, "fight adventure," and for good measure, since he hadn't had a sniff of kzinrret in years, "female interest."

He got a bad virtual adventure of a Pride of Heroes swept beyond the Border of the Patriarchy by a Warp Storm. They fought giant worms who chased them into the crystalline ruins of a civilization that had been born during the Fireball of Creation, so old it had died before the galaxies could form. Just as the largest worm was about to eat them for slaying its worm warriors, they fell into a crystal room with a perfectly preserved superluminal device that glowed malevolently when they touched it.

Unable to resist temptation, they were transported to the inner glory of the galaxy, to a dark cool world guarded by giants. The giants were protecting the galaxy from the sight of creatures that would destroy all who looked upon them, such was their beauty. Over the dead bodies of the giants they found the svelte kzinrret-like creatures deep at the center of the dark forest, at a wondrous waterhole. Then kzin warriors fell upon each other, slicing, stabbing, clawing until only the greatest warrior remained. Faster than light, he brought his kzinrret-like harem back to the ancient crystalline mysteries and lived happily ever after, hunting throughout the grassy plains beyond his palace.

In the morning Trainer-of-Slaves tried gentle questioning of the lieutenant-beast about her ship. She was not yet fit enough for torture. She volunteered only her name and rank, a puzzling concept for Trainer. He did discover that she was interested in a picture of her youngest sister and so he went through the personal effects of the *Shark*'s crew which had survived. That was how he came to be caught up in the illustrations of a "comic book," copyright date: January 2420 After the Damning. Purple-caped flying monkeys KAPOWed ferocious red kzin who were defending the walls of their captured Elvis Presley Monastery.

Something made him check the data-link files on the material they were receiving from Man-home. He didn't keep it in his head but their dating system was well known because of its oddity. All events were referenced from the time they had tortured a Trinity of Criminals on Golgotha Hill, nailing the Father and the Son and the Grandfather to wood so that buzzards (a carrion bird) might feast upon their livers.

The latest events to come in from the *Patriarch's Nose* and the *Tigripard's Ear* carried the Man-sun date: November 2415 After the Damning. By the immutable laws of physics any Solar event later than that was forbidden to Alpha Centauri. 2420 was essentially a taboo future.

Trainer-of-Slaves pondered alien copyright law for a day. Did they have a five-year grace period in which plagiarism was allowed before the copyright applied? In the meantime, his Jotoki disassembled a burned controller. All the intricate electronic parts were labeled *We Made It*. That would have been an ear tickler—if you didn't know that We Made It was a monkey colony more than eleven light-years from Man-sun and thirteen light-years from Alpha Centauri.

There wasn't any economical way that such standard parts could be shipped via ramscoop or slowboat.

It was time for another devious conversation with the lieutenant-animal. He researched the transcripts from the First and Second Black Prides, selecting non-military items that she might be willing to talk about. He had an ally in Long-Reach. His Jotok had discovered that she liked the sweet-bitter berries his slaves enjoyed with their ration of leaves.

He came armed with berry ice cream. She was still suffering from extensive burns and the after-effects of a concussion, but she could remain out of the autodoc for hours at a time, if she was properly chained.

"Fur Face, when does my uniform come back from the cleaners?"

He grinned at her around his fangs in response to her insolence, though his liver wasn't in the expression. The indignities one had to put up with from kzinrretti! He was confused. He wasn't sure which rules applied to sentient females. The grin was purely reflexive.

"All right, already. Sire! I abjectly request some decent clothing, and will kiss the ground you sit on when they appear."

He put on his goggles to consult his English Vocoder, spitting and growl-hissing requests. "I can inject you with chemicals that will make your fur grow," said the elegant voice of the machine. Then a rougher voice. "Auburn hair. Your head," said Trainer-of-Slaves who hated to rely on translators, but he had to give up and let the machine finish his thought. "Your fur will grow in fine and attractive. I have already done the experiments and can guarantee a positive result."

So much for having 98 percent of the genes of a chimpanzee, thought Nora wryly. "Sire! I'm sure your five-armed sewing machine over there could stitch together an elegant little outfit for me in no time at all! *He* gets to wear livery. Why can't *I*? *Please*."

The monstrous yellow-orange cross between a Basketball Center and Football Tackle didn't understand, but politely listened to the catfight coming out of his translator.

His eyes lit up as he comprehended. "Yes. Livery. Will make red-green garters for—" he consulted his Vocoder—"knees and elbows. You like?"

"I think I need some of that ice cream," she groaned. She had already consulted with Long-Reach about the fish in kzinti ice cream, and he'd promised a fix. He proffered a golden dish of vanilla with purple spots. He'd already stolen some of the berries, an irresistible temptation. She didn't complain. She just ate in silence, sometimes twirling her little curl nervously.

"Long-Reach will now sing Top Ten Songs of 2415 years after torture of Christ Gang. English I can speak. Sing no. Now, Number One on your Hot Shot Hour!" What else could he say? He was taking the words straight off the recording.

The green and red liveried being who was also a quintet began to sing to the naked prisoner of war as she sat among the cramped gray bulkheads of a warship, in chains, eating ice cream. She did not know that she was being deviously questioned. She did not know that this was a substitute for torture, that the answers to his questions were vital to him. Was she a seer? Could she see the future? Could she tell Trainer-of-Slaves of events between 2415 and 2420 that weren't permitted yet at Alpha Centauri?

The five voices that came from the five lung slits in the arms weren't human, but they knew harmony and each word was enunciated with passionate clarity though the accent was no sound that she'd ever heard in her short life.

"When the night is cold,
and my arms are bold
and you are very far away . . ."

It was the song they'd been singing everywhere at the time of her graduation prom, at the end of High School, when the two year Military Academy course was just a kid's dream. She had to cry. She tried not to, but that only made the bawling worse when it came. Charlie was dead. Prakit was dead. Those tough thugs in the hold, so gung ho to kill kzin, were wasted. Her mission had failed. She had failed her Dad. And she didn't have the least idea about what to do with a seven-foot tall kzin who courted her with a five-armed singing comedian.

"Humans cry when the ice cream is good," she sniffed to cover herself.

"Berries, ptui!" said Trainer-of-Slaves.

"I think too much," continued Nora, wiping her face.

"That can be corrected," said Trainer-of-Slaves. "I have done the experiments."

"How did you learn these songs?"

"You animals do not keep radio silence."

"You listen to *that*? All the way out here?"

"In past-gone hour, I watch beastly holo, *Blaze of Glory!*"

She wasn't crying anymore. She was grinning. "Lots of kzin killing in that one. I loved it! You monsters killed my beloved Dad. That holo won an award for its acting. Passion, the spirit of mankind that you'll never crush!"

Won an award. She was predicting the future. In November 2415 *Blaze of Glory* had only been *nominated* for an award, one of sixteen. "Bad acting," said Trainer-of-Slaves. "Monkey in kzin-suit, too slow. Wrong emotions. Liver was sick."

He pulled the lieutenant-animal further into the conversation, letting her vent her anger at the kzinti. When she was angry she leapt before she thought. Three more times he caught her predicting the future.

By then he was sure.

He reported his suspicions immediately to Grraf-Hromfi, though the timelag between the *Nesting-Slashtooth-Bitch* and the main body of the Pride was still too great for conversation.

Trainer's old mentor took the news well. His return message read: "So the old warrior can still sniff out a different scent. A superluminal drive is exciting. But it compromises our whole strategic position. We'll have to react quickly. Keep me informed."

In the vast hangar in the belly of the *Nesting-Slashtooth-Bitch* Trainer drove his Jotoki slaves in their dissection of the wreck. How could such a little thing, lost in the spotlights of the hangar, bring back the awful fear he thought he had lost forever? He paced around the hangar, looking down at the alien shape, keeping his feet inside the local gravitic field of the catwalk. His liver was telling him to run in panic. He was no longer the mighty Hero willing to take on the whole Man-system, and after conquering it, to ride elephants to the hunt with monkeys carrying his bedding and his equipment and his kzinrretti in palanquins.

He returned to Lieutenant Argamentine in the middle of the day and opened the autodoc coffin, waking her, to ask her his question directly. "You came here faster than light!" he accused.

She smiled at him without showing her teeth. There were dimples in her furless cheeks. "That's not for me to say."

The answer terrified him and he went away.

With a superluminal drive the animals could penetrate the Patriarchy with impunity. Every system

would be isolated, on its own, unable to call on nearby
warriors for aid. Heroism would be a sham. A new-
born kit could kill his father with unopened eyes. In
the face of such unnaturalness, run! The Fifth Fleet
should run, should disperse, should hide!

Kzin warriors are taught to obey orders on penalty
of death. But it is also instinct for them to create their
own orders. A superior officer might be only light-
hours away but the skirmish will be decided in
minutes. The General Staff might be only light-days
away, but battles can be decided in hours. The Patriarch who orders a warrior to the borderspaces, gives
his order only once. After that the warrior makes his
own orders for a lifetime and trains his sons to train
his grandsons to report back that the mission has been
accomplished.

The Patriarch requires obedience, but the ruthless
Emperor of Light executes all warriors who are not
their own Chief of Staff.

Trainer-of-Slaves's internal Chief of Staff was telling
him to flee. *How can I be such a coward?* He thought
he had conquered cowardice. He'd tried so hard! Desperately he recalled words that Grraf-Hromfi had once
tossed away casually—almost unaware of their profound wisdom—words which had found a fertile home
in Trainer's mind: "To flee one's duty is cowardice,
but to flee while retaining a grip on duty can be the
act of a Hero!" Perhaps his mentor would condone
fleeing in this extreme case. The thought that he might
have an ally in his fear was comforting.

Trainer vowed by his grandfather that wherever he
fled, he would bring duty with him. He was in turmoil.
He had conquered fear only to be trapped by his own
prey. Short-Son of Chiirr-Nig was running on the surface of Hssin with no place to go, every door guarded
by the enemy.

He knew that this little engine mounted in the

wreck of a tiny ship was the most valuable asset in the
whole of the Patriarchy. The entire Fifth Fleet must
be devoted to protecting it. If a hundred thousand
Heroes died in its defense, that would not be too great
a sacrifice. He could flee, but there could be no honorable fleeing without the engine.

By the time the *Nesting-Slashtooth-Bitch* had rees-
tablished its station within the Third Black Pride,
Lieutenant Argamentine was well enough for the
cages. The berries in the ice cream had done no good
at all. She became violent when she was introduced
to the cage room, incoherent with rage at the sight of
the orphans, even though there were only three of
them left uneaten and they had ample room.

"They are children! You monster, they are just
children!"

She actually attacked him. To defend himself he
had to hold her by the forearms off the floor. That
didn't help him because of the well placed kicks. She
had hands-and-feet combat training! He had to toss
her away. It was a true kzinrret rage. But most kzinretti did not get that angry unless you were about to
eat *their* kits!

To appease her he did what any kzintosh would
have done—he gave her the children and put them
all in the same cage and left her alone.

He found it remarkable how quickly that single act
calmed her down. She forgot her bruises as she lav-
ished attention upon his experimental tots. He liked
that. She was going to make very good breeding stock.
The cage was too small for them all—he noticed
that—but he did nothing about it because he was
interrupted by an urgent message.

There is a kzin saying: *Trouble does not give the
single finger; trouble comes with four claws*.

Detection staff reported three more gravitic pulses
with the signature of the superluminal drive—but at

distances too far to intercept. And Detection was reporting the appearance of an armed feral navy in the Serpent's Swarm. Trainer-of-Slaves had received a priority query from Grraf-Hromfi.

Could Man-sun, as in *right now*, be using superluminal craft to deliver weapon supplies for the feral fleet?

Then Traat-Admiral began to send out ominous directives. The messages were fresh, but their source events were two days old.

Grraf-Hromfi ordered an emergency goggle-briefing of all officers of the Third Black Pride. He wasn't waiting for them to reach his lecture room on the *Sherrek's Ear*, he wasn't even waiting for a quorum of goggle-connects. By the time Trainer-of-Slaves was in link, the chaotic meeting was at full tempest, and though he could not smell it, he could see that the air was redolent of aggression. When Trainer moved his goggled head, he saw no less than five warriors, lips twitching, barely able to repress their fightfever.

His claws extended, almost in self-defense, though he was alone.

Astonishingly, Grraf-Hromfi wasn't analyzing the attack that Man-system had launched with their deadly new weapon. He had gone crazy. He was ranting about mythological warriors who had risen out of the misty past and were attacking the Fifth Fleet along a whole section of the Serpent's Swarm. He was screaming about superkzin mental powers and super technology. He was raving about Wunderkzin Traitors. He was snarling about cyclopean terrors. And he was exhorting warriors to their Final Bravery.

He had already ordered the full Third Black Pride into battle, repositioning all ships down to Alpha Centauri to reinforce Traat-Admiral's fight. Even as Trainer watched through his goggles in awe, Hrith-Master-Officer gave the command for the *Nesting-*

Slashtooth-Bitch to move downstar. It wasn't the way Chuut-Riit had taught them to fight.

They were in mid-leap without a thought in their heads. Pure rage.

Without thought himself, Trainer-of-Slaves ripped off his goggles and raced to the hangar where he requisitioned a *Ztirgor* from the upper racks. Long-Reach and Joker scampered to unhook it and swing it down to the airlock tracks for release.

"You are agitated, master!"

"Old Smelly Fur is trying to get us all killed! He wants you dead and he wants me dead! And he's willing to claw the Patriarch in the bargain!"

Long-Reach froze in fear at such wrath in Mellow-Yellow.

Trainer-of-Slaves sped across the heavens to the *Sherrek's Ear* which had already abandoned its great antenna to the blackness—its antenna, its strength! Calmer now, he checked the *Ztirgor* into a receiver bay.

Why was Grraf-Hromfi doing this? *Think before you leap.* Was that his motto because he knew in his liver that he was impulsive, his reflexes faster than thought? Had he needed all these years the constant image of that motto across his eyes to keep his blood in check?

The communications officer knew Trainer-of-Slaves, and knew of his close relationship with Grraf-Hromfi, yet still he tried to discourage Trainer from his call. Trainer insisted, and surprisingly, when Grraf-Hromfi learned he was there, found himself ordered to the Command Center immediately.

"I have a question for you about your captive. Was she behaving like a slave in thrall?"

"Sire! She strikes me as highly feral."

Grraf-Hromfi's eyes were maddeningly bright as they pierced through to Trainer-of-Slaves. "Did you feel the commanding pulse this morning that came with the wallop of a religious revelation driving you to obey?"

"My alarm clock?"

"The Slaver! The scaly green monster with one eye!"

"Sire! I came here because the superluminal drive in the hangar of the *Bitch* is the only one we've got."

"Yes? And?" growled Hromfi.

Trainer was in a rage that this stupid old fossil couldn't see the obvious. "We are leaping without a thought in our head! Think before you leap! Remember? We have to get that drive to Kzin-home!"

Grraf-Hromfi bared his fangs and fell into his dangerous fighting crouch. "You mock me!" he threatened. "You mock me with my own words, a son stabbing his father!" At this commotion the Lord's Second Officer turned to watch, almost ready to interfere should Trainer become dangerous. Hromfi was virulent. "You haven't been listening, youngling! What do you know of ancient empire and craft and war? Nothing."

Trainer-of-Slaves was already regretting his insolence and moved into a more propitiative posture. "I could never be so great a student of mythology as you, Dominant One."

"Mythology!" Grraf-Hromfi was now *grievously* enraged. "Five octal-squared years past, these audacious monkeys who are giving us so much trouble found and revived one of those one-eyed monsters. That is mythology?"

"I am glad that it amuses my Lord to wander among the fairy tale shelves of the Munchen library." *Why am I goading him?* Trainer-of-Slaves was terrified by the ferocity he had unleashed in his mentor who was now clearly angry as well as insane.

Hromfi was circling Trainer, growling out his words, slowly, threateningly. "They found this horror. They released him out of monkey curiosity and he took over the minds of all the monkey vassals within range. They'd still be in thrall—but 'monkey-daffy; monkey-lucky.' They tricked him back into his stasis suit and turned it on. And *then* do you know what those hollow-brains did? They put him in a museum. Their silver Sea Statue."

Grraf-Hromfi spun from the confrontation to calm himself. He dropped into one of the command chairs and growled and spat out his rage at the instrument panels. Then he turned over his shoulder and spoke to Trainer-of-Slaves again.

"You speak to me of that superluminal drive of yours. Where do you think it came from? You've seen monkey technology. You destroyed their pitiful ramscoop. You've refitted their quaint torchships with gravitics. You've seen their weapons. Could they have created a superluminal driver for spaceships? Not likely. *Impossible*. But from evidence on a dozen worlds, students of the ancient mysteries suspect that the Slavers could travel faster than light.

"We are confronted with a W'kkai puzzle. And I have put it together with no protrusions. The monkeys have released their Sea Statue again. The ultimate weapon against the Patriarchy. It was this ancient beast who must have given them their superluminal ships and he is here now, in the Serpent's Swarm, because I *felt* his mind and my officers are with me because they, too, *felt* that mind which would make slaves of kzinkind! If you hadn't been asleep, you too would believe!"

Trainer-of-Slaves was always awed by Grraf-Hromfi's ability to convince. Still it was foolish to take as true a tale told five lifetimes ago by the member of a race whose individuals were known to lie at every opportunity. Indeed! One eye and green scales!

"Sire! I am here to request permission to take the superluminal drive unit to Kzin-home."

Grraf-Hromfi rose from his chair. He walked over to Trainer-of-Slaves. His nose came to Trainer's forehead and his shoulders were broader. "Permission denied. Do you think you'll get anywhere if we fail to destroy this menace? His mind will pluck you right out of the sky and bring you whimpering to his feet."

The fear was overpowering. Never in his life had Trainer-of-Slaves defied anyone, not his father, Chiirr-Nig, not Puller-of-Noses, not Jotok-Tender, not his friend, Ssis-Captain. He was universally sweet-tempered with his military associates. He had always accommodated Grraf-Hromfi's wishes, and the wish of every officer who held authority above him. His inclination now was to flatter Grraf-Hromfi into letting him disappear into interstellar space with the wreck of the *Shark*.

"Sire! In your great wisdom you have advocated thinking before leaping . . ."

Grraf-Hromfi slashed this impudent warrior's vest through to the flesh of his chest beneath. "Do you think that I would let *you* flee from a battle, Eater-of-Grass? Only Heroes who are eager to die in battle can carry the burden of flight." He gestured to two tall kzin guards. "I cannot kill this coward. Take him back to the *Bitch* and put him in hibernation. He'll die there in battle, and if we survive . . . I'll deal with him then."

The Lord Commander of the Black Pride was desperate to eliminate the smell of abject fear from his command room.

CHAPTER 23
(2420 A.D.)

Long-Reach was in a panic argument with himselves. The ship was no longer a safe place. Mellow-Yellow was in danger. Mellow-Yellow was in hibernation. Kzin warriors were talking about slashing the throat of Mellow-Yellow for cowardice. They were rough with him when they put him away. After the battle they would take him out and kill him. Joker had heard them say so while he was relining the gravity walks. Long-Reach felt grief in the tips of his thumb-fingers. No more card games. No more currying that fine pelt.

He felt an unexplainable desolation.

Fourteen Jotoki were directly bonded to Mellow-Yellow. In the slave quarters these fourteen bundled together, avoiding conversation even with Jotoki who were bonded to other kzin. Arms entwined, they chattered and moaned and sifted thoughts among their brains. The need to help Mellow-Yellow was unsettling and painful because they could *not* help him. Disoriented, they set about their tasks mechanically, then returned to the slave quarters to share their agony.

Long-Reach knew that the man-beasts had to be fed, but while he went through the motions he was remembering another such terrifying time of threat—long ago on another world. Simpler times. Only one kzin had been menacing Mellow-Yellow then, not a ship full. The challenge had taken place in the birth-haven of Long-Reach among the trees and swamps and caverns that had nurtured himselves during the growing-up and were almost alive enough to come to his aid when he needed to call upon a glen or ridge between hillbanks. The very land had helped him kill that other kzin.

Now there were only the cold corridors of a ship and pipes and snaking power lines and catwalks and patrolling warriors. Killing one kzin to save his master had been the most troubling horror of his life. To kill a whole shipload was unthinkable, enough to make his arms disconnect from each other and send him stumbling in an uncoordinated scramble of arm-legs.

Nevertheless, that is what he, himselves, was thinking.

Lieutenant Argamentine knew that her routine had been upset. That bizarre kzin who was called Mellow-Yellow by his five-armed followers disappeared to be replaced by a taciturn kzin who was larger and redder, whose only function seemed to be that of interrogator. He took her from her cage, never very gently, never so roughly that he hurt her. Together they rode a capsule to his tiny torture chamber. He questioned her. He brought her back to the charge of the slaves, forgetting her until the next time he needed to torture her.

She had grown up dealing with difficult people, including her father, and she had long ago developed a facility of manner with intractable personalities—but this one fitted none of her patterns. He was *disturb-*

ingly alien. He was impatient with chitchat. He was impossible to reason with about anything like her living conditions or the needs of the children. He was interested only in answers and he was impatient with devious answers.

When she did not give him what he wanted he turned immediately to torture, preferring agonizing nerve-stim to mutilation. But she got no feeling that he was interested in torture. He had an uncanny sensitivity, almost as if he was a latent telepath. When she didn't *have* answers to his questions, he blandly moved on to the next question. But if she did have answers and tried to withhold them, he became ruthlessly persistent.

Desperately, she tried to get an angle on him. He was curious about the strangest things.

"Sea Statue at UN Comparative Cultures Exhibit. You know?"

She knew, but like most flatlanders, she'd never really wanted to know much about the one-eyed thrintun monster who lived inside, frozen in stasis. It was a story three hundred years old. She was tortured into remembering.

Had the Sea Statue been moved?

Had the Sea Statue been transported to Alpha Centauri?

Had the Sea Statue provided the principles of superluminal flight?

Were the UNSN officers in thrall?

War bred the strangest paranoias from its soup of deceptions, misinformation, misdirection, and poor communication. And lack of any cultural basis for understanding.

When she was thrown back into her cage after her last session, the silent children seemed to know that she was hurting and her mind half incoherent. They just held her. They were too numb, and too maltreated themselves, to be able to give her much. Finally the food came.

"You're late. We're starving," said Lieutenant Argamentine. She wasn't even ready to try to figure out a five-brained spider.

The three children were very quiet around Long-Reach. He fed them—but he was also the chief lab technician in a place where they were mere lab animals. She couldn't read Long-Reach's emotions. He had no face. A mottled pot-belly where his face should have been. His eyes and arms were expressive but she didn't know how to read their mobility.

"Bean mash on kzin bones," said Long-Reach's translator with an appropriately apologetic melody. Short(arm) took umbrage with the vocoder and offered an English translation. "Not kzin bones! Shudder. Groundified bone and marrow, rolled to cracker shape. Bonding heated. Kzin rations for ship. Not kzin bones! Kzin not cannibals except with kits of wrong father."

Freckled(arm) made an interjection to correct an aspect of short(arm)'s terrible English grammar.

"Are you going to stay around for another English lesson?" asked Nora. She didn't really want this strange creature to go. The torture was demoralizing her.

"No. Must go. Mellow-Yellow in trouble," lamented Long-Reach. "Bad, bad, bad," commented three of his arms in a round-robin.

"I haven't seen him for a while." Was she better off with Mellow-Yellow or Redfur?

A pause while the vocoder sorted out the conversation. "We are all doomed by death," said its speaker. "A big battle," kibitzed skinny(arm). "Ship has been recalled to Alpha Centauri," intoned big(arm).

She decided to exact some intelligence of her own. "Why are they interested in thrintun slavers?"

"What?" Long-Reach consulted the vocoder and drew a blank.

"One-eyed scaly monsters who take over minds. They died in a war with the tnuctipun billions of years ago. I've just had my memory forcibly refreshed," she said ruefully.

"Kzin worry about free-will," said Long-Reach. "All the time, worry. Warrior fetish. Always must be in control. Didn't you feel the wave of intrusion? Myselves went right to the kitchen and made up hot soup for Mellow-Yellow, then wondered why I do this. Pleasant feeling to serve others. Kzin no like."

Suddenly Nora was remembering an impulse of feeling that had overwhelmed her just days ago. Devotion. An enormous need to *help* someone. She had supposed it was something Mellow-Yellow had put in her food to make her talk. "There's a Slaver loose down there?"

"Was. Big explosion, hour ago here, days ago there. Don't know what's happening today. Tomorrow we find out. We're all doomed."

"Are you a slave?" she asked, curious about the creature's response. She found out that his vocoder couldn't translate the word for him, and she couldn't explain it to him. The nearest he could come was the English word "friend." As in "only friend."

Redfur the Torturer didn't come back. But a delegation of four Jotoki did. They seemed ill at ease in their body motions. It was impossible for her to stop trying to read expressions off the belly-faces that sat on their mouths even though she knew they weren't faces. The shoulder-mounted eyes watched her. They wanted something. They gave her a delicate dish of stuffed leaves that tasted like Greek *dolmadakia*, vine leaves, almost as if it were a ceremony. Another presented her timidly with green and red garters for her elbows and knees.

They were bargaining! "Yes?" she asked, gently, not knowing what to do with her revelation.

"Our master wished to take this ship out of the battle," intoned their translator, which had been carefully pre-programmed.

"An interesting idea," replied Nora, warily.

The four were talking among themselves in a spitting language that sounded like a corruption of the Hero's Tongue. Finally the translator spoke again. "Your race and the kzinti are enemies."

"Perhaps someday . . ."

The translator wasn't listening to her. It continued. "Men kill kzinti. Kzinti kill men. Is this not so?"

"It's war."

"You are military man," said Long-Reach, impatient with the machine. "Your ice cream desire is to kill all kzin. I understand mankind."

No you don't, she thought while she twiddled with her curl.

"We work, side together, like many arms."

What she was hearing sounded like mutiny. It also sounded like they had an exaggerated respect for her powers. A naked woman with garters was a threat to no one. "I have been defanged and you will notice that I am locked behind bars."

Long-Reach opened the cage and quickly closed it. "Bargain," he said. "We make bargain." She could hear the tremor in his voices, and she was sure she could see his arms shaking. He was terrified. She could almost see him running. The tremors came from inhibiting the flight.

"What can I do for you?"

"You kill all kzin, but one. We free Mellow-Yellow. Bargain? Mellow-Yellow live."

"I'm quite willing to let Mellow-Yellow live," she lied. She almost saw the four of them relax. "What makes you think I might be able to kill all kzin?"

"Ferocious monkey warriors defeat kzin. We know. Monkey squash kzin ships. We repair. We scrape kzin off wall."

Were they thinking that if they let her out of her cage she might not settle for anything less than the death of *all* kzin on board? As if she had a hope of killing even one of the behemoths! It hadn't slipped her notice that her interrogator had two sets of human ears casually attached to his belt.

"Mellow-Yellow live. Bargain?" Long-Reach repeated.

Why were these creatures so bonded to Mellow-Yellow? Why was he different from the others? His name translated as something like Overseer of Inferiors, or Animal Manipulator. Perhaps he had a chemical hold on them? Perhaps he was an expert at some kind of hypnotic conditioning? No matter. The irrational loyalty was there. She remembered the day she had attacked Mellow-Yellow, ready to die, because he was cruel to children, and Long-Reach had been watching her with four eyes. If she had hurt Mellow-Yellow, Long-Reach would have killed her.

It was a strange bargain. If she protected their master (from her cage?), the Jotoki were hers.

Was it a good bargain? It was dangerous to have naïve allies. Were they as naïve as they seemed? Were they treacherous? How much did the kzin trust their slaves? How reliable were these Jotoki? What skills did they have? What skills did *she* have? What weapons did she have? Nothing. She knew the formula for a nerve gas that would kill kzin and was harmless to men, but even given the equipment, she wouldn't have known how to manufacture it. This whole situation wasn't part of her Gibraltar Base training.

No, it wasn't a good bargain, but it was the only bargain she had.

"I'm no match for a kzin," she said. She wanted them to tell her something.

"You have military mind. We have arms. Ship is our playground."

They began to feed her more often. They cleaned cages and when they moved her to a new cage, she found a ship map on the floor. She was surprised that they controlled the cage locks. They *were* trusted. Or was it just that Mellow-Yellow trusted them and in the heat of battle that kzin's duties had not been fully reapportioned? Why was he in disgrace?

Her allies came up with vicious little plans. They had molecular trip-wire that they could set up that would cut a kzin's legs off. They knew how to rig a gravity floor plate into a booby trap that would grab a kzin in a sudden six-g field. But when she tried to plan with them, she understood why they needed her. What they didn't have was an overall strategic sense. When one starts a battle, it sets off an avalanche of activity. The good commander is able to predict where the avalanche will go, and have his responses already in place.

She could make detailed plans, but could they follow orders? Can a slave follow orders? She was willing to bet that they could.

Some of the events she wasn't going to be able to predict. So far as Nora knew, the human hyperfleet was already fighting at Alpha Centauri. That was one wild card—she could be vaporized by her comrades before the mutiny even started. On the other hand, the *Nesting-Slashtooth-Bitch* was the most sluggish ship of the Third Black Pride and so would reach its new station many days later than the maneuverable elements of its squadron. *If* the mutiny could be carried out before they reached the battle, their chances were much better. Haste was in order.

Lieutenant Nora Argamentine did not expect to sur-

vive the mutiny, so she was optimizing her strategy
for maximum kzin kill. She wanted as many kzin dead
as possible before the inevitable moment when her
plans fell apart. Meticulously, with the information the
slaves gave her, she targeted every kzin on board the
Bitch. Mellow-Yellow was at the bottom of the list.
He could be killed by flooding his hibernation cell
with liquid nitrogen—but not while she still needed
her Jotoki allies.

They were able to manufacture her nerve gas. That
surprised her at first until she remembered what Mellow-Yellow had been doing to the children. He had
some kind of "grant" to do "medical research" on
humans. No, she was not going to spare that one.

The Jotoki fiends even cobbled together hand weapons. They had a spaceman's usual devout respect for
high-velocity projectiles and high-energy cutting tools.
The result was a launcher for a concussion pellet that
could hemorrhage a kzin's insides but wouldn't damage bulkheads.

The *Bitch*'s manufacturing shop was designed for
interstellar war. You didn't fly in spare parts to an
interstellar battle, you tooled up for anything, on the
spot, at a moment's notice and burped out one-of-a-
kind items. It was incomprehensible to Nora that such
facilities could be trusted to slaves, but then she wasn't
a kzin.

The attack began in the dorm. The airseal bulkheads sealed without triggering alarms—gas flooded
the rooms, stayed, and was flushed out—the airseal
bulkheads unlocked. A gas-killed kzin looks like he's
asleep except that he's not breathing.

Jotoki who were not already at their stations on regular jobs began to move to their assigned position.
The Command Center was gassed. Hrith-Master-
Officer was comprehending what was happening to
him at the same time his nervous system was failing

to obey his order to sound a gas alarm. The officer farthest from the air purifier did issue that alarm before he died.

The surviving kzinti moved efficiently into their battle armor, which was gas-proof—alert, thoroughly alarmed, and ready for action. They were primed for orders, and they got them: "Battle Stations!" That was the wrong order. The ship was being attacked internally, not from an external threat. "Boarding Stations!" would have been a better order. "Damage Containment!" might have worked. Even "Abandon Ship!" would have collected them into a defensible position. "Battle Stations!" just dispersed them to known destinations, along known routes, across Jotok-devised booby traps. A Jotok, in a rack-held *Ztirgor*, picked off the kzin who tried to pass through the hangar.

Lieutenant Argamentine was master-minding the battle from a tiny munitions closet which had been jury-rigged into the *Bitch*'s main communications net, finally wearing trousers and a shirt she'd *ordered* her Jotoki allies to make for her, plus an ugly kzin oxygen mask, retailored for her head. She knew the jig was up when a kzin commando team retook the Command Center, killing the occupying Jotoki, and cut off her contact.

They could trace her location.

She evacuated instantly, taking the best position she could, facing down both legs of an L-shaped corridor, her only weapon the improvised concussion-pellet launcher. Hunkering behind her portable stun-gun barricade, she knew that this was where she was going to die. She wondered what the kids would think when they came out of sedation. She was damned if she wanted to die in a cage.

Without warning, a stun-bolt ripped down the corridor, covering the advance of a kzin clean-up team.

The barricade hardly did any good at all. She felt the bolt hit her back, probably from a bounce off a wall, numbly noting that her fingers were now so frozen that she could hardly fire off the concussion rounds— one at the lead kzin, one at the kzin behind, and one for good measure at the blind bend from whence they had appeared. The blasts went off. She was suddenly deaf and her paralyzed legs refused to propel her out of the way but she saw the disabled kzinti carried toward her down the gravityless corridor. She felt the thuds on the wall as she was buried in kzin armor.

When a little girl studied war, odd things stuck in her memory. Now she was remembering the fragment of a twentieth century Frenchman's letter from a hospital near Reims describing how he had spent four days buried with eight dead comrades on top of him in a shell-destroyed trench.

The duty of a soldier is to wait. And while one is waiting, paralyzed, life goes on. Three Jotoki raced around the corner, chattering in their pseudo–Hero's Tongue. Efficient hands rolled the kzinti over, removed their helmets and slit their throats. They stripped the corpses of weapons, piled the armored bodies in a neat barricade for Nora, reloaded her launcher, and propped her up facing down the L. Two of the beasts skittered away. The third remained just long enough to give her a shot of paralysis antidote— effective for a kzin but no better than a bee sting for a human. Hands rearranged her trousers, and then he, too, was gone.

The duty of a soldier is to wait, soaked in the blood of an enemy, fingers unable to fire, praying that the fingers will come back to life before it is necessary to kill again.

Daddy had been burned alive.

Eventually Long-Reach arrived, arguing with himselves about how to help Nora. Three Jotoki carried her away for a bath by multitudinous arms. While her mouth was still only able to make the noises of a baby trying to discipline its tongue, she learned of their impossible victory.

Lieutenant Argamentine couldn't speak her joy but her eyes could leak. *If General Fry could see me now, naked and being bathed by monster slaves!*

Long-Reach was combing out her hair with three hands, caressing the auburn richness of it, fluffing it, adding proteins to it to give body. He knew how to take care of a pelt!

"Did . . . Mellow . . . Yellow . . . survive?"

"Slept through it all. Like a kit."

Nora grinned to herself. *One to go!* A half an hour later, when she could speak coherently, she suggested the dehibernation of Mellow-Yellow.

Long-Reach was uneasy. The other Jotoki became somber in their fear. "Not now. First we clean up ship. Blood! Dents! Awful mess!" Big(arm) added somberly, "He must never know." Freckled(arm) shivered. "The rage if he finds out . . ."

"Lie to a kzin, and it's the torture chamber for you," said Nora knowingly.

"The mutiny never happened!" said Long-Reach adamantly. "All is as it was."

The Jotoki knew enough about gravity polarizers to alter course. They were almost at turnover by the time of the revolt and were doing a quarter of the velocity of light. They didn't try to decelerate. They just changed direction—with deep space as their only destination.

One team spaced the kzin corpses. Each corpse was ejected violently by the polarizer field in a transient restabilization of the ship's energy and momentum balance. Other teams cleaned and scrubbed and repaired. Long-Reach slaughtered all Jotoki who were bonded to deceased kzin, dressing and storing them for Mellow-Yellow's table.

For the first time in millennia, the ancient conquerors of the barbarian warlords of Kzin-home commanded their own warship.

CHAPTER 24
(2420 A.D.)

Hibernation did damp the immediacy of the thoughts and rages with which one went into hibernation, but there was no memory loss upon revival. Waking up and expecting to confront Grraf-Hromfi and possible death, to find oneself instead the master of a kzinless lumbering drydock headed off in the general direction of kzinspace was a disorienting experience. At the minimum he should have rated a navigator and crew.

Trainer-of-Slaves's first assumption had been that Grraf-Hromfi had undergone a drastic change of liver, had seen the reasonableness of the request to flee the battle with the superluminal motor and had simply sent him on his way. It was the only *logical* assumption. Everything was in order. The *Shark* was still in the hangar—the first thing he checked—and the *Bitch* was shipshape.

But Grraf-Hromfi *didn't trust Jotoki to massage his pelt*, let alone take command of a ship. Something else had happened. Trainer didn't have the time to ponder.

He was new to ship command and priority tasks kept cropping up and demanding his attention. Still, he noticed things.

The record of orders was absent. The log file was too clean. The transfer of command was broken. *When* had his Jotoki been forced to take command? He couldn't even locate information about how the developing battle at Alpha Centauri had ended. The last he'd heard it had been chaos—UNSN superluminal vehicles winking on, Grraf-Hromfi foaming at the mouth about mythical green-scaled monsters trying to take over his mind, a feral flotilla of animal rockjacks converging on the monster, and a massive mobilization of the Fifth Fleet to the wrong rendezvous at the wrong time.

Now not a word of that. Not a sniff of kzin fur. Not a trace of kzinti hierarchy. Almost, a discontinuity.

In all this pastoral calm—no battles, no emergencies—serenity should have been master. But his Jotoki, who had clearly been in command of the ship in violation of standing admiralty orders, were terrified—that's what was wrong.

His slaves were honest. If Grraf-Hromfi had found himself in a hopeless situation and had ordered the *Bitch* to flee under Jotoki control, they would have said so and been proud of Grraf-Hromfi's trust. But they were all running around, tripping all over their arms, trying to please him, inventing orders to be obeyed—and keeping their mouths shut.

It was plain that they were expecting their mild-mannered Mellow-Yellow to murder them all. Each of them had the fear of the Fanged God in all of their five hearts. Trainer couldn't bear to question them. He insisted, absolutely, upon the truth from his slaves—but sometimes the truth was better left unsaid. He had never, ever, questioned Long-Reach or Joker or Creepy about the death of Puller-of-Noses. The subject had always been taboo.

Murder in the service of loyalty.

Jotok-Tender had mumbled about Jotok loyalty as if it were a sin when he was drinking too deeply of his contraband sthondat blood. The rumors about their treachery were true but Trainer had always put that down to poor slavecraft. Was it more? Did a threatened bond sometimes lead to a murderous frenzy?

He examined the ship for evidence of murder, and found not a mark. His suspicion was absurd, of course. He knew his Jotoki very well. Perhaps they were capable of well-meaning murder, but they were *not* capable of *organized* mutiny. Their education had been standardized for ages. Military prowess was not part of it. Indeed, military prowess had been systematically bred out of their root stock.

But there was something else he was noticing. His Jotok slaves were carefully shielding him from that she-man Lieutenant Argamentine. They were taking care of the cages all too well. He purred at such a revealing insight. In the mystery surrounding his revival, he had forgotten her, and no one had reminded him.

He had pity for his Jotoki, but he had no scruples about questioning a man-beast. She must be healthy by now.

While he thought about it, he spent time in the Command Center checking the *Bitch*'s course towards faint R'hshssira. Navigation was not his specialty, but he'd spent half his life out under the interstellar heavens absorbed by the majesty of the celestial sphere. He had the lore of perhaps twice octal-cubed stars etched into the passion lobe of his liver. Finding his way was no problem. It was avoiding the treacherous shoals of mass that was the navigator's art and pride and nightmare—and at that Trainer was an amateur.

Nora Argamentine was in a sullen mood when he found her in the cages. His Jotoki had exceeded their authority by merging four of the barred boxes into one large space for her and the children, but he had to agree that the new arrangement was a better one. The three children cried when they saw him.

"Silence, slaves!" he said, and they were silent.

"So, your little tricksters let you out of the cold box, did they? They had the command of a whole warship to themselves, and they let *you* out."

"I trust my Jotoki in all things. But Grraf-Hromfi would never have trusted this vessel to any Jotok without a wide-awake kzin on hand," he said. "I'm curious how that happened."

"Ask them!"

He unlocked the cage, and turned to the apprehensive children to reassure them. "I'll only be questioning her for a short while. She'll be right back."

He pulled her out by the arm, and kept her more or less at arm's reach so that she couldn't attack him, thus propelling her to the inter-floor capsule station. She tried to shake off his arm. "I'm not fighting." But she was resisting every Patriarch's toe-length of the way.

In the kzin-sized chair of the torture chamber, he strapped her down and attached the instruments. He set up the vocoder to monitor their conversation so that there would be no misunderstandings. "Tell me the truth and there will be no pain," he said gently.

"I've been here before and I *killed* my torturer."

The muddled situation was beginning to clear. Female acumen could only be a tiding of vast troubles. "Hr-r, this is the truth?"

"Why should I cover for your perfidious little tricksters?"

"They betrayed you?"

"They tranquilized me and put me back in the cages. They betrayed *themselves*."

"What happened? I can't question them—their fear produces an agony of pity in my liver regions. My shame is that they are my friends."

"Friends? Together we cleaned you ratcats out of this ship in half an hour. They took a positive pleasure in the mayhem. I made one mistake." She spat at him. "I let *you* live."

There was a low growl in his voice despite himself. Here was the leader of the mutiny. Now events made sense. "Details!" he insisted.

She told him where he could stuff his tail.

He turned on the nerve-stim.

"All right, all right. Why should I cover for your monsters?" There was no way for her to withhold the story of the mutiny—but she could make him work for it. She described the attack as if it were a spontaneously lucky uprising, careful not to mention the nerve gas, steeling herself to resist "offering" its chemical structure if he pressed her—but he didn't ask for details. He was too appalled by the total picture. She sensed, surprised, that he didn't *want* to see his Jotoki as killers. He even released her restraints as a way of telling her that he wanted no more answers.

"I should space them all!" he roared.

"Why don't you? I'll help!"

"I've had that dilemma before. Then who would cover my back? Kzin who hunt alone are vulnerable." He whacked his tail against the bulkhead in annoyance. "You led them astray," he accused.

"Will you execute me?"

"Females are not responsible for their actions. It is not your fault that you are intelligent. The Fanged God has his jokes."

"I can see you on my living room rug by the fireplace," she snarled, twisting her curl.

He did not reply. Her story of massacre had sobered him. What *other* terrible consequences of female intelligence were there? A thinking, talking female could severely disturb a household by teaching what she knew to her litter. His mind reeled at the thought of female military genius within a kzinrret palazzo! They would steal the younglings! They would turn youth against wisdom!

How unlucky for a race to have been cursed with such a cruel twist of evolution. He felt his first stab of pity for mankind. In the last two hundred generations, just on Man-home alone, there had been more wars than in all the expanse of Kzinspace and more death by war on that one planet than in all of the wars waged by Heroes to protect the Long Peace. What else could arise while female quickness sowed dissent between father and sons?

Such a waste of the feminine essence which could be better employed in play with kits and on the mating couch with males.

He put the torture implements away. A black-fingered paw touched her auburn tresses. He was missing his long lost Jriingh. "Do not be afraid of me. I am a strange kzintosh, known for the unwarlike feelings I have in my liver for my slaves. You have beautiful natural hair. I shall see to it that you grow a fine pelt over your nakedness. You have your feral flaws, but your intelligence can be improved."

This female was perfectible. No hurry. It was a long journey home.

CHAPTER 25
(2420–2423 A.D.)

The *Nesting-Slashtooth-Bitch* was sluggish but her cruising velocity was as high as any large kzin warship. Three and a half years was the estimated trip-time to Hssin, which was 2.6 light-years from Alpha Centauri. Detection was unlikely even though they might now be traveling through hyperdrive infested space. Hssin lay 5.6 light-years to the north of Man-sun. Nobody could patrol that much volume any more than an acorn could patrol an ocean.

He was going to have problems with his female. Keeping experimental animals caged was expedient, but a cage would not do for slave breeding and he was anxious to begin his breeding program. He had a sufficiency of frozen sperm. He probably *did* need to do more experimentation, but without a source of experimental animals, that was no longer an option. He'd have to use what he already knew.

But if he gave the Nora-beast the breeding room a female needed, even built her a kzinrret palazzo with enough space for her children, he was leaping into trouble. He picked the larger of the crew dormitories for her, but left her in her cage while he refitted the room—think before you leap!

The original dorm layout was not sabotage-proof. If he were building an ordinary palazzo, that would not matter. But he knew very well that she was dedicated to destroying the *Shark*—and would give her life to do so. Next on her priority list was killing the one kzin she'd missed when she'd used his Jotoki against the Patriarchy. Feral intelligence in a female was a captivating nuisance. He dare not underestimate her.

The walls he had his Jotoki armor-plate. He built in monitors to watch her for dangerous behavior. They weren't the most intelligent of monitors but they probably wouldn't gas her too frequently if she was careful.

When her chambers were ready, he took her for a visit. She was wearing clothes again, he noted disapprovingly. They weren't decorative but they did cover her tail-like baldness.

"I like it," Nora said laconically. "It reminds me of the *Alabama*. The munitions room."

"The Alabama?"

"You wouldn't know the war. The USN *Alabama* was a seagoing battleship with a steelclad munitions room that could take an internal explosion—hopefully without sinking the ship."

He listened and then ran her words through his vocoder to make sure of what he'd heard. Dangerous memories. For all he knew, she could make high explosives out of paper and spit. Her memories would have to be replaced, and her emotions would have to be altered, and her facility with language crippled. While she had her memories and her full repertoire of skills, she was dangerous. Perhaps he could add some aesthetically pleasing fur. Then he would be able to relax and enjoy her.

In the meantime he needed her memories.

To please the Nora-beast he let her design the furniture for herself and the children.

"You're really going to let me have whatever I want?" She looked at him with a whimsical smile that he knew was amusement, but which he couldn't help but read as a subliminal warning of attack. Her fingers were twirling with that long curl of hers.

"No weapons," he admonished.

"I want a big stuffed pillow that I can flop into."

His mind worked on that one. How could a pillow be turned into a weapon to kill him when he least suspected it? This was a nerve-racking game. He imagined himself being smothered. His mind's eye watched her soaking the stuffings in nitric acid to make high explosive, while she wove a noose out of the shreaded covering. None of the scenes were plausible. "All right," he said.

He was astonished at the ornate furniture she designed. A bed with a satin roof and adjustable gravity? Golden man-babies with wings, dancing on the headboard? He grumbled but had his Jotoki make them for her, scrounging substitutes for satin and wood. They had to reprogram the weavers and the plastic molders.

The time went quickly because there was so much to do. Deciphering the superluminal drive was top priority. Trainer-of-Slaves couldn't be reckless with the device, couldn't test it to destruction because it was the only one he had. He developed a two-pronged approach.

(1) Analysis. Isolate the sub-units. Attempt to craft a duplicate of the subunit. Test. The *Bitch* was a repair facility that could make any part in the kzin arsenal. He practically owned a prototype factory and he had the slave power to utilize it.

(2) Explore the military memories of Lieutenant Nora Argamentine.

Trainer-of-Slaves had had many years with his experimental animals to determine that human memory was very plastic, approximately five times as plastic as the kzin memory.

Torture could get at gross detail quickly, but it didn't work well with nuances. Every time a human memory was recalled, it was altered in some way. If the memory was recalled to relieve pain—while the brain was saturated in the chemical stew brought on by agony—the memory trace was *drastically* mutated. Torture gradually obliterated the nuances it was meant to recover. He had to veto the use of torture.

Slowly, he worked out other methods.

Trainer-of-Slaves got his best results with Lieutenant Argamentine when he doped her into a sleep state from which she couldn't waken, but in which she remained on the verge of dreaming. He strapped her into a mock-up of the *Shark*'s cockpit and fed her dreaming-mind virtual images of combat conditions in which she was being attacked by kzin warcraft. Winning kept up her interest in the dreams and reduced her anxiety.

While she was dreaming, he read off her motor responses. That told him what she was doing to counter the images he was feeding to her eyes. From that he learned the combat characteristics of the *Shark*. For one thing, he discovered that phasing into hyperspace took half an hour to set up. For another thing, he learned that the *Shark* had only been captured because of an engine malfunction.

All this while Trainer-of-Slaves was studying his female as an evolutionary curiosity. In a bisexual animal, the rational female was clearly an unwanted trait for domestication. If kzinti were to husband properly obedient human slaves—and the Nora-beast was not properly obedient—child-animal care would have to be divorced from male-child teaching. With second, third, and fourth, etc., voices from the harem subverting the patriarch's word, a household would disintegrate into chaos. Monkey society must be shifting around like the surface of a quake-world!

He explained all this to Nora, but she was just as stubborn as Grraf-Hromfi's sons while she sat under her canopy, arguing back with inappropriate aggressiveness for a female. She didn't know how to listen. It was proof that females couldn't use the gift of language even when it was given to them.

In idle moments, when the analysis of the hyperdrive motor had exhausted him, he toyed with hypothetical ways of using chromosome engineering to cure the man-females of male language skills. The daydreams went nowhere because such a neat answer probably wasn't practical.

The kzin solution, which was genetic, wouldn't work.

During Heroic reproduction the male egg combined with the female egg to form a doubled nucleus. The kzincode-groups, not unlike human chromosomes, were then distributed, leaving the super-egg to divide into two fertile male and female eggs which then migrated to the kzinrret's pouch in pairs, a litter always containing an even number of kits, half kzintosh, half kzinrret.

Reproduction wasn't all that dissimilar among monkeys—but there were unfortunate differences. The nuclei of kzincells were more complicated than those of mancells, containing three distinct kinds of protein coding, sexual, major-group, and lumpy-constellation.

The kzincode-strands that determined kzinsex were enormous, four times as large as any strand in the major kzincode-group, and several octals larger than any member of the lumpy kzincode-constellation. In male cells the kzintosh-strand appeared *twice*, while in female cells a dominant kzintosh-strand was lord over the *single* kzinrret-strand, the latter acting to edit physical size and repress language in the female who carried it.

It would be difficult to genetically engineer male sex dominance in the man-beasts because with these animals it was the *female* who carried the twinned sex chromosome! A perverse reversal of the normal situation. Given their genetic makeup one might well wonder how *male* monkeys, balding and hemophiliac, came to be intelligent! Worse, the male and female sex-chromosomes of the man-beast were normal-sized, the male chromosome runtish, even, and unlike the kzintosh-strand or the kzinrret-strand, were not major centers of developmental switching.

In any event, Trainer-of-Slaves wasn't in a hurry to destroy the Nora-beast's intelligence. As a younger, more reckless researcher his haste had ruined many promising experiments. *Think before you leap.*

Intelligence had many facets, and it was disastrous to confuse its parts, to destroy one thing when you thought you were destroying another. It was better to be patient, to alter only small pieces of her mind at a time—and then carefully observe the incremental change as a guidepost to the next change.

Several months into their journey, the Lieutenant actually did try to destroy the ship. She used furniture parts to escape. She assembled a makeshift gas mask to keep herself conscious during the breakout, and she headed straight for the ship's vital parts through an airconditioner she'd learned about from the Jotoki at the time of the mutiny. She had memorized the ship too well!

He found her unconscious. She had been stopped by a whimsical trap he had set up more as a paranoid afterthought than as a serious line of defense. He had been reading too much Chuut-Riit who believed in covering low-probability events.

The Nora-beast insisted on wearing clothes, to her downfall. He had tried to argue her out of it, to reach her sensibilities by creating virtual images for her eyes of elephants in sombreros and boleros, of newts in weskits, of giraffes in middies, of yaks in yoke skirts, but she had only laughed until her curls shook and told him that she had been brought up on books in which animals wore clothes. Obscene! Imagine having to unbutton a *vatach*'s vest before devouring him!

When Trainer lost the argument he had simply booby-trapped her trousers to release a nerve poison into her skin if she ever came too close to electromagnetic triggers in certain vital installations.

Lying beside her was a lethal firebomb. Where had she obtained the oxidizer? From the air! Trainer-of-Slaves growled in disgust at his oversight. What would a monkey do with a harem of these creatures! How did the males survive?

That incident decided Trainer. Her memories had to go. She was already clamped to the operating table when she recovered consciousness.

"We're still here. I goofed," she said sadly, near tears.

If she'd been kzin, she would have earned a partial name as a break-out artist. "Forget it," he growled. "The *Alabama* was designed not to sink."

"Are the kids all right?" Now she *was* crying. The three cage- and brain-damaged orphans were her responsibility. She didn't know whether she was a mother or a UNSN Lieutenant.

"Long-Reach is in there teaching them how to play cards."

"Louie won't be able to learn. You *hurt* him. He can't concentrate."

Trainer-of-Slaves was unmoved. He had grown up in a society with a high kit mortality rate. The younglings died routinely by violence and neglect. There were always more where they came from. Suffering was the way to Heroism.

"You're going to hurt me now, too, aren't you? You're going to carve me up? Make a drooling idiot out of me?"

She was afraid. He had an unnatural compassion in his liver for that combination, fear and bravery. "I'm going to sew a tail on your backside," he growl-hissed. It was his way of trying to crack a joke.

She came out of the operation with artificial gland implants in her brain. She didn't feel any different. Her mind was clear. She was still driven to destroy the *Shark*. She still hated kzin.

Trainer-of-Slaves had been spending his spare time away from the *Shark* completing his mathematical model of the human brain. It wasn't all that difficult. The data-link did most of the work. All he had to do was enter the special human conditions (taken from the autodoc and his experiments) into the generalized model that kzin physiologists had developed eons ago to cover diverse organic brains—Jotok, Kzin, kdatlyno, Chunquen, etc. They were all different and they were all the same.

Memory erasure was a delicate matter. Memories were all interrelated like a giant n-dimensional crossword puzzle. No memory could be erased without snipping out pieces of a myriad of other memories. And the erased memory could always be reconstructed by "filling in" the empty puzzle blanks. The reconstruction went on automatically by the mere act of using the remaining memories. The missing pieces were "interpolated" during recall. If the erasure had been caused by wetware destruction, the "interpolated" information was simply stored elsewhere.

Organic brains, having evolved over hundreds of millions of years of deadly struggle, were systems designed to military specs. They could take great damage with minimal degradation of performance. No single location was vital for system operation. And efficient redundancy insured that even heavy losses of data were recoverable.

That meant that Trainer couldn't erase the whole of the Nora-beast's memory at once without killing her. What he could do was set up a steady degradation of memory that didn't overwhelm the general homeostatic balance. He could alternately shrink and accelerate the dendritic root growth of her neurons, disconnect and randomly reconnect. He could arbitrarily change the strength of the synaptic coefficients. He could switch on or off the machinery that converted short-term memory into long term memory.

He could turn on or off specific neural receptor sites in a way that unbalanced her brain so that it had to compensate with rapid neural learning. He could chemically accelerate learning by up to a factor of twenty, a dangerous game which if continued caused a kind of self-reference that left the mind fixated upon one event. Rapid learning overwrote old memories faster than they could be reconstituted.

The brain normally learned in spurts. Neural disequilibrium induced by failure turned learning on until a new equilibrium state was reached. Success turned learning off. *Constant* learning degraded old memories without ever giving them time to reintegrate into a new equilibrium state.

The Wunderland autodoc had taught Trainer-of-Slaves another neat trick. Using a carrier pseudo-virus, he could induce a neuron to suicide by budding. The bud killed its parent upon detaching but the bud then either reproduced itself (under one kind of stimulus) or began to sprout an axion (under a second stimulus). If the neural attachment sites were active, the axion would sprout dendrites and hardwire itself into the brain. That was another way of nondestructively degrading old memories.

The fur-growing gland he had implanted was only a whim.

He was not yet ready to tackle the disassembly and rewiring of her language processor. One leap at a time.

When the Nora-female recuperated he had an ice cream party for her in her rebuilt palazzo. Probably it was still not "monkey-proof" but it was the best he could do. The major improvement was a removable barricade across the nursery, so that she could get some peace from the little monsters if she wanted it. Louie was indeed impulsively destructive. The girls were all right. They fought each other like two kzinti in a tournament ring, and each was jealous of the attention that the Nora-beast gave the other. Brunhilde would die in a few years of too many brain cells.

Long-Reach played with the children while Trainer-of-Slaves was lounging on the giant pillow eating his liver-and-kidney ice cream. He spoke to Nora, unable to keep his eyes off her face.

"Hrr-r. You are very precious to me. I want you alive. But the hyperdrive motor is even more precious. It is precious to the Patriarchy. If you try to escape again, I will kill you."

"If I don't kill you first." She was picking out the purple berries and eating them before tasting her ice cream. She had dimples. It was the first time he noticed.

He grinned, trying hard to imitate a human smile by forcing a curl to his lips. "Forget you ever said that."

When they reached R'hshssira Nora's fur was coming in nicely. She wore a lustrous pelt that had changed her from an ugly pink "tail" into a stunningly handsome animal. She could still argue fluently in English, after a fashion, between the pauses, and he hadn't yet found a way to impregnate her with twins.

CHAPTER 26
(2423 A.D.)

Short-Son of Chiirr-Nig, alias Eater-of-Grass, alias Trainer-of-Slaves, was home and excited. Why did he love that hot stove, R'hshssira? What was Hssin to him? Why was he looking forward to wandering through the old Jotok Run and gossiping with Jotok-Tender?

He sat in the Command Center trying to read the instruments long before they got there. He was baby-sitting Louis for his Nora-female because the boy's hostility was running her ragged and she needed a rest.

"Grrough! Stay away from that!" he commanded in slave patois. He whacked the boy, not too hard, and returned to his seat. "Come over here. I'll have something to show you soon." He was hoping to interest Louis in the stars. Younglings brought out the father in a kzin, no matter how badly they behaved, and this one was his only male.

The electromagnetic silence disturbed Trainer. Had his instrument gone dead?

Louis was already back into mischief, glancing warily at the kzin to see if he dared do what he really wanted to do. He decided that he could. The kzin was busy.

When the *Bitch* had maneuvered closer into the R'hshssira system, the electronic telescope confirmed the awful truth. Trainer-of-Slaves let out a wretched scream of anguish. Destruction. The man-ghouls had been here first! They had come and gone. There wasn't a glimmer of any spacefaring. He howled and clawed the walls!

Louis dived under the astrogator's desk, terrified, leaving the fragment of plastic wall-stripping half stuffed into the computer slot.

The wrathful kzin saw only a monkey trying to destroy his machine. A claw scooped the screaming child out from under the desk, ripping jaws beheading him to silence the shriek. Angrily Trainer shook the child apart, the bloodlust driving him to devour an arm. But he wasn't hungry. He dropped the corpse and beat his breast.

The Fanged God had forsaken them without warning! Hssin would have had no news from Ka'ashi—he reverted to the kzin name for Wunderland, unable to speak or think the human words. He howled! Death would have come from the heavens with superluminal surprise! His family wouldn't have had a chance. His mother! He tore his mane with bloody claws, bellowing. Hamarr the beautiful, his beloved comforter, his youth, his earliest friend! Dead! He stormed around the Control Center, smashing his Ka'ashi relics, things he had collected from that planet with love. Hamarr would have been fascinated by the porcelain, shattered now against the bulkhead.

The rage of a kzin knows no bounds. But it subsides, sometimes into anguished mewling. He went to his oldest friends—Long-Reach, Joker, Creepy, who stared, shocked by the blood on his vest.

"Jotok-Tender is dead," he wailed, and they grieved with him for grief is the universal emotion that does not even need intelligence to wrack the soul. It comes from the liver.

They helped him clean up the Control Center. A trip to the planet showed the details of the fury of the man-monsters. In some places the destruction was total. Where the power plant had been was only slag. But it doesn't take much to kill a space colony. Holes in the roofs.

In the Jotok Run they found a desiccated Jotok, one of the wily ferals, clinging to his tree, the powder-dry leaves still green. They found giant Jotok-Tender in his kitchen with a dehydrated grin defiantly threatening a bowl of preserved *vatach*. His Jotok slave had died trying to help him, now convulsed into an emaciated heap.

By torchlight they found Hamarr holding three tiny mummified kits; not her own, for she was too old to bear such a litter. He hunched beside his mother, taking her dried corpse in his arms, howling in his helmet. Her face still seemed to be whimpering silently, almost alive. Even the flesh-rotting bacteria had died. They found a roomful of suffocated kzinretti and kits, the room sealed against the poisonous Hssin atmosphere.

Somewhere there must be survivors? Without rest, he searched. A shelter, a special life support unit must have withstood the attack? A city that lives in a deadly atmosphere is not one single unit, it is a collection of self-contained cells built around the *assumption* of disaster. The death of cells is possible—but *some* cells survive! Trainer searched, for days, with tireless Joker whose arms slept in rotation. Then the kzin had to sleep. All he found were signs of human infantry who had been there after the air attack in a thorough campaign of genocide.

Exile. The crew of the *Bitch* was still in exile. They were still alone. Eleven Jotoki, one man-female, two orphans and a kzin.

Back on the ship Nora asked him what had happened down there. She wanted to ask him what had become of Louis, but she didn't dare. She felt his rage. Poor maltreated Louis who hated everybody and would only obey and smile when you were looking straight into his eyes and being stern.

Trainer-of-Slaves had stopped talking to Nora in English, had broken off all her access to her own culture. He spoke to her now in the corrupt form of the Hero's Tongue which he used to communicate with his Jotoki. "No one lives on Hssin," he spat-growled. "Your Navy has murdered them, kits and all."

I shouldn't have let him baby-sit Louis, she thought. She had had a theory that kzin males must have lots of paternal abilities inside somewhere, since their females were so mentally limited. *I was trying to stimulate his compassion. Compassion? That was my excuse.*

Actually, Nora had needed time off from Louis. Stupid. Louis could work even "love-everybody Nora" into a murderous rage. Imagine what he could do to a kzin who had just lost his family and nation?

I think My Hero killed Louis. "What happened to Louis?" she asked in the staccato patois because she wanted a reply.

He wouldn't tell her. He turned away, as contrite as a kzin who has just eaten one of his own kits.

But later, as he was making plans to move her down to Hssin, he did talk to her about Louis, however obliquely. He told a story about his own family. He was reminiscing about Hssin and recalled for Nora the

day his father murdered a youngling half-brother on
a point of discipline.

*Poor doomed Louis. I saved him and then I fed him
back to the lion's den.* She felt horrible that all she
felt was relief. Maybe with her pelt of chimpanzee/
kzinrret fur she really was turning into a kzin.

constructed—and invisible to curious eyes. I don't know what to make of its contents. Found trinkets, I would call them. What kind of a mind would think such things beautiful enough to cherish? Dare I make the analogy of a dog hiding precious bones from his master?

I was touched as I stared at the trinkets. Is that what I am to become, a mind who values such simple things and knows somewhere in her soul that her master will not let her keep such junk?

I am living a nightmare. I can't kill myself because of the girls, who are pathetic in their need for me, and I can't escape. My brain is dissolving slowly and I don't know enough about the human mind to know what parts of it he's going to leave me. I can't feel the difference from day to day—except for the temporary rushes and blackouts he triggers with his gizmo—but I *can* tell the difference from last year and I fear the future. For instance, I'm not sure I'm qualified anymore to lead a mutiny.

Sometimes I don't believe that My Hero is doing this to me, and then I stroke the soft auburn fur on my body and know that, yes, he is. I can't argue with him. I've tried. He is like some men I know. He listens. I feel his kindness, even his love—but he doesn't *listen*!

Brunhilde is dying of some malady of perception that has grown markedly worse in the last year. Some days she can't take care of herself or eat. Jacin is thin, chronically insecure, and epileptic. I expect neither of them to live, but I try. Louis was beyond my meager skills—poor abandoned, caged, brutalized child!

Once, back on the ship, when I was going out of my mind with worry, I asked My Hero for help with the children's health. He had the *practical* suggestion that they be destroyed. Yet he surprised me. He actually read my horror at his suggestion and came back a day later with an experimental program of damage control. Wetware revision and editing. He couldn't promise results.

How can I bear this life—to let my girls die, perhaps like Louis, or to ask My Hero to experiment on them again to fix what he has botched? Would *anyone* trust him with girls?

Day 4
The kzin use an octal clock and a hopelessly complicated dating system. I really have lost track of what time it is, what day it is, what month it is. Females aren't supposed to care about such things. The year, I think, is 2423. I have periods of blankness, where whole days are missing. Of these I remember nothing. That makes keeping track of time even harder. I could put X's on my prison wall. Would that mean anything? How do I know when it is a new day? I'm arbitrarily assigning this day the number four, counting from the day of planetfall.

Writing is easier than talking for me now. When I write I have time to remember the words, to pause and rebuild what I've lost or to think my way around any mental block. Nora-From-My-Future, if you are reading this over and do not understand it, I am writing it because my memory is going. The loss is subtle. But I have noticed that if I *practice* remembering, I can hold on to things. It is when I forget to remember, that I forget how to remember what I want to remember.

Practice. Practice. Practice. Remember that.

THIS IS MY MEMORY. If you've forgotten something, Nora, maybe you'll find it here. Maybe. My ability to learn doesn't seem to be impaired, except during the blanks. My Hero has told me that I'll always be able to learn as well as I do now, I just won't be able to talk or think with words. He's phasing out English and phasing in Heroic patois. Then he's going to phase out the patois. Thanks a lot, buster!

He's also phasing out the Earth. All the early parts of my life.

I try to remember Earth. I do not want to forget Earth. I remember my home town and the cornfields. I can see the afternoon sun on the church steeple. I know where I went to high school. I remember holding Benny's wrist when he was trying to kiss me and fondle my breasts at the same time. It was in the gazebo behind the lilacs in the backyard of the Yankovich place. But I can't for the life of me remember the *name* of my home town. How could I forget that?

Day 5

Sin is a wonderful moniker for this planet. That is as close as I can come to the hiss-rumblings that pass for its name in the Hero's Tongue. It is an awful place.

I no longer have a hope of getting to the *Shark*. I can only pray that the UNSN finds it like they found Sin, then blows it to hell. Maybe My Hero will never fix the hyperdrive engine, but don't count on that. He is obsessive about his work and the hyperdrive is always on his mind. Those five-armed mechanics of his are *good*. I think kzin science is much better than we supposed back on ... dammit, I can't even remember the name of my base. It begins with

a J, I'm sure. It has the same name as the rock
at the head of the Mediterranean Sea. Tomorrow
I'll remember.

I have no idea whether My Hero is a great
scientist or only a mediocre one. I do know that
the aids he has available to him terrify me. I've
seen him tackle problems that make me chuckle.
I relish the decade he's going to spend beating
his brains out—and then he just looks up the
answer in that ding-bat of his, tailors the answer
to his needs and zips on to the next problem. An
answer might be buried in the work of some
obscure kzin scholar who lived when the Romans
were raping the . . . whoever the hell they were
. . . and he can zero in on that answer faster than
I can slurp a bowl of soup even if he starts with
the wrong question. The ease with which he can
search makes up for his lack of curiosity. God
help us if they get the hyperdrive!

And then again maybe it doesn't matter about
the *Shark*. Nobody has a monopoly on science.
My grandfather used to say that you can't build
a dike with a single brick. There . . . I should
remember the name of my grandfather and I
can't. He had a white beard and a silver handled
cane. Grandmother? Should I remember a
grandmother? It is gaps like that which drive me
wild.

Day 12
I've been neglecting my journal. Brunhilde has
been sick. My Hero surprised me and ran off a
simulation on his ding-bat's human brain model
and came up with some medicine that helps. He
says it won't work for long. Brunhilde doesn't
have a normal human brain anymore (he says).
Something is running amok in there and doing

irreversible haywiring. A side effect of the long ago experiment.

Day 17
I never thought a ratcat had a sense of beauty. But when My Hero looks at me I know he is seeing beauty. He didn't used to see me as beautiful. On Earth, I remember Earth, they have stories about what happens to sailors who spend so much time away from their women. Am *I* starting to think My Hero is beautiful? He's graceful. But I go cross-eyed when I look at him. After all these years, he still scares the shit out of me. I'm living in a palazzo for kzinrretti. *He* put me there. *That* scares the shit out of me.

Day 21
Today My Hero took me out into the City of Sin to show me what my UNSN colleagues have done. He cobbled together an atmosphere suit for me, awkward but servicable. I wouldn't want to take it into space.

General Whatzisname was right. War is hell. Parts of the city around the power station are utterly devastated. That kind of annihilation is so complete that the horror is muted and melted into a dissonant abstract sculpture.

It is the least damaged parts of Sin that give me the heebie-jeebies. The preserved corpses make it a museum of horror.

I flashed on Earth, vividly. I once walked over an American Civil War battlefield. It was only a pile of well-tended mounds that *might* once have been trenches if you exercised your imagination. The thousands of corpses spread over that field disappeared without a trace within months—five centuries before I was born. I suspect that the trenches had collapsed within a year, by then already overgrown with weeds.

Here there are no weeds. Here the corpses remain, freeze-dried and pickled in the gases of Sin. How long will it take to banish the horror? Sin *does* have an active atmosphere. Eventually I suspect that drifting dust will sanitize this speck of man-kzin history.

I can't describe how strange it was for me to walk through the gloom of the Chiirr-Nig household with my giant Hero, trying to imagine how a kzin patriarch ran all that, trying to imagine My Hero as a kit. He showed me the very spot where his father murdered his son, the half-brother of my power-driven master. In this one walk I saw a greater range of kzin emotion than I knew existed. He introduced me to his father, quite formally, still frozen in the rictus agony of suffocation, trying to reach his oxygen mask. The evidence of a total surprise attack is everywhere.

Long ago My Hero gave his mother the funeral rites. His father he won't touch.

We took a long walk in the old Jotok Run, climbing down through a hole in the roof. Why did My Hero want to show me the very spot where he met Long-Reach? He stayed there lost in contemplation and then he showed me all the trails that Long-Reach had once shown him. I can't imagine what it was like with smells and breezes, with waving leaves and baby Jotoki crawling out of the marshes. All I saw was a petrified forest from hell. When you stand in the light of R'hshssira you know you are in hell.

Why does he want to show me this when he is going to erase it all from my mind, and then erase my ability even to put it into poetry?

Day 62

Brunhilde died today. That rat-tailed Seventh Son-of-a-Ghoul wanted to *eat* her! God knows we are short of fresh meat. I had to pull a fit. There is a strange power in being a kzinrret. I can rage at him without triggering his anger. He just gives me what I want. We cremated her. I put the ashes in a delicate little box, carved and inlaid, once owned by a noble kzinrret of the very palazzo that is now mine. The box must have been given as a gift by some male.

Day 63

There is only so much power in rage. My Hero does not *always* give me what I want. He won't strike me, but when I cross some line, he just becomes stubborn: kindly stubborn, amused stubborn, arrogantly stubborn, angrily stubborn, passively stubborn—implacable, in other words. (I keep words like implacable on a list so I won't forget them. My list is hidden with the trinkets that no kzintosh must see.)

What did we fight about? A subject dear to me: The Second Phase of his attack on my brain. He's going to start chipping away at my ability to process language. I think I'm in for another "operation." He can black me out with his gismo that runs the gland implants in my brain. When I start remembering again there will be a blank of unknown length. I'll never know whether or not I've had an operation.

He isn't going to do brain surgery. He's going to set up a disassembler and hardwire reorganizer. Neural networks resist such changes so the whole effect will be a transition rather than a discontinuity.

He says it is safe. He says that the language

processing ability was added last to the functions of the human brain and so is the easiest to disconnect. He says I don't need language to think with. Of course, I won't be able to *communicate* what I'm thinking to anyone else and won't be able to tap into anyone else's thoughts, but I'll be able to think! Great! *Isolated* is what I'll be. And I'll start to hoard trinkets or something.

My Hero swears by the Fanged God and his mother's nipples that he isn't the Wild Leaper that he was in his youth when he did all those botched experiments on helpless orphans. He's checked out what he intends to do to me on the model of the human brain that he built out of the genetic codes he took from the autodoc. He says he built that model so he wouldn't have to risk hurting me! I'm having apoplexy! (Hurrah! Yesterday I tried all day to remember the word "apoplexy"! Is that the way to spell it?)

Sometimes I love the bastard as a kind of strange friend of fate, but I'd kill My Hero if I could. I would! I would! He says that's why I must change, so I won't hate him enough to kill him, so I won't be intelligent enough to figure out a way to kill him. He doesn't understand that I only plot to kill him to save myself! He doesn't *understand* that we could be friends. Yes, I'm some kind of possession. I'm to be a slave.

I can't kill him. If I did kill him, his Jotoki would kill me quick as a flash. I could kill them, too. Great. Me and epileptic Jacin up against the universe.

My Hero actually patted me on the head, the paternalistic ... Poor me, what he's doing is working, I can't even remember my naval vocabulary and I used to be able to curse with the best of them!

"Now, now," he said. "Changing our personality is very difficult. I tried for many years on myself and despaired often, but still I persevered and triumphed. You will, too." He thinks of female intelligence as a disease that can be cured.

I think about murder! That is, when I'm not crying.

Jacin follows me around all the time. She won't leave me. She crawls into my bed when I'm asleep. If she knows I want to be alone, she hides behind my back so I won't see her. I've found her under my pillow. I've found her behind my curtains.

Day 243
How can I tell him?

My intelligence is all I have. My language is my way of seeing a greater world. There must be mercy somewhere in that heart of his??????? I try to remember Earth. I no longer know if Ceres is in New York or San Francisco.

After Day 479, Argamentine's day headings become incoherent, and sometimes are missing altogether. The following is one of the last journal entries.

Day is a pretty word. Night and day.
He told me I will talk 500 words. I know that is clump which kzinrret can talk. I tried remember Earth. I saw cornfields. I saw a red scarf. Cornfield cornfield cornfield cornfield ears of yellow corn, red scarf red scarf red scarf around neck, but remember only facts. Earth is 4.3 light years from Wunderland. Earth whirls in space. Whirl pretty word. Cornfield cornfield cornfield.

Remember sight of Earth from space. Earth is
blue with clouds. Pretty Earth.

Sin I remember. House in Sin. Death in Sin.
My Hero won't let me talk English. Write secret
dictionary of Hero-English words. Mnemonic
trick. Clever me. Clever Nora. Clever is pretty
word. Can read English. Practice. Practice day
and night. Easy talk Hero, talk in spits and
snarls. Hard speak English. Write English
because I practice. Practice. Nora is clever. Now
I copy some of words I save.

inkwell pocket shepherd's pie microscope
ultramarine harmonize plumbing joystick wind-
mill insect crawl cornfield tired never-never land
tip-of-tongue tanj . . .

The Nora-beast paced through her palazzo and
always when she came to the great circular rug she
followed the design around in circles because that
seemed to focus her thinking. She was concentrating.
She wore trousers. It was something she wouldn't give
up. A narrow-faced girl, nakedly furless, followed
behind her closely, sporadically complaining in the
Female Tongue.

The furry woman did not forget the girl, and sometimes stroked the child's hair, but she was busy and
concentrating. What she wanted was on the tip of her
tongue but it wouldn't come. Simple Heroic words got
in the way. She had to concentrate.

She gave up for a while and ate a meal. She fed
the girl. She cleaned up the kitchen. She toured the
palazzo to spruce up the rooms. Then she returned to
her single-minded concentration.

It started with a hiss.

She knew that much. Finally a broad grin of triumph crossed her face, dimpling her cheeks. She said
the word aloud, relishing the sounds, all three sylla-

bles. The word did indeed begin with a hiss! She knew it! She repeated the English word over and over again so that she might learn it faster than she forgot it.

When she was sure of her mastery she went to the little niche and took out the book from among the pretty baubles. She opened the book to a fresh page, not looking at the writing because the words no longer meant anything to her and she had a hard time pronouncing them. She knew they were words just like the hissing-staccato words of Her Hero.

She picked up the stylus and wrote her word very carefully, eighteen times, pronouncing it each time with a smile. She knew exactly what it represented. She had the picture in her head. It was important because it *wasn't* a Heroic word. Then she hid the book and hid the stylus. It was the last entry she ever made in her journal.

She couldn't stop smiling. No kzinrret ever smiled like that; it wasn't part of the hardwiring of their brains to do so. She waited impatiently for Her Hero to arrive. He *always* came to lie in her bed with her, stroking her fur, making her feel cozy.

When she heard him at the entrance, heard the airlock cycling, she began to mumble to herself. This time she didn't greet him. She waited coyly for him to come into the stone room with the round rug. She waited until he was right beside her before she turned to him and said her word straight to his face, grinning happily in her victory.

"Centipede," she said, hissing it out. She had the image clearly in her mind, a tiny centipede furry with legs, legs, legs.

For twelve years the crew of the *Nesting-Slashtooth-Bitch* stayed among the ruins of Hssin, living alternately on the ship and in the buildings they had refurbished. The kzin's Jotoki slaves rebuilt the body of the

Shark. The secrets of its hyperdrive motor came less quickly. Without a UNSN operations and repair manual, puzzles that should have been solved in days, took years.

Trainer-of-Slaves learned how to impregnate the Nora-female with sperm extracted from the bodies of his previous experiments. He was delighted to discover that he could always arrange to give her a normal birth of one son and one daughter. Jacin died of a brain seizure. Nora never forgot her and the memory made her fiercely protective of her own twins. She loved Her Hero but she did not trust him with children.

In that twelve years of exile the refugees from Alpha Centauri had to hide from one patrolling UNSN vessel. Two kzin ships arrived and fled, and one unsuspecting kzin flotilla coming into Hssin—probably not even aware that a superluminal war was happening—ran into a UNSN ambush while decelerating. They were wiped out to the last kzin, as a cautious *Bitch* later determined.

The final tests of the refurbished *Shark* took three months. Trainer-of-Slaves was not aware that the war was already over.

CHAPTER 28
(2435 A.D.)

On the fourth dropout from hyperspace, W'kkai-sun was the brightest star in the heavens, two light-days away. It was fifteen light-years from here to Hssin, and they had made it in a miraculous forty-four days. The Empire of the Patriarch would never be the same. They had reached mighty W'kkai!

Trainer-of-Slaves paused for a moment to consider the event. Fifty-eight years ago, bargaining among the rumor-laden bazaars of this illustrious star-system, the great Chuut-Riit had first sniffed the scent of the man-beast and laid his plans for the Patriarch's Glory. In that same year, inside the humble Fortress Walls of Hssin, the runt of Hamarr's new litter had been given the name Short-Son of Chiirr-Nig. Nobody had expected him to live—except his protective mother.

From W'kkai it had taken Chuut-Riit's caravan nineteen years to reach the outpost Hssin. From Hssin it had taken Short-Son of Chiirr-Nig fifty-eight years to reach the legendary W'kkai—by means of a short cut of forty-four days at the end.

In the meantime how had the warriors of Riit and Nig fared? Chuut-Riit was dead, his sons dead, his entourage slaughtered. Chiirr-Nig, who had chosen to stay at Hssin and breed sons, was dead. His brothers were fried corpses circling Man-sun or dead at Ka'ashi. His "warrior" sons had died in the Fourth Fleet or found valiant martyrdom during that final valiant cataclysm at Ka'ashi-suns.

One son had survived. Only one. The runt, the short-son, the eater-of-grass. The coward. The lowly trainer-of-slaves. *The survivor*.

The Nora-beast beside him was suckling her third pair of twins at milk-swollen breasts, fascinated by the heavens as she always was. She didn't like the shutters that were in place during hyperspatial travel, or the dim electric glow of the cabin. Her dimples told him that she was excited that her world had opened up again.

There was a slight hint of human urine on Nora's fur—the boy's soaker needed to be changed again. The baby girl suddenly opened up her eyes for a burp, then closed them and went back to her obsessive sucking. She was going to grow up to be a beauty. She ought to be very marketable as a breeder if he could manage her verbal development to peak at 500 words.

The softly furred female was thinking that she had been very patient with her Mellow-Yellow, but enough was enough! Ex-Lieutenant Argamentine wanted her big room back. With its colors and furs and its baby beds. Where were her other babies? It made her uncomfortable to see them frozen in the hold. They didn't move!

Bad Mellow-Yellow! He'd kept them all cooped up too long in his silly ship. Poor Long-Reach, funny Long-Reach, with no place to put his arms back there. The return of the stars was welcome but big old Mellow-Yellow had tricked her before with those. It didn't

necessarily mean they were home. "We home?" asked
Nora in the elementary hiss-spits of the Female
Tongue. She no longer remembered any English at
all.

The kzin warrior spent a day scanning the sky. He
was looking for the gravitic pulse of a UNSN ship,
worried that they might have inflicted on W'kkai the
same horrible fate they had delivered to Hssin. It
wasn't likely. That was why he had picked W'kkai. The
UNSN ships could outflank the worlds of the Patriarchy. They could lay siege to whole systems. They could
disrupt trade. But siege wasn't conquest. W'kkai-sys-
tem had the resources to resist siege for a dozen
generations!

His sensors detected only kzin.

He was moving in on the system using the same
careful plan that he had extracted from Lieutenant
Argamentine's mind, the same maneuver she had been
using to close in on a hostile Alpha Centauri.

They jumped in, one light-day closer. It took Long-
Reach half an hour to phase in the motor for that
jump and fifteen minutes to arc through hyperspace.

W'kkai! Trainer-of-Slaves was already dream-seeing
his noble household. He saw the stone walls. There
would be a vast Jotok Run out back, bigger than the
whole Run on Hssin had ever been. He had some
nice little bungalows in mind for the man-slaves.
They'd need a common dormitory, too. Monkeys were
communal animals.

And the palazzo for his kzinrretti: that would be a
marvel of carved red sandstone and tall wrought iron
walkways to let the light in, W'kkai style—all laid out
with cool inner corridors, and mazed plazas for the
chasing and leaping games. He could almost smell the
perfume of kzinrret fur. To stock his harem he'd be
able to walk into the most noble of households—

carved woods, tapestries, trophies, ancient heir-
looms—and take his pick of their favorite daughters.

Still nothing but the electromagnetic hubbub of a
thriving civilization, and the characteristic gravitic signature of polarizer-driven interplanetary commerce.

Another jump, and then he knew they were near a
military base.

He beamed out an identification code, so hoary in
its use among the worlds of the Patriarchy that it was
conjured in base twenty-five mathematics—which
probably meant that it had been invented by the
ancient Jotoki and learned by the kzin while they were
still mercenaries. The code was a royal tail-pain to use.
But changing standard regulations in a sublight empire
could be impossibly complex.

The man-monkeys weren't any different. He had
often wondered why the navigation instruments in the
Shark were calibrated to odd intervals of twenty-four
and sixty, translated to base ten mathematics. It was
a minor miracle that he'd been able to find W'kkai
using them. The custom probably reflected something
that the humans had inherited from their chimpanzee
ancestors.

He wasn't expecting a fast response to his signal.
The *Shark* was eleven light-minutes from the nearest
kzin military unit, well out of "leap first and ask questions later" range. He'd have to wait twenty-two
minutes for a reply.

Eventually that reply arrived. "Kppukiss-Guardian
speaking. Identification code incompatible with vessel
type. You are putting out the neutrino profile of a
UNSN ghostship. You are presently trespassing, I
repeat, *trespassing* the defense sphere permitted to
W'kkai by the MacDonald-Rishshi Peace Treaty of the
2433rd year honoring the torture of the Fanged
Father, the Monkey Son, and the Unseen Grandfather." The rest of the message was unstated but the

242242 *Man-Kzin Wars IV*

menace was there—no truce existed *inside* the treaty
perimeter. Good. That meant that they were within
kzin controlled space.

Trainer-of-Slaves decided that now was the time to
use a new name. Then he would never have to reveal
his duty names—and no one could ever flaunt them
to insult him. Self-promotion wasn't unknown in the
Patriarchy—if a Hero had the swinging-claw to make
it stick. And this Hero's swinging-claw moved faster
than light!

"Lord Grraf-Nig acknowledging Kppukiss-Guardian. Grraf-Nig here. Grraf-Nig receiving." In taking
this name he was honoring his mentor, Grraf-Hromfi
(out of affection) and his father, Chiirr-Nig (out of
spite). For the rest of his life he intended to spread
the wisdom of Grraf, and for the rest of his life he
intended to be such a fulgent Nig that all other Nigs,
especially his father, would fade from the sky.

His beamcast continued. "This servant of the Patriarch does indeed travel in a salvaged UNSN vessel,
unfettered by the luminiferous bondage. We come
from the wreckage of Ka'ashi-system and from the
martyrdom of Hssin. Light will not yet have delivered
its message of these distant woes to W'kkai, so you
must only have heard the version spoken to you by
the superluminal man-beasts who tell lies to suit the
mood of their livers.

"Grraf-Nig's desire is to settle upon the lush plains
of W'kkai to breed a new generation of warriors for
which I will need the aid of your magnificent
daughters.

"I come in poverty and lamentation from our
wasted worlds. I bring with me only a superluminal
drive and a functioning hyperwave receiver, neither of
which I can fully comprehend without the help of
W'kkai scholarship and neither of which can be comprehended by W'kkai scholarship without the fifteen

years of sweat and thought given to these devices by
me and my slaves.

"I come in poverty without a warrior entourage,
with only the memory of martyred Heroes. My pitiful
wealth is reduced to ten Jotoki-slaves of mechanical
bent who know gravitic and superluminal mechanics,
and one female breeder of a new slave race and her
litter of six child-slaves.

"The Lord Grraf-Nig requests a full military escort
to W'kkai. The vessel *Shark* is unarmed. Your Heroes
are welcome aboard for inspection. Lord Grraf-Nig
out. Standing by."

Grraf-Nig was almost shaking in his fear. After fifteen years of living a kzinless life he had forgotten
what contact was like. The frightened Short-Son had
been impressed by the speech but appalled that it had
been coming out of *his* mouth. Trainer-of-Slaves was
just glad that the W'kkai warriors couldn't smell the
fear in the *Shark*'s cabin. He was going to have to
request a talcum rubdown by Nora to get the evidence
of cowardice out of his fur. Then he'd replace the
entire cabin air supply minutes prior to the boarding.

He expected the next contact to be visual. That gave
them twenty-two minutes to dress. He pulled out the
case from behind the box that had been made on We
Made It and held up the best kzin finery he had been
able to salvage from the ruins of Hssin.

Grraf-Nig had fresh livery for Long-Reach who was
sitting on his mouth atop the hyperdrive motor, three
brains asleep and two arms holding sleeping babies.
That pose would have to be changed. He wanted his
slaves to appear as well-groomed animals. He combed
the Nora-beast's fur on her torso and legs until the
soft down glimmered. It pleased him to do things for
her. She was able to perform miracles upon *his* pelt.
Then he gave her new lace garters for her video
debut. She slipped them on, her dimples in her

cheeks. That meant she liked them. Of course she didn't understand about the video.

I've gone crazy from loneliness, thought Grraf-Nig. *I love my five-armed sons and my wonderfully feminine man-kzinrret*. It was a venal sin to become attached to slaves but that was the risk a slave-master had to take.

The twenty-two minutes were up. The radio came to life. "Honored Grraf-Nig! This unworthy Kppukiss-Guardian offers you a military escort of six *Screamers*. W'kkai welcomes its Rescuing Hero! Our wealth is your wealth! My only daughter will comfort your couch! A thousand of our sons will be your Warrior's Guard . . ."

Though Long-Reach was mostly asleep, short(arm) had been keeping an eye on things. "Dominant Master, don't let all that sthondat excrement overheat your liver."

"Trip over?" asked Nora brightly.

Grraf-Nig banged the box from We Made It. "We Made It!" he exclaimed in English.

Nora didn't understand a word. But she knew what to do. She snuggled up to Mellow-Yellow. "My Hero," she purred-spat in her charming human accent.

THE MAN WHO WOULD BE KZIN

Greg Bear & S.M. Stirling

"I am become overlord of a fleet of transports, supply ships, and wrecks!" Kfraksha-Admiral said. "No wonder the First Fleet did not return; our Intelligence reports claimed these *humans* were leaf-eaters without a weapon to their name, and they have destroyed a fourth of our combat strength!"

He turned his face down to the holographic display before him; it was set for exterior-visual, and showed only bright unwinking points of light and the schematics that indicated the hundreds of vessels of the Second Fleet. Here beyond the orbit of Neptune the humans' sun was just another star ... *we will eat you yet*, he vowed silently. A spacer's eye could identify those suns whose worlds obeyed the Patriarch. More that did not, unvisited, or unconquered yet like the Pierin holdouts on Zeta Reticuli. *Yes, you and all like you!* So many suns, so many ...

The kzin commander's tail was not lashing; he was beyond that, and the naked pink length of that organ now stood out rigid as he paced the command deck

247

of the *Sons Contend With Bloody Fangs*. The orange fur around his blunt muzzle bristled, and the reddish washcloth of his tongue kept sweeping up to moisten his black nostrils. The other kzinti on the bridge stayed prudently silent, forcing their batwing ears not to fold into the fur of their heads at the spicy scent of high-status anger. The lower-ranked bent above the consoles and readouts of their duty stations, taking refuge in work; the immediate staff prostrated themselves around the central display tank, laying their facial fur flat. Aide-to-Commanders covered his nose with his hands in an excess of servility; irritated, Kfraksha kicked him in the ribs as he went by. There was no satisfaction to the gesture, since they were all in space-combat armor save for the unhinged helmets, but the subordinate went spinning a meter or so across the deck.

"Well? Advise me," the kzin admiral spat. "Surely *something* can be learned from the loss of a squadron of *Gut Tearer*–class cruisers?"

Reawii-Intelligence-Analyst raised tufted eyebrows and fluttered his lips against his fangs.

"Frrrr. The . . . rrrr, humans have devoted great resources to the defense of the gas-giant moons, whose resources are crucial."

As Kfraksha-Admiral bared teeth, the Intelligence officer hurried on. Reawii's Homeworld accent irritated Kfraksha-Admiral at the best of times. His birth was better than his status, and it would not do to anger the supreme commander, who had risen from the ranks and was proud of it. He hurried beyond the obvious.

"Their laser cannon opened fire with uncanny accuracy. We were unprepared for weapons of this type because such large fixed installations are seldom tactically worthwhile; also, our preliminary surveys did not indicate space defenses of any type. It is worth the risk to further fleet units to recover any possible Intelligence data from wreckage or survivors on appropriate trajectories."

Kfraksha-Admiral's facial pelt rippled in patterns equivalent to a human nod.

"Prepare summaries of projected operations for data and survivors," he said. Then he paused; now his tail did lash, sign of deep worry or concentration. "Hrrr. It is time we stopped being surprised by the Earthmonkeys and started springing unseen from the long grass ourselves. Bring me a transcript of all astronomical anomalies in this system."

The staff officers rose and left at his gesture, and Kfraksha-Admiral remained staring into the display tank; he keyed it to a close-in view of the animal planet. Blue and white, more ocean than Homeworld, slightly lighter gravity. A rich world. A soft world, or so the telepaths said, no weapons, a species that was so without shame that it deliberately shunned the honorable path of war. Thousands of thousands squared of the animals. Unconsciously, he licked his lips. *All the more for the feeding.*

The game was wary, though. He must throttle his leap, though it was like squeezing his own throat in his claws.

"I must *know* before I fight," he muttered.

He was the perfect spy.

He could also be the perfect saboteur.

Lawrence Halloran was a strong projecting telepath.

He could read the minds of most people with ease. The remaining select few he could invade, with steady concentration, within a week or two. Using what he found in those minds, Halloran could appear to be anybody or anything.

He could also make suggestions, convincing his subjects—or victims—that they were undergoing some physical experience. In this, he relied in large measure on auto-suggestion; sometimes it was enough to plant a subliminal hint and have the victims convince themselves that they actually experienced something. The problem was that the Earth of the twenty-fourth century had little use for spies or saboteurs. Earth had been at peace for three hundred years. Everyone was prosperous; many were rich. The planet was a little crowded, but those who strongly disliked that could leave. Psychists and autodocs saw that nobody was violent or angry or unhappy for long. Most people were only vaguely aware that things had ever been very different, and the ARM, the UN technological police, kept it that way, ensuring that no revolutionary changes upset the comfortable status quo.

Lawrence Halloran had an unusual ability that seemed to be completely useless. He had first used his talents in a most undignified way, appearing as the headmaster of his private Pacific Grove secondary school, *sans* apparel, in the middle of the quad during an exercise break. The headmaster had come within a hair's-breadth of being relieved of duty; an airtight alibi, that he had in fact been in conference with five teachers across the campus, had saved his job and reputation. Halloran's secret had not been revealed. But Halloran had learned an important object lesson—foolish use of his talents could have grave consequences. He had been raised to feel strong guilt at any hint of aggression. Children who scuffled in the schoolyard were sick and needed treatment.

Human society was not so very different from an ant's nest, at the end of the Long Peace; a stick, inserted from an unexpected direction, could raise hell. And woe to the wielder if he stayed around long enough to let the ants crawl up the stick.

That Halloran had not manifested his ability as an infant—not until his sixteenth year, in fact—was something of a miracle. The talent had undoubtedly existed in some form, but had kept itself hidden until five years after Halloran's first twinges of pubescence.

At first, such a wild talent had been exhilarating. After the headmaster fiasco, and several weirder if less immediately foolish manifestations (a dinosaur on a slidewalk at night, Christ in a sacristy), and string of romantic successes everyone else found bewildering, he had undergone what amounted to a religious conversion. Halloran came to realize that he could not use his talent without destroying himself, and those around him. The only thing it was good for was deception and domination.

He buried it. Studied music. Specialized in Haydn.

In his dreams, he became Haydn. It beat being himself.

When awake, he was merely Lawrence Halloran Jr., perpetual student: slightly raucous, highly intuitive (he could not keep his subconscious from exercising certain small forays) and generally regarded by his peers as someone to avoid. His only real friend was his cat. He knew that his cat loved him, because he fed her. Cats were neither altruists nor hypocrites, and nobody expected them to be noble. If he could not be Haydn, he would rather have been a cat.

Halloran resented his social standing. *If only they knew how noble I am.* He had a talent he could use to enslave people, and by sublimating it he became an irritating son of a bitch; that, he thought, was highly commendable self-sacrifice.

And they hate me for it, he realized. *I don't much love them either. Lucky for them I'm an altruist.*

Then the war had come; invaders from beyond human space. The kzinti: catlike aliens, carnivores, aggressive imperialists. Human society was turned upside down once again, although the process was swift only from a historical perspective. With the war eight years along, Halloran had grown sick of this masquerade. Against his better judgment, he had made himself available to the UN Space Navy; UNSN, for short. Almost immediately, he had been sequestered and prepared for just such an eventuality as the capture of a kzinti vessel. In the second kzin attack on the Sol system, a cruiser named *War Loot* was chopped into several pieces by converted launch lasers and fell into human hands.

In this, Earth's most desperate hour, neither Halloran nor any of his commanding officers considered his life to be worth much in and of itself. Nobility of purpose . . .

And if Halloran's subconscious thought differently—

Halloran knew himself to be in control. Had he not sublimated the worst of his talent? Had he not let girls pour drinks on his head?

Halloran's job was to study the kzin. Then to *become* one, well enough to fool another kzin. After all, if he could convince humans he was a dinosaur—which was obviously an impossibility—why not fool aliens into seeing what they expected?

The first test of Halloran-Kzin was brief and simple. Halloran entered the laboratory where doctors struggled to keep two mangled kzin from the *War Loot* alive. In the cool ice-blue maximum isolation ward, he approached the flotation bed with its forest of pipes and wires and tubing. Huddled beneath the apparatus, the kzin known to its fellows as Telepath dreamed away his final hours on drugs custom-designed for his physiology.

Telepaths were the most despised and yet valued of kzinti, something of an analogue to Halloran—a mind reader. To kzinti, any kind of addiction was an unbearably shameful thing—a weakness of discipline and concentration, a giving in to the body whose territorial impulses established so much of the rigid Kzinti social ritual. To be addicted was to be less self-controlled than a kzin already was, and that was pushing things very close to the edge. And yet addiction to a drug was what produced kzinti telepaths.

This kzin would not have looked very good in the best of times, despite his two hundred and twenty centimeters of height and bull-gorilla bulk; now he was shrunken and pitiful, his ribs showing through matted fur, his limbs reduced to lumpy bone, lips pulled back from yellow teeth and stinking gums. Telepath had been without his fix for weeks. How much this lack, and the presence of anesthetics, had dulled his talents nobody could say, but his kind offered the greatest risk to the success of Halloran's mission. The kzin had been wearing a supply of the telepath drug on a leather belt when captured. Administered to him now, it would allow him to reach into the mind of another, with considerable effort . . .

Halloran-Kzin had to pass this test.

He signaled the doctors with a nod, and from behind their one-way glass they began altering the concentration of drugs in Telepath's blood. They added some of the kzinti drug. A monitor wheeped softly, pitifully, indicating that their kzin would soon be awake and that he would be in pain.

The kzin opened his eyes, rolled his head, and stared in surprise at Halloran-Kzin. The dying Telepath concealed his pain well.

"I have been returned?" he said, in the hiss-spit-snarl of what his race called the Hero's Tongue.

"You have been returned," Halloran-Kzin replied.

"And am I too valuable to terminate?" the kzin asked sadly.

"You will die soon," Halloran-Kzin said, sensing that this would comfort him.

"Animals . . . eaters of plants. I have had nightmares, dreams of being pursued by herbivores. The shame. And no meat, or only cold rotten meat . . ."

"Are you still capable?" Halloran-Kzin asked. He had learned enough about kzinti social structure from the relatively undamaged prisoner designated Fixer-of-Weapons to understand that Telepath would have no position if he was not telepathic. Fixer was the persona he would assume. "Show me you are still capable."

The kzin had shielded himself against stray sensations from human minds. But now he closed his eyes and knotted his black, leathery hands into fists. With an intense effort, he reached out and tapped Halloran's thoughts. Telepath's eyes widened until the rheumy circles around the wide pupils were clearly visible. His ears contracted into tight knots beneath the fur. Then he emitted a horrifying scream, like a jaguar in pain. Against all his restraints, he thrashed and twisted until he had torn loose the internal connections that kept him alive. Orange-red blood pooled around the flotation bed and the monitor began a steady, funereal tone.

Halloran left the ward. Colonel Buford Early waited for him outside; as usual, his case officer exuded an air of massive, unwilling patience.

"Just a minor problem," Halloran said, shaken more than he wished the other man to know.

"Minor?"

"Telepath is dead. He saw my thoughts."

"He thought you were a kzin?"

"Yes. He wouldn't have tried reading me if he thought I was human."

"What happened?"

"I drove him crazy," Halloran said. "He was close to the edge anyway . . . I pushed him over."

"How could you do that?" Colonel Early asked, brow lowered incredulously.

"I had a salad for lunch," Halloran replied.

*   *   *

Halloran knew better than to wake a kzin in the middle of a nightmare. Fixer-of-Weapons had not rested peacefully the last four sleeps, and no wonder, with Halloran testing so many hypotheses, hour by hour, on the captive.

The chamber in which the kzin slept was roomy enough, five meters on a side and three meters high, the walls colored a soothing mottled green. The air was warm and dry; Halloran had chapped lips from spending hours and days in the hapless kzin's company.

Thinking of a kzin as hapless was difficult. Fixer-of-Weapons had been Chief Weapons Engineer and Alien Technologies Officer aboard the invasion cruiser *War Loot*, a position demanding great strength and stamina even with the wartime dueling restrictions, for many other kzinti coveted such a billet.

War Loot had been on a mission to probe human defenses within the ecliptic; to that extent, the kzinti mission had succeeded. The cruiser had been disabled within the outer limits of the asteroid belt by converted propulsion beam lasers three weeks before, and against all odds, Fixer-of-Weapons and two other kzin had been captured. The others had been severely injured, one almost cut in half by a shorn and warped bulkhead. The same bulkhead had sealed Fixer-of-Weapons in a cabin corner, equipped with a functional vent giving access to seven hours of trapped air. At the end of six and a half hours, Fixer-of-Weapons had passed out. Human investigators had cut him free . . .

And brought him to Ceres, largest of the asteroids, to be put in a cage with Halloran.

To Fixer-of-Weapons, in his more lucid moments, Halloran looked like a particularly clumsy and socially inept kzin. But Halloran was a California boy, born and bred, a graduate of UCLA's revered school of music. Halloran did not look like a kzin unless he wanted to.

Four years past, to prove to himself that his life was not a complete waste, he had spent his time learning to differentiate one Haydn piano sonata or string quartet from another, not a terribly exciting task, but peaceful and rewarding. He had developed a great respect for Haydn, coming to love the richness and subtle invention of the eighteenth century composer's music.

To Earth-bound flatlanders, the war at the top of the solar system's gravity well, with fleets maneuvering over periods of months and years, was a distant and dimly perceived threat. Halloran had hardly known how to feel about his own existence, much less the survival of the human race. Haydn suited him to a tee. Glory did not seem important. Nobody would appreciate him anyway.

Halloran's parents, and their fathers and mothers before them for two and a half centuries, had known an Earth of peace and relative prosperity. If any of them had desired glory and excitement, they could have volunteered for a decades-long journey by slowboat to new colonies. None had.

It was a Halloran tradition; careful study, avoidance of risk, lifetimes of productive peace. The tradition had gained his grandfather a long and productive life—one hundred and fifty years of it, and at least a century more to come. His father, Lawrence Halloran Sr., had made his fortune streamlining commodities distribution; a brilliant move into a neglected field, less crowded than information shunting. Lawrence Halloran Jr., after the death of his mother in an earthquake in Alaska, had bounced from school to school, promising to be a perpetual student, gadding from one subject to another, trying to lose himself . . .

And then peace had ended. The kzinti—not the first

visitors from beyond the Solar System, but certainly the most aggressive—had made their presence known. Presence, to a kzin, was tantamount to conquest. For hundreds of thousands of kzin warriors, serving their Patriarchy, Earth and the other human worlds represented advancement; many females, higher status, and lifetime sinecures, without competition.

Humans had been drawn into the war with no weapons as such. To defend themselves, all they had were the massive planet- and asteroid-mounted propulsion lasers and fusion drives that powered their starships. These technologies, some of them now converted to thoroughgoing weapons by Belters and UN engineers, provided what little hope humans had . . .

And there was the bare likelihood—unconfirmed as yet—that humans were innately more clever than kzinti, or at least more measured and restrained. Human fusion drives were certainly more efficient— but then, the kzinti had gravity polarizers, not unlike that found on the Pak ship piloted by Jack Brennan, and never understood. The Brennan polarizer still worked, but nobody knew how to control it—or build another like it. Gradually, scientists and UNSN commanders were realizing that capture of kzinti vessels, rather than complete destruction, could provide invaluable knowledge about such advanced technology.

Gravity polarizers gave kzin ships the ability to travel at eight-tenths the speed of light, with rapid acceleration and artificial gravitation . . . The kzinti did not *need* super-efficient fusion drives.

Halloran waited patiently for the Fixer-of-Weapons to awaken. An hour passed. He rehearsed the personality he was constructing, and toned the image he presented for the kzin. He also studied, for the hundredth time, the black markings of fur in the kzin's face and along his back, contrasting with the brownish-red undercoat. The kzin's ears were ornately tattooed in patterns Halloran had learned symbolized the intermeshed bones of kzinti enemies. This was how the kzinti recognized each other, beyond scent and gross physical features; failure to know and project such facial fur patterns and ear tattoos would mean discovery and death. The kzinti's own mind would supply the scent, given the visual clues; their noses were less sensitive than a dog's, much more so than a human's.

Another hour, and Halloran felt a touch of impatience. Kzinti were supposed to be light and short-term sleepers. Fixer-of-Weapons seemed to have joined his warrior ancestors; he barely breathed.

At last, the captive stirred and opened his eyes, glazed nictitating membranes pulling back to reveal the large, gorgeous purple-rimmed golden eyes with their surprisingly humanlike round irises. Fixer-of-Weapons's wedge-shaped, blunt-muzzled face froze into a blank mask, as it always did when he confronted Halloran-Kzin, who stood on the opposite side of the containment room, tapping his elbow with one finger. Distance from the captive was imperative, even when he was "restrained" by imaginary bonds suggested by Halloran. A kzin did not give warning when he was about to attack, and Fixer-of-Weapons was being driven to emotional extremes.

The kzin laid back his ears in furious misery. "I have done nothing to deserve such treatment," he growled. He believed he was being detained on a kzinti fleet flagship. Halloran, had he truly been a kzin, would have preferred human capture to kzinti detention. *I can't say I like the ratcat,* he thought, with a twinge of guilt, quickly suppressed. *But you've got to admit he's about as tough as he thinks he is.*

"That is for your superiors to decide," Halloran-Kzin said. "You behaved with suspected cowardice, you allowed an invasion cruiser to be disabled and captured—"

"I was not Kufcha-Captain! I cannot be responsible for the incompetence of my commander." Fixer-of-Weapons rose to his full two hundred and twenty centimeters, short for a kzin, and flexed against the imaginary bonds. The muscles beneath the smooth-furred limbs and barrel chest were awesome, despite weight loss under weeks of captivity. "This is a travesty! Why are you doing this to me?"

"You will tell us exactly what happened, step by step, and how you allowed animals—plant-eaters—to capture *War Loot*."

Fixer-of-Weapons slumped in abject despair. "I have told, again and again."

Halloran-Kzin showed no signs of relenting. Fixer-of-Weapons lashed his long pink rat-tail, sitting in a tight ball on the floor, swallowed hard and began his tale again, and again Halloran used the familiar litany as a cover to probe the kzin's inner thoughts.

If Halloran was going to be a kzin, and think like one for days on end, then he had to have everything exactly right. His deception would be of the utmost delicacy. The smallest flaw could get him killed immediately.

Kzinti, unlike the UN Space Navy, did not take prisoners except for Intelligence and culinary purposes.

Fixer-of-Weapons finished his story. Halloran pulled back from the kzin's mind.

"If I have disgraced myself, then at least allow me to die," Fixer-of-Weapons said softly.

That's one wish you can be granted, Halloran thought. One way or another, the kzin would be dead soon; his species did not survive in captivity.

Halloran exited the cell and faced three men and two women in the antechamber. Two of the men wore the new uniform—barely ten years old—of the UN

Space Navy. The third man was a Belter cultural scientist, the only one in the group actually native to Ceres, dressed in bright lab spotter orange. The two women Halloran had never seen before; they were also Belters, though their Belter tans had faded. All three wore the broad Belter Mohawk. The taller of the two offered Halloran her hand and introduced herself.

"I'm Kelly Ysyvry," she said. "Don't bother trying to spell it."

"Y-S-Y-V-R-Y," Halloran said, displaying the show-off mentality that had made his social life so difficult at times.

"Right," Ysyvry said, unflappable. "This," she nodded at her female companion, "is Henrietta Olsen."

Colonel Buford Early, the shortest and most muscular of the three men, nodded impatiently at the introductions; he was an Earther, coal-black and much older than he looked, something Ultra Secret in the ARM before the war. Early had recruited Halloran four years ago, trained him meticulously, and shown remarkable patience toward his peculiarities.

"When are you going to be ready?" he asked Halloran.

"Ready for what?" Halloran asked.

"Insertion."

Halloran, fully understanding the Colonel's meaning, inspected the women roguishly.

"I'm confused," he said, smiling.

"What he means," Ysyvry said, "is that we're all impatient, and you've been the stumbling block throughout this mission."

"What is she?" Halloran asked Early.

"We are the plunger of your syringe," Henrietta Olsen answered. "We're Belter pilots. We've been getting special training in the kzinti hulk."

"Pleased to meet you," Halloran said. He glanced back at the hatch to the cell airlock. "Fixer-of-Weap-

ons will be dead within a week. I can't learn any more
from him. So . . . I'm ready for a test."

Early stared at him. Halloran knew the Colonel was
restraining an urge to ask him, *Are you sure?*, after
having displayed such impatience.

"How do you know Fixer-of-Weapons will die?" the
black man said.

Halloran's smile stiffened. He disliked being challenged. "Because if I were him, and part of me is, I
would have reached my limit."

"It hasn't been an easy assignment," the cultural
scientist commented.

"Easier for us than Fixer-of-Weapons," Halloran
said, smirking inwardly as the scientist winced.

There would be many problems, of course. Halloran
would never be as strong as a kzin, and if there were
any sort of combat, he would quickly lose . . .

Halloran, among the kzinti, thinking himself a kzin,
would have to carefully preprogram himself to avoid
such dangerous situations, to keep a low profile con-
comitant with his status, whatever that might be. That
would be difficult. A high-status kzin had retainers,
sons, flunkies, to handle status-challenges; many of the
retainers picked carefully for a combination of dim
wits and excellent reflexes. An officer with recognized
rank could not be challenged while on a warship; pun-
ishments for trying included blinding, castration, and
execution of all descendants—all more terrible than
mere death to a kzin. Nameless ratings could duel as
they pleased, provided they had a senior's permission
. . . and Halloran-Kzin would be outside the rank
structure, with no protector.

Fixer-Halloran, when he returned to the kzinti fleet,
would likely find all suitable billets on other vessels
filled. To regain his position and keep face among his
fellows, he could not simply "fit in" and be docile. But

there were more ways than open combat to gain social status.

The kzinti social structure was delicately tuned, though how delicately perhaps not even the kzinti understood. Halloran could wreak his own kind of havoc and none would suspect him of anything but overweening ambition.

All of this, he knew, would have to be accomplished in less than three hundred hours: just twelve days. His body would be worn out by that time. Bad diet—all meat, and raw at that, though digestible, with little chance for supplements of the vitamins a human needed and the life of a kzin did not produce; mental strain; luck running out.

He did not expect to return.

Halloran's hope was that his death would come in the capture or destruction of one or more kzinti ships.

The chance for such a victory, however negligible it might be in the overall strategy of the war, was easily worth one's life, certainly his own life.

The truth was, Halloran thought he was a thorough shit, not of much use to anyone in the long run, a petty dilettante with an unlikely ability, more a handicap than an asset.

Self-sacrifice would give him a peculiar satisfaction: *See, I'm not so bad.*

Nobility of purpose.

And something deeper: *to actually be a kzin.* A kzin could be all the things Halloran had trained himself not to be, and not feel guilty about it. Dominant. Vicious. Competitive.

Kzinti were allowed to have fun.

The short broadcast good-byes to his friends and relatives on Earth, as yet unassailed by kzinti:

His father, now one hundred and twenty, he was able to say farewell to; but his grandfather, a Struldbrug and still one of the foremost collectors of Norman Rockwell art and memorabilia, was unavailable.

He disliked his father, yet respected him, and loved his grandfather, but felt a kind of contempt for the man's sentimental passion.

His grandfather's answering service did not know where the oldest living Halloran was. That brought on a sharp tinge of disappointment, against which he quickly raised a shield of aloofness. For a moment, a very young Lawrence—Larry—had surfaced, wanting, desperately needing to see Grandpa. And there was no room for such active sub-personalities, not with Fixer-of-Weapons filling much of his cranium. Or so he told himself, drowning the disappointment as an old farmer might have discarded a sack of unwanted kittens.

Halloran met his father on the family estate at the cap of Arcosanti Two in Arizona. The man barely looked fifty and was with his fifth wife, who was older than Halloran but only by five or ten years. The sky was gorgeous robin's egg at the horizon and lapis overhead and the green desert spread for ten kilometers around in a network of canals and recreational sluices. Arcosanti Two prided itself on its ecological balance, but in fact the city had taken a wide tract of Arizona desert and made it into something else entirely, something in which bobbing lizards and roadrunners would soon go crazy or die. Halloran felt just as much out of place on the broad open-air portico at two kilometers above sea level. Infrared heaters kept the high autumn chill away.

"I'm volunteering for a slowboat," Halloran told his father.

"I thought they'd been suspended," said Rose Petal, the new wife, a very attractive natural blond with oriental features. "I mean, all that expense, and we're bound to lose them to the, mmm, outsiders . . ." She looked slightly embarrassed; even after nearly a decade, the words *war* and *enemy* still carried a strong flavor of obscenity to most Earthers.

"There's one going out in a few weeks, a private venture. No announcements. Tacit government support; if we survive, they send more."

"That does not sound like my son," Halloran Sr. ventured.

When I tried to assert myself, you told me it was wrong. When I didn't, you despised me. Thanks, Dad.

"I think it is wonderful," Rose Petal said. "Whether characteristic or not."

"It's a way out from under family," Halloran Jr. said with a little smile.

"*That* sounds like my son. Though I'd be much more impressed if you were doing something to help your own people . . ."

"Colonization," Halloran Jr. interjected, leaving the word to stand on its own.

"More directly," Halloran Sr. finished.

"Can't keep all our eggs in one basket," his son continued, amused by arguing a case denied by his own actions. *So tell him.*

But that wasn't possible. Halloran Jr. knew his father too well; a fine entrepreneur, but no keeper of secrets. In truth, his father, despite the aggressive attitude, was even more unsuited to a world of war and discipline than his son.

"That's not what you're doing," Halloran Sr. said. Rose Petal stood by, wisely keeping out from this point on.

"That's what I'm saying I'm doing."

His father gave him a peculiar look then, and Halloran Jr. felt a brief moment of camaraderie and shared secrets. *He has a little bit of the touch too, doesn't he? He knows. Not consciously, but . . .*

He's proud.

Against his own expectations for the meeting and farewell, Halloran left Arcosanti Two, his father, and Rose Petal, feeling he might have more to lose than he had guessed, and more to learn about things very close to him. He left feeling good.

He hadn't parted from his father with positive feelings in at least ten years.

There were no longer lovers or good friends to take leave of. He had stripped himself of these social accoutrements over the last five years. It was difficult to have friends who couldn't lie to you, and he always felt guilty with women. How could he know he hadn't influenced them subconsciously? Knowing this, as he returned to the port and took a shuttle to orbit, brought back the necessary feeling of isolation. He would not be human much longer. Things would be easier if he had very little to regret losing.

Insertion. The hulk of the kzin cruiser, its gravity polarizer destroyed by the kzin crew to keep it out of human hands, was propelled by a NEO mass-driver down the solar gravity well to graze the orbital path of Venus, piloted by the two Belter women to the diffuse outer reaches of the asteroids, there set adrift with the bodies of Telepath and the other unknown kzin restored to the places where they would have died. The Belters would take a small cargo craft back home. Halloran would ride an even smaller lifeboat from *War Loot* toward the kzin fleet. He might or might not be picked up, depending on how hungry the kzin strategists were for information about the loss.

The fleet might or might not be in a good position; it might be mounting another year-long attack against Saturn's moons, on the opposite side of the sun; it might be moving inward for a massive blow against Earth. With the gravity polarizers, the kzin vessels were faster and far more maneuverable than any human ships.

And there could be more than one fleet.

The confined interior of the cargo vessel gave none of its three occupants much privacy. To compensate, they seldom spoke to each other. At the end of a week, Halloran began to get depressed, and it took him another week to express himself to his companions.

While Henrietta Olsen buried herself in reading, when she wasn't tending the computers, Kelly Ysyvry spent much of her time apparently doing nothing. Eyes open, blinking every few seconds, she would stare at a bulkhead for hours at a stretch. This depressed Halloran further. Were all Belters so inner-directed? If they were, then what just God would place him in the company of Belters during his last few weeks as a human being?

He finally approached Olsen with something more than polite words to punctuate the silence. *A kzin wouldn't have to put up with this*, he thought. Kzinti females were subsapient, morons incapable of speech. *That would have its advantages*, Halloran thought half-jokingly.

Women frightened him. He knew too much about what they thought of him.

"I suppose lack of conversation is one way of staying sane," he said.

Olsen looked up from her page projector and blinked. "Flatlanders talk all the time?"

"No," Halloran admitted. "But they talk."

"We talk," Olsen said, returning to her reading. "When we want to, or need to."

"I need to talk," Halloran said.

Olsen put her book down. Perversely guilty, Halloran asked what she had been reading.

"Montagu, *The Man Who Never Was*," she replied.

"What's it about?"

"It's ancient history," she said. "Forbidden stuff. Twentieth century. During the Second World War— remember that?"

"I'm educated," he said. As much as such obscene subjects had been taught in school. Pacific Grove had been progressive.

"The Allies dressed up a corpse in one of their uniforms and gave him a courier's bag with false information. Then they dumped him where he could be picked up by the Axis."

Halloran gawped for a moment. "Sounds grim."

"I doubt the corpse minded."

"And I'm the corpse?"

Olsen grinned. "You don't fit the profile at all. You're not *The Man Who Never Was*. You're one of those soldiers trained to speak the enemy's language and dropped behind the lines in the enemy's uniforms to wreak havoc."

"Why are you so interested in World War Two?"

"Fits our times. This stuff used to be pornography— or whatever the equivalent is for literature about violence and destruction, and they'd send you to the psychist if they caught you with it. Now it's available anywhere. Psychological refitting. Still, the thought of . . ." She shook her head. "Killing. Even thinking like one of *them*—so ready to kill . . ."

Ysyvry broke her meditation by blinking three times in quick succession and turned pointedly to face Halloran.

"To the normal person of a few years ago, what you've become would be unspeakably disgusting."

"And what about now?"

"It's necessity," Ysyvry said. That word again. "We're no better than you. We're all soldiers now. Killers."

"So we're too ashamed to speak to each other?"

"We didn't know you wanted to talk," Olsen said.

Throughout his life, even as insensitive as he had tried to become, he had been amazed at how others, especially women, could be so ignorant of their fellows. "I'll probably be dead in a month," he said.

"So you want sympathy?" Olsen said, wide-eyed. "The Man Who Would be Kzin wants sympathy? Such bad technique . . ."

"Forget it," Halloran said, feeling his stomach twist.

"We learned a lot about you," Ysyvry continued. "What you might do in a moment of weakness, how you had once been a troublemaker, using your abilities to fool people . . . Belters value ingenuity and independence, but we also value respect. Simple politeness."

Halloran felt a deep void open up beneath him. "I was young when I did those things." His eyes filled with tears. "Tanjit, I'm sacrificing myself for my people, and you treat me as if I'm a bleeping dog turd!"

"Yeah," Olsen said, turning away. "We don't like flatlanders, anyway, and . . . I suppose we're not used to this whole war thing. We've had friends die. We'd just as soon it all went away. Even you."

"So," Ysyvry said, taking a deep breath. "Tell us about yourself. You studied music?"

The turnabout startled him. He wiped his eyes with his sleeve. "Yes. Concentrating on Josef Haydn."

"Play us something," Olsen suggested, reaching into a hidden corner slot to pull out a portable music keyboard he hadn't known the ship carried. "Haydn, Glenn Miller, Sting, anything classical."

For the merest instant, he had the impulse to become Halloran-Kzin. Instead, he took the keyboard and stared at the black and white arrangement. Then he played the first movement of Sonata Number 40 in E Flat, a familiar piece for him. Ysyvry and Olsen listened intently.

As he lightly completed the last few bars, Halloran closed his eyes and imagined the portraits of Haydn, powdered wig and all. He glanced at the Belter pilots from the corners of his eyes.

Ysyvry flinched and Olsen released a small squeak of surprise. He lifted his fingers from the keyboard and rotated to face them.

"Stop that," Olsen requested, obviously impressed.

Halloran dropped the illusion.

"That was beautiful," Ysyvry said.

"I'm human after all, even if I am a flatlander, no?"

"We'll give you that much," Olsen said. "You can look like anything you want to?"

"I'd rather talk about the music," Halloran said, adjusting tones on the musicomp to mimic harpsichord.

"We've never seen a kzin up close, for real," Ysyvry said. The expression on their faces was grimly anticipatory: Come on, scare us.

"I'm not a freak."

"So we've already established that much," Olsen said. "But you're a bit of a show-off, aren't you?"

"And a mind-reader," Ysyvry said.

He had deliberately avoided looking into their thoughts. Nobility of purpose.

"Perfect companion for a long voyage," Olsen added. "You can be whatever, whomever you want to be." Their expressions had become almost salacious. Now Halloran was sorry he had ever initiated conversation. How much of this was teasing, how much— actual cruelty?

Or were they simply testing his stability before insertion?

"You'd like to see a kzin?" he asked quietly.

"We'd like to see Fixer-of-Weapons," Ysyvry affirmed. "We were told you'd need to test the illusion before we release the hulk and your lifeship."

"It's a bit early—we still have two hundred hours."

"All the more time to turn back if you don't convince us," Olsen said.

"It's not just a hat I can put on and take off." He glanced between them, finding little apparent sympathy. Belters were polite, individualistic, but not the most socially adept of people. No wonder their mainstay on long voyages was silence. "I won't wear Fixer-of-Weapons unless I become him."

"You won't consciously know you're human?"

Halloran shook his head. "I'd rather not have the dichotomy to deal with. I'll be too busy with other activities."

"So the kzinti will think you're one of them, and . . . will *you*?"

"I will be Fixer-of-Weapons, or as close as I can become," Halloran said.

"Then you're worse than the fake soldiers in World War II," Olsen commented dryly.

"Show us," Ysyvry said, over her companion's words.

Halloran tapped his fingers on the edge of the keyboard for a few seconds. He could show them Halloran-Kzin—the generic kzin he had manufactured from Fixer-of-Weapons's memories. That would not be difficult.

"No," he said. "You've implied that there's something wrong, somehow, in what I'm going to do. And you're right. I only volunteered to do this sort of thing because we're desperate. But it's not a game. I'm no freak, and I'm not going to provide a sideshow for a couple of bored and crass Belters."

He tapped out the serenade from Haydn's string quartet Opus 3 number 5.

Ysyvry smiled: "All right, Mr. Halloran. Looks like the UNSN made a good choice—not that they had much choice."

"I don't need your respect, either," Halloran said, a little surprised at how deeply he had been hurt. *I thought I was way beyond that.*

"What she's saying," Olsen elaborated, "is that we were asked to isolate you, and harass you a little. See if you're as much of a show-off as your records indicate you might be."

"Fine," Halloran said. "Now it's back to the silence?"

"No," Ysyvry said. "The music is beautiful. We'd appreciate your playing more for us."

Halloran swore under his breath and shook his head.

"Nobody said it would be easy, being a hero . . . did they?" Ysyvry asked.

"I'm no hero," Halloran said.

"I think you have the makings for one," Olsen told him, regarding him steadily with her clear green eyes. "Whatever kind of bastard you were on Earth. Really."

Will a flatlander ever understand Belters? They were so mercurial, strong, and more than a little arrogant. Perhaps that was because space left so little room for niceties.

"If you accept it," Ysyvry said, "we've decided we'll make you an honorary Belter."

Halloran stopped playing.

"Please accept," Olsen said, not wheedling or even trying to placate; a simple, polite request.

"Okay," Halloran said.

"Good," Ysyvry said. "I think you'll like the ceremony."

He did, though it made him realize even more deeply how much he had to lose . . .

And why do I have to die before people start treating me decently?

*   *   *

The Belter pilots dropped the hulk a hundred and three hours after his induction into the ranks. They cut loose the kzin lifeship, with Halloran inside, five hours later, and then turned a shielded ion drive against their orbital path to drop inward and lose themselves in the Belt.

There were beacons on the lifeship, but no sensors. In the kzinti fleet, rescue of survivors was strictly at the discretion of the commanding officers. Halloran entered the digitized odor-signature and serial number of Fixer-of-Weapons into the beacon's transmitter and sat back to wait.

The lifeship had a month's supplies for an individual kzin. What few supplements he dared to carry, all consumable, would be gone in a week, and his time would start running out from that moment.

Still, Halloran half hoped he would not be found. He almost preferred the thought of failure to the prospect of carrying out his mission. It would be an ordeal. The worst thing that had ever happened to him. His greatest challenge in a relatively peaceful lifetime.

For a few days, he nursed dark thoughts about manifest destiny, the possibility that the kzinti really were the destined rulers of interstellar space, and that he was simply blowing against a hurricane.

Then came a signal from the kzinti fleet. Fixer-of-Weapons was still of some value. He was going to be rescued.

"Bullshit," Halloran said, grinning and hugging his arms tightly around himself. "Bullshit, bullshit, bullshit."

Now he was *really* afraid.

Wherever you are, whether in the crowded asteroid belt or beyond the furthest reaches of Pluto, space appears the same. Facing away from the sun—negligible anyway past the Belt—the same vista of indecipherable immensity presents itself. You say, yes, I know those are stars, and those are galaxies, and nebulae; I know there is life out there, and strangeness, and incident and death and change. But to the eye, and the animal mind, the universe is a flat tapestry sprinkled with meaningless points of fire. Nothing meaningful can emerge from such a tapestry.

The approach of a ship from the beautiful flat darkness and cold is itself a miracle of high order. The animal mind asks, *Where did it come from?*

Halloran, essentially two beings in one body, watched the kzinti dreadnought with two reactions. As Fixer-of-Weapons, now seating himself in the center of Halloran's mind, the ship—a rough-textured spire with an X cross at the "bow"—was both rescue and challenge. Fixer-of-Weapons had lost his status. He would have to struggle to regain his position, perhaps wheedle permission to challenge and supplant a Chief Weapons Officer and Alien Technologies Officer. He hoped—and Halloran prayed—that the positions on the rescue ship were held by one kzin, not two.

The battleship would pick up his lifeship within an hour. In that time, Halloran adjusted the personality that would mask his own.

Halloran would exist in a preprogrammed slumber, to emerge only at certain key points of his plan. Fixer-of-Weapons would project continuously, aware and active, but with limitations; he would not challenge another kzin to physical combat, and he would flee at an opportune moment (if any came) if so challenged.

Halloran did not have a kzin's shining black claws or vicious fangs. He could project images of these to other kzinti, but they had only a limited effectiveness in action. For a moment, a kzin might think himself slashed by Fixer-of-Weapons's claws (although Halloran did not know how strong the stigmata effect was with kzinti), but that moment would pass. Halloran did not think he could convince a kzin to die . . .

He had never done such a thing with people. Exploring those aspects of his abilities had been too horrifying to contemplate. If he was pushed to such a test, and succeeded, he would destroy himself rather than return to Earth. Or so he thought, now . . .

Foolishness, Fixer-of-Weapons's persona grumbled. *A weapon is a weapon.*

Halloran shuddered.

The battleship communicated with the lifeship; first difficulty. The coughing growl and silky dissonance of the Hero's Tongue could not be readily mimicked, and Halloran could not project his illusion beyond a few miles; he did not respond by voice, but by coded signal. The signal was not challenged.

The kzinti could not conceive of an interloper invading their fold.

"Madness," he said as the ships closed. Humming the Haydn serenade, Lawrence Halloran Jr. slipped behind the scenes, and Fixer-of-Weapons came on center stage.

The interior of the *Sons Contend With Bloody Fangs*—or any kzinti vessel, for that matter—smelled of death. It aroused in a human the deepest and most primordial fears. Imagine a neolithic hunter, trapped in a tiger's cave, surrounded by the stench of big cats and dead, decaying prey—and that was how the behind-the-scenes Halloran felt.

Fixer-of-Weapons salivated at the smells of food, but trembled at the same time.

"You are not well?" the escorting Aide-to-Commanders asked hopefully; Fixer's presence on the battleship could mean much disruption. The kzin's thoughts were quite clear to Fixer: *Why did Kfraksha-*

Admiral allow this one aboard? He smells of confine-
ment . . . and . . .

Fixer did not worry about these insights, which might be expected of a pitiful telepath; he would use whatever information was available to re-establish his rank and position. He lifted his lip at the subordinate, lowest of ranks aboard the battleship, a *servant* and licker-of-others'-fur. Aide-to-Commanders shrank back, spreading his ears and curling his thick, unscarred pink tail to signify non-aggression.

"Do not forget yourself," Fixer reminded him. "Kfraksha-Admiral is my ally. He chose to rescue me."

"So it is," Aide-to-Commanders acknowledged. He led Fixer down a steep corridor, with no corners for hiding would-be assailants, and straightened before the hatch to Kfraksha-Admiral's quarters. "I obey the instructions of the Dominant One."

That the commander did not allow Fixer to groom or eat before debriefing signified in how little regard he was held. Any survivor of a warship lost to animals carried much if not all the disgrace that would adhere to a surviving commander.

Kfraksha-Admiral bade him enter and growled to Aide-to-Commanders that they would be alone. This was how the kzin commander maintained his position without losing respect, by never exhibiting weakness or fear. Loss of respect could mean constant challenge, once they were out of a combat zone with its restrictions. As a kzin without rank, Fixer might be especially volatile; perhaps deranged by long confinement in a tiny lifeship, he might attack the commander in a foolish effort to regain and then better his status with one combat. But Kfraksha-Admiral apparently ignored all this, spider inviting spider into a very attractive parlor.

"Is your shame bearable?" Kfraksha-Admiral asked,

a rhetorical question since Fixer was here, and not immediately contemplating suicide.

"I am not responsible for the actions of the commander of *War Loot*, Dominant One," Fixer replied.

"Yes, but you advised Kufcha-Captain of alien technologies, did you not?"

"I now advise you. Your advantage that I am here, and able to tell you what the animals can do."

Kfraksha-Admiral regarded Fixer with undisguised contempt and mild interest. "Animals destroyed your home. How did this happen?"

This is why I am aboard, Fixer thought. *Kfraksha-Admiral overcomes his disgust to learn things that will give him an edge.*

"They did not engage *War Loot* or any of our sortie. There is still no evidence that they have armed their worlds, no signs of an industry preparing for manufacture of offensive weapons—"

"They defeated you without weapons?"

"They have laser-propulsion systems of enormous strength. You recall, in our first meetings, the animals used their fusion drives against our vessels—"

"And allowed us to track their spoor back to their home worlds. The Patriarchy is grateful for such uneven exchanges. How might we balance this loss?"

Fixer puzzled over his reluctance to tell Kfraksha-Admiral everything. Then: *My knowledge is my life*.

"I am of no use to the fleet," Fixer said, with the slightest undertone of menace. He was gratified to feel—but not see—Kfraksha-Admiral tense his muscles. Fixer could measure the commander's resolve with ease.

"I do not believe that," Kfraksha-Admiral said. "But it is true that if you are no use to me, you are of no use to anybody . . . and not welcome."

Fixer pretended to think this over, and then showed

signs of submission. "I am without position," he said sadly. "I might as well be dead."

"You have position as long as you are useful to me," Kfraksha-Admiral said. "I will allow you to groom and feed . . . if you can demonstrate how useful you might be."

Fixer cocked his fan-shaped ears forward in reluctant obeisance. These maneuvers were delicate—he could not concede too much, or Kfraksha-Admiral would come to believe he had no knowledge. "The humans must be skipping industrialization for offensive weapons. They are converting peaceful—"

Kfraksha-Admiral showed irritation at that word, not commonly used by kzinti.

"—propulsion systems into defensive weapons."

"This contradicts reports of their weakness," Kfraksha-Admiral said. "Our telepaths have reported the animals are reluctant to fight."

"They are adaptable," Fixer said.

"So much can be deduced. Is this all that you know?"

"I learned the positions from which two of the propulsion beams were fired. It should be easy to calculate their present locations . . ."

Kfraksha-Admiral spread his fingers before him, unsheathing long, black and highly polished claws. Now it was Fixer's turn to tense.

"You are my subordinate," the commander said. "You will pass these facts on to me alone."

"What is my position?" Fixer asked.

"Fleet records of your accomplishments have been relayed to me. Your fitness for position is acceptable." The days when mere prowess in personal combat decided rank were long gone, of course; qualifications had to be met before challenges could be made. "You will replace the Alien Technologies Officer on this ship."

"By combat?" A commander could grant permission . . . which was tantamount to an order to fight. Another means of intimidating subordinates.

"By my command. There will be no combat. Your presence here will not be disruptive, so do not become *too* ambitious, or you will face me . . . on unequal terms."

"And the present officer?"

"I have a new position he will not be unhappy with. That is not your concern. Now stand and receive my mark."

Halloran-Fixer could not anticipate what the commander intended quickly enough to respond with anything more than compliance. Kfraksha-Admiral lifted his powerful leg and swiftly, humiliatingly, peed on Halloran-Fixer, distinctly marking him as the commander's charge. Then Kfraksha-Admiral sat on a broad curving bench and regarded him coldly.

Deeply ashamed but docile—what else could he be?—Fixer studied the commander intently. It would not be so difficult to . . . what?

That thought was swept away even before it took shape.

Fixer-of-Weapons had no physical post as such aboard the flagship. He carried a reader the size of a kzin hand slung over his shoulder—with some difficulty, which did not immediately concern him—and went from point to point on the ship to complete his tasks, which were many, and unusually tiring.

The interior spaces of the *Sons Contend With Bloody Fangs* were strangely unfamiliar to him. Halloran had not had time (nor the capacity) to absorb all of his kzin subject's memories. He did not consciously realize he was giving himself a primary education in kzinti technology and naval architecture. His disorientation would have been an infuriating and goading sign of weakness to any inferior seeking his status, but he was marked by Kfraksha-Admiral—physically marked with the commander's odor, like female or a litter— and that warned aggressive subordinates away. They would have to combat Kfraksha-Admiral, not just Fixer.

And Fixer was proving himself useful to Kfraksha-Admiral. This aspect of Halloran's mission had been carefully thought out by Colonel Early and the Intelligence Staff—what could humans afford to have kzinti know about their technology? What would Fixer logically have deduced from his experience aboard the *War Loot*?

Kfraksha-Admiral, luckily, expected Fixer to draw out his revelations for maximum advantage. The small lumps of information deemed reasonable and safe— past locations of two Belter laser projectors that had since burned out their mirrors and lasing field coils, now abandoned and useless except as scrap—could be meted out parsimoniously.

Fixer could limp and cavil, and nobody would find it strange. He had, after all, been defeated by animals and lost all status. His current status was bound to be temporary. Kfraksha-Admiral would coax the important facts from him, and then—

So Fixer was not harassed. He studied his library, with some difficulty deciphering the enigmatic commas-and-dots script and mathematical symbologies. Unconsciously, he tapped the understanding of his fellows to buttress his knowledge.

And that was how he attracted the attention of somebody far more valuable than he, and of even lower status—Kfraksha-Admiral's personal telepath.

Kzinti preferred to eat alone, unless they had killed a large animal by common endeavor. The sight of another eating was likely to arouse deep-seated jealousies not conducive to good digestion; the quality of

one's food aboard the flagship was often raised with
rank, and rank was a smoothly ascending scale. Thus,
the officers could not eat together safely, because
there were no officers at the same level, and if there
was no difference in the food, differences could be
imagined. No. It was simply better to eat alone.

This suited Fixer. He had little satisfaction from his
meals. He received his chunks of reconstituted meat-
substitute heated to blood temperature—common
low-status battle rations from the commissary officer,
and retired to his quarters with the sealed container
to open it and feed. His head hurt after eating the
apparent raw slabs of gristle, bone and meager muscle;
he preferred the simulated vegetable intestinal contents and soft organs, which were the kzinti equivalent
of dessert. A kzin could bolt chunks the size of paired
fists . . . But none of it actually pleased him. What he
did not eat, he disposed of rapidly: pitiful, barely
chewed-fragments it would have shamed a kzin to
leave behind. Fixer did not notice the few pills he
took afterwards, from a pouch seemingly beneath his
chest muscles.

After receiving a foil-wrapped meal, he traversed
the broad central hall of the dining area and encoun-
tered the worst-looking kzin he had ever seen. Fur
matted, tail actually *kinked* in two places, expression
sickly-sycophantic, ears recoiled as if permanently
afraid of being attacked. Telepath scrambled from Fixer's path, as might be expected, and then—

Addressed him from behind.

"We are alike, in some respects—are we not?"

Fixer spun around and snarled furiously. One did
not address a superior, or even an equal, from behind.

"No anger necessary," Telepath said, curling obei-
santly, hands extended to show all claws sheathed.
"There is an odd sound about you . . . it makes me

curious. I have not permission to read you, but you are strong. You send. You *leak*."

Halloran-Fixer felt his fury redouble, for reasons besides the obvious impertinence. "You will stand clear of me and not address me, *Addict*," he spat.

"Not offending, but the sound is interesting, whatever it is. Does it come from time spent in solitude?"

Fixer quelled his rage and bounded down the Hall—or so it appeared to Telepath. The mind reader dropped his chin to his neck and resumed his halfhearted attempts to exercise and groom, his thoughts obviously lingering on his next session with the drug that gave him his abilities.

Fixer could easily tell what the commander and crew were up to, if not what they actually thought at any given moment. But Telepath was a blank slate. Nothing "leaked."

He returned to his private space, near the commander's quarters, and settled in for more sessions in the library. There was something that puzzled him greatly, and might be very important—something called a ghost star. The few mentions in the library files were unrevealing; whatever it was, it appeared to be somewhere about ten system radii outside the planetary orbits. It seemed that a ghost star was nothing surprising, and therefore not clearly explicated; this worried Fixer, for he did not know what a ghost star was.

Kzinti aboard spaceships underwent constant training, self-imposed and otherwise. There were no recreation areas as such aboard the flagship; there were four exercise and mock-combat rooms, however, for the four rough gradations of rank from executive officers to servants. When kzinti entered a mock-combat room, they doffed all markings of rank, wearing masks to disguise their facial characteristics and strong mesh

gloves over their claws to prevent unsheathing and
lethal damage. Few kzinti were actually killed in
mock-combat exercise, but severe injury was not
uncommon. The ship's autodocs could take care of
most of it, and kzinti considered scars ornamental.
Anonymity also prevented ordinary sparring from
affecting rank; even if the combatants *knew* the other's
identity, it could be ignored through social fiction.

Fixer, in his unusual position of commander's
charge, did not receive the challenges to mock-combat
common among officers. But there was nothing in the
rules, written or otherwise, that prevented subordinates from challenging each other, unless their officers
interfered. Such combats were rare because most
crewkzin knew their relative strengths, and who would
be clearly outmatched.

Telepath, the lowest-ranked and most despised kzin
aboard the flagship, challenged Fixer to mock-combat
four day-cycles after his arrival. Fixer could not refuse;
not even the commander's protection would have prevented his complete ostracization had he done so. His
existence would have been an insult to the whole
kzinti species. A simple command not to fight would
have spared him—but the commander did not imagine
that even the despised Fixer would face much of a
fight from Telepath. And Fixer could not afford to be
shunned; ostensibly, he had his position to regain.

So it was that Halloran faced a kzin in mock-combat. Fixer—the kzin persona—did not fall by the wayside, because Fixer could more easily handle the
notion of combat. But Halloran did not remain completely in the background. For while Fixer was "fighting" Telepath, Halloran had to convince any
observers—including Telepath—that he was winning.

Fixer's advantages were several. First, both combatants could emerge unharmed from the fray without

raising undue suspicions. Second, there would be no remote observers—no broadcasts of the fight.

The major disadvantage was that of all the kzinti, a telepath should be most aware of having psychic tricks played on him.

The exercise chambers were cylindrical, gravitation oriented along one flat surface at Kzin normal, or higher for more strenuous regimens. The walls were sand-colored and a constant hot dry wind blew through hidden vents, conditions deemed comfortable in the culture that had dominated Kzin when the species achieved spaceflight. The floor was sprinkled with a flaked fluid-absorbing material. Kzinti rules for combat were few, and did not include prohibitions against surprise targeting of eye-stinging urine. The flakes were more generally soaked with blood, however. The rooms were foul with the odors of fear and exertion and injury.

Telepath was puny for a kzin. He weighed only a hundred and fifty kilograms and stood only two hundred and five centimeters from crown to toes, reduced somewhat by a compliant stoop. He was not in good shape, but he had little difficulty bending the smallest of the ten steel bars adjacent to his assigned half of the combat area—a little gesture legally mandated to give a referee some idea how the combatants were matched in sheer strength. This smallest bar was two centimeters in diameter.

Halloran-Fixer made as if to bend the next bar up, and then ostentatiously re-bent it straight, hoping nobody would examine it closely and find the metal completely unmarked. Probably nobody would; kzinti were less given to idle curiosity than humans.

Telepath screamed and leaped, arms spread wide. The image of Fixer was a bare ten centimeters to one side of his true position, and that allowed one of the kzin's feet to pass a hair's-breadth to one side of Halloran's head. Halloran convinced Telepath he had received a glancing blow across one arm. Telepath recovered somewhat sloppily, for a kzin, and sized up the situation.

There were only the mandated two observers in the antechamber. This fight was regarded as little more than comedy, and comedy, to kzinti, was shameful and demeaning. The observers' attentions were not sharply focused. Halloran-Fixer took advantage of that to dull their perceptions further. This allowed him to concentrate on Telepath.

Fixer did not crouch or make any overt signs of impending attack. He hardly breathed. Telepath circled at the outside of the combat area, nonchalant, apparently faintly amused.

Halloran had little experience with fighting. Fortunately, Fixer-of-Weapons had been an old hand at all kinds of combat, including the mortal kind that had quickly moved him up in rank while the fleet was in base, and much of that information had become lodged in the Fixer persona. Halloran waited for Telepath to make another energy-wasting move.

Kzinti combat was a matter of slight advantages. Possibly Telepath knew this, and sensed something not right about Fixer. Something weak . . .

But Telepath could not read Fixer's thoughts in any concentrated fashion; that required a great effort for the kzin, and debilitating physical weakness afterward. Halloran's powers were much more efficient and much less draining.

Fixer snarled and feigned a jump. Telepath leaped to one side, but Fixer had not completed his attack. He stood with tail twitching furiously several meters from the kzin, needle teeth bared in a hideous grin.

Telepath had good reason to be puzzled. It was rare for a threatened attack to be aborted, from a kzin so much larger and stronger than his opponent. Now the miserable kzin was truly angry, and afraid. Several times he rushed Fixer, but Fixer was never quite where he appeared to be. Several times, Halloran came near to having his head crushed by a passing swipe of the weak kzin's gloved hand, but managed to avoid the blow by centimeters. Something was goading Telepath beyond the usual emotions aroused by mock combat.

"Fight, you sexless female!" Telepath shrieked. A deeply obscene curse, and the observers did some of their own growling now. Telepath had done nothing to increase their esteem.

Fixer used the kzin's anger to his own advantage. The fight would have to end quickly—he was tiring rapidly, far faster than his puny opponent. Fixer seemed to run to a curved wall, leaping and rebounding, crossing the chamber in a flash—and bypassing Telepath without a blow. Telepath screamed with rage and tried to remove his gloves, but they were locked, and only the observers had the keys.

While Telepath was yowling fury and frustration, Fixer-Halloran delivered a bolt of suggestion that staggered the kzin, sending him to all fours with an apparent cuff to the jaw. The position was not as dangerous for a kzin—they could run more quickly on fours than erect—but Halloran-Kzin's image loomed over the stunned Telepath and kicked downward. The observers did not see the maneuver precisely, and Telepath was on the floor writhing in pain, his ear and the side of his head swelling with auto-suggestion injury.

Fixer offered his gloves to the observers and they were unlocked. He had not harmed Telepath, and had not received so much as a scratch himself. Fixer had acquitted himself; he still wore Kfraksha-Admiral's stink, but he was not the lowest of the kzinti on *Sons Contend With Bloody Fangs*.

*   *   *

"The humans obviously have a way of tracking our ships, yet they do not have the gravity polarizer ..." Kfraksha-Admiral sat on his curved bench, legs raised, black-leather fingers clasped behind his thick neck, seeming quite casual and relaxed. "What is our weakness, that they spy on us and can aim their miserable adapted weapons upon us?"

Fixer's turmoil was not apparent. He knew the answer—but of course he could not give it. He had to maneuver this conversation to determine if the commander was asking a rhetorical question, or testing him in some way.

"By our drives," he suggested.

"Yes, of course, but not by spectral signatures or flare temperatures, for in fact we do not use our fusion drives when we enter the system. And without polarizer technology, gravitational gradient warps cannot be detected ... short of system wide detectors, which these animals do not have, correct?"

Fixer rippled his fur in agreement.

"No. They detect not the effects of our drives, but the power sources themselves. It is obvious they have discovered magnetic monopoles. I have suspected as much for years, but now plans are taking shape ..."

Fixer-Halloran was relieved, and horrified, at once. This was indeed how kzinti ships were tracked; in fact, it was a little slow of the enemy not to have thought of it before. The cultural scientists back on Ceres had been puzzled as well; the kzinti had a science and technology more advanced than the human, but they seemed curiously inept at pure research. Almost as if the knowledge had been pasted onto a prescientific culture ...

Every Belter prospector had monopole detection equipment; mining the super-massive particles was a major source of income for individual Belters, and for huge Belt corporations. Known monopole storage centers and power stations were automatically compensated for in even the cheapest detector. In an emergency, a detector could be used to determine position in the Belt—or anywhere else in the solar system—by triangulation from those known sources. An unknown—or kzinti—monopole source set detectors off throughout the solar system. And the newly-converted propulsion lasers could then be locked onto their targets . . .

"This much is now obvious. It explains our losses. Do you concur?"

"This is a fact," Fixer said.

"And how do you know it is a fact?" Kfraksha-Admiral challenged.

"The lifeship from *War Loot* is not powered by monopoles. I survived. Animals would not distinguish monopole sources by the size of the vessel—they would attack all sources."

Kfraksha-Admiral pressed his lips tight together and twitched whiskers with satisfaction. "Precisely so. We must have patience in our strategies, then. We cannot enter the system using our monopole-powered gravity polarizers. But there is the ghost star . . . if we enter the system without monopoles, and without approaching the gas-giant planets, where we might be expected . . . We can enter from an apparently empty region of space, unexpectedly, and destroy the animal populations of many worlds and asteroids. This plan's success is my sinecure. Many females, much territory—glory. We are moving outward now to pass around the ghost star and gain momentum."

Fixer-Halloran again felt a chill. Truly, without the monopoles, the kzinti ships would be difficult to detect.

Fixer pressed his hands together before his chest, a sign of deep respect. Kfraksha-Admiral nodded in condescending fashion.

"You have proven valuable, in your own reluctant, rankless way," he acknowledged, staring at him with irises reduced to pinpoints in the wide golden eyes. "You have endured humiliation with surprising fortitude. Some, our more enlightened and patient warriors, might call it courage." The commander drew a rag soaked in some pale liquid from a bucket behind his bench. He threw it at Fixer, who caught it.

The rag had been soaked in diluted acetic acid— vinegar. "You may remove my mark," Kfraksha-Admiral said. "Henceforth, you have the status of full officer, on my formal staff, and you will be in charge of interpreting the alien technologies we capture. Your combat with Telepath . . . has been reported to me. It was not strictly honorable, but your forbearance was remarkable. In part, this earns you a position."

Fixer now had status. He could not relax his vigilance, for he would no longer be under the commander's protection, but he could assume the armor of a true billet; separate quarters, specific duties, a place in the ritual of the kzinti flagship. Presumably the commander would not grant permission for many challenges, and as a direct subordinate he would count as one of the commander's faction, who would retaliate for any unprovoked attack.

The *Sons Contend With Bloody Fangs* had pulled its way out of the sun's gravity well at a prodigious four-tenths of the speed of light, faster than was safe within a planetary system, and was racing for the ghost star a hundred billion kilometers from the sun. Sol was now an anonymous point of light in the vastness of the Sagittarius arm of the galaxy; the outer limits of the solar system were almost as far behind.

The commander's plans for the whiplash trip around the ghost star were secret to all but a few. Fixer was still not even certain what the ghost star was—it was not listed under that name in the libraries, and there was obviously a concept he was not connecting with. But it was fairly easy to calculate that to accomplish the orbital maneuvers the commander proposed, the ghost star would have to be of at least one-half solar mass. Nothing that size had ever been detected from Earth; it was therefore dark and absolutely cold. There would be no perturbed orbits to give it away; its distance was too great.

So for the time being, Fixer assumed they were approaching a rendezvous with either a dark, dead hulk of a star, or perhaps a black hole.

A hundred billion kilometers was still close to the solar neighborhood, as far as interstellar distances were concerned. That kzinti knew more about these regions than humans worried the sublimated Halloran. What other advantages would they gain?

The time had come for Halloran to examine what he had found. With his personality split in half, and locked into a kzin mentality, he might easily overlook something crucial to his mission.

In his quarters, with the door securely bolted, Halloran came to the surface. Seven days in the kzinti flagship had taken a terrible toll on him; in a small mirror, he saw himself almost cadaverous, his face deeply lined. Kzinti did not use water to groom themselves, and there were no taps in his private quarters— the aliens were descended from a pack-hunting desert carnivore, and had efficient metabolisms—so his skin and clothing would remain dirty. He took a medicinal towelette, used to treat minor scratches received during combats, and wiped as much of his face and hands clean as he could. The astringent solution in the towelette served to sharpen his wits. After so long in Fixer's charge, there seemed little brilliance and fire left in Halloran himself.

And Fixer is just not very bright, he thought sourly. *Think, monkey, think!*

He looked *old*.

"Bleep that," he murmured, and picked up the library pack. As Fixer, he had subliminally marked interesting passages in the kzinti records. Now he set out to learn what the ghost star was, and what he might expect in the next few hours, as they approached and parabolically orbited. A half-hour of inquiry, his eyes reddening under the strain of reading the kzinti script without Fixer's intercession, brought no substantial progress.

"Ghost," he muttered. "Specter. Spirit. Ancestors. A star known to ancestors? Not likely—they would have come on into the solar system and destroyed or enslaved us centuries ago . . . what the tanj *is* a ghost star?"

He queried the library on all concepts incorporating the words ghost, specter, ancestor, and other synonyms in the Hero's Tongue. Another half-hour of concentrated and fruitless study, and he was ready to give up, when the projector displayed an entry. *Specter Mass.*

He cued the entry. A flagged warning came up; the symbol for shame-and-disgrace, a Patriarchal equivalent of Most Secret.

Fixer recoiled; Halloran had to intervene instantly to stop his hand before it halted the search. Curiosity was not a powerful drive for a kzin, and shame was a *very* effective deterrent.

A basic definition flashed up. *"That mass created during the first instants of the universe, separated from kzinti space-time and detectable only by weak gravitational interaction. No light or other communication possible between the domain of specter mass and kzinti space-time."*

Halloran grinned for the first time in seven days.

Now he had it—he could *feel* the solution coming. He cued more detail.

"*Stellar masses of specter matter have been detected, but are rare. None has been found in living memory. These masses, in the specter domain, must be enormous, on the order of hundreds of masses of the sun*"—the star of Kzin, more massive and a little cooler than Sol—"*for their gravitational influence is on the order of .6 [base 8] Kzin suns. The physics of the specter domain must differ widely from our own. Legends warn against searching for ghost stars, though details are lost or forbidden by the Patriarchy.*"

Not a black hole or a dark star, but a star in a counter-universe. Human physicists had discovered the possible existence of *shadow mass* in the late twentieth century—Halloran remembered that much from his physics classes. The enormously powerful superstring theory of particles implied *shadow mass* pretty much as the kzinti entry described it. None had been detected . . .

Who would have thought the Earth was so near to a ghost star?

And now, Kfraksha-Admiral was recommending what the kzinti had heretofore forbidden—close approach to a ghost star to gain a gravitational advantage. The kzinti ships would appear, to human monopole detectors, to be leaving the system—retreating, although slowly. Then the fleet would decelerate and discard its monopoles, sending them on the same outward course, and swing around the ghost star, gaining speed from the star's angular momentum. No fusion drives would be used, so as not to alarm human sentries. Slowly, the fleet would swing back into the solar system, and within a kzinti year, attack the worlds of men. Undetected, unsuspected, the kzinti fleet could end the war then and there. The monopoles would be within retrieval distance.

And all it would require was a little kzinti patience, a rare virtue indeed.

Someone scratched softly at the ID plate on his hatch. Halloran did not assume the Fixer persona, but projected the Fixer image, before answering. The hatch opened a safe crack, and Halloran saw the baleful, rheumy eye of Telepath peering in.

"I have bested you already," the Fixer image growled. "You wish to challenge for a shameful rematch?" Not something Fixer need grant in any case, now that his status was established.

"I have a problem which I must soon bring to the attention of Kfraksha-Admiral," Telepath said, with the edge of a despicable whimper.

"Why come to me?"

"You are the problem. I hear sounds from you. I *remember* things from you. And I have dreams in which you appear, but not as you are now ... sometimes I am you. I am the lowest, but I am important to this fleet, especially with the death of *War Loot*'s Telepath. I am the last Telepath in the fleet. My health is important—"

"Yes, yes! What do you want?"

"Have you been taking the telepath drug?"

"No."

"I can tell ... you speak truth, yet you hide something."

The kzin could not now deeply read Halloran without making an effort, but Halloran was "leaking." Just as he had never been able to quell his "intuition," he could not stop this basic hemorrhage of mental contents. The kzin's drug-weakened mind was there to receive, perhaps more vulnerable because the subconscious trickle of sensation and memory was alien to it.

"I hide nothing. Go away," the Fixer-image demanded harshly.

"Questions first. What is an 'Esterhazy'? What are

these sounds I hear, and what is a 'Haydn'? Why do
I feel emotions which have no names?"

The kzin's pronunciation was not precise, but it was
close enough. "I do not know. Go away."

Halloran began to close the door, but Telepath
wailed and stuck his leathery digits into the crack.
Halloran instinctively stopped the hatch to prevent
damage. A kzin would not have . . .

"I cannot see Kfraksha-Admiral. I am the lowest . . .
but I feel danger! We are approaching very great danger. My shields are weakening and my sensitivity
increases even with lower doses of the drug . . . Do
you know where we are going? I can feel this danger
deep, in a place my addiction has only lightly touched
. . . Others feel it too. There is restlessness. I must
report what I feel! Tell the commander—"

Cringing, Halloran pressed the lever and the door
continued to close. Telepath screamed and pulled out
his digits in time to avoid loosing more than a tip and
one sheathed claw.

That did it. Halloran began to shake uncontrollably.
Sobbing, he buried his face in his hands. Death
seemed very immediate, and pain, and brutality. He
had stepped into the lion's den. The lions were closing
in, and he was weakening. He had never faced anything so horrible before. The kzinti were insane. They
had no softer feelings, nothing but war and destruction
and conquest . . .

And yet, within him there were fragments of Fixer-
of-Weapons to tell him differently. There was courage,
incredible strength, great vitality.

"Not enough," he whispered, removing his face
from his hands. Not enough to redeem them, certainly, and not enough to make him feel any less revul-
sion. If he could, he would wipe all kzinti out of
existence. If he could just expand his mind enough,

reach out across time and space to the distant home-world of kzin, touch them with a deadliness . . .

The main problem with a talent like Halloran's was hubris. Aspiring to god-like ascendancy over others, even kzinti. That way lay more certain madness.

A kzin wouldn't think that way, Halloran knew. *A kzin would scream and leap upon a tool of power like that.* "Kzin have it easier," he muttered.

Time to marshal his resources. How long could he stay alive on the kzinti flagship?

If he assumed the Fixer persona, no more than three days. They would still be rounding the ghost star . . .

If he somehow managed to take control of the ship, and could be Halloran all the time, he might last much longer. And to what end?

To bring the *Sons Contend With Bloody Fangs* back to human space? That would be useful, but not terribly important—the kzinti would have discarded their gravity polarizers. Human engineers had already studied the hulk of *War Loot,* not substantially different from *Sons Contend*.

But he wanted to *survive*. On that Halloran and Fixer-Halloran were agreed. He could feel survival as a clean, metallic necessity, cutting him off from all other considerations. The Belter pilots and their initiation . . . Coming to an understanding of sorts with his father. Early's wish-list. What he knew about kzinti . . .

That could be transmitted back. He did not need to survive to deliver that. But such a transmission would take time, a debriefing of weeks would be invaluable.

Survival.

Simple life.

To *win*.

Thorough shit or not, Halloran valued his miserable life.

Perhaps I'm weak, like Telepath. Sympathetic. Particularly towards myself.

But the summing up was clear and unavoidable. The best thing he could do would be to find some way to inactivate at least this ship, and perhaps the whole kzinti fleet. Grandiose scheme. At the very top of Early's wish-list. All else by the wayside.

And he could not do it by going on a rampage. He had to be smarter than the kzinti; he had to show how humans, with all their love of life and self-sympathy, could beat the self-confident, savage invaders.

No more being Fixer. Time to use Fixer as a front, and be a complete, fully aware Halloran.

Telepath whimpered in his sleep. There was no one near to hear him in this corridor; disgust could be as effective as status and fear in securing privacy.

Hands were lifting him. *Huge* hands, tearing him away from Mother's side. His own hands were tiny, so tiny as he clung with all four limbs to Mother's fur.

She was growling, screaming at the males with the Y-shaped poles who pinned her to the wicker mats, lashing out at them as they laughed and dodged. Hate and fury stank through the dark air of the hut.

"Maaaa!" he screamed. "Maaaa!"

The hands bore him up, crushed him against a muscular side that smelled of leather and metal and *kzintosh*, male kzin.

They will eat me, they will eat me! cried instinct. He lashed out with needle-sharp baby claws, and the booming voice above him laughed and swore, holding the wriggling bundle out at arm's length.

"*This one has spirit,*" the Voice said.

"*Puny,*" another replied dismissively. "*I will not rear it. Send it to the creche.*"

They carried him out into the bright sunlight, and he blinked against the pain of it. Fangs loomed above him, and he hissed and spat; a hand pushed meat into his mouth. It was good, warm and bloody; he tore loose chunks and bolted them, ears still folded down. From the other enclosures came the growls and screams of females frightened by the scent of loss, and behind him his mother gave one howl of grief after another.

Telepath half-woke, grunting and starting, pink bat-ears flaring wide as he took in the familiar subliminal noises of pumps and ventilators.

He was laughing, walking across the quadrangle. Faces turned toward him

—naked faces?—

Mouths turning to round O shapes of shock.

—Flat mouths? Flat teeth?—

Students and teachers were turning toward him, and he knew they saw the headmaster, buck-naked and piriapically erect. He laughed and waved again, thinking how Old Man Velasquez would explain *this—*

Telepath struggled. Something struck him on the nose and he started upright, pink tongue reflexively washing at the source of the welcome, welcome pain. The horror of the nightmare slipped away, too alien to comprehend with the waking mind.

"Silence, *sthondat*-sucker!" Third Gunner snarled, aiming a kick that thudded drumlike on Telepath's ribs. Another harness-buckle was in one hand, ready to throw. "Stop screaming in your sleep!"

Telepath widened his ears and flattened his fur in propitiation as he crouched; Third Gunner was not a great intellect, but he was enormous and touchy even for a young kzin. After a moment the hulking shape turned and padded off down the corridor to his own doss, grumbling and twitching his whiskers. The smaller kzin sank down again to his thin pallet, curling into a fetal ball and covering his nose with his hands, wrapping his tail around the whole bundle of misery. He quivered, his matted fur wrinkling in odd patterns, and forced his eyes to close.

I must sleep, he thought. His fingers twitched toward the pouch with his drug, but that only made things worse. *I must sleep; my health is important to the fleet.* Unless he was rested he could not read minds on command. Without that, he was useless and therefore dead, and Telepath did not want to die.

But if he slept, he dreamed. For the last four sleeps the dreams of his kittenhood had been almost welcome. Eerie combinations of sound plucked at the corners of his mind as he dozed, as precise as mathematics but carrying overtones of feelings that were not *his*—

He jerked awake again. *Mother*, he thought, through a haze of fatigue. *I want my mother.*

The alienness of the dreams no longer frightened him so much.

What was really terrifying was the feeling he was beginning to *understand* them . . .

Halloran flexed and raised his hands, crouching and growling. Technician's-Assistant stepped aside at the junction of the two corridors, but Fire-Control-Technician retracted his ears and snarled, dropping his lower jaw toward his chest. Aide-to-Commanders had gone down on his belly, crawling aside. Beside the disguised human Chief-Operations-Officer bulked out his fur and responded in kind.

Sure looks different without Fixer, Halloran thought as he sidled around the confrontation.

The kzinti were almost muzzle-to-muzzle, roaring at each other in tones that set the metal around them to vibrating in sympathy; thin black lips curled back from wet half-inch fangs, and the ruffled fur turned their bodies into bristling sausage shapes. The black-leather shapes of their four-fingered hands were almost skeletal, the long claws shining like curves of liquid jet. Dim orange-red light made Halloran squint and peer. The walls here in this section of officer country were covered with holographic murals; a necessity, since kzinti were very vulnerable to sensory deprivation. Twisted thorny orange vegetation crawled across shattered rock under a lowering sky the color of powdered brickdust, and in the foreground two Kzinti had overturned something that looked like a giant spiked turtle with a bone club for a tail. They were burying their muzzles in its belly, ripping out long stretches of intestine.

Abruptly, the two high-ranking kzin stepped back and let their fur fall into normal position, walking past each other as if nothing had happened.

Nothing did, a ghost of Fixer said at the back of Halloran's head; the thin psychic voice was mildly puzzled. *Normal courtesy.* Passing by without playing at challenge would be an insult, showing contempt for one not worthy of interest. Real challenge would be against regulations, now.

Chief-Operations-Officer scratched at the ID plate on the commander's door, releasing Kfraksha-Admiral's coded scent. A muffled growl answered.

Kfraksha-Admiral was seated at his desk, worrying the flesh off a heavy bone held down with his hands. A long shred of tendon came off as he snapped his head back and forth, and his jaws made a wet *clop* sound as he bolted it.

"Is all proceeding according to plan?" he asked.

"Yes, Dominant One," Chief-Operations-Officer said humbly.

"Then why are you taking up my valuable time?" Kfraksha-Admiral screamed, extending his claws.

"Abasement," Chief-Operations-Officer said. He

flattened to the floor in formal mode; the others joined him. "The jettisoning of the monopoles and gravity polarizer components has proceeded according to your plans. There are problems."

"Describe them."

"A much higher than normal rate of replacement for all solid-state electronic components, Kfraksha-Admiral," the engineer said. "Computers and control systems particularly. Increasing as a function of our approach to the ghost star. Also personnel problems."

Kfraksha-Admiral's whiskers and fur moved in patterns that meant lively curiosity; discipline was the problem any Kzin commander would anticipate, although perhaps not so soon.

"Mutiny?" he said almost eagerly.

"No. Increased rates of impromptu dueling, sometimes against regulations. Allegations of murderous intent unsupported by evidence. Superstitions. Several cases of catatonia and insanity leading to liquidation by superiors. Suicides. Also rumors."

"*Hrrrr!*" Kfraksha-Admiral said. Suicide was an admission of cowardice, and very rare.

Time to fish or be bait, Halloran decided.

Gently, he probed at the consciousness of the kzin, feeling the three-things-at-once sensation of indecision. Kfraksha-Admiral knew something of why the Patriarchy forbade mention of phenomenon; because the Conservors of the Ancestral Past couldn't figure out what was involved. Inexplicable and repeated bad luck, usually; the kzin was feeling his fur try to bristle. Kzinti *believed* in luck, as firmly as they believed in games theory. Eternal shame for Kfraksha-Admiral if he turned back now. His cunning suggested aborting the mission; an unwary male would never have become a fleet commander. Gut feeling warred with it; even for a kzin, Kfraksha-Admiral was aggressive;

otherwise he could never have achieved or held his position.

Shame, Halloran whispered, ever so gently. It was not difficult. Easier than it had ever been before, and now he felt *justified*.

Eternal disgrace for retreating, his mind intruded softly. *Two years of futility already. Defeat by plant-eaters.* Sickening images of unpointed grinding teeth chewing roots. *Endless challenges.* A commander turned cautious had a line of potential rivals light-years long, waiting for stand-down from Active Status. Kzin were extremely territorial; modern kzin had transferred the instinct from physical position to rank.

Glory if we win. More glory for great dangers overcome. Conquest Hero Kfraksha-Admiral—no, Kfraksha-Tchee, a full name, unimaginable wealth, planetary systems of slaves with a fully industrialized society. Many sons. Generations to worship my memory.

The commander's ears unfolded as he relaxed, decisions made. "This is a perilous course. Notify *Flashing Claws*"—a Swift Hunter–class courier, lightly armed but lavishly equipped with drive and fuel—"to stand by on constant datalink." The Patriarchy would know what happened. "The fleet will proceed as planned. Slingshot formation, with *Sons Contend With Bloody Fangs* occupying the innermost trajectory."

That would put the flagship at the point of the roughly conical formation the fleet was to assume; the troopships with their loads of infantry would be at the rear. "Redouble training schedules. Increase rations." Well-fed kzin were more amenable to discipline. And—"Rumors of what?"

"That we approach the Darkstar of Ill-Omen, Dominant One."

Kfraksha-Admiral leaned forward, his claws prickling at the files of printout on his desk. *"That was confi-*

dential information!" He glared steadily at Chief-
Operations-Officer, extreme discourtesy among carnivores. The subordinate extended hands and ears, with
an aura of sullenness.

"I have told no one of the nature of the object we
approach," he said. Few kzinti would trouble to prod
and poke for information not immediately useful,
either. "The ship and squadron commanders have
been informed; so have the senior staff."

"Hrrr. Chirrru. You—" a jerk of the tail towards
Aide-to-Commanders. "Fetch me Telepath."

Halloran slumped down on the mat in his quarters,
head cradled in his hands, fighting to control his nau-
sea. *Murphy, don't tell me I'm developing an allergy
to kzin*, he thought, holding his shaking hands out
before him. The mottled spots were probably some
deficiency disease, or his immune system might be
giving up under the strain of ingesting all these not-
quite-earthlike proteins. He belched acid, swallowed
past a painfully dry throat, remembering his last meeting with his father. A kzin ship was like the *real* Arizona desert, and it was sucking the moisture out of
his tissues, no matter how much he drank. A dry cold,
though. It held down the soupy smell of dried rancid
sweat that surrounded him; that had nearly given him
away half a dozen times.

A sharp pain thrilled up one finger. Halloran looked
down and found he had been absently stropping nonexistent claws on the panel of corklike material set
next to the pallet. A broken fingernail was bent back
halfway. He prodded it back into place, shuddering,
tied one of the antiseptic pads around it and secured
it with a strip of cloth before he lowered himself with
painful slowness to his back. Slow salt-heavy tears
filled the corners of his eyes and ran painfully down
the chapped skin of his face.

It was easier to be Fixer. Fixer did not hurt. Fixer was not lonely. Fixer did not feel guilt; shame, perhaps, but never guilt.

Fixer doesn't exist. I am Lawrence Halloran Jr. He closed his eyes and tried to let his breathing sink into a regular rhythm. It was difficult for more reasons than the pain; every time he began to drop off, he would jerk awake again with unreasoning dread. Not of the nightmares, just dread of *something*.

Intuition. Halloran had always believed in intuition. Or maybe just the trickle of fear from the crew, but he should not be *that* sensitive, even with fatigue and weakness wearing down his shields. His talent should be weaker, not stronger.

Enough. "My status is that of a complete shit, but my health is important to the mission," he mumbled sardonically to himself. Sleep was like falling—

—and the others were chasing him again, through the corridors of the creche. Pain shot in under his ribs as he bounded along four-footed, and his tongue lolled dry and grainy. They were all bigger than him, and there were a double handful of them! Bright light stabbed at his eyes as he ran out into the exercise yard, up the tumbled rocks of the pile in the center, gritty ocher sandstone under his hands and feet. Nowhere to run but the highest . . .

Fear cut through his fatigue as he came erect on the central spire. He was above them! The high-status kits would think he was challenging them!

Squalls of rage confirmed it as the orange-and-spotted tide boiled out of the doorway and into the vast quadrangle of scrub and sand. Tails went rigid, claws raked toward him; he stood and screamed back, but he could hear the quaver in it, and the impulse to grovel and spread his ears was almost irresistible. Hate flowed over him with the scent of burning ginger, varied only by the individual smells of the other children.

Rocks flew around him as they poured up the minia-
ture crags; something struck him over one eye. Vision
blurred as the nictitating membranes swept down, and
blood poured over one. The smell of it was like death,
but the others screeched louder as they caught the
waft.

Hands and feet gripped him as he slumped down
on the hard rock, clawing and yanking hair and lifting,
and then he was flying. Instinct rotated his head down,
but he was already too stunned to get his hands and
feet well under him; he landed sprawling across an
edge of sandstone and felt ribs crack. Then the others
were on him, mauling, and he curled into a protective
ball but two of them had his tail, they were stretching
it out and raising rocks in their free hands and *crack*
and *crack*—

Halloran woke, shuddering and wincing at pain in
an organ he did not possess. Several corridors away,
Telepath screamed until the ratings dossed near him
lost all patience and broke open an arms locker to get
a stunner.

"Dreams? Explain yourself, *kshat*," Kfraksha-Admiral
growled.

Telepath ventured a nervous lick of his nose, eyes
darting around, too genuinely terrified to resent being
called the kzin equivalent of a rabbit.

"Nothing. I said nothing of dreams," he said, then
shrieked as the commander's claws raked along the
side of his muzzle.

"*You dare to contradict me?*"

"I abase mysel—"

"Silence! You distinctly said 'dreams' when I asked
you to determine the leakage of secret information."

"Leaks. First Fixer-of-Weapons was leaking. He is
strong. He *leaks*. I run from him but I cannot hide in
sleep. Such shame. Now *more* are leaking. The officers

dream of the Ghost Star. Ancestors who died without honor haunt it . . . their hands reach up to drag us down to nameless rot. One feels it. All feel it—"

"Silence! Silence!" Kfraksha-Admiral roared, striking open-handed. Even then he retained enough control not to use his claws; this thing *was* the last Telepath in the fleet, after all, even if insanity was reducing its usefulness.

And even such a sorry excuse for a kzin shouldn't be much harmed by being beaten unconscious.

"You find time to groom?" Kfraksha-Admiral asked sullenly.

Finagle, Halloran swore inwardly, drawing the Fixer persona more tightly around him. The last sleep-cycle had seen a drastic deterioration in *everyone's* grooming, except his memorized projection. The commander's pelt was not quite matted; it would be a long time before he looked as miserable as Telepath—Finagle alone knew what Telepath looked like now, he seemed to have vanished—but he was definitely scruffy. The entire bridge crew looked peaked, and several were absent, their places taken by younger, less-scarred understudies. Some of those understudies had new bandages, evidence that their superiors' usefulness had deteriorated to the point where the commander would allow self-promotion. The human's talent told him the dark cavern of the command deck smelled of fear and throttled rage and bewilderment; the skin crawled down his spine as he sensed it.

Kzinti did not respond well to frustration. They also did not expect answers to rhetorical questions.

Kfraksha-Admiral turned to Chrung-Fleet-Communications Officer. "Summarize."

"*Hero's Lair* still does not report," that kzin said dully.

That was the first of the troop-transports, going in

on a trajectory that would leave them "behind" the cruisers, dreadnoughts, and stingship carriers when the fleet finally made its out-of-elliptic slingshot approach to Earth. Kfraksha-Admiral had calculated that Earth was probably the softest major human target, and less likely to be alert. Go in undetected, take out major defenses and space-industrial centers, land the surface-troops; the witless hordes of humankind's fifteen billions would be hostages against counterattack.

If things go well, Halloran thought, easing a delicate tendril into the commander's consciousness. *Murphy rules the kzin, as well as humans.* Wearily: *When do things ever go well?*

—and the long silky grass blew in the dry cool wind, that was infinitely clean and empty. His Sire and the other grown males were grouped around the carcass, replete, lapping at drinks in shallow, beautifully fashioned silver cups. He and the other kits were round-stomached and content, play-sparring lazily, and he lay on his back batting at the bright-winged insect that hovered over his nose, until Sire put a hand on his chest and leaned over to rasp a roughly loving tongue across his ears—

"It is well, it is well," Kfraksha-Admiral crooned softly, almost inaudibly. Then he came to himself with a start, looking around as heads turned toward him.

Finagle, I set him off on a memory-fugue! Halloran thought, feeling the kzin's panic and rising anger, the tinge of suspicion beneath that.

"All must admire Kfraksha-Admiral's strategic sense," Halloran-Fixer said hastily. "Light losses, for a strategic gain of the size this operation promises."

Kfraksha-Admiral signed curt assent, turning his attention from the worthless sycophant. Behind Fixer's mask, Halloran's human face contorted in a savage grin. Manipulating Kfraksha-Admiral's subconscious was more fun than haunting the other kzin. *Even for a ratcat, he's a son-of-a . . . pussy, I suppose. Singleminded, too.* Relatively easy to keep from wondering what was causing all this—*I wish I knew*—and tightly, tightly focus on getting through the next few hours. Closest approach soon.

And it was all so *easy.* He was *unstoppable . . .*

Scabs broke and he tasted the salt of blood. *I'm not going to make it.* He ground his jaws and felt the loosening teeth wobble in their sockets. Death was a bitterness, no glory in it, only this foul decay. *Maybe I shouldn't make it. I'm too dangerous.* His face had been pockmarked with open sores, the last time he looked. Maybe that was how he looked inside.

So easy, sucking the kzinti crews down into a cycle of waking nightmare. As if they were doing it to themselves. Fixer howled laughter from within his soul.

"I have the information by the throat, but I still do not understand," Physicist said, staring around wildly. He was making the *chiruu-chiruu* sounds of kzinti distress. *Dealer-With-Very-Small-and-Large* was a better translation of his name/title. "I do not understand!"

Most of the bridge equipment was closed down. Ventilation still functioned, internal fields, all based on simple feedback systems. Computers, weapons, communications, all had grown too erratic to trust. A few lasers still linked the functioning units of the fleet.

Outside, the stars shone with jeering brightness. Of the Ghost Star there was no trace; no visible light, no occlusion of the background . . . and instruments more sophisticated had given out hours ago. Many of the bridge crew still stayed at their posts, but their scent had soured; the steel *wtsai* knives at their belts attracted fingers like unconscious lures.

"Explain," Kfraksha-Admiral rasped.

"The values, the records just say that physical law

in the shadow-matter realm is unlike kzinti timespace
. . . and there is crossover this close! The effect
increases exponentially as we approach the center of
mass; we must be within the radius the object occu-
pies in the other continuum. The cosmological con-
stants are varying. Quantum effects. The U/R
threshold of quantum probability functions itself is
increasing, that is why all electronic equipment becomes unreliable—probability cascades are approaching the macrocosmic level."

Kfraksha-Admiral's tail was quivering-rigid, and he
panted until thin threads of spittle drooled down from
the corners of his mouth.

"Then we shall win! We are nearly at point of closest approach. Our course is purely ballistic. Systems
will regain their integrity as we recede from the area
of singularity."

Murphy wins again, Halloran thought wearily,
slumping back against the metal wall. His body was
shaking, and he felt a warm trickle down one leg. *He's
right*. The irony of it was enough to make him laugh,
except that that would have hurt too much. Halloran
had done the *noble* thing. He had put everything into
controlling Kfraksha-Admiral, blinding him to the
voices of prudence . . .

And the bleeping ratcat was right *after all*.

His shields frayed as the human despaired. Frayed
more strongly than he had ever felt, even drunk or
coming, until he felt/was Kfraksha-Admiral's ferocious
triumph, Physicist's jumble of shifting equations, Telepath's hand pressing the ampule of his last drug capsule against his throat in massive overdose, *why have
the kzinti disintegrated like this*—

Halloran would never have understood it. He lacked
the knowledge of physics—the ARM had spent centuries discouraging that—but Physicist was next to him,
and the datalink was strong. No kzinti could have

understood it; they were simply not introspective enough. Halloran-Fixer *knew*, with the whole-argument suddenness of revelation; knew as a composite creature that had experienced the inwardness of Kzin and Man together.

The conscious brain is a computer, but one of a very special kind. Not anything like a digital system; that was one reason why true Artificial Intelligence had taken so long to achieve, and had proven so worthless once found. Consciousness does not operate on mathematical algorithms, with their prefixed structures. It is a quantum process, indeterminate in the most literal sense. Thoughts became conscious—decision was taken, will exercised—when the nervous system amplified them past the one-graviton threshold level. So was insight, a direct contact with the paramathematical frame of reality.

They couldn't know, Halloran realized. Kzinti physics was excellent but their biological sciences primitive by human standards.

And I know what's driving them crazy, he realized. Telepathy was another threshold effect. Any conscious creature possessed *some* ability. The Ghost Star was amplifying it to a terrifying level, even as it disabled the computers by turning their off/on synapses to off *and* on. Humans might be able to endure it; Man is a gregarious species.

Not the kzinti. Not those hard, stoic, isolated killer souls. Forever guarded, forever wary, disgusted by the very thought of such an involuntary sharing . . . whose only glimpse of telepathy was creatures like Telepath. Utter horror, to feel the boundaries of their personalities fraying, merging, becoming *not-self*.

Halloran knew what he had to do. *It's the right thing*. Fixer-of-Weapons stirred exultantly in his tomb of flesh. *Die like a Hero!* he battle-screeched.

Letting go was like thinning out, like dying, like

being free for the first time in all his life. Halloran's awareness flared out, free of the constraints of distance, touching lightly at the raw newly-forged connections between thousands of minds in the Ghost Sun's grip. *I get to be omnipotent just before the end*, he thought in some distant corner. To his involuntary audience: *MEET EACH OTHER.*

The shock of the steel was almost irrelevant, the reflex that wrenched him around to face Telepath automatic. Undeceived at last, the kzin's drug-dilated eyes met the human's. Halloran slumped forward, opening his mouth, but there was no sound or breath as

—he—

"Get out of my dreams!"

—the human—

—fell—

—released—

"Shit," Halloran murmured. His heels drummed on the deck. *Mom.*

The roar from Colonel Buford Early's office was enough to bring his aide-de-camp's head through the door. One glance at his Earther superior was enough to send it back through the hatch.

Early swore again, more quietly but with a scatological invention that showed both his inventiveness and his age; it had been *many* generations since some of those Anglo-Saxon monosyllables had been in common use.

Then he played the audio again; without correction, but listening carefully for the rhythm of the phrasing under the accent imposed by a vocal system and palate very unlike that of *Homo sapiens sapiens*:

"—so you see"—it sounded more like *zo uru t'zee*—"it's not really relevant whether I'm Halloran or whether he's dead and I'm a kzinti with delusions.

Halloran's . . . memories were more used to having an alien in his head than Telepath's were, poor bleeping bastard. The Fleet won't be giving you any trouble, the few that are still alive will be pretty thoroughly insane.

"On the other hand," the harsh nonhuman voice continued, "remembering what happened to Fixer I really don't think it would be all that advisable to come back. And you know what? I've decided that I really don't owe any of you that much. Died for the cause already, haven't I?"

A rasping sound, something between a growl and a purr: kzinti laughter. "I'm seeing a lot of things more clearly now. Amazing what a different set of nerves and hormones can do. My talent's almost as strong now as it was . . . before, and I've got a *lot* less in the way of inhibitions. It's the Patriarchy that ought to be worried, but of course they'll never know."

Then a hesitation: "Tell my Sire . . . tell Dad I died a Hero, would you, Colonel?"

EPILOGUE

The kzin finished grooming his pelt to a lustrous shine before he followed Medical-Technician to the deepsleep chamber of the Swift Hunter courier *Flashing Claws*. His face was expressionless as the cover lowered above him, and then his ears wrinkled with glee; there would be nobody to see until they arrived in the Alpha Centauri system a decade from now.

The Patriarchy had never had a Telepath who earned a full name before.

Too risky! Telepath wailed.

Kshat, Fixer thought with contempt.

Shut up both of you, Halloran replied. *Or I'll start thinking about salads again*. All of them understood the grin that showed his/their fangs.

The Patriarchy had never had one like Halloran before, either.